KT-426-307

Ret
or ɛ
Plea
by p

WITHDRAWN

BRYANT & MAY AND THE INVISIBLE CODE

Two young children are playing a game called Witch-Hunter, cursing a woman sitting in a church courtyard they wait for her to die. And die she does in St Bride's Church. Unfortunately Bryant and May are refused the case. Instead they're investigating why the wife of their greatest enemy has suddenly started to behave strangely; she believes she's the victim of witchcraft. There's a brutal stabbing in a London park and suddenly a connection is found between the two investigations. Probing behind the city's facades, they uncover a world of hidden passageways, covert loyalties and murder.

BRYANT & MAY AND THE INVISIBLE CODE

Bryant & May And The Invisible Code

by

Christopher Fowler

Magna Large Print Books
Long Preston, North Yorkshire,
BD23 4ND, England.

British Library Cataloguing in Publication Data.

Fowler, Christopher
    Bryant & May and the invisible code.

    A catalogue record of this book is
    available from the British Library

    ISBN   978-0-7505-3805-3

First published in Great Britain in 2012 by Doubleday
an imprint of Transworld Publishers

Published in Large Print 2013 by arrangement with
Transworld Publishers

Magna Large Print is an imprint of Library Magna Books Ltd.

Printed and bound in Great Britain by
T.J. (International) Ltd., Cornwall, PL28 8RW

This book is a work of fiction and, except in pre-
sentations of fact, any resemblance to actual
persons, living or dead, is purely coincidental.

For Peter Chapman

'Money can't buy friends,
but it can get you a better class of enemy.'

Spike Milligan

'It started with me. It ends with me.'

**Unnamed teenager,
when asked about the history of London**

ACKNOWLEDGEMENTS

'Make your leading characters younger and put in more sex and violence if you want them to be a success,' a critic warned me as I embarked on the first Bryant & May mystery. Blithely ignoring his advice I ploughed on, determined to create a pair of intelligent Golden Age detectives who are forced to deal with the modern world. I knew I'd have fun just watching Arthur Bryant trying to use a smartphone.

Luckily, there were others who always agreed with me. Simon Taylor, my editor at Transworld, is so wonderfully enthusiastic that I sometimes doubt his sanity but never his *savoir faire*. Thanks too, to Lynsey Dalladay, who has restored my faith in publishing PR. Both she and Mandy Little, my charming agent, prove it's not all standing around drinking champagne and that we can also have fun going to secluded libraries on wet winter Wednesdays.

I really hope there are further Bryant & May adventures to come, as each book is more pleasurable to write than the last. Remember, the strangest parts of these tales are true. You can uncover lots more information at www.christopherfowler.co.uk

Peculiar Crimes Unit
The Old Warehouse
231 Caledonian Road
London NI 9RB

STAFF ROSTER FOR MONDAY 18 JUNE

Raymond Land, Acting Unit Chief
Arthur Bryant, Senior Detective
John May, Senior Detective
Janice Longbright, Detective Sergeant
Dan Banbury, Crime Scene Manager/InfoTech
Giles Kershaw, Forensic Pathologist
(St Pancras Mortuary)
Jack Renfield, Sergeant
Meera Mangeshkar, Detective Constable
Colin Bimsley, Detective Constable
Crippen, staff cat

BULLETIN BOARD

Housekeeping notes from Raymond Land to all staff:

As you know, we now have a fully activated secure swipe-card entry system on the front door. It worked perfectly for two whole days, until Arthur Bryant accidentally inserted an old Senior Service 'Battle of Britain' cigarette card into the slot instead of his electronic keycard and somehow jammed it. The engineers hope to have the system working again by Thursday.

The new common room is to be used as a neutral zone for calm reflection and the sharing of information. It is not an after-hours bar, a video-game parlour or a place where you can stage chemical experiments, impromptu film shows or arm-wrestling matches for beers.

When the fire inspector came to test the smoke detector in the first-floor corridor last week, he found a box of Bryant & May matches wedged in place of the alarm battery. Obviously only a disturbed, selfish and immature individual would risk burning his colleagues alive in order to smoke a pipe indoors. I'm not mentioning any names.

I want to put the rumours to rest about our new building once and for all. While it appears to be true that a Mr Aleister Crowley once held meetings here (and decorated the wall of my office with inappropriate images of young ladies and aroused livestock), the building is most emphatically not 'haunted'. It's an old property with a colourful history, and has Victorian pipes and floorboards. The noises these make at night are quite normal and certainly don't sound like the 'death-rattles of trapped souls', as I overheard Meera telling someone on the phone. May I remind you that you are British officers of the law, and are not required to have any imagination.

There's a funny smell in the kitchen. It might be a gas leak. Our builders, the two Daves, are coming back to rip everything out. If I find one of you dropped a kebab behind the units, you'll be on unpaid overtime for a month.

Finally, I was under the impression that Crippen, our staff cat, was a neutered tom, but this appears not to be the case as she is clearly pregnant. Can someone please take care of this? I DO NOT want anyone unexpectedly giving birth in this unit.

PART ONE

The Case

1

CLOSE TO GOD

There was a witch around here somewhere.

The Fleet Street office workers who sat in the cool shadow of the church on their lunch breaks had no idea that she was hiding among them. They squatted in the little garden squares while they ate their sandwiches, queued at coffee shops and paced the pavements staring at the screens of their smartphones, not realizing that she was preparing to call down lightning and spit brimstone.

On the surface the witch was one of them, but that was just a disguise. She had the power to change her outward appearance, to look like anyone she was standing near.

Lucy said, 'She won't be somebody posh. Witches are always poor.'

Tom said, 'I can't tell who's posh. Everyone looks the same.'

He was right; to a child they did. Grey suits, black suits, white shirts, grey skirts, blue ties, print blouses, black shoes. London's workforce on the move.

Lucy pulled at her favourite yellow T-shirt and felt her tummy rumble. 'She'll have to appear soon. They often travel in threes. When a witch starts to get hungry, she loses concentration and lets go of her disguise. The spell will weaken and she'll turn back into her real self.'

She was crouching in the bushes and wanted to stand up because it was making her legs hurt, but knew she might get caught if she did so. The flowerbeds bristled with tropical plants that had spiny razor-sharp leaves and looked as if they should be somewhere tropical. A private security guard patrolled the square, shifting the people who looked as if they belonged somewhere else too.

'What does she really look like?' asked Tom. 'I mean, when she drops her disguise?'

Lucy answered without hesitation. 'She has a green face and a hooked nose covered in hairy warts, and long brown teeth and yellow eyes. And her breath smells of rotting sardines.' She thought for a moment. 'And toilets.'

Tom snorted in disgust as he looked around the courtyard for likely suspects. Nearby, an over-weight woman in her mid-thirties was standing in a doorway eating a Pret A Manger crayfish and rocket sandwich. She seemed a likely candidate. The first of the summer's wasps was hovering around, scenting the remains of office lunches. The woman anxiously batted one away as she ate.

'It can't be her,' said Lucy.

'Why not?' asked Tom.

'Witches don't feel pain, so she wouldn't be scared of a stupid wasp.'

'Can a witch be a man?'

'No, that would be a warlock. It has to be a woman.'

Tom was getting tired of the game. Lucy seemed

to be making up extra rules as she went along. The June sun shone through a gap in the buildings and burned the back of his neck. The sky above the courtyard was as blue as the sea looked in old films.

He was starting to think that this was a stupid way to spend a Saturday morning when he could have been at football. He had been looking forward to seeing the Dr Who exhibition as well, but right at the last minute his dad had to work instead, and said, 'You can come with me to the office,' as if it was a reasonable substitute. There was nothing to do in the office. You weren't allowed to touch the computers or open any of the drawers. His dad seemed to like being there. He always cheered up when he had to go into the office on a Saturday.

The only other father who had brought his child in that morning was Lucy's, so he was stuck playing with a girl until both of their fathers had finished their work. At least Lucy knew about the game, which was unusual because most girls didn't play games like that. She explained that she had two older brothers and always ended up joining in with them. She didn't tell him they had outgrown the game now and spent their days wired into hip-hop and dodgy downloads.

'How about that one?' said Lucy, taking the initiative. Her brothers could never make up their minds about anything, and always ended up arguing, so she was used to making all the decisions.

'Nah, she's too pretty,' said Tom, watching a slender girl in a very short grey skirt stride past

23

to the building at the end of the courtyard.

'That's the point. The prettier they look on the outside, the uglier they are inside. Too late, she's gone.'

'I'm bored now.'

'Five more minutes. She's here somewhere.' There were only a few workers left in the square, plus a motorcycle courier who must have been stifling in his helmet and leathers.

'It's this one. I have a feeling. I bet she belongs to a coven; that's a club for witches. Remember, we have to get them before they get us. Let's check her out. Come on.' Lucy led the way past a sad-looking young woman who had just seated herself on the bench nearest the church. She had opened a paperback and was reading it intently. Lucy turned to Tom with an air of theatrical nonchalance and pointed behind the flat of her palm.

'That's definitely her.'

'How can we tell if she's a witch?' Tom whispered.

'Look for signs. Try to see what she's reading.'

'I can't walk past her again, she'll see. Wait, I've got an idea.' Tom had stolen a yellow tennis ball from his father's office. Now he produced it from his pocket. 'Catch, then throw it back to me in her direction. I'll miss and I'll have to go and get it.'

Lucy was a terrible actress. If the sad-faced young woman had looked up, she would have stopped and stared at the little girl gurning and grimacing before her.

'I'm throwing now,' Lucy said loudly, hurling

24

the ball ten feet wide of the boy. Tom scrambled in slow motion around the bench, and the young woman briefly raised her eyes.

Tom ran back to Lucy's side. 'She's reading a book about babies.'

'What was it called?'

'*Rosemary's Baby*. By a woman called Ira something.'

'Then she's definitely a witch.'

'How do you know?'

Lucy blew a raspberry of impatience. 'Don't you know anything? Witches eat babies! Everyone knows that.'

'So she really is one,' Tom marvelled. 'She looks so normal.'

'Yeah, clever isn't it?' Lucy agreed. 'So, how are we going to kill her?'

2

DEATH IN THE WEDDING CAKE

Even though the presses of the Fourth Estate had been shifted to London's hinterlands by Rupert Murdoch, St Bride's Church was still known to many as the Printers' Cathedral. Tucked behind Fleet Street, it stood on a pagan site dedicated to Brigit, the Celtic goddess of healing, fire and childbirth. For two thousand years the spot had been a place of worship, and for the past five hundred it had been the spiritual home of journalists. Samuel Pepys, no mean reporter himself, had been born in Salisbury Court, right next to the church, and had later bribed the gravedigger of St Bride's to shift up the corpses so that his brother John could be buried in the churchyard.

St Bride's' medieval lectern had survived the Great Fire and the Luftwaffe's bombs. It still stood bathed in the lunchtime sunlight, barely registered by the tourists who stopped by to take photographs of just another London church. The building had been badly damaged in the fire-storm of 29 December 1940, but had now been restored according to Wren's original drawings.

With the paperback in her hand, the sad young woman walked into the church and looked about. Amy O'Connor had been here many times before, but her visits had never brought her the satisfaction she'd hoped for. She knew little about the church except the one thing everyone knew: that the shape of a wedding cake came from its tiered spire. It was usually empty inside, a place where she could sit still and calm herself. Her encounter with the children in the courtyard had disturbed her. It was as if they had been slyly studying her.

Before her the great canopied oak reredos dedicated to the Pilgrim Fathers stood in front of what appeared to be a half-domed apse, but it was actually a magnificent *trompe l'oeil*. A striking oval stained-glass panel, like an upright eye holding the image of Christ, shone light down on to the polished marble floor, which was laid with black Belgian and white Italian tiles.

Amy looked around the empty pews with their

homely little lampshades. If there had been any lunchtime worshippers here, they had all gone back to work now. The churchwarden was still on his break and had probably headed up the road for a pie and a pint in the Cheshire Cheese. Someone had taken over for him, and was manning the little shop selling books and postcards near the entrance.

Seating herself in one of the oak chairs arranged near the pulpit, she closed her eyes and let the light of God shine through the dazzling reds, blues and yellows of the stained glass on to her bare freckled arms and upturned face. It was like being inside a gently shifting kaleidoscope. The light divided her into primary colours. She swayed back and forth, feeling the changing patterns on her eyelids. She thought of lost love, wasted time and missed opportunities.

She was still furious with herself for losing the only man she had ever loved. She had been angry for more than two years now, and only coming to St Bride's could dull the ache of loss. If she had taken him more seriously and tried harder to help, she was sure he would still be with her.

His death had hastened the end of her trust in God, but here in the church he must have loved she felt a connection between the present and the past, the living and the dead. She could believe that angels were watching and guiding her thoughts.

But when she opened her eyes, she found that pair of children still peering through the door at her. Where were their parents, and why were they staring?

They looked as if they were waiting for something to happen.

The church's thick walls kept it cool even in the heat of summer. The chill radiated from the stones. But now, after just a few minutes, the interior started to seem hot and airless. The light from the windows hurt her eyes. She could feel her face burning.

Suddenly aware that she was perspiring, she wiped her forehead with the paper tissue she kept tucked in her sleeve, and looked up at the drifting motes of dust caught in the sunlight coming through the plain glass on either side of the nave. Perhaps it was her imagination, but today she really did feel closer to some kind of spiritual presence in here.

The sensation was growing, starting to envelop her. Perhaps God had finally decided to make himself known, and would apologize for screwing up her life. The colours in the oval window above the altar grew more vivid by the second. Even the oak pews that faced each other across the church seemed to give off waves of warmth.

It wasn't her imagination. The church was definitely getting hotter. The light streaming through the glass was tinged crimson. The floor was rippling in the heat. It was as if the entire building had divorced itself from its moorings and was sinking down to hell.

Suddenly she felt very close to a watchful being, but it wasn't God – it was the Devil.

She twisted her head to see the children leaning in from outside the church door, still staring at her intently. And someone or something no more than a stretched silhouette was behind them, dark and faceless, willing them on to evil deeds.

I am going to suffer, she thought. *This is all wrong. I can't die before knowing the truth.*

As the church tipped and she fell slowly from her chair, all she felt was frustration with the incompleteness of life.

3

HEALTH CHECK

'You need to start acting your age,' said Dr Gillespie.

'If I did that, I'd be dead.' Arthur Bryant coughed loudly, causing the doctor to tear off his stethoscope.

'Would you kindly refrain from doing that when I'm listening to your heart?' he complained. 'You nearly deafened me.'

'What?' asked Bryant, who had been thinking about something else.

'Deaf,' said Dr Gillespie. 'You nearly deafened me.'

'Yes, I'm quite deaf, but don't worry, it's not catching. You're a doctor, you should know that. I've got a hearing aid but it keeps picking up old radio programmes. I put it on yesterday morning and listened to an episode of *Two-Way Family Favourites* from 1963.' He coughed again.

Dr Gillespie coughed too. 'That's not possible.

How long have you been coming here?' he asked, thumping his chest.

'Forty-two years,' said Bryant. 'You ought to cut down on the oily rags.'

'The what?'

'The fags. The snouts. Gaspers. Coffin nails. Lung darts.'

'All right, I get the picture.'

'The doctor I had before you is dead now. He was a smoker, too.'

Dr Gillespie coughed harder. 'He was run over by a bus.'

'Yes, but he was on his way to the tobacconist.'

'You smoke a pipe.'

'My tobacco has medicinal properties. Is there anything else wrong with me?'

'Well, quite a lot, but nothing's actually dropping off. It's mostly to do with your age. How old are you, exactly?'

'My date of birth is right there in your file.' Bryant reached forward and slapped an immense sheaf of yellowed paperwork.

Dr Gillespie donned his glasses and searched for it. 'Good Lord,' he said. 'Well, I suppose, all things considered, you're doing all right. Mental health OK?'

'What are you implying?'

'I have to ask these things. No lapses of memory?'

'Well of course there are, all the time. But I know if I'm at the park or the pictures, if that's what you mean. It proves quite convenient sometimes. Birthdays, anniversaries and so on.'

'Jolly good. Well, you should make sure you get

30

adequate rest, take a snooze in the afternoons.'

Bryant was apoplectic. 'I can't suddenly go for forty winks in the middle of a case.'

'Yes, but a man of your age...'

'Do you mind? I am certainly not a man of my age! I'm running national murder investigations, not working for the council,' Bryant bellowed.

'Well, there's nothing wrong with your voice.' Dr Gillespie made a tick on his list. 'You could always take up a hobby.'

'What, run the local newsletter or work in a community puppet theatre? Have you met the kind of busybodies who do that sort of thing? I'm not interested.'

'That's not what I heard.' Dr Gillespie coughed again and blew his nose. 'I think I'm coming down with something. What was this about you thinking someone had been murdered by a Mr Punch puppet recently?'

'Where did you hear about that?'

'Your partner Mr May is one of my patients too. He's in very good nick, you know. Takes care of himself. He's got the body of a much younger man.'

'Well, he should give it back.'

'He's wearing much better than you.'

'Thank you very much. I'm so pleased to hear that. We solved the Mr Punch case, by the way. Beat people a quarter of our age.'

'Well done. Good appetite? Bowels?'

'I'm sorry?'

'Are they open?'

'Not right at this minute, no, but they will be if you keep me here much longer.'

'I'm almost through. How's your eyesight?'

'It's like I'm living in a thick fog.'

'You should try cleaning your glasses occasionally.' Dr Gillespie's cough turned into a minute-long hack. 'God, I'm dying for a cigarette.'

'If you need one that badly, I'll wait.'

'Can't,' Dr Gillespie wheezed, 'no balcony.'

Bryant absently patted him on the back, waiting for him to catch his breath. 'You don't sound too good. Ciggies just bung up your lungs. I bet your chest feels sore right now.'

'You're right, it does.' The doctor hacked again.

'Like a steel strap slowly tightening around your ribs. Hands and feet tingling as well, no doubt. You're probably heading for a stroke.'

'I've tried to give up.'

'Lack of willpower, I expect.'

'I know, it drives me mad.'

'Perhaps you should think about retiring.'

The doctor bristled. 'Don't be ridiculous, I'm perfectly capable of doing my job.'

'There, now you know how I feel.' Bryant was triumphant. 'Let's call it quits.'

'Fair enough. Put your – whatever that is – back on.'

'It's my under-vest. Then I have my vest, my shirt and my jumper.'

'Aren't you hot in that lot? It's summer.'

'Ah, I thought the rain was getting warmer. I need these layers. They keep my blood moving around.'

'I saw a case that was right up your street the other day,' said Dr Gillespie as Bryant dressed. 'Young woman, Amy O'Connor, twenty-eight, pretty little thing, dropped dead in a church on Saturday.'

'Where was this?'

'St Bride's, just off Fleet Street. It was in the *Evening Standard*.'

'Why do you think that's a case for us, then?'

'You run the Peculiar Crimes Unit, don't you?' said Dr Gillespie. 'Well, her death was bloody peculiar.'

After the doctor had outlined what he knew about the case, Arthur Bryant left the GP's scruffy third-floor office situated behind the Coca-Cola sign in Piccadilly Circus and set off towards the Peculiar Crimes Unit in King's Cross, to check out the case of a lonely death in a City of London church.

Bryant ambled. In Paris he would have been a *boulevardier*, a *flâneur*, but in London, a city that no longer had time for anything but making money, he was just slow and in the way. Accountants, bankers, market analysts and PR girls hustled around him, cemented to their phones. The engineers and artists, bootmakers, signwriters and watch-menders had long fled the centre. Who worked with their hands in the City any more? The ability to make something from nothing had once been regarded with the greatest respect, but now the Square Mile dealt in units, its captains of industry preferring to place their trust in flickering strings of electronic figures.

Bryant would not be hurried though. He was as much a part of London as a hobbled Tower raven, a Piccadilly barber, a gunman in the Blind Beggar, and he would not be moved from his determined path. He was, everyone agreed, an annoying, impossible and indispensible fellow who had long ago decided that it was better to be disliked than forgotten.

And over the coming week, he would find himself annoying some very dangerous people.

4

STRING

'Why did I have to hear about this from my doctor, of all people?' asked Bryant petulantly.

'It's not our jurisdiction,' replied John May, unfolding his long legs beneath the desk where he sat opposite his partner. 'The case went straight to the City of London Police. They're a law unto themselves. You can't just cherry-pick cases that take your fancy, they'll come around here with cricket bats.'

Bryant was aware that the City of London's impact extended far beyond its Square Mile inhabitants. Marked out by black bollards bearing the City's emblem and elegant silver dragons that guarded the major entrances, it contained within its boundaries more than 450 international banks, their glass towers wedged into Palladian alleyways and crookbacked Tudor passages. As the global axis of countless multi-national corporations, it demanded a bespoke police force equipped to protect this unique environment with special policies and separate uniforms.

'If there's a reason why we should take over the investigation we can put in a formal request,' he suggested.

'True, but I can't think of one.'

'How did you know about it?'

'I picked up the details as they came in,' said May. 'It was kept away from us because Faraday wanted it to be handled by the City of London.'

Leslie Faraday, the Home Office liaison officer charged with keeping the Peculiar Crimes Unit in line, was under instruction from his boss to reduce the unit's visibility, and therefore decrease their likelihood of embarrassing the government. His latest tactic was to starve them of new cases.

'But you made some notes, I see.'

'Yes, I did, just out of interest.'

'Well?' asked Bryant, peering over a stack of old Punch annuals at May's papers like an ancient goblin eyeing a stack of gold coins.

'Well what?' May looked innocently back across the desk, knowing exactly what Bryant was after.

'The details. What are the details of the case?' He waved his ballpoint pen about. 'There, man, what have you got?'

'Look at you, you're virtually salivating.'

'I have nothing else to concern myself with this morning, unless you happen to know where my copy of *The Thirteen Signs of Satanism* has got to.'

'All right.' May pulled up a page and held it at a distance. Vanity prevented him from wearing his newly prescribed glasses. 'It says here that at approximately two twenty p.m. on Saturday, a twenty-eight-year-old woman identified as Amy

35

O'Connor was found dead in St Bride's Church, just off Fleet Street. Cause of death unknown, but at the moment it's being treated as suspicious. No marks on the body other than a contusion on the front of the skull, assumed by the EMT to have been incurred when she slipped off her chair and brained herself on the marble floor.'

'So what did she die of?'

'It looks like her heart simply stopped. There was a lad running the church shop, but he left his post to go for a cigarette a couple of times and didn't even notice her sitting there. She was found by one of the wardens returning from lunch, who called a local med unit. The only note I have on the initial examination is an abnormally high body temperature. The building has CCTV, which the City of London team requisitioned and examined. They know she entered the building alone, and during the time that she was in there nobody else came in. That's about all they have.'

'Where was she before she entered St Bride's?'

'She was seen sitting on a bench in the courtyard outside the church. A lot of the area's local workers go there at lunchtime. Quite a few work on Saturdays. O'Connor was alone and minding her own business, quietly reading a book.'

'Was she working in the area?'

'No. She had a part-time job as a bar manager at the Electricity Showroom in Hoxton.'

'Why would an electricity showroom have a bar?'

'They kept the name from the building's old

usage. It's a popular local hostelry. There aren't any electricity showrooms as such any more, Arthur, even you must have noticed that.'

'What about her movements earlier in the morning?'

'Nobody's too sure about those. She was renting a flat in Spitalfields, had been there a couple of years. Her parents live on the south-west coast. She'd never been married, had no current partner, no close friends. There, now you know as much as anyone else.'

'Where was her body taken?'

'Over to the Robin Brook Centre at St Bart's, I imagine. They handle all the cases from the Square Mile. But you can't go near the place.'

'Why not? I know the coroner there. We used to break into empty buildings together before my knees packed up.'

'Why did you do that?'

'Oh, just to have a look around. I think I'll pop over.'

'No, Arthur. I absolutely forbid it. You can't just walk into someone else's case and stir things up.'

'I'm not going to, old sport. I'll be visiting an old friend. There's a big bowling tournament coming up. He's a keen player. I think I should let him know about it.' Bryant rose and jammed a mouldy-looking olive-green fedora so hard on his head that it squashed his ears. 'Want me to bring you anything back?'

The hospital and the meat market occupied the same small corner of central London, the saviours and purveyors of flesh. In Queen Square, the doctors lurked like white-coated gang members, grabbing a quick cigarette before returning to their wards to administer health advice. Not far from them, in Smithfield, the last of London's traditional butchers did the same thing. Both areas were at their most interesting before 7.00 a.m., when the doctors were intense and garrulous, the butchers noisome and amiably foulmouthed.

Dr Benjamin Fenchurch's parents had been among the first Caribbean passengers to dock in Britain from the SS *Empire Windrush* in 1948. He had spent his entire working life in the St Bartholomew's Hospital Coroner's Office. Over the decades, he had become so institutionalized that he hardly ever left the hospital grounds. He owned a small flat in an apartment building that was so close to his office he could see into it from his kitchen window. He ate in the St Bart's canteen and always volunteered for the shifts that no one else wanted. Perfectly happy to cover every Christmas, Easter, Diwali and Yom Kippur, he actively avoided the living, who were loud and messy and unreliable, and always let you down. Bodies yielded their secrets with far more grace.

It seemed to Arthur Bryant that this was not a healthy way to live, and yet in many ways he was just as bad, preferring the company of his staff to the world beyond the unit. Working for public-service institutions had a way of making conscientious people feel as if they were always running late. They spent their lives trying to catch up with themselves, and Fenchurch was no exception.

Threading his way through a maze of overlit basement corridors, Bryant reached the immense mortuary that served both the two nearby hospitals and the City of London Police. In the office at the farthest end, Fenchurch was at his lab desk, hunched over his notes, lost in a world of his own.

Bryant cleared his throat.

'I know you're there, Arthur. You don't have to make that absurd noise. I know the sound of your shoes.' Even after all these years, Fenchurch had retained his powerful Jamaican accent. He removed his glasses and raised a huge head of grizzled grey hair.

Bryant was surprised. 'Really? My Oxford toe-caps?'

'Nobody else I know still wears Blakey's.' He was referring to the crescents of steel affixed to Bryant's toes and heels that saved leather and ruined parquet floors. 'I haven't seen you since that disgusting business with the Limehouse Ratboy.'

'Yes, that was rather nasty, wasn't it?' Bryant looked around. 'All by yourself today?'

'Do you see anyone else? My assistant's off having a baby. I mean it's his wife who's having the baby. Why he has to be there as well is a mystery to me. It's a simple enough procedure. So, what have I done to deserve a visit?'

'Amy O'Connor.'

'Oh yes. Thought you might be sniffing that one out. Very interesting.'

'That's just what I thought.'

'Pity it's not your jurisdiction.'

39

'It should have been. She died in a church. Part of our remit is to ensure that members of the general public aren't placed in positions of danger. If people can't trust the sanctuary of a church, what can they trust? But I'm not here in an official capacity. I thought you might like some company. Here, I brought you some sherbet lemons.'

Bryant rustled the corner of a paper bag. Fenchurch sniffed. 'Not much of a bribe, is it?' He fished inside and took one anyway.

'We're playing the Dagenham Stranglers at the Hollywood Lanes Saturday week. I'll put you on our team.' For some peculiar reason, bookish Bloomsbury was the home of two decent central London bowling alleys.

'I thought you'd been banned after that incident with the nutcases.'

'New ownership. Don't think you should call them nutcases.' Bryant sucked ruminatively on a sherbet lemon, clattering it loudly against his false teeth. Last year he had fielded a team of anger-management outpatients to play in a bowling tournament against a group of Metropolitan Police psychotherapists. The outpatients had proven to be sore losers. One of them had tried to make a psychotherapist eat his shoes before knocking him unconscious with a bowling pin. 'Have you carried out a post-mortem yet?'

'Last night. I'm afraid it's going to be an open verdict.'

'Why so?'

'You know I'm not allowed to tell you.'

'Oh come on, Ben, who am I going to tell? I'm

40

old. Most of my friends are either dead, mad or on the way out.'

'How's John?'

'Well, he's fine, obviously. And he's not a friend; he's the other half of my brain. I'd discuss it with him, I admit, but it would go no further.'

'Promise?'

'Cross my hardened heart.'

'To be honest it's a bit of a puzzler, and I could do with some feedback. She had a slight contusion to the orbital frontal region, but was otherwise clean of any marks.'

'You mean falling from the chair and banging her head wasn't enough to kill her?'

'Our bodies are a little tougher than that, Mr Bryant. Otherwise we'd be smashing ourselves to bits like bone-china teacups.'

'Then what else could it have been?'

'With the heightened body temperature it *feels* like toxicosis – systemic poisoning of some kind – but there's no agent present that I could trace. No oesophageal trauma, so she hadn't ingested anything severe. Stomach's fine. That's the thing with City of London workers – you always find the same gut contents, courtesy of our friends at Pret A Manger. The City workers tend to favour the crayfish and rocket sandwiches.'

'She wasn't a City worker. She had a job in a bar in Hoxton. No other marks on the body at all?'

'None that I could see. The admitting officer says they checked the CCTV and she'd been alone outside the church and inside it. There was a boy working in the shop, but he was in and out

– a smoker – and went nowhere near her. There's a witness report from him that's the blankest document I've ever seen. She was completely alone except for a couple of kids.'

Bryant's ears pricked up. 'What kids?'

'The officer said it looked like she had an argument with two small children a few minutes before going into the church. She was trying to read. They were playing ball near her, annoying her apparently. Not hoodies – well dressed.'

'Has anyone tried to track the children down?'

'I wouldn't have thought so. What would be the point? What could a small child do?'

'You never know these days. Nothing else un-usual at all? Clothes, personal belongings, mobile, handbag?'

'You'd have to ask someone else about that. I'm only dealing with the physical remains. Wait a minute – there was one thing.' He rose and went over to a stack of steel drawers labelled alpha-betically. 'Hang on, it's gone.'

'Not "C",' said Bryant. 'Try "O" for "O'-Connor".'

'Don't know my own filing system.' Opening the lower drawer, Fenchurch pulled out a clear plastic bag and held it up. 'I hung on to this because I had to cut it off her body. She had a piece of red string knotted around her left wrist.' He threw it over to Bryant. 'My first thought was Kabbalah.'

'No,' said Bryant. 'A Kabbalah string is usually a single strand of red woollen thread, and it's associated with Judaism. It's called a *roite bindele* in Yiddish. With a name like O'Connor she cer-

42

tainly wasn't Jewish, and it wasn't her married name because she'd never had a husband. St Bride's is the church of St Bridget of Ireland, so I daresay it attracts Irish worshippers.'

'Then maybe it was just decoration.'

Bryant turned it in the light, thinking. 'St Bride's. An interesting place to die. It's one of the oldest churches in London, at least the seventh to have stood on that site. Wedding cakes.'

'I'm sorry?'

'A baker called William Rich saw the spire from his window and had the idea for the shape of his daughter's wedding cake. Oh, and journalists always used it. A few old ones still do. Suggestive, don't you think?'

'No, I don't, Arthur. My mind doesn't store things up for later use like yours does. I prefer to have a brain, not a shed.'

'A couple of things,' said Bryant. 'You had to cut the string off, yes?'

'Yes, the knot–'

'Precisely. Not the sort of knot you could do up by yourself. So someone else tied it on for her.'

'What's the other thing?'

Bryant had second thoughts. 'Well, the colour is indicative – but I'll have to do some research on it.'

'Except that it's not your case.'

'I know, everybody keeps saying that.' Bryant jammed his hat back on and walked to the door. 'Ben, will you do me one favour for old times' sake? Don't file your conclusions for a couple of days. Say the printer ran out of paper or something. I want to try and get the investigation

43

transferred to the unit.'

'All right,' said Fenchurch. 'There's no one pressuring me, and we're short-staffed. I suppose I can sit on it for forty-eight hours without too much trouble.'

'You're a pal. Saturday night, weekend after next, bowling, you're playing for us. Eight p.m. sharp for warm-up drinks at the Nun and Broken Compass.'

'I won't do it,' said Raymond Land, shaking his head angrily.

'I don't see why not,' said John May. 'The City of London's on a high alert because of the banking protests, their resources are overstretched and I'm sure they'd appreciate the offer of help.'

'You just don't get it, do you?' Land hissed. 'They hate us. All of them, from the Commissioner downwards. Not just us. They especially hate Arthur. He makes them look bad. He swans in and nicks all the high-profile work, solves the cases and gets the column inches, and accidentally forces up their targets. Why should they give him a case that's already been assigned? He's been in to see me about it and I said no. Absolutely not. We have to keep our noses clean for a while.'

'Fair enough,' said May, raising his hands. 'The others wanted me to ask.'

'Wait, what others?'

'Everyone. Janice, Jack, Meera, Colin, all of them.'

'Are you telling me you've been going around canvassing support behind my back?'

44

'Of course not. But you know when Arthur gets a hunch it usually turns out to be right.'

Land caught sight of himself in the mirror and saw the usual mix of puzzlement, frustration and anger stirred together like a pudding in a bowl. The little hair he had left was turning grey. He wanted to show authority, but how could he when his detectives defied him at every turn? 'Look, it's bad enough having to fight everyone else in the police service without internal divisions as well. Bryant is a detective, not a mystic. He chases these cases because he fancies having a crack at them, not because he has some strange psychic ability to know exactly when–'

Land's office door opened and Bryant shambled in, his hands thrust deep in the pockets of a shapeless, patched corduroy jacket, his unlit pipe jutting from the side of his mouth. 'Wind's changed direction. It's in the east,' he said meaningfully. 'Looks like there's a storm coming.'

'Where have you been?' asked Land, annoyed.

'Ah. I was on my veranda having a quiet smoke and a think.'

'You haven't got a veranda. This is King's Cross, not New Orleans. It's a rickety old loading platform and it's unsafe. Please don't stand on it.'

Bryant gave a derisive snort. 'It doesn't matter at my age. These days I'm amazed if I just wake up in the morning. Senior citizens should take more chances, not less. Teenagers sleep all the time and us oldies manage four hours a night. Life is upside down. I have a hypothesis about how Amy O'Connor died.'

'You can't possibly know anything about her,'

45

Land protested as a faint but ominous roll of thunder rattled the windows. He glanced out at the seething grey skies above the station, unnerved.

'The old insurance office,' said Bryant, removing his pipe. 'They were tearing down a Victorian building in Salisbury Court, right behind the bench where O'Connor was sitting, but work stopped while they excavated a Roman floor in the basement. Some very nice mosaics. I've just been over there. I looked down into the ruined brickwork and saw something lying in the shadows. It might have been the reason for her death.' The raising of his eyebrow was a study in Stanislavskian method acting.

Land was dumbfounded. His attempts to show leadership were always undermined by his utter amazement at the abilities of others. As a student of human nature he would have made a fine pastry chef. 'Are you telling me that she was murdered?'

'I didn't say that. But I can see how she might have died. I need to find the children who were playing ball in the courtyard.'

'Well you can't, it's not your case.'

'No,' said Bryant, 'but it soon will be.'

'So you're some kind of clairvoyant now?' said Land, exasperated.

'Answer the phone,' said Bryant, pointing to the desk. 'It's your wife.'

The phone suddenly rang, making Land jump. He gingerly raised the receiver. 'Raymond Land. Oh, Leanne, it's you. Yes, I know. I won't be late. All right.' He put the phone down. 'How

46

did you...?'

'The same way I know that you've developed a fear of rats, that you think you're undergoing a mid-life crisis and you've recently started to believe in the supernatural,' said Bryant.

'You can't possibly – who have you been speaking to?'

Bryant rolled his eyes knowingly and grinned, exposing an amount of white ceramic not seen since the reduction of the East Midlands Electrification Programme had resulted in a surfeit of semi-conductors on the London black market.

'I know everything about you, Raymondo, even things you don't know yourself.' Bryant gave a lewd wink as Land stared at him in ill-disguised horror.

Suddenly, the eerie sound of a theremin started up, the *oooo-weee-oooo* call sign of a hundred old monochrome science-fiction films. 'That's my mobile,' said Bryant, 'I must take this call. If anyone wants me, I shall be in my boudoir.'

'You haven't got a boudoir,' Land called after him helplessly, 'you've got an office!'

'All right, what's with the Sherlock Holmes stuff?' asked May, closing the door behind him. 'You're really getting up Raymond's nose.'

'Oh, it was a dreadfully cheesy trick, I know,' said Bryant airily, 'but I couldn't resist getting him back for refusing to let me try for the case. He's so adorable when his mouth is hanging open, like a spaniel trying to understand house-training instructions.'

'How did you know all that stuff about him? Or did you just make it up?'

'It's easy. His wife just called me by mistake and I rerouted it. He left a card from a rodent exterminator on his desk. We had rats at the old headquarters in Mornington Crescent and they never bothered him, but ever since Janice mentioned she's heard noises in the walls in this building late at night, he's been on edge.'

'The mid-life crisis?'

'He found out about his wife's affair, yes?'

'Only because you told him.'

'Now she's talking about divorce and he's suddenly realized he'll be back on the dating scene, hence his recent purchase of several appallingly unsuitable shirts. Oh, and that horrible after-shave he's starting pouring over himself. You must have noticed that he's smelling like a perfumed drain. And before you ask, he's started to believe in the supernatural because I can see that he's borrowed some books from my top shelf, notably *Psychogeographical London*, *Great British Hauntings* and my 1923 copy of *Mortar and Mortality: Who Died in Your House?* He's been upset ever since he discovered that Aleister Crowley ran a spiritualism club in our attic. Nearly every London house has been lived in by somebody else, and Crowley was all over this town like a cheap suit. It's hardly anything to get upset about.'

'You could try being nice to him for a change,' said May. 'He's been very supportive lately. I feel sorry for him, stuck in a job he hates, having to look after us lot. He can't understand how you think.'

'I should hope not,' said Bryant indignantly. 'I would be most offended if he could. But perhaps you're right. I'll make it up to him.'

'No.' May hastily held up his hand. 'Don't do anything unusual. Just do what he says for a while.'

'You mean don't push for the Amy O'Connor case.'

'Exactly.'

'All right,' said Bryant, 'but don't say I didn't warn you.'

'What do you mean?'

'"By the pricking of my thumbs, something wicked this way comes."' He sauntered to the door. I'm going to the terrace for a pipe of St Barnabas Old Navy Rough Cut Shag. But I'm telling you, there's more to Amy O'Connor's death than meets the eye.'

'Because of what you saw in a Roman excavation?' asked May.

'That, and because of the string that was tied around her wrist.'

5

THE ENEMY

'You're not going to be happy about this,' warned John May. 'Home Office Security has backed up the City of London. They won't let you have the O'Connor case.'

'Why not? What's it to them?' Bryant asked, as he and May made their way across Bloomsbury's sunlit garden squares towards the Marchmont Street Bookshop.

'Your pal Fenchurch has already tipped someone off about his likely verdict, although he seems to be holding back the full official report. Once that's been filed, the case is technically closed unless you get Home Office dispensation, and they won't grant it.'

'That's odd. I was with him this morning and he said he'd delay the process by forty-eight hours. Why would he have told someone?'

'You weren't supposed to go there. Maybe he's being pressured.'

'That makes no sense unless someone at the Home Office thinks the case is more important than it looks. Amy O'Connor was a low-paid bar manager. Apparently she studied biology at Bristol University, but dropped out. She's not connected to anyone important. Unless there's something in her past. I could take a look at her employment records and see if—'

'Arthur, maybe she really did just black out and fall.'

'Without a cause of death? Next you're going to tell me she was struck down by the hand of God. Nobody dies without a reason, and no reason has been found. If I can just go back through her history…'

'But it's not your—'

'Don't say it again, all right? Here we are.' Bryant stopped in front of the bookshop and pointed proudly at the window. 'Sally's given me pride of place.' Bryant's wrinkled features peered up from the cover of a slim volume entitled *The Casebook of Bryant & May*, by Arthur Bryant, as told to Anna Marquand. Beside it, a joss stick protruded from the head of a green jade Buddha, as if in funereal remembrance.

'It's just the first volume, as you know, but it covers quite a few of our odder investigations, from the Leicester Square Vampire and the Belles of Westminster, to the Billingsgate Kipper Scandal and the hunt for the Odeon Strangler.'

'And you honestly think the public wants to read this stuff? People aren't interested in the past any more. The young want to get on and make something of their lives. They don't want to wallow about in ancient history.'

'I didn't write it for the ambitious young,' said Bryant primly. 'I wrote it for the mature and interested. And, if you don't mind, it isn't ancient history, it's my life. Yours, too.' Privately, though, Bryant had to admit that the events of his life were receding into history. Last Christmas the

51

milkman had come in for a warm-up and had asked his landlady if she collected art deco. 'No,' Alma had replied, 'this happens to be Mr Bryant's furniture.' Yesterday's fashions were today's antiques.

The owner of the small bookshop greeted Arthur. Now in her early fifties, Sally Talbot was an attractive blue-eyed blonde with the natural freshness of someone raised on a warm coastline. John May was a great appreciator of beautiful women, and his pride required him to smooth his hair and pull in his stomach.

'Nice to see me in the window,' Bryant commented. 'I'm not sure about the incense, though. It looks as if I've died.'

'Oh, we've got damp,' said Sally. 'It's better than the smell of mildew. Thank you for coming by to sign the stock. You only went on sale this morning but we've already sold a few copies.'

'One of them wasn't to a man who looks like a vampire bat, was it?' asked Bryant. Oskar Kasavian, the cadaverous Home Office Security Supervisor, had made it publicly known that he objected to Bryant writing his memoirs, and had been trying to get hold of the manuscript so that he could vet it for infringements. The Peculiar Crimes Unit was the flea in his ear, the pea under his mattress, the ground glass in his gin, but at least he had lately abandoned his attempts to have it closed down. So long as the unit's strike rate remained high, there was little he could do to end its tenure. He was not against the idea of the place so much as its method of operation, which defied all attempts at rational explanation, beyond a vague sense of modus vivendi among its staff.

'No, they went mostly to sweet little old ladies who love murder mysteries,' said Sally.

Bryant dug out his old Waterman's fountain pen, uncapped it and shook it, splodging ink about. 'How many do I have to sign?' he asked.

'Well, five if you don't mind.'

'Is that all you have left?' Bryant beamed at the bookseller. 'How many did you sell?'

'Three.'

'Oh. What's your bestselling biography?'

'*Topless* by Katia Shaw,' said Sally. 'She's a glamour model.'

Bryant turned to his partner in irritation. 'You see? This is what's wrong with the world. A young lady with bleached hair, an estuarine accent and unfeasible breasts can outsell a respected expert with decades of wisdom and experience.'

'She's human interest,' replied May. 'You're not. People reading her story will feel that if she can make it without talent, maybe they can.'

'Well, I find that phenomenally depressing.' Bryant's theremin call sign sounded once more. 'Well, speak of the Devil,' he said, checking the number, 'it's Mr Kasavian himself. I bet I know what this is about. I'd better take it outside.'

Ten minutes later, the detectives had hailed a taxi and were heading south towards Victoria. 'My guess is he wants an explanation about the memoir,' said Bryant.

'Then why would he ask to see me as well?'

'You're mentioned in the title of the book, John. You're as involved in this as I am. I think he

53

might have found something unpalatable in one of the chapters and taken objection.'

'I wonder if it's the part where you refer to MI7 as a secure ward for the mentally disenfranchised, or the bit where you describe his department as a hotbed of paranoid conspiracy theorists with a looser grip on reality than a stroke victim's hold on a bedpan handle?'

'I'm impressed you remembered that,' said Bryant, pleased. 'There's nothing in the book that breaches the Official Secrets Act, and that's the only thing he can get me on. Anna triple-checked it.'

'Yes, but Anna Marquand is dead.' Bryant's biographer had supposedly died of septicaemia in the South London home she shared with her mother, but she had passed away shortly after being mugged by an unknown assailant. The case remained unsolved.

'You know my feelings about that,' said Bryant. 'I'm sure Kasavian's department is implicated somehow. He might not have been directly involved, but I bet he knows who was.'

'I'm not so convinced any more,' said May. 'You honestly think the Home Office found something in your memoirs that was so damaging they would commit murder to cover it up? They're part of the British government, not the Vatican.'

'I think they might have gone as far as condoning an unlawful killing, if it involved the Porton Down case.' Bryant sucked his boiled sweet ruefully.

Porton Down was a military science park in Wiltshire, the home of the Ministry of Defence's

54

Science & Technology Laboratory, DSTL. The executive agency had been set up and financed by the MOD to house Britain's most secretive military research institute. Three years ago there had been a rash of suicides at a biochemical company outsourced by the DSTL. The project leader at the laboratory had turned whistle-blower, and had been found drowned. At the time, Oskar Kasavian had been employed as the head of security in the same company. It might have been coincidence – government defence officials moved within a series of tightly over-lapping circles – but the absence of information made Bryant suspicious.

'Why do something so dramatic?' asked May. 'Why not simply slap an injunction on the book?'

'That would be the best way to draw attention to it, don't you think? Do you honestly imagine governments can't make people disappear when they want to? Looks like we're here.'

The taxi was pulling up in Marsham Street, the new Home Office headquarters. The building had won architectural awards, but to Bryant's mind its interior possessed the kind of anonymous corporate style favoured by corrupt dictators who enjoyed picture windows in the boardroom and soundproofed walls in the basement.

'A word of advice, Arthur,' May volunteered. 'The less you say, the better. Don't give him anything he can use as ammunition.'

'Oh, you know me, I'm the soul of discretion.'

May's firm hand on his shoulder held him back. 'I mean it. This could go very badly for us.'

'That's fine, John, so long as you remember

that he is our enemy. Anna Marquand was more than just my biographer, she was fast on her way to becoming a good friend; someone I trusted with the secrets of my life. And she may have paid for it with her own.'

In the immense open atrium, the detectives appeared as diminished as the figures in a Lowry painting. A blank-faced receptionist asked for their signatures and handed them plastic swipe cards.

Three central Home Office buildings were connected from the first to the fourth floors by a single walkway. This formed part of a central corridor running the length of the site, commonly known as the Bridge. Kasavian's new third-floor office was in the only part of the building that had no direct access to sunlight. As the detectives entered his waiting room, they felt the temperature fall by several degrees.

Kasavian's assistant looked as if she hadn't slept for months. 'Perhaps he drains her blood,' Bryant whispered from the side of his mouth. She beckoned them into an even dimmer room. Kasavian was standing at the internal window with his back to them, his hands locked together, a tall black outline against a penumbra of dusty afternoon light. In this corner of the new century's high-tech building it was forever 1945.

May glanced across at his partner. Arthur Bryant had no interest in what others thought of his appearance. His sartorial style could most easily be described as 'Postwar Care Home Jumble Sale'. It was usually possible to see what he had been eating just by glancing at his front. John May prided himself on a certain level of elegance, although his police salary did not run to hand-made suits. When Kasavian turned, May instantly recognized the Savile Row cut of charcoal-grey cloth, the lustrous gleam of Church's shoes, the dark glitter of Cartier cufflinks, and felt a twinge of jealousy.

'Take a seat, both of you. I'm sorry about the light. Sometimes when I'm stressed my eyes become hypersensitive.'

Bryant shot his partner a meaningful look. *Something's wrong here.* Kasavian never revealed anything that could be interpreted as a human flaw; it wasn't in his DNA to do so.

Kasavian sighed and absently ran a palm against the side of his oiled black hair. As yet he had looked neither of them in the face. He stalked around his chair, picked up an onyx-handled letter opener and set it back down, then suddenly seemed at a loss. Searching about in vague confusion, he eventually planted himself on the edge of the desk and carefully studied each of them in turn.

'This isn't about your memoir,' he said finally. 'Our legals gave it a cursory glance when it was still proofing.'

'That's odd,' said Bryant. 'The galleys were locked away.'

Kasavian waved the implication aside. 'We let you off because it appears your early cases weren't covered by actionable security regulations, and the department has resolved not to take a stance on your more provocative jibes. We like to think we can take a joke, and besides, your personal opinions don't matter to us. This – well, it's about something else entirely. And it occurred to me that you might be able ... that is, you might be the only ones ... who could help me out.'

'What do you mean?' asked May.

'Perhaps I'm not making myself clear,' said Kasavian, rising and starting to pace about. 'I want to hire your services.'

6

PERSECUTED

Bryant was taken aback by the tone of Kasavian's voice. The civil servant he knew had a steely grimness that turned the lightest remark into the pronouncement of a death sentence, Judge Jeffreys with a gastric complaint. Now he sounded unsure of himself and almost human.

'I know there has been a certain level of ... dissension between us in the past, but I want to put that behind us.'

'Fine,' said Bryant, 'but could you sit down? You're making me nervous.'

Kasavian went behind his desk and sat. Bryant was amazed. It was the first time the security chief had ever heeded one of his requests. Steepling his long, crab-leg fingers, Kasavian thought for a moment. 'I don't want this to go beyond my office, do you understand?'

'Of course,' May readily agreed, inching forward on his chair. Bryant shot him a jaundiced look.

'I have a problem. It has nothing to do with the antagonism between your unit and my department. This is a purely personal matter.'

Bryant was clearly fighting to suppress a grimace. He liked his enemies cold and bitter, like his beer. Anything less weakened them in his eyes.

'I don't know if either of you has ever met my wife?'

'Certainly not,' said Bryant. 'I never pictured you being married to a—' He was thinking of *human being*, but hastily ended the sentence.

'She's – very beautiful. Very young. Perhaps too young.' He lifted a framed photograph from his desk and showed it to them. 'In this job one expects to be vetted for many different degrees of security clearance, but one thing they don't do is decide whom you fall in love with. Perhaps they should do. How can I describe Sabira? She's wilful and easily bored. Rather like a Christmas tree: beautifully adorned but likely to burn the house down if left unattended.'

For Bryant, this was intolerable. The last thing he wanted was to know about the private life of his arch-nemesis, but the framed photograph was extraordinary. It showed an extremely attractive woman with a heart-shaped face, an absurdly flat stomach and cantilevered breasts, lying in a cheesecake pose on a sun lounger in a candy-striped bikini. It looked less like she was absorbing the rays of the sun than radiating them. She did indeed appear to be very young. If Kasavian had to be married at all, surely his wife should have had a face that could send a dog under a table?

Meanwhile, May was taking another look at the security supervisor and trying to imagine how on earth women could find him attractive. There was, he supposed, power and gravity in his bearing, authority in his saturnine features. A wife would be able take shelter if not comfort, and some were more concerned with finding a safe harbour than igniting passion.

'She is the light of my life. Everything changed after I met her. But now there's something wrong between us. It's hard to explain. In the last six weeks her personality has undergone an extraordinary transformation. She is angry all the time – very angry. Not just with me but with everyone around her.'

'We're detectives, not marriage-guidance counsellors,' said Bryant. 'Have you tried taking her to the pictures occasionally?' May fired off a warning look.

'I'm not explaining myself very well. I'm not used to having this kind of conversation. Let me tell you more.'

Bryant's intestines cringed. He forced out a staggeringly insincere smile.

'We've been married for almost four years. Sabira is eighteen years younger than me.'

May gave a low whistle. Kasavian glared at him before continuing. 'Yes, I know it's a big gap. And on the surface, we have few common points of interest. She left school at fifteen to work in a biscuit factory; I went to Eton and King's College, Cambridge. Her parents used to manage an

60

industrial aluminium smelting plant in Albania and still live on the contaminated site; mine are landowners in Herefordshire and breed horses. She was raised a Muslim, I was High Anglican.'

'But you love each other very much,' said May, leaning further forward in his seat. Disgusted, Bryant unwrapped a Hacks cough sweet and crunched it noisily.

'Our affection for each other is beyond question. I don't want you to think this is some kind of lovers' quarrel – there's been a tangible and dangerous psychological change in her.'

'Can you give us an example of her behaviour?'

'I knew Sabira was raised in a religious household, but by the time she left home she was no longer a practising Muslim. I discovered she was superstitious when she began covering all the mirrors in the house.'

'Why did she do that?'

'She said there was an evil presence nearby.' Kasavian shook the thought aside, impatient with its absurdity. 'She said she could feel something following her around, intending harm. Believe me, I am fully aware how ridiculous this sounds.'

'Not at all,' said May. 'Please go on.'

'At first it just seemed like another of her quirks. Albania is one of the most religious countries in Europe, and she was raised in a small village, the kind of place about which they have a saying: "In order to live peacefully here, you must first make war with your neighbours." Coming to London must have been a profound shock for her. Lately her belief in this so-called evil presence has escalated. She started ransacking the house, but wouldn't tell me what she was looking for. One evening I came home and found her burning books and letters in the garden. She talked about devils taking human form, about satanic conspiracies and witchcraft and a plot against her and God knows how many other crazy notions. It's not as if this happened slowly; the change occurred over two, perhaps three weeks.'

'How did you cope with this?'

'I was very busy here. I had just taken over the development of the new UK border-control directive, so I wasn't at home much. It's by far the largest project the department has ever undertaken, a pan-European initiative designed to curtail the movement of members of terrorist organizations within the EU. As the head of the UK delegation I'm representing the wishes and intentions of Her Majesty's Government.'

'What does that mean exactly?' asked Bryant. Kasavian levelled ebony eyes at him. 'It means I don't get home in time for supper.'

'Does your wife have many friends here?'

'Hardly any. We met during her second London visit, and soon after she moved here to be with me.'

'You said the psychological change in her was dangerous – what do you mean by that?'

'Mr May, my job is to establish a rational explanation for why things go wrong and come up with practical solutions. But what do you do when your wife suddenly announces that she is being chased by demons? She swears there's someone in the grounds of the house at night, someone who watches her all the time and wishes her harm. She believes she's the victim of a witch-hunt. She says she only feels safe in a place of worship, so she spends more and more time in mosques and churches. One night she dragged me into the garden to look at a pattern carved on a tree and said it was a satanic sign, that she had been marked as a victim. I can't talk to any of my colleagues about this, and I certainly couldn't go to the police without any evidence. There's no proof, no consistency to these absurd stories. I thought if anyone could understand, it would be you. You seem to know a lot of abnormal people.'

'I'll take that as a compliment. Has she seen a doctor?'

'She absolutely refuses to do so, and I can't force her. She tells me there is a history of mental instability in her family, and fears becoming like her grandmother or her aunt, both of whom were sectioned after years of aberrant behaviour. She thinks a doctor will look at her past and make assumptions about her mental health.'

'But if she's delusional it seems she needs a therapist, not a detective.'

'You don't understand,' said Kasavian. 'I and my entire department operate within the confines of the Official Secrets Act, and although I've told her virtually nothing about my work over the time we've been together, she is my wife. Within a marriage there can be no absolute guarantee of privacy. And now she is running around talking to complete strangers, telling them people are casting spells on her. I have no idea what else she's saying to them. My position here is being compromised. It's as if she's two people, ecstatic one minute, suicidal the next. If I thought she was going mad I would force her to seek psychiatric help, but I suspect there's something more to it.'

'Why do you think that?'

'Because this cult of Devil-worshippers she imagines lurking behind every car and tree – I have a feeling she thinks I'm their leader.'

'Well, you must admit you do look–' Bryant began, but once again thought the better of it. 'What do you imagine brought on this sudden change in her behaviour?'

'I can only think something happened around six weeks ago – perhaps she met someone unsavoury, or did something foolish. Got herself into some kind of trouble. She won't give me a straight answer.'

'Then what do you expect us to do?'

'I need you to find out if there's anything behind these fantasies of hers,' said Kasavian. 'Obviously I wouldn't be able to grant the case official status, but if you get to the root of the problem I think I can promise a very agreeable recompense.'

'What did you have in mind?' asked Bryant.

'A full exoneration for the unit, an amnesty on your memoirs and a permanent guarantee of official status within the City of London Police structure. You'd no longer face challenges from the Met or the Home Office.'

'We'd be reinstated and officially recognized?' asked Bryant, staggered.

'I just want my wife back,' said Kasavian, looking suddenly pitiful. 'Please, find a way to make her sane again.'

'I haven't felt this revolting since we wormed Crippen,' said Bryant as they headed towards Victoria Station. 'Dracula seeks our services and asks us to sort out his barking wife's persecution complex? The very unit he's spent the last few years trying to close down?'

'You heard him,' said May. 'He has no one else to turn to.'

'Of course not, everybody hates his guts. But we're not experts on mental health. Quite the reverse, if anything. Besides, if I know Kasavian he's less concerned about his wife's sanity than he is about making sure his department isn't brought into disrepute.'

'That's understandable. He's about to represent British interests in Europe. The last thing he needs right now is something that will break his concentration and damage his reputation. And we might be able to deal with the problem quickly. It sounds as if Sabira's parents live on a chemically contaminated site, and presumably she was raised there as well, which might explain her mental problems now. We have nothing to lose by taking on the case.'

'Oh no? What if we fail? He'll have the perfect ammunition against us.'

'You heard him say that our involvement would be kept strictly off the record. He won't be able to blame us if we fail. What have we got to lose?'

'Do I have to remind you?' asked Bryant. 'Anna Marquand may have been murdered because somebody wanted to destroy the notes she made from my interviews.'

'It would help if you could remember what you told her about your past cases.'

'The sessions took place over a two-year period. I have no idea what I might have said. You know what my memory's like. I can't even remember where I'm living.'

'Good Lord, I'd forgotten you were moving at the weekend. How is it?'

'I don't know, I haven't been there yet.'

'But you must have seen the place.'

'No, I left it all to Alma.' Alma Sorrowbridge had been Bryant's long-suffering landlady for over thirty years, and had arranged to find a new flat for them after their old home had received a compulsory purchase order. 'That's not important right now. The important thing is... I've forgotten the important thing.'

'Anna Marquand.'

'Anna, yes. Her attacker had been to Oskar Kasavian's office. There was a Home Office slip in his pocket with Kasavian's department named on it.'

'But their new premises doesn't use entrance slips any more – it operates on a swipe-card system.'

'You're right. I hadn't thought of that,' said Bryant. 'A swipe card wouldn't have led us to Kasavian.'

'Exactly – so maybe somebody was trying to implicate him.'

Bryant groaned. 'This is dreadful. Not only do I lose my only suspect, I gain Dracula as a client.'

'I thought it would be right up your street – his

wife thinking she's being hunted down by a satanic cult.'

'Well, it is actually. Except that Kasavian should turn out to be the culprit, not the client. He looks like the sort of man who'd try to drive his wife mad, doesn't he? He's a cold-blooded bureaucrat. He can make children cry just by staring at them.'

'But he'd gain nothing by coming to us. His career is about to come under the microscope, and the last thing he'd want is to draw attention to his marital problems. He's giving us the power to wreck his career, Arthur. That's not the action of a man who wants his own complicity uncovered. It's the act of someone who's desperate and has been forced to turn to his enemies for help.'

'Fair enough, but it's Occam's razor, if you ask me. When a man looks like Christopher Lee with irritable bowel syndrome, it's hard to suddenly imagine him buying flowers and patting puppies. Never mind, I shall set aside my personal antipathy while we figure out what's behind it all. Just don't ask me to be friends with him afterwards.'

The detectives descended into the muggy tunnels of Victoria tube station.

7

THE ENGLISH DISEASE

Like most of the venerable institutions in London, the Guildhall was more impressive than beautiful. It had been the corporate home of the City of London for eight hundred years, and tonight was illuminated to welcome six European heads of state, from Finland, the Czech Republic, Spain, the Netherlands, Poland and Italy.

The chevrons and monograms of previous reigning monarchs and Lord Mayors shone down on the Great Hall's assembled guests, who were seated beneath monuments to Nelson, Wellington, Chatham, Pitt and Churchill. It was in this room that Dick Whittington had entertained Henry V, paying the delicate compliment of burning His Majesty's bonds on a fire of sandalwood. Gog and Magog, the short-legged, flame-helmeted giants who founded London before the time of Christ, glowered over the oblivious diners, who were finishing their desserts and moving on to coffee.

Sabira Kasavian was growing more upset by the minute. Sandwiched between a moth-eaten City alderman and a twitchy, crow-faced woman named Emma Hereward, she tried to spot her husband. Oskar was seated on the top table between the Deputy Prime Minister and the Chief of the Metropolitan Police. The intense conversation did not allow him time to look up and offer her a complicit smile. She had been relegated to an unimportant table because regulations prevented her from being within earshot of private ministerial conversations.

After almost four years of marriage she should have become used to such snubs, but each one still came as a shock. Her security clearance for visiting her husband at his place of work was one of the department's lower grades, because other wives had longer-serving spouses. She was not permitted to call him between certain hours, nor ask Oskar any questions about his work. There were rooms in the house she was forbidden from entering because they contained sensitive documents; she was not allowed access to any of his electronic devices. In times of a security crisis her friends, family members and correspondents were vetted, and sometimes, during those periods when the city was on the highest level of security alert, a guard was posted outside their flat.

She had thought she was freeing herself from her lunatic ex-boyfriend and her own impossible family, from the endless financial worries and the painful peculiarities of Albanian life, but instead she had stepped into a secretive gilded prison.

So she drank. Downing the dregs of her red wine, she snatched the brandy bottle away from the alderman, filling her water glass from it. She looked around at the other guests: the florid businessmen and their badly dressed wives; the desiccated accountants and corporate lawyers;

the frumpy horse set; the charmless couples who couldn't wait to get back to their dogs and their mock-Tudor Thames Valley houses; the so-called cream of the *nouveaux riches*. They all treated her as if she was a fool and a foreigner, as if those states were synonymous. None of them had bothered to get to know her. If they had, they would have found out that she was well read and intelligent, and spoke flawless, if accented, English. The other wives could speak only their own language plus a smattering of restaurant French.

She knew the real reasons for their enmity. She was young and attractive, and liked to dress glamorously. She was wearing a red dress edged with silver bugle-beads, a look none of the other wives would have dared to try and pull off, and she simply wasn't apologetic enough about not being English.

'Of course, we've largely stopped going to Capri because these days it's full of the most ghastly people.' Emma Hereward was talking across her. 'The budget airlines all fly into the region now.' As usual, Emma was seated with Anastasia Lang and Cathy Almon. The three of them were hardly ever apart and were as poisonous as scorpions. Cathy was the plainest and therefore the most picked on. All were married to men in Oskar's department.

'We go to a marvellous little island off Sicily—'

'Isn't that where Giorgio Armani has his villa?' asked Ana Lang, also talking across Sabira. 'The Greek islands are ruined, of course. Do you still have the place in Tuscany?'

'We gave it to the children. Better for the tax

70

man.' Emma noticed Sabira listening. 'Does your husband have a bolt-hole?'

'I'm sorry?' She didn't understand the question. What was *bolt-hole?*

'A second home – you know...' She walked her fingers. 'Somewhere you can whizz off to in the school holidays.'

'He has a house in Provence,' Sabira replied, 'but I have never been there.'

'Why ever not? I mean, the French are frightful, obviously, but you must get so bored being stuck in London.'

'I go home to see my family in Albania, but Oskar is usually too busy to accompany me.'

'Of course it's different for you, not having any children,' said Ana. 'But what would Oskar do in Albania?'

'We go to the beach there.'

'You have beaches?' Ana exclaimed. 'How extraordinary.'

'Yes, we have very nice ones.'

'That's a surprise. I always assumed the country was mainly industrial. We have a Polish chap – you must have met him, Emma. He built our patio. A terrible one for the vodka, but then all Eastern Europeans drink like fish.'

Sabira dropped out of the conversation and refilled her glass.

The speeches dragged on. Someone from the Animal Procedures Committee was talking about a new initiative, but he had a habit of moving his face away from the microphone, and whole sentences dropped out of earshot. The Deputy Prime Minister, a fair, faded little man who might easily have been mistaken for the manager of a discount software firm, was whispering in her husband's ear. She was so far away from the speaker's table that she could barely see who was talking.

'These initiatives are a waste of time,' Cathy Almon was saying. 'Democratic governmental procedures are hopeless. People respond better to a benign dictatorship; it saves them having to take responsibility.'

'I don't agree,' said Sabira, jumping in. 'Surely the key to any democratic process is represent-ation.'

Cathy stared at her as if she expected frogs to start falling from her mouth. 'I'm sorry,' she said. 'Remind me who you are again?'

'I'm Sabira Kasavian. We have met a dozen times.'

'Goodness, of course, you must forgive me. I have absolutely no memory for faces. You must be very proud of your father.'

'I am, but Oskar Kasavian is my husband.'

'Then you must be more mature than you look.' She meant it as a compliment, Sabira de-cided, a very English kind of compliment, the sort that offended as it flattered.

'No, I am not,' she said in a louder voice than she intended. 'He is forty-five and I am twenty-seven. There is an eighteen-year age difference between us.'

Ana Lang laid a beringed claw on her arm. 'There's no need to take offence, dear. You mustn't be so sensitive.'

'But I do take offence,' said Sabira hotly. 'You know where Giorgio Armani has his holiday villa

72

but seem unaware that Albania has a coastline. That one, Mrs Almon, likes to pretend we've never met, and makes me introduce myself again. And you just accused my countrymen of being alcoholics. You've been patronizing and condescending to me ever since we sat down.'

'I think you're overreacting,' said Ana, who could only cope with indirect criticism. 'There's no need to get so overwrought. This is simply dinner conversation. How long have you been married to Oskar?'

'Nearly four years,' Sabira replied.

'Then I'm sure you must be familiar with at least some of our social customs by now, just as we are with yours. For example, your drinking habit could hardly go unnoticed, and while you might consider it part of a noble heritage there are others who could misconstrue it as intemperance.' Ana bared her teeth in a mirthless smile, daring her to answer back.

'Then you'll know that, according to my noble heritage, when someone is insulted custom requires them to take revenge,' said Sabira.

She felt her hand going towards her full water glass. She intended to take a sip of brandy to steady her frayed nerves.

'The girl has some spirit, Ana. I think Oskar's done rather well for himself.' Emma Hereward laughed.

'I think you should stop picking on her,' said Cathy Almon, who knew what it was like to be constantly bullied.

'If you think I'm beneath him, you should say so to my face,' said Sabira. 'Hypocrisy is the

English disease, isn't it?'

'I imagine dear Oskar probably woke up on an Albanian fact-finding mission and found you beneath him,' said Ana Lang, chuckling softly with the others.

Sabira's grip on the brandy-filled glass tightened.

8

SABIRA

'You've got to admit it's a great photo.' Detective Sergeant Janice Longbright threw the newspaper at Jack Renfield. 'Look at her, she's a real wildcat.'

'Blimey, that'll sell a few copies.' Sergeant Renfield grinned approvingly. 'I wonder why they stuck a blurry box over the top of her thighs.'

'According to the *Daily Mail* she didn't have any knickers on,' said Longbright. 'She said she took them off before the dinner began because it was too hot in the room. It looks like a very tight dress. She probably didn't want a VPL.'

'Typical of a woman to think it was about fashion. Perhaps she was just feeling horny.'

'She was attending a dinner to welcome heads of state at the Guildhall, not hitting on guys in a Nottingham nightclub, Jack. It says there that she threw a glass of brandy in some old bag's face.'

'That "old bag" is Lady Anastasia Lang,' said

74

John May, snatching up the paper as he entered on Tuesday morning. "'Sabira Kasavian was arrested for being drunk and disorderly last night, and was taken to Wood Street Police Station." The arresting officer told me that Oskar tried to get her off the hook, but they had no choice but to run her in. Ana Lang was ready to press charges.'

'Wait a minute,' said Longbright, 'it's "Oskar" now? Since when did you switch to first-name terms?'

'Since he hired us to investigate his wife,' said May. Everyone in the common room turned to look at him. 'What can I say? I know. He's always been the enemy, and now he's the client.'

'After all the terrible things he's done in the past, I'm amazed he would trust us with something so personal.'

'Kasavian didn't have anyone else he could turn to. He managed to get his wife released from Wood Street a short while later, but by that time the damage had been done.'

'I wonder what upset her so much?' Longbright asked. 'It says here the Finnish Minister for Finance was forced to stop his speech.'

'This is a big deal,' said May. 'Three months ago our Deputy PM made a speech in Finland that was halted by hecklers halfway through, so now everyone's saying this was payback. But Sabira Kasavian says it wasn't planned; she'd been insulted all evening and finally had enough of it.'

'OK, she was drunk, but she must have known it would reflect badly on her husband. Kasavian's in line for one of Europe's top security posts, isn't he?'

'He may not be after this. Check the rest of the online press; see if there are any more details. I bet they're having a field day. Then fix up an appointment with the wife this morning. If she refuses to meet with us, I'll get Oskar to call her.'

'He's on the line right now,' said their detective constable, Meera Mangeshkar, covering the phone. May took the call with a certain amount of trepidation.

'I suppose you've seen the news this morning,' said Kasavian.

'I could hardly have missed it.'

'My wife was carried from the Guildhall kicking and screaming last night. *The Guildhall*. She smashed a tray of glasses and threw a shoe at one of my colleagues' wives, then swore at the arresting officer and tried to run off down the street.' He sounded exhausted.

'But you got the charges dropped.'

'Yes, but I can't keep her locked up at home. I'm not putting her under house arrest: I'm her husband, not her jailer. I don't know what to do. In an ideal world I'd take her away for a holiday, but this border-control thing is taking up all my time. And I can't send her home to Albania. Imagine how that would look just ahead of the talks.'

'Then I suggest you concentrate on your work and allow us to take care of her,' said May. 'You know our methods are unorthodox, but you'll simply have to trust us. We're going to need a level of access that may cause problems for you.'

'I've a stack of reports on your past activities from Leslie Faraday. I'm fully aware of the lines you cross to get results, Mr May. But in this case, I need you to do whatever you can for my wife. Go and see her, and I'll get you any other access you need. I have half a dozen important social occasions this month, and Sabira is expected to accompany me to them. If she suddenly stops turning up, my opposite numbers will be quick to make capital of it. The trouble is, I no longer know what she's likely to do.'

'First we'll look at your calendar and take her out of the more sensitive events.'

May prided himself on his understanding of women, but he felt uncomfortable knowing that if he failed to get to the cause of Sabira Kasavian's problem, her husband would have good reason to come down hard on the unit. Her behaviour could derail his career and wreck a European-wide initiative. The Americans would be watching, and would step in fast.

He swung into the office he shared with Bryant. 'Get your hat and scarf on, Arthur,' May instructed. 'Kasavian's granted us clearance. Let's catch his wife by surprise and find out what she's up to.'

'They have a house in Henley, but his London apartment is in Smith Square,' said May, opening the badly rusted door of Victor, Bryant's leprous yellow Mini. 'I'll drive.'

'You'll need this,' said Bryant, handing him an apostle spoon.

'What am I supposed to do with it?'

77

'Stick it down the side of the gear stick. It seems to hold it in place.'

May gave up trying to move the seat back, and set off into the traffic, heading towards the river. There was something wrong with Victor's gears. 'I'm surprised this thing passed its MOT,' he said as the car leapfrogged across the Euston Road.

'It passed under certain conditions,' replied Bryant vaguely. 'I think one of them was that I must never drive it anywhere.'

'Then it's an illegal vehicle.'

'No – I'm not driving, am I?'

Smith Square, just south of the Palace of Westminster, was dominated by the immense white frontage of St John's, a baroque church now used as a concert hall. Surrounding it were the offices of the Department for Environment, Food and Rural Affairs, the Local Government Association and the headquarters of the European Parliament. Sandwiched between these grandly appointed workspaces were a number of elegant flats.

'I wouldn't want to live here,' sniffed Bryant, pulling his scarf tighter as he gazed up at the grand buildings.

'Why not?' asked May.

'The noise.'

'There isn't any.'

'Not now, but whenever there's a government crisis the BBC sends its outside-broadcast vans over here, and they're so full of electronic equipment that the technicians have to leave their air-conditioning units running all night, and they keep everyone awake.'

'You're a mine of useless information, do you know that? Come on.' May trotted up the stairs and rang the doorbell.

A porter admitted them into a hallway chequered with black and white diamond tiles. 'Janice texted me to say that she'd cleared the way, but leave the talking to me for once, OK?' May instructed.

The second-floor front door opened to reveal a slender, delicate-boned young woman with large, expressive eyes, her blonde hair knotted in a graceful chignon. She was wearing a black and silver T-shirt that read 'Wild Girl', very tight jeans and high heels. For a moment, Bryant assumed it was the maid. Then he remembered the photograph.

She studied the detectives in puzzlement. 'I'm sorry, I was expecting you to be more, well, Scotland Yard, you know? At home we used to have an old English television programme with a detective, always doing crossword puzzles and breaking secret codes.'

'Ah, you were expecting someone in a gabardine mackintosh with a pencil moustache and a pipe,' said Bryant. 'Possibly wearing a bowler hat. Actually, I'm very good at breaking codes and I do have a pipe.'

'No,' said Sabira, 'I just meant he was younger.' Her blue eyes widened and her hand rose to her mouth. To their surprise, she started giggling. 'Oh God, I've done it again,' she said, horrified and amused in equal measure. 'Lately I seem to have offended every English person I've spoken to.' She ushered them into a narrow painting-filled hall that led to the drawing room.

'It's quite all right,' said Bryant, revealing a crescent of bleached false teeth. 'I don't suppose there's any chance of a cup of tea?'

'Of course – the tea, always the tea!' Settling the detectives, she ran to the kitchen, her heels clicking on the oak floor, and called back over her shoulder: 'Do either of you know a cure for a hangover? I feel terrible this morning.' She sounded unrepentant.

Bryant had already found an armchair. He pointed back at the wall mirror behind him; a bolt of black velvet material had been thrown over the glass. 'She's behaving very oddly,' he whispered. 'You'd better go and see to her.'

May raised his hand. 'Leave this to me.'

He joined Sabira in the kitchen. 'Mrs Kasavian–' he began.

'Oh, call me Sabira, I can't bear being so formal.'

'I have something that might sort out your head. But I'll need–'

'Just dig around in the cupboards for anything you want. I have a tiny man with a road-drill behind my eyes.' She was racing around in the tiny space, boiling water, spilling milk, rattling cups, nearly dropping them.

May found what he needed. Filling a tumbler with milk, he added a dash of Worcester sauce, chilli sauce and black pepper, and cracked an egg into the mixture. 'You must drink it straight down without breaking the yolk,' he explained. 'The egg contains cysteine, which helps fight the free radicals in your liver.'

Sabira gave the tumbler a mischievous sidelong

glance, and then grabbed it and downed it in one, slamming the empty glass into the sink. '*Gëzuar!*' she shouted. She wiped her lips with the back of her hand, flicked a loose blond curl away from her eyelashes and grinned. 'That was truly – disgusting.' She laughed again.

Bryant had settled so deeply into the armchair that he looked as if he came with the room. 'You were a long time,' he complained, helping himself to biscuits.

'We were getting rid of an annoying little man,' said Sabira, dropping on to the sofa opposite. 'I suppose you're here to tell me off.'

'I think it goes beyond that,' said May. 'I'm sure I don't need to remind you that you're married to a very high-powered official, and he has many enemies. They watch and wait for incidents like last night's, and use them against your husband's department.'

'Oh, the woman was rude, the speeches were long and boring, and I got drunk. In my country such a thing is not important. We laugh because there is so much pain in our lives. Sometimes there is nothing else to do but laugh – you understand this?'

'But your situation is very different now. Your husband is a very important man.'

'I know! Everyone keeps telling me about the important man! Don't you think I know that I have shamed him? Of course I know! But there are things you don't know.' She stabbed a painted nail at both of them in turn.

'Perhaps you'd like to tell us,' said Bryant.

'How do I know I can trust you?'

'I'm too old for games,' said Bryant. 'If you can't trust a man of my advanced years, who can you trust?'

'That is a fair point,' Sabira conceded. 'I'll try to answer your questions.'

'Was this the first time such an incident has occurred?'

'In public, yes. I've been upset for a while now.'

'What about? Why are you so upset?'

Sabira leaned forward with her head in her hands, trying to compose her thoughts. 'This is the fine English society I heard so much about. When I married Oskar, I knew things would not go easily for me, but I did not think I would be shut out so completely. Right from the start, I would walk into a room and feel it go cold. The women are the worst. At least the men fancy me. The women look at my clothes, my face and go – *poof!*' She flicked up her nose, imitating their disdain. 'They ask who are my people, where do they live, what do they own and I tell them with complete honesty. I say I was born Sabira Borkowski, and I grew up with the smell of a smelting plant in my nostrils. Oskar always said I would have to be less honest, but it's not in my nature. About a year ago I came to the ... understanding? Is that the word? ... that this was how it would always be from now on. I would be a social outcast.' She looked from one of her guests to the other, anxious to make them understand. 'I thought my marriage would open the doors, not slam them in my face. They think I'm stupid, common, a gold-digger, a whore. I was largely self-educated, but I am a clever woman. Since coming here I have studied English literature and art history as well as the history of London. I am better than these dried-up snobs, but perhaps not as confident.'

'Why not?' asked May, 'You seem to know your own mind.'

'I'll never be accepted by the people closest to my husband, and I really don't care. The old ones with their inherited furniture, their horses and boat races and seasons at Glyndebourne – boring, boring. Who cares? They talk about breeding, they trace their history back through the centuries but it's really just about who owns the most. Many of these people are Oskar's colleagues. It's as if they all belong to some big private club that no one else is allowed to enter. I smile and keep my mouth shut. I dress nicely and behave well and I outsmile every last one of them.'

'You didn't last night.'

'No, a demon came out of the brandy bottle.' She laughed again.

'But something else happened, didn't it? Tell me what occurred six weeks ago.'

'Did Oskar tell you that?' For the first time the pair saw a flicker of fear in her eyes.

'He says he saw a change in your behaviour from that time.'

'I don't want to talk about it. Some things are personal.'

'Then we can't help you,' said Bryant, putting down his cup. 'Ta for the biscuits.' He made to get up, but couldn't get out of the armchair.

'No, wait, please. Ask me something else.'

'All right. How do you get on with your husband's colleagues?'

'Which ones? The people in his department?'

'Yes, Edgar Lang, Stuart Almon and Charles Hereward,' said May. He saw Bryant mouthing '*Who?*' at him. 'They're all in Mr Kasavian's division, and they're also his business partners. That's correct, Sabira, isn't it?'

'Yes, they own a company together. Oskar is very careful about declaring his interests. He places great value on honesty.'

'Pegasus Holdings provides intelligence to the scientific community,' May told his partner. 'They check for security leaks and make sure data doesn't get passed to the wrong parties. It's part-funded by British and American homeland security interests.'

'There's no conflict with the ministry?' Bryant asked.

'It's the kind of public–private initiative this government loves. There are guidelines governing the running of such companies. The Home Office isn't allowed to out-source to Pegasus without holding an open tender.'

'Stuart Almon fell out with Oskar and is now just doing the books,' said Sabira. 'They are colleagues but not friends.'

'You didn't answer my question,' said Bryant. 'You must meet these people socially. It was Edgar Lang's wife you threw the drink over, wasn't it?'

'I don't care for Edgar or his wife. I find them insufferable. Charlie seems less pompous. I don't think he went to Eton. Stuart is simply invisible. I've met him dozens of times but can't even remember what he looks like.'

'And their wives?'

'They don't like me, of course. They spent their lives being groomed to marry powerful men, and along I come and steal their husbands' boss. I hate them all. But it doesn't matter what I think. I suppose they are all very clever men, and their wives – well, they do what such wives are trained to do.'

'Why did you cover up the mirror?' asked Bryant.

'There are bad things here.'

'What kind of things?'

'Devils. In my country we call them devils. I don't know what you call them.'

'You mean spirits?'

'They can be in many forms. They can be the ghosts of the dead, or people who are not what they say they are.'

'Who are these people?'

'They take different shapes,' Sabira warned. 'Some of them are Oskar's friends. Some of them can walk through the walls.'

'Walk through walls?'

'Yes, in places where they should not be.'

May felt a growing sense of frustration. Each time he thought they were getting somewhere, Sabira's answers became abstract.

'Let's see if we can cut through some of the mystery,' said Bryant impatiently. 'You covered the mirrors because you didn't want to see these spirits? Or you didn't want them to see you?'

'That spirit waits for me in the dark. He glares over my shoulder. He will kill me if he can.'

Bryant clambered to his feet and walked over to

85

the mirror. With a flourish, he whipped away the bolt of black cloth. Sabira gasped and turned her face aside. To May, it seemed like a piece of terrible overacting.

Bryant stepped back and examined the mirror's surface. 'See? There's nothing.'

'He's not there now.'

'Your husband says you talk to strangers in churches.'

'Certainly. Why not? I feel safe there. When I was a little girl, if I ever felt sad or frightened I would go to the mosque and the feeling would go away.'

'So why do you go to churches?'

'What, you think because I was once a practising Muslim I cannot enter a church? It is a sanctuary to me, nothing more. A mosque is where my thoughts can be heard, but a church will do almost as well.' She laughed. 'I'm glad my parents can't hear me say that.'

'But your husband also says you believe there is some kind of … satanic club–'

'You have met Oskar's colleagues. They all belong to clubs, Boodle's, the Devonshire, White's, but sometimes there are clubs inside of clubs and this – this' – she stamped her palms together – 'is where they plan their evil.'

'But you don't honestly mean they're *satanic*?'

'Well – perhaps this is the wrong word.'

'Do you have many friends of your own age?' asked May, changing tack. 'Anyone in whom you can confide, have a good honest conversation?'

'Only in Albania. No English. My husband does not approve of my Albanian friends because they are low class.'

'You're not wearing any jewellery,' said Bryant, cutting in. 'Do you normally?'

The question took Sabira by surprise. 'Sometimes, for formal occasions only. But not like the other women. You hang baubles from a straggly tree to distract from the meanness of its branches.'

Bryant laughed but May could see they were not going to get any further. 'I think that's all we have to ask you today,' he said, rising. 'I hope we'll meet again.'

'I hope so too,' said Sabira, smiling warmly. 'My head is feeling much better now.'

'Well, I thought she was delightful,' said May as they headed back across the square. The sky had clouded over and a strand of grey shadow was massing above the church. 'But highly strung. All the paranoid stuff, it's just in her mind. She feels cut off from her friends, she hates the circles she's forced to mix in, and when she picks a fight I imagine her husband refuses to take her side.'

'I think it's something more than that,' murmured Bryant. 'Come over here. Children don't use this square. Hardly anyone cuts across it because the back gate is kept locked, and they certainly don't deviate from the path if they do. Take a good look at the grass.'

He wandered over to a patch of green within the boundary of the church and poked at it with his walking stick. Then he looked back at the Kasavians' second-floor apartment.

'This is the area of the street she sees reflected in the mirror. That's why she keeps it covered.

87

Look.' He directed his stick at a lamp-post on the path. 'She sees a man standing under the lamp-light at night, watching her.'

He bent and examined the flattened area. 'It rained on Saturday night. Someone stood here on the wet grass.' There were several cigarette butts tightly grouped in among the crushed blades. 'I think he stood here and watched her. And she's terrified of him.'

9

PERMISSIBLE MATERIAL

Alma Sorrowbridge dragged the last of the cardboard cartons inside the front door and kicked it shut with her slippered foot. When the removal men refused to pack up Bryant's chemistry experiments and transport them, citing health-and-safety regulations, her church group had kindly undertaken the task.

Now everything from his reeking Petri dishes to his mummified squirrels and the stuffed bear inside which Kensington Police had once discovered the body of a gassed dwarf had been shifted into the new flat's spare room, in an almost perfect replica of Bryant's old study.

Alma picked up a book and checked its spine: *Intestinal Funguses Volume 3*. None of Mr Bryant's books seemed to have been arranged alphabetically, but were grouped by themes and the vagaries of his mind. She set the tome between *A User's Guide to Norwegian Sewing Machines* and *The Complete Compendium of Lice* and hoped it would eventually find its place. After setting his green leather armchair behind his stained old desk and arranging what he referred to as his 'consulting chair' before it, she satisfied herself that everything was in its rightful place, gave the shelves a final flick of her duster and sat down to await her lodger's arrival. Bryant had been sleeping in his office, and had yet to see his new home.

The move to number 17, Albion House, Harrison Street, Bloomsbury, had been delayed because the council painters had decorated the wrong flat, but as she checked each of the rooms she saw much that was to her liking. The windows were large and let in plenty of light. The oven had already been put to good use and the kitchen was filled with the smell of freshly baked bread. Best of all, her bedroom was at the far end of the corridor away from Mr Bryant, so she wouldn't be disturbed by his appalling snoring.

The impatient knock at the door suggested that he had already mislaid his keys. 'You never told me we were on the third floor,' he complained before she had even managed to open the door wide.

'There's a lift. Why didn't you take it?'

'It smells of wee.'

'Don't be ridiculous, I just bleached it.'

'Aha, then it *did* smell of wee.'

'Of course not, I just knew you would make a fuss.'

'I really didn't realize we'd be all the way up

here.' Bryant sniffed and peered about himself in vague disapproval. 'There are lots of bicycles chained to the railings downstairs, and there's an Indian man in a string vest watering some kind of vegetable patch. He offered me a turnip.' He unwound his moulting green scarf and took a tentative step inside. 'Hm. Nice paintwork. Did you do that?'

'No, the council sent someone round.'

'What, they paid for it?'

'Yes, they pay for maintenance and upkeep.'

'That's a good wheeze. I don't know why we didn't think of this years ago. And you say the rent's very low?'

'You're classed as an essential worker, Mr Bryant, although I can't imagine why.'

'Where's my study?'

Alma pushed open the study door with a little pride, although pride was technically regarded as a sin by her church. 'Here we are,' she said, stepping out of his way.

Bryant walked around his desk, shifting books and ornaments by an inch here, an inch there. 'Where's my Tibetan skull?'

'Exactly where it always is,' said Alma. 'In your office at work.'

'And my Mexican Day of the Dead puppets?'

'You gave them to Mr May's sister's children the last time you went down to see them. She confiscated them from her boys after one of them cut himself on a crucifix and came up in boils.'

'Just testing. My books are out of order.'

'Well, that will give you something to do when you're home, won't it?'

'And where's my marijuana plant?'

'This is a council block. You can't keep it here any more, the police have dogs.'

'I am the police, you silly woman.'

'I sent it to your office. Honestly, I thought you'd be pleased. It took half a dozen of us to move all your stuff in and lay it out correctly. There's a nice southerly light.'

Bryant sniffed. 'I suppose it'll have to do.'

'It'll have to do,' Alma repeated. She was a large, cheerful woman predisposed to a kind smile, but right now the smile was fading to a scowl. *It'll have to do?* You ungrateful, miserable old man! You didn't help me in any way. I had to attend the court hearings and deal with the compulsory purchase order of our old place, then search for accommodation and apply for the flat and deal with the council, a job I wouldn't wish on a dog, then move everything by myself and reinstall it here without a single thing broken, missing or out of place, and all you had to do was walk out of your old home and into this one with nothing more than the clothes on your back. I still have relatives in Antigua; I could have left you and gone home to live somewhere happy and sunny, but I stayed here. If I wasn't a good Christian I'd smack you around the head until your ears rang.'

'All right, you've made your point,' Bryant mumbled. 'It's very nice. What's for tea?'

'There's ginger cake and banana bread laid out in the kitchen, and a spiced chicken salad later.' She stood with her hands on her hips and resisted the temptation to give him a whack on the ear as he passed.

Longbright was staying late at the unit, transferring John May's interview notes. Downloading all the images she could find of Sabira Kasavian, including those in her social-networking profiles, she reassembled them by date and location. *She has a hell of a clothing allowance,* thought Longbright. *Skinny women can wear anything.* There were hardly two photographs where she was in the same outfit.

Longbright dreamed of a clothing allowance, although that would have been a slippery slope. She would have soon lavished it on impractical corsetry and 1950s sheath gowns.

The next thing she noticed was how closely Sabira stayed by her husband's side. In the few photographs that showed her seated with other people at government dinners, she appeared to be mutely listening. Her attitude was demure, as if she had been advised not to speak by her husband.

Around the end of the last week of May there was a noticeable change in the pictures. Sabira was rarely photographed without a drink in her hand, and appeared introspective, sullen, even startled. In the few Facebook shots she had put up from public events she looked flushed and nervous. Perhaps her drinking just got out of control, thought Longbright. *It happens.*

She spotted something else: a uniformity of style in the official press pictures. Checking the provenance of the images, she found that the same news agency had taken them, which probably meant that Sabira had been targeted by one specific photographer. She called the agency but it was shut for the night, so she checked Photo-Net's list of clients and found *Hard News* at the top of the supply list. She rang the editor, Janet Ramsey, on her mobile.

'Janice, you'd better have a damned good reason for calling me on my private number,' Janet warned. The unscrupulous editor was well known to the staff of the PCU.

'Do you have someone at PhotoNet permanently assigned to cover Sabira Kasavian?'

Janet sounded as if she was in a crowded cocktail bar. 'I wouldn't say he's permanently assigned. We have a special-interest list of public figures and their partners, as I'm sure you're well aware.'

'I guess you've been waiting for her to screw up.'

'Of course. We all want a good story, darling. And she has, hasn't she? I assume that's why you're calling me.'

'Who took the shot of her being carried out of the Guildhall last night?'

'You'd have to take that up with PhotoNet.'

'Obstruction, Janet. You know how that goes.'

'OK, it's no secret. His name is Jeff Waters. He likes taking shots of her. She's a very photogenic girl. She brightens a page on a slow news day.'

'Do you or Mr Waters get any instruction on the taking of photographs? I mean, from the Home Office. Her husband's—'

'—in the security department, I know. There are guidelines. The smudgers aren't usually allowed inside the ministerial venues, and if they are, they have to stay within specifically defined spaces. It's implicit that we don't take shots if they're tipsy, but negotiable. There are other protocols which you'd have to speak to the HO about.'

'How did you get away with last night's shot?'

'You're slipping, Janice. Take a careful look at the sequence. She's off the front step of the building. That's pavement under her shoes. Technically public space. She'd been cautioned by the police, which made her fair game. Permissible material.'

Longbright rang off. Sabira Kasavian must have noticed that she was being targeted by the same photographer every time she appeared in public. Perhaps that was part of the reason why she thought there was a conspiracy against her.

The detective sergeant pushed back from her desk and rubbed her eyes. It didn't seem like much of a case. But there was something else in Sabira's photographs – a certain look in her eyes, a certain angle of the head. Unable to put her finger on it, she closed down her screen for the night and decided to head home.

Jack Renfield stuck his head around the door. Although the room was cold, he was sweating. 'I've been whacking the punchbag upstairs. Didn't realize you were still here. I wouldn't get too close to me if I were you. D'you fancy a quick beer?'

'Not tonight, Jack,' said Longbright.

'You don't have to worry, I'm not going to jump on you or anything. At least, not without a shower. Joke.'

'No, I'm really not up for it.'

94

'A drink is just a drink, y'know. You look like you're going out later in that clobber anyway.'

Longbright toned down her look for work, but there was still a touch of the nightclub hostess about her. She had long ago decided that she would die in high heels. 'I'm just in a bit of a weird mood tonight.'

'Gonna start thinking you're avoiding me soon.'

'I'll take you up on the offer, I promise.' She knew how much Jack liked her, and was slowly getting used to his rough-and-ready manner, but while she thought of him as a tree or a fence-post, something strong you could lean on or shelter under, he seemed a bit too rooted to the soil. She still dreamed of achieving something beyond her work on murder investigations. 'What do you think about Kasavian's wife?' she asked.

Renfield shrugged. 'She's rich and bored and feeling neglected. Give it a few years, she'll start studying horoscopes and supporting cat charities; it's what they all do.'

'Thank you for your rich insight into the female psyche.'

'I mean it; she's going against the grain to try and assert some power, to tell him she's still got free will and that he can't take her for granted.'

'John and Arthur say she thinks she's being sort of – hunted.'

'Maybe someone has decided that she's a security risk and is keeping an eye on her movements.'

'Perhaps you're right.'

'See you in the morning, beautiful. Did I tell you that you look beautiful?'

'Jack, bugger off.'

As he headed out, Longbright turned back to her computer and reopened the photo file, to try to understand what she might have missed.

10

INVISIBLE CODE

Sabira Kasavian hated Fortnum & Mason.

The department store's pastel shades, its veiled windows, the airless, hushed old-world atmosphere that was meant to be charming felt merely repressive to her. She imagined wandering around its food hall with her mother, who would marvel at the jars of apricots in brandy, the tins of caviar and miniature hat-boxes of champagne truffles that cost as much as her family's weekly food bill. It seemed to be a store for people who disliked the simple pleasures of eating.

The wives of the Home Office officials met in the Fountain Restaurant every third Wednesday to boast about their holidays and luncheons and to complain about their husbands. Lately attendance seemed to have become compulsory, if only to ensure that no one was talking about you behind your back. They would have preferred to meet in the more expensive fourth-floor St James's Restaurant, but its bloated sofas and armchairs squatted around the tables like sumo wrestlers, and prevented the ladies from being seated closely together.

There were eight wives today, presided over by the impermeable Anastasia Lang. Everyone had turned up to see if further sparks would fly. Sabira had decided to attend because she needed to show that she was unrepentant about her behaviour on Monday night. The first few minutes were made all the more awkward by the wives' determination to act as if everything was normal between them all.

There was no air-kissing and no cocktails; they were not footballers' wives. Instead they went straight to the table and ordered the lightest and most complex starters, less salads than fragile ecosystems of exotic greenery. The wine list was considered with the gravity a juror might reserve for convicting a rapist.

'That is, if you're drinking wine?' Ana asked her foe pointedly as the other wives fell silent.

'I'll have a glass of anything red and full-blooded, a large one,' said Sabira, fixing the group with an open I-dare-you-to-argue smile.

Lunch progressed through the usual roster of subjects, dinners and weekend trips, charity work and the difficulties of finding reliable nannies and gardeners, but inevitably it arrived, as it always did, at husbands.

With little to contribute, Sabira listened and drank. She heard the chatter of birds on a fence: creatures noted more for their colourful plumage than their songs. If Sabira had known that she would be required to give up her voice, she might not have been persuaded to move to England and get married.

'I don't mind that he comes to bed with his

laptop,' one of the women said, 'but he puts it between us. He might as well stick an electrified fence down the middle of the duvet. I get the message; he's working. He doesn't need to point it up.'

'Perhaps you should consider having an affair, darling,' said Cathy Almon, already bored by the conversation.

'That's easy for you to say. Your husband is an accountant. He's not required to think about anything but totting up numbers.'

'Actually he heads up the Home Office's Workforce Management Data System, and has a number of very important functions within the ministry,' Mrs Almon recited.

'Aren't there websites that arrange affairs for you?' asked the woman opposite her.

'God, you couldn't leave a data trail. It would have to be the butcher's boy or someone like that.'

'Someone uncouth and inarticulate.' They all laughed.

Ana Lang turned to Sabira. 'But, of course, we should ask you, shouldn't we? I hear you already have someone uncouth waiting in the wings, don't you?' Her smile was as venomous as ever.

'I don't know what you mean,' Sabira replied, sipping her wine.

'Oh come on, darling, your little secret is safe with us,' said Emma Hereward, looking around the table. 'Spill the beans.'

'There is only my husband.'

'It's perfectly understandable. You're *au mieux de votre forme*. You must have at least fift– ten years on the rest of us. You're among friends here. You can tell all.'

'There's nothing to tell. I would never dream of being unfaithful. I was raised a Muslim.'

'We know all about the Muslims, sweetie, they're the worst. Half of them operate double standards. I don't know why you insist on pretending that you're more virginal than anyone else. We all heard you weren't wearing any underwear at the Guildhall dinner.'

'We know who he is,' said Ana. 'We've all seen him.'

'Have I?' asked Cathy, confused.

'Yes, darling, outside the Spanish Embassy – dark-haired, rather dishy.'

'You mean... He's just a photographer,' said Sabira, colouring.

'Yes, but we've all seen the way he looks at you.'

'He means nothing to me.'

'So you are seeing him!' Ana was triumphant.

'No, of course not!'

'It's funny how you always seem to be wearing more make-up when he's around.'

'If I wore as much make-up as you I'd suffocate,' Sabira replied, draining her wine. She had yet to master the subtle art of English sarcasm. The joke fell flat.

'You're supposed to sip that,' said Ana, pointing to the glass. 'It's a Montrachet, not potato vodka.'

Sabira meant to slap her face, but in the process Ana's earring came loose somehow and gashed her left cheek. Ana yelped as she saw the smear of blood on her fingers. As the others came to her aid, Sabira realized that none of them

99

would take her side. Dipping her napkin in her water glass, she tried to help but Ana slapped her hand aside. 'Get away from me,' she hissed. 'Go back to the pig farm where you were raised.'

'If I'd been raised like a pig I'd still have better manners than any of you,' she said, rising sharply. Her chair went back and the shoulder bag she had draped over it fell to the floor, spilling papers.

Ana looked down, clutching at her face. 'What the hell are you doing with my husband's private correspondence?' she said.

And that was when all hell broke loose.

'She's done it again,' said Meera Mangeshkar, running into the office. 'And this time it's on Sky News.' She reached over and opened a fresh screen on Longbright's computer. 'She attacked the same woman over lunch. Two security guards just took her away.'

'That looks like Fortnum and Mason,' said Longbright. 'I made a shoplifting arrest there once.' As she watched, a red banner rolled across the footage: 'Home Office official's wife in restaurant brawl'. 'They'll have taken her to West End Central in Savile Row.'

'No,' said Mangeshkar. 'I called them. She's been driven to the Home Office. This is serious.'

'One of us needs to be there as an independent observer,' said Longbright. 'You'd better tell John.'

May arrived in Victoria forty minutes later and found that Sabira Kasavian had been taken to a private room on the ground floor of the building opposite her husband's department. The trapezoid of grey concrete in which he found himself was far less welcoming than the airy glass atrium it faced. The staff security passes had jumped a couple of grades.

'You can't see her at the moment,' warned the scrubbed young man who came out to find him. 'This is out of your jurisdiction.'

'You're Andy Shire, aren't you?' said May, squinting at the laminated ID pinned on the security official's breast pocket. 'We met with the Police Commissioner a few months back.' May was owed a favour after he had helped Shire locate a suspected arsonist.

'I remember,' said Shire, 'but I still can't give you access.'

'I can obtain written permission from Sabira's husband if need be. Why wasn't she taken to West End Central?'

'I think you know the answer to that one, John. In matters of national security we override the police.'

'The PCU isn't part of the Met, it's a Home Office unit, so we're working on your side. I'm just trying to understand why she was brought here. I don't want to have to ask Oskar. I know he's got a lot on his plate right now.'

Shire knew that his boss would complain if his staff failed to shield him from unnecessary interruptions. 'All right,' he said. 'It appears a number of sensitive papers were found on her when she was removed from the restaurant. We don't yet know if they were taken from this building.'

'You mean she's going to be held on a spying charge?'

'We're trying to ascertain the importance of the documents at the moment. If she took them without authorization, it looks as if this is going to fall under the Terrorism Investigation Act. You interviewed her, so I assume you know she's still in contact with her Russian ex-boyfriend.'

'No, I didn't,' he admitted. 'How is she?'

'She came in here kicking and screaming, having a real panic attack. It looked like a full-blown psychotic episode to me. Her doctor gave her a sedative and she's feeling a little better now, but she keeps calling for her husband. He's still in a meeting.'

May knew that Kasavian was preparing to present the UK's case for the European border-security initiative in just over a week's time. As it was likely that his future career relied upon driving the deal through, he wouldn't take kindly to being disturbed, even to help his wife. May dreaded to think what his reaction would be when he heard the details of Sabira's latest outburst.

'Andy, I'm working with her husband to try and sort this out,' he explained. 'When do you think I can get to see her?'

'Obviously we don't want to hold her any longer than is necessary, but we need an explanation as to why she had a classified file in her handbag. This isn't half an hour in the cop shop and a slapped wrist. We're following protocol now, and you have to realize it could lead to a prosecution.'

'It could be a set-up, Andy. Maybe Kasavian has an enemy who's using his wife to get at him.'

Shire gave a cold laugh. 'Are you kidding? Oskar has nothing but enemies. They're required to sustain the department. Just don't ask us to narrow down the suspects.'

The South Bank Centre and the Royal Festival Hall were bedecked with fluttering blue and red flags, turning the promenade into an urban seaside town. Artificial sandbanks had been placed against the embankment walls and topped with beach huts as part of an arts festival.

'What a mess,' said May, leaning on the cool stone balustrade of Waterloo Bridge.

'I don't know, I quite like it,' said Bryant, screwing the pieces of his pipe together and digging around for his tobacco pouch. 'The juxtaposition of sand and grubby old buildings. It's a bit like Margate.'

'I mean the investigation. We didn't ask any of the right questions. It's my fault. I let her charm me. It was completely inappropriate behaviour.'

'I'm glad you pointed that out. You've always been a sucker for a pretty face. She played you like a Stradivarius, matey. We should have run a thorough background check on her first. I didn't know about the ex-boyfriend or her past mental-health issues. I'm losing my touch.'

'I thought it was strange to find her in such an upbeat mood the morning after she'd made a spectacle of herself. I asked Janice to find out if she's on prescription medication, but she says apparently not. She's being assessed by her doctor later this afternoon.'

'Have you ever read Henry Mayhew?' asked

Bryant, looking out over the olivine water as he drew flame into his pipe bowl. 'London Labour and the London Poor, 1851. Fascinating stuff. Conversations with ordinary working-class Londoners. Of course we still have a tremendous class divide, but the disenfranchised weren't always outsiders. If anything, they knew more about what was really going on. Mayhew met rat-catchers and fire-jugglers, pickpockets and sewer-hunters, and the thing you notice most when you read their accounts is this: a poor man will tell you everything, and someone in society will tell you nothing.'

'That's true enough,' May agreed. 'It seems the further up you go, the less you find out.'

'There are only a handful of major landowners in London, but we never fully discover the truth about them. It's all part of the invisible code of English conduct that baffles foreigners.'

'So you think we're wasting our time even talking to Sabira?'

'No, I believe she feels she's been genuinely ill treated.'

'Isn't that just naivety on her part?' asked May.

'Maybe. When you reach a certain level it's not about how much money you have, but your background. Knightsbridge and Notting Hill may be home to wealthy New York bankers and Dubai businessmen, but even they have trouble reaching the inner circles of power. It's certainly not something that's automatically conferred upon you by marriage. The Foreign Office and the Home Office have always been run by men like Kasavian. I'll bet you his entire family moves in

104

government circles. He may well worship the ground she walks on, but he'll never let her in.' Experience had encouraged Bryant to hold bleak views about the British class system.

'So it's his fault she's behaving like this? You don't think she just has anger-management issues?'

'Don't say "anger-management issues". What's wrong with the word "temper"? I'm not saying it's a conscious act, John. A job at the most senior level of government is a Mephistophelean deal. In return for power you surrender your peace of mind.'

'Are you sure you're not just siding with her because of your own working-class background?'

'Look, I remember standing at the end of Petticoat Lane with my father one freezing Sunday morning. All around us were men selling chickens and canaries and skinned rabbits, and my old man – who was sober for once – lifted me up so I could look into the window of Arditti's restaurant, and he said, "There'll always be a pane of glass between you and these fine gentlemen. Even when you think it's gone, it will still be there."' As if to illustrate the point, a cyclist passing behind them waved two fingers at the diplomatic vehicle that had just cut him up on the bridge.

'Oh, you've always had a chip on your shoulder about your background. You enjoy being an outsider.'

'I made the best of it because I never had a choice,' Bryant pointed out. 'Your father used to take you to the Wigmore Hall for classical concerts when you were a little boy.'

'Because he was a musician and wanted me to appreciate the finer things in life. But he never had any money. Our family was always hard up.'

'But your parents gave you ambition. Mine just wanted me to have a job. The fear of poverty is never far away from the working-class mind, and all the plasma TVs, PlayStations and iPhones are just talismans warding off that darkness. I think Sabira Borkowski married to free herself from the fear of poverty, and now she's paying the price.'

'Fine, but in her husband's eyes the situation is worsening and we're not helping. If you take her side, you'll be setting us against the government.'

'You know diplomacy has never been my strong point. I think everyone already assumes we're against the government.'

'Then what do you suggest we do next?'

'We go to this address.' Bryant held up the crumpled piece of paper he had used for wrapping up his sherbet lemons.

'I can't read your writing.'

'Neither can I, but don't worry, Janice put it in my phone. The Home Office is looking into the possibility of the spying charge. Let's talk to a more rational enemy – the woman Sabira Kasavian assaulted in Fortnum and Mason.'

11

THE GLASS

Edgar Lang and his wife lived in a redbrick Edwardian house with a wrought-iron veranda overlooking a wide, calm section of the Thames at Barnes, just past Hammersmith Bridge. Anastasia Lang was not at all pleased to find a pair of detectives standing in her porch, and reluctantly invited them in. She had covered the cut on her cheek with taped cotton wool, but her left eye was now turning a lurid shade of mauve.

'I'm fully prepared to press charges; I won't let anybody talk me out of that,' she said with ice in her voice. 'Not for the physical attack, but for stealing private documents.' She waved them into an immense glass-roofed kitchen that had been added to the rear of the already substantial house. 'I can't offer you anything, I've sent the maid home.'

'Nice gaff,' said Bryant, walking to the wall-sized window with his hands in his pockets. 'A very popular look, this. Classic at the front, modern at the back. Architectural hypocrisy. Should I call you Lady Anastasia?'

'Mrs Lang will do.'

'We're not here to ask you about the argument. What do you think Mrs Kasavian was doing with your husband's property in her handbag?'

107

'She must have taken it from the Pegasus offices in Great Portland Street. Edgar never keeps documents anywhere else.'

'You have children?'

'No, we have a dog.'

'Do any of the directors have kids?'

'Yes, Cathy and Emma do. I can't see what that has to do with–'

'Do you think Sabira was being paid to spy?' It was Bryant's technique to keep his witness wrong-footed.

'She's hardly short of money, the number of new outfits she wears. No, I don't think she was being paid to spy. I think she did it because she's jealous. She wishes she had my husband. Do you know how they met? My husband and Oskar were in a wine bar in the city. She started talking to Edgar first and, being a married man, he turned her down, so she went after Oskar. She was on a mission to find a successful man, operating with a fairly limited arsenal and a tight time limit on her sex appeal. Eastern European girls blow up like zeppelins when they hit thirty. Edgar said no, so she switched her attention to Oskar, who at that point had been divorced for over three years and was vulnerable to a pretty face.'

May could not imagine Kasavian ever being vulnerable. 'You're saying Mr Lang turned her down over four years ago, so she stole papers from his office? Doesn't that seem a little pointless to you?'

'I don't understand the point of anything she does,' said Ana Lang, touching her face lightly as if checking that nothing had shifted.

'How well do you and Mrs Kasavian know each other?'

'I meet her at social events, but we have nothing to say to one another. Her every utterance is a mystery to me. All I know is that she drinks too much and has an uncouth personality. You'll take her side, of course. You're a policeman. But what you must understand is that women of our social standing remain by our men, no matter how wrong we think they might be. It's part of the deal, it's what we signed up for.'

A tinkle of metal made them both turn around. Bryant had pulled the head off a small but rather valuable sculpture. Mrs Lang ploughed on with determination. 'When I want to know what a British politician really thinks, I ignore what he's saying and talk to his wife, Mr May. Neil Hamilton and Jeffrey Archer both had strong women at their sides to support and further their careers.'

'Archer went to jail, Mrs Lang, and Hamilton got into a fair bit of trouble himself.'

'I was merely illustrating the point. Sabira could have had it all, and now she'll have nothing. No one will have anything to do with her after this. I suppose you know she was having an affair?'

'I understand you accused her of having one, yes,' said May. 'We called your fellow lunch guests.'

'I did not "accuse" her, I merely stated what everyone already knew. It's the Australian photographer who always takes her pictures.'

'We know about him.'

Ana Lang was surprised. 'How?'

'He has an exclusive deal with a magazine called *Hard News*, Mrs Lang. He's assigned to follow Mrs Kasavian to social events. Do you have evidence that they're having an affair?'

'You only have to look at the way he photographs her.'

'So no actual proof.'

May heard the front door open and shut. A broad-bodied man in his late forties came in and set down his briefcase. With his slicked grey hair and pinstriped blue suit, he had the appearance of a stockbroker or an auction-house expert. 'Who's this?' he asked. 'What on earth's that on your face?'

'They're detectives,' Edgar Lang's wife explained. 'I was attacked today, but of course I couldn't get hold of you.'

'You should have pulled me out of my meeting. Why are they here?'

Bryant resented being discussed as if he was invisible. 'We needed to ask your wife a few questions,' he said.

'Not without a lawyer present,' warned Lang. 'I think you'd better leave now. I'm a very good friend of the Commissioner, and he'll have something to say about this.'

'No, it was better to make you leave right then,' said May as they walked along the footpath that ran beside the river. Ahead of them, a pair of swans swooped down to the water and folded their wings, looking like funfair love boats. 'I could see you were about to open your mouth. It seems Mr Lang's first concern was the impropriety of our

110

presence and not his wife's health. You realize this is impossible, don't you? They've built a wall around themselves. How are we supposed to find out anything? Anyway, how can you help a woman who behaves so irrationally? It's as if Sabira deliberately set out to wreck her life. Why would she risk throwing her marriage away by stealing classified documents?'

'Oh, they weren't classified,' said Bryant cheerily. 'There's nothing in the paperwork of any value whatsoever.'

'What are you talking about? Why is the Home Office holding her if she's not suspected of spying?'

'Well, they don't yet know that there's nothing of value in the papers.'

'But you do.'

'Yes.'

'Would you care to explain how you know?'

'I made a few inquiries.'

'Then why didn't you tell me?'

'I wanted Mrs Lang to think they were important for now. If we admitted they weren't, she wouldn't have talked to us at all. We need to find out what happened to Sabira six weeks ago.' He patted his partner's broad back. 'Don't worry: I'll fill you in as we go along. But we have to act fast. I think something very bad is about to happen.'

'If you're trying to convince me that you're clairvoyant, it won't work,' said May. 'I've shared an office with you for most of my adult life. I know how you think.'

'Well, I wish you'd tell me,' said Bryant. 'I have absolutely no idea how my brain operates.'

111

'I think it's a sort of intelligent threshing machine. It chews up bits of information and spits them back out in a different order. They should pickle it when you die.'

'I'd quite like to end up in a glass jar in the Wellcome Institute.'

'Yes, I thought you would.' With a despairing sigh, May led his partner back to Barnes Bridge Station.

At the unit, Longbright had summoned all members of staff to the common room. Raymond Land sulked in his office for a few minutes, upset that he hadn't been in charge of calling the meeting, but then, worried that nobody would miss him, he reluctantly attended.

'I just had a call from the Home Office,' said Longbright. 'There was nothing sensitive in the paperwork. It was just a folder of Edgar Lang's taxi receipts and dinner expenses. Sabira says she doesn't know how the file got into her bag. She's agreed to be placed in a private clinic. Based on her past history her doctor feels she's at risk, and is admitting her tonight.'

'Can we get our mitts on her medical records?' asked Renfield.

'No, they're off limits.'

'I wonder if this is for her health or because she's become a major embarrassment,' said May. 'Which clinic?'

Longbright checked her notes. 'Somewhere in Hampstead. It's called the Cedar Tree Centre, just off Fitzjohn's Avenue. She's not allowed any visitors tonight.'

'She's at risk, but not from herself,' said Bryant. 'Bring her smudger in. I want to meet him.'

Jeff Waters arrived in the doorway of Bryant and May's office a little over an hour later. The handsome Australian was in his late thirties, unshaven and long-haired, still slung with cameras. He plucked at his lapel and grinned. 'I don't need the photographers' jacket now that we're fully digital, but I can't bring myself to give it up. I'm on my way to work.'

'I suppose you keep late hours,' said Bryant.

'It's mostly night assignments, and when I've not got a schedule I make sure I'm outside the Ivy by eleven p.m. Then I do the rounds of the clubs to see if anything's going on.'

'How do you know who's going to be there?'

'There's a network of tip-offs. We bung some of the maître d's.'

'You've got some misdemeanours on your record, I see.'

'Small stuff. In this job it happens.'

'Grab a seat, Jeff,' said May. 'We need to know just how well you know Sabira Kasavian.'

'Janet Ramsey appointed me to tag her. I cover about fifteen women for PhotoNet. Sabira photographs like a dream. You get to know your clients pretty quickly.'

'Do they want to know you?'

'Most of them act like they don't care about having their photos taken, but they love it. I can always tell the ones who want to get their faces in the press. They find excuses to slow down when they walk past us, stop and talk to their partners, turn and laugh about nothing. If a woman adjusts her dress as she passes you, you know she wants her shots done. But they never want to speak to you. I'm careful, I only have one chance to get the right shot, so with some of them I stick to "Over here, love, turn to your left" – that sort of thing. Sabira Kasavian isn't like that. She's always happy to be photographed. She loves the camera; the camera loves her.'

Bryant watched the photographer's hands. He was glib, fast, hard as nails, but there was something else. He was smoothly moving the conversation on, trying to control it.

'So the two of you never get to talk?'

'No, not at all, you can't when you've been railed into a ten-by-eight with a dozen other paps, security all around, and you've got maybe ten seconds for each target. Overstep your mark and you risk being blacklisted.'

'Have you ever spoken to Mrs Kasavian privately?'

'No, not so much as a single word. I'm sure she'd be fine with it if I did, though. She seems honest and friendly, a bit more fun, not like the others.'

'But you do form some kind of relationship with your subject?'

'What do you mean?'

'You fancy her – she appeals to you.'

'No, nothing like that.' Waters laughed. 'We're not in the same class, are we? Christ, I used to push a vegetable barrow in Melbourne. I mean, I know her background but even so ... there might as well be bullet-proof glass between us. It's all over this city, the glass.'

'Is she always with her husband?'

'No. One evening outside a conference centre in Canary Wharf he had to take the driver and it took fifteen minutes to find her another car. She was standing there with a friend – they were speaking to each other in Albanian. Not many people speak it, so I guess she's glad when she finds someone who does.'

'Do you know any Albanian?'

'I know a little of every language. In this job you have to. I got talking to the friend while they waited. Sabira was standing off to one side, a bit aloof. Then I realized she was shy. It was raining hard, so I lent the pair of them my umbrella. The friend told me how much Sabira hated going to the embassy dinners. She said she'd rather go and eat pizza in a café.' He smiled, but it faded with the memory. 'I thought Sabira was very – nice.' Both of the detectives could see that it wasn't what he had been about to say.

'Do you remember the name of the friend?' Bryant asked.

'I would have written it down. You always do; it's a habit.' He pulled out a BlackBerry and thumbed through his notes. 'Edona. I guessed the spelling. Didn't get the last name – probably too many consonants for me to handle. I took a picture of her for fun. I wasn't going to use the shot.'

'What did you talk about?'

'Nothing much, we were just filling in the time.' He suddenly rose to his feet. 'Is that it? Can I go now?'

'One last thing,' said May. 'When was this?'

Waters checked his BlackBerry again. 'I made

the note in early June. So, nearly a month ago.'

'Mr Waters,' said Bryant sharply, 'did you really not talk to Sabira Kasavian? The woman your camera loved so much?'

'I told you, no.' He did not catch Bryant's eye. As he left, he passed Detective Constable Fraternity DuCaine in the passageway. DuCaine looked back as he entered.

'Who was that?'

'A photographer who knows Sabira,' said May.

'Why?'

'So that's Waters. I've seen him around. He's always outside West End clubs, chatting up women. A real eye for the ladies. Did you find a connection?'

May went to the window and watched Waters crossing the street. 'No,' he said, puzzled. 'According to him, he stood next to her for fifteen minutes and they never exchanged a single word. He's stretching the truth, but I have no idea why.'

12

THE ENGLISH HEART

Hampstead had always prided itself on being a cut above other London areas. The homes of Byron, Dickens, Keats and Florence Nightingale had now been usurped by financiers who had turned the village into one of the most expensive places in the world. Its street names were printed

116

in elegant reverse text, white lettering out of black tiles, its avenues were sumptuously leafy, its houses gabled and slightly suburban, set back from the sight of vulgar vehicles. It had lakes and the largest open heathland in London, and looked down on everyone else from a windswept peak where the city temperatures cooled, and on a summer day like this you could almost believe you were deep in countryside until you saw the high-street prices.

May wondered aloud who lived there, and Bryant was delighted to enlighten him; in 1951, he explained, the Church Commissioners, who owned most of Hampstead, were advised by their estate agent to sell everything off as prices were about to plunge. They sold, prices soared, and Hampstead Man, the pipe-smoking chap who wrote books that didn't sell and supported nuclear disarmament, moved down the hill to shabbier postcodes, leaving Hampstead to rapacious property developers. Even the politicians moved to cheaper areas.

The Cedar Tree Clinic was founded in a house formerly owned by an English composer who had chosen the spot for its tranquillity. In 1937 it was bought by a wealthy American benefactress who came to paint and stayed to heal. The clinic's gardens sloped to manicured woodlands and had provided a sheltered spot for officers recuperating from a devastating war. Now the main house was used by burned-out musicians and detoxing media executives, but the east wing was for more troubled souls, those with recurring addictions and nervous disorders.

'Put that out,' John May instructed. 'The last thing they want is the smell of tobacco drifting over their lawns.'

'Lightweights.' Bryant knocked out his pipe, unscrewed the stem and without checking for embers dropped the bowl into his jacket pocket. He stamped his feet on the porch steps. 'Bloody English summer, my feet are frozen.'

'You should try wearing thicker socks.'

'I shouldn't have to. I've already got the linings from my carpet slippers tucked inside my boots. It's not like this on the continent. Everyone's in flip-flops and Bermuda shorts. They smile at each other and eat vegetables that still have earth on them. They're happy. If I lived over there I'd have retired by now. I'd be living a life of luxury and deceit. Instead I'm stuck here with a pension that wouldn't buy a beach hut. They have sunlight. What do we have? Sublight. D'you know, I accidentally caught sight of myself when I shaved this morning. I looked like a very old apple. Slightly green with a wrinkled skin, probably full of worms. I need a suntan.'

'If you don't stop complaining, I'll leave you here.'

'You couldn't afford to.'

'If you dressed smarter, you'd feel better about yourself.'

'You can't pour a pint of bitter into a cocktail glass.'

May sighed. 'I don't know where you get these sayings.'

The door was opened by one of the senior nurses, who introduced herself as Amelia Med-

118

way. She led them through to the wing where Sabira Kasavian had been settled. 'The main thing is to ensure that you don't upset her,' she said as they passed the empty dining room. 'We try to avoid medication wherever possible, preferring to encourage our guests to participate in holistic programmes and natural therapies.'

'Is she allowed out?' asked Bryant.

'Sabira isn't a prisoner, Mr Bryant. She is free to come and go as she pleases, although she is required to keep us informed of her whereabouts at all times.'

'What's to stop her from doing a runner?'

'Her access to money is limited. Her credit cards have been put away, and she is provided with a daily cash allowance. There's a wardrobe restriction, and for bigger trips she's required to wear a bracelet that allows us to track her movements, although we find that's rarely necessary. Most of our guests only go as far as the heath or the high street. They like to return in time for meals and special events; there's always something going on. Many of our guests soon find they enjoy having a structure imposed on them, and try their best to maintain the regime, but it can prove challenging for some.'

'You mean they either become institutionalized or they get stroppy with the staff. I suppose getting them into a load of smells-and-bells therapy is better than doping them up.'

May could see the nurse was trying not to be defensive. Considering his partner believed in all manner of bizarre alternative practices, it surprised May that he was so sceptical about private

119

clinics, but consistency had never been Bryant's strong point.

Inside, the atmosphere was calm, relaxed and low-key. There were no locks or bars, just carers and guests and a full schedule of daily activities with which to occupy fretful minds. Banning definitions like 'nurses' and 'patients' was meant to speed the journey to recovered health.

Sabira Kasavian was sitting in the morning room wearing a thick white towelling robe. Without make-up she looked diminished and ghost-like. 'They're bringing you some herbal tea whether you want it or not,' she whispered. 'I'm going to be a model patient.' She raised her hand to her mouth. 'Sorry, I said the forbidden word – I keep forgetting we are all *guests* here, except guests don't usually have to pay their hosts five hundred pounds a day.'

'How are you feeling?' asked May.

'Fine for a woman who has just been locked away in a madhouse by her husband.'

'It's hardly a madhouse. It was your doctor who recommended your admission, and you agreed that it was a good idea.'

'I met some of the inmates this morning and they are pretty crazy. There's a TV talent-show winner who has to be kept out of the kitchens because he knows how to make drugs from household items, and some PR woman who had a screaming fit this morning because they took her mobile away from her. But it's fine, I am safe here.'

'Safe from what?'

She looked blankly at them. It was as if she

disconnected from their questions when faced with anything uncomfortable. 'My mind. Being poisoned. I think they are putting spells on me. It's some form of witchcraft, but I don't know how it works. Do you think there are books on witchcraft in the local library? Why did you come to see me?'

'Why do you think Mrs Lang accused you of having an affair? Is that why you attacked her?'

'How is she – have you seen her? Does she have a scar? I hope so. I think they're deliberately trying to manufacture a scandal to humiliate me and drive me back home.'

'Who are *they?*'

'The establishment. The members of the club.'

'Including your husband?'

'Of course. He has no choice but to go along with the others. If he refuses, his initiative will fail and he won't get his promotion. Without a vote of confidence, his career will be over.'

May leaned forward. 'Mrs Kasavian ... Sabira, this makes no sense. I understand the anger you feel at being excluded, but why would anyone go to so much trouble?'

'Because I know what's going on.'

'And what is going on?'

'I can't tell you that. At least, not yet, until I have more proof.'

May tried another tack. 'Why did you steal papers from Edgar Lang's office?'

'I didn't steal them. They were important documents.'

'You didn't steal them? Then how do you know they were important?'

121

A cloud of doubt crossed Sabira's features. 'I'm – I get confused. They were taxi receipts.'

'I don't think you're telling us the whole truth,' said May.

'It is true. I saw them for myself. I am the victim. You cannot make this sound as if it is my fault!'

'What do you mean, your fault?'

'The press says I am trying to damage my husband's reputation, but they don't know what he's like.'

'Has he ever hurt you, threatened you, subjected you to mental cruelty?' May asked.

'No, of course not. He has always been wonderful to me, but don't you see, that is all part of the trick.'

Bryant could tell that his partner was losing patience, and made a rare attempt to be the voice of reason. 'Sabira, we know there's no truth in the rumour that you were having an affair with your photographer. But I think you spoke to him. He knows a little of your language. I'd like to know what you talked about.'

She looked away, watching a crow hopping about on the lawn. 'I asked him if he had ever had to photograph a dead body. I asked him to do something for me. Something it was impossible for me to do.'

'And what was that?'

'I asked him to explain what was in the English heart. He didn't know the answer, and that is why I must die.'

'If it wasn't for the fact that the man in charge of

our future personally requested the investigation, I'd have walked away from this by now,' said May when they reached Hampstead Tube station. 'I told you what I thought of her at the outset. She's one of those women.'

'One of what women?'

'You know, the ones who always need an audience, an attention-seeker.'

'She's overwrought and imaginative, I agree. But what if she really is being victimized?'

'Over *what*, Arthur? We haven't had one word from her that's made a lick of sense.'

'That's because she's frightened. I think she honestly believes someone is going to try and harm her. And we know someone's been watching her. Renfield talked to the neighbours in Smith Square. A couple of dog-walkers remember seeing someone standing on the grass at night, but they didn't get a good look at him. She's safer where she is, but I don't want her leaving the place and wandering about. I'll have a word with the nurse.'

'If she's that scared, why won't she tell us anything that will help catch him?'

'Because she doesn't trust us. She thinks we're part of the problem, and for all I know she may be right.'

'What do you mean?'

'If Sabira's life is being threatened, it can only be by someone she knows through her husband. She has no friends of her own here except this Albanian woman Waters saw her with. We should try and talk to her.'

'If she can't tell us what's wrong I don't see

how anyone else will be able to help.'

'That's the trouble. We answer to the same people Sabira hates. It's a closed circle. I think Jeff Waters was given information that holds the key to her behaviour. If she won't tell us, we have to get the truth from him.'

'What makes you think he has any inkling of what she's talking about?'

'He lied to us, didn't he?' said Bryant.

13

IN CORAM'S FIELDS

The motorcycle rider had been following the photographer all day. Now he watched as Waters slipped between the tables outside Carluccio's, and wondered what the hell he was doing. He seemed to be searching for someone, but it was hard to tell from here. The enclosed concrete rectangle of Brunswick Square was crowded with shoppers and diners enjoying the sunny afternoon.

He saw Waters clearly for a moment, and spotted the object of his search: the small girl in a yellow T-shirt and jeans. He only glanced away briefly, but when he looked back the pair had disappeared.

Pushing his way through the pedestrians, he headed into the walkway beside the Renoir Cinema. It was the only exit on the east side. Waters was a hundred yards ahead, hurrying down the street with the girl in his arms, and looking as guilty as hell. The rider followed at a safe distance, trying to see where they were going, then realized they were heading for Coram's Fields. Waters would be able to enter, but he would be turned away.

Smart idea, he thought, *but it's not going to keep you alive.*

'Christ, I'm going to be arrested for abducting a bloody minor,' Jeff Waters muttered as he looked down at the little girl. He already had quite a few arrests on his police file. Adding *Suspected Paedophile* to the list wasn't going to do him any favours when it came to getting visas for overseas assignments.

'It was just a game,' said Lucy. 'We didn't mean to hurt anyone.'

'I know you didn't, darling, but something went wrong and we have to see if we can put it right. This is the best place to talk, trust me.'

Setting her down, he led her across the busy road to the entrance of the playground. Coram's Fields was a unique seven-acre park for children in the centre of the city, constructed on the site of the old Foundling Hospital. At the gates a sign read: 'No ADULTS UNLESS ACCOMPANIED BY A CHILD'. Right now, it was the safest place for Waters to be.

He had followed the child all morning, starting at her school in Belsize Park, then to her father's office off Fleet Street, heading across to Hamley's toy store in Regent Street, where Lucy was bought a talking pink poodle ('Comes with Built-in Wi-Fi!' said the box) and finally to the crowded farmers' market that filled the central courtyard of the Brunswick Centre in Bloomsbury.

He had used his Nikon zoom to track the girl in the yellow T-shirt and jeans as she trotted behind her father with the toy poodle under her arm. His name was Mansfield; Waters called the office just after the pair had left and asked a few questions; he was good at teasing out answers from suspicious receptionists. Apparently Mansfield was taking care of his daughter today because she had an appointment at Moorfields Eye Hospital to have her new glasses fitted, which meant that either the wife worked or he was divorced.

Waters had kept the Nikon trained on the yellow shirt. It darted behind the Portuguese food stall, reappeared briefly by a woman selling iced cupcakes, and then slipped between a fence of dark blurs that proved to be a line of Chinese tourists taking photographs of London litter bins.

The crowd was denser on this side of the square because it was directly in the sun, and people were sitting on the edge of the fountains that never seemed to be working, eating sausage baguettes, waiting for friends, talking on their phones.

Lucy's father had released her hand and was walking over to a bookstall, where he turned his back for a moment to examine a hefty volume of New York City photographs.

It was long enough. Waters had lifted the girl off her feet and made a run for it before she could cry out, slipping away down the steps and beneath the raised concrete platform of the precinct. To his surprise Lucy didn't cry out. 'You again,' was all she said. Waters's great advantage was his face, handsome, wide and friendly. Girls turned to him and smiled even before they realized that he was a photographer.

He had been following Lucy for days, and they had reached the point of smiling and tentatively waving, but Waters was under no illusions – Lucy was likely to turn and shriek in the way that only little girls could if he put a foot wrong now.

He figured he had less than ten minutes before her father thought of searching the park and all hell broke loose.

'Why are we here?' Lucy asked, clutching her pink poodle. 'You said you knew about the witch.'

'I do, Lucy, I just wanted to ask you something very quickly before we go back to your daddy.' He crouched beside her, reducing his height to something more manageable and safe. 'About the lady who went into the church. The one on Saturday.'

'It wasn't my fault,' Lucy warned him. 'Tom agreed with me. His father works with my father. I'm nine months and seven days older than him, and I know all the rules of the game because my brothers used to play it, but they got bored with it and gave it to me.'

'What game? Is this the game you were playing on Saturday morning?' Waters checked over his shoulder, watching the plaza steps, expecting to see Mansfield appear on them at any minute.

'Yes,' said Lucy loudly and clearly in her best

explaining voice, which you had to do because adults were slow. 'It's called *Witch Hunter* and you have to find the witches and kill them. And me and Tom looked for a witch and found the lady who was one, and we put a curse on her to make her die.'

'How did you put a curse on her, Lucy?' Waters's sight-line remained fixed on the steps, watching for a distraught father.

'You have to make her pass a test,' said Lucy. 'The man showed me how to do it.'

'What man?'

'He works with my dad but I don't know his name. He brings the food.'

'What do you mean, he brings food?'

'You know, pizzas. He has a big bike.'

'What exactly happened?' asked Waters. 'I mean from when you saw the lady?'

'She was sitting eating a sandwich and she was reading a book about how to eat babies.'

There was a sudden movement across the road. Mansfield's Ray-Bans flared in the sunlight. He was running down the steps, taking them in pairs, watching the traffic, seeing when he could cross the road to the park.

'Shit,' said Waters under his breath, rising.

'You mustn't say that,' said Lucy.

'I have to go. You mustn't mention this to anyone, do you understand? It has to be our secret. Like your game.'

Lucy remembered the rules of *Witch Hunter* and smiled. 'All right.'

He turned and checked the park for cover. It was a bright, clear afternoon, but there was deep green shade beneath the immense plane trees and oaks that lined the path to the petting zoo.

'That's him,' said Lucy softly, 'he's here.' But Waters didn't hear her.

A young man in a black motorcycle jacket and black jeans was shifting out of the shadows, moving swiftly towards Waters. Judging by the bulk of his chest he'd either been in jail or spent his life on a bench press.

Waters was still checking Mansfield's progress across the road. He stepped back from the little girl and waved her away. 'Lucy, I can see your daddy, he's coming to get you right now, and it's very important you don't say anything about us being–'

He didn't finish the sentence.

The motorcycle rider was up close and turning Waters to him. A slender blade found an entry point between the photographer's ribs, slicing directly into the chambers of his heart. Waters tried to finish his warning but hot coppery blood filled his throat and he was frightened of spitting it on to her, so he dropped as quietly as he could to his knees, trying not to fall on his injured side. It was important to him that the girl didn't see there was something wrong. She was safe; she had her back to him now.

The knife was smoothly extracted and re-inserted. The searing heat appeared further up, then again to the right, and all he could think was *She didn't see, she got away,* because he could hear the girl running back to her father, back into the sunlight where she belonged.

14

CONNECTIONS

The mock-Gothic windows of the St Pancras Mortuary and Coroner's Office peered out on to a Victorian graveyard gilded with scrolled gates. The Regent's Canal wound around it, sparkling in the milky evening sunlight. Beyond was an Edwardian crescent of terraced houses, a third-century church, giant blue cement tanks preparing to create a new town square and several six-floor blocks of council flats, crammed into a messy collage so typical of the capital city that Londoners never noticed its strangeness.

Inside the coroner's office, Giles Kershaw was thinking about knife wounds. 'There's a mandatory minimum four-month prison sentence for sixteen- and seventeen-year-olds found guilty of aggravated knife offences now,' he said, checking over his new arrival. 'Every Tory government returns to the old "lock 'em up" policy eventually, just as every Labour one tries to introduce a more liberal penal attitude to stabilize the prison population.'

'Will either of them stop kids from tooling up?' asked John May.

'Unlikely. The anti-knife campaigns are endless and well meaning but they don't make it any easier for a kid to walk down a street at night,

130

staying out because his mum's got a new boy-friend.'

On the steel tray before Kershaw was the stripped body of Jeffrey Martin Waters, a grey plastic mesh sheet arranged above his hips. He was lying face down, so his wounds were not visible from this side. It looked as if he was waiting to have a massage.

'We were about to bring Waters back in,' said May. 'We interviewed him yesterday but didn't get very far. He knew more than he was willing to tell us.'

'So he knew his attacker?'

'It looks that way.'

'Before we get into the question of how you managed to pre-empt a murder victim, John, let me quickly outline what happened,' said Kershaw. 'I can turn him over – do you want to see?'

'Not unless the killer signed his work,' said May.

'Good. He's a big lad and I put my back out last week playing squash. There are five narrow but very deep puncture wounds over and around the heart, no serrations on the blade. At first I thought the weapon had penetrated so deeply because it had been incredibly well sharpened, but then I found traces of oil inside the wound. The blade had been sprayed with WD40 and all the cuts were pointing towards the heart itself. Waters was wearing a baggy T-shirt and a jacket with lots of pockets, so stabbing should have been a hit-and-miss affair. This was someone attacking with a decent knowledge of anatomy and an intent to kill, not wound. That's pretty rare.

Knives are kept to be brandished, to ward off, to mark territory. This one was ... well, you remember that business with Mr Fox and his sharpened skewer? I don't suppose he's out on the streets again.'

'He's safely behind bars,' said May.

'OK, but it's someone like that. I'd say he set out to remove your witness and did a very neat job. How did Waters get into Coram's Fields? You're not allowed inside the perimeter without a child.'

'He had a little girl with him,' said May. 'Coram's Fields has several CCTVs around the outer railing. Unfortunately, Mr Waters was standing behind a very large plane tree when he was stabbed.'

'Then how did his attacker get in?'

'He vaulted the fence covered by some bushes – the council had been due to cut them back – and made his way straight towards Waters. He knew his target.'

'Waters was with – who, his daughter?' Kershaw's interest always extended beyond the bodies on his table.

'We don't know. We've got a muddy shot of a girl running away, maybe nine or ten years old, that's all. We've only just started piecing together the witness reports. She ran off moments before he was attacked and carried on until she reached the far side of the park railing. It looks like Waters warned her away. We've got a brief shot of his arms outstretched, then we lose him.'

'Did you get a description of the killer?'

'It's useless,' May said. 'Black motorcycle

helmet, black leathers, boots, broad build, young and obviously fit. Thanks to the helmet we don't even know if he was Caucasian. No branding on the jacket, which is unusual. Probably removed it to avoid identification, which also suggests intent.'

'Well, I think our crime scene manager is probably going to disappoint you on particle evidence, assuming we can afford any proper tests. There isn't much to go on. I get the feeling our man stuck his right arm out, gripped with the left, hauling Waters into close contact by keeping him off balance. You can't see anything on the CCTV?'

'Not a sausage. My guess is he knew where the cameras were positioned, and avoided walking on the grass, so there are no prints to speak of.'

'About the intent to kill. I'd say Waters was targeted and dropped as neatly as a bull at a corrida. There's a fresh abrasion on the left knee.' Kershaw picked up his telescopic indicator – a bequest from his predecessor – and flicked it at the corpse's leg. The Victorian device served no real purpose but was a trade accessory, like a journalist's pencil. 'It's a textbook army hit.'

'So you think it was a professional job?'

'It seems the likeliest scenario. Do you want to tell me what this is all about? You interviewed a – what, suspect, witness? – who was then murdered. And you don't have the case, because it came to me direct. So what on earth's going on?'

'You remember Oskar Kasavian?'

'Of course. Is he still trying to close the unit down?'

'He commissioned us to investigate his wife. She's been suffering from behavioural problems and has turned into a security risk. She was being shadowed by Waters here, who was commissioned to take photos of her, but we think she told him something that got him killed. Oh, and his killer matches the description of the man who mugged Arthur's biographer, Anna Marquand.'

'Well, that's as clear as creosote,' said Giles, covering the body. 'It's a bit of a tenuous link, isn't it?'

'Not at all. There were two murders in London today, in a city of eight million people. One was the victim of a gang stabbing on a Tower Hamlets estate and the other was Waters, who appeared in my office just a day before he was killed. I'd say we have a link, wouldn't you?'

'Then where does the kid fit in?'

'No idea yet. There's no reason to assume there's a connection between her and Mrs Kasavian, although I'm sure Arthur is looking hard. I've sent Dan Banbury over to Waters's apartment to retrace his final day on earth. He enjoys jobs like that. I have to say, it feels like we're pulling on threads that may unravel something big.'

'Like what?' asked Giles.

'I don't know,' May admitted gloomily. 'Something that'll probably come down and crush us all.'

Dan Banbury was the only member of the unit who still knocked on the door of Bryant and May's shared office, or at least he knocked on the lintel, as the door had been removed by the decorators because it was sticking and had yet to be put back because they had lost the screws between the floorboards. 'I've got Waters's movements for the full day,' he said. 'Do you want to come and see?'

'Why can't you just print them out?' asked Bryant, looking over the top of his spectacles. He was completely surrounded by loose pages with scrawled-in margins, Prospero marooned on his island of books.

'Because nobody uses paper any more.'

'Well, I do.'

'You mean you want me to create a document and print it so that you can read it, screw it into a ball and then throw it away? That's very old-fashioned and wasteful.'

'So am I. Just do it.'

Banbury sighed and returned a minute later, setting the sheet on Bryant's desk. 'Waters wasn't driving to assignments, because they're usually all in the centre of town and he hates paying the congestion charge. He took the Tube, and touched in and out with his Oyster card. So we get eight fifty a.m. out of Belsize Park, then just after one p.m. back in at Belsize Park, touching out at Blackfriars. The cameras picked him up in Fleet Street, Salisbury Court, then St Bride's Church–'

'He went into St Bride's?'

'He was inside for about five minutes. Cameras show him waiting around but you can't see much in the courtyard because of the trees. It's a problem at this time of the year, most of them should have been trimmed back but the weather–'

'Get on with it.'

'OK, the next one is Piccadilly Circus, then

135

back in at Oxford Circus, suggesting he walked up Regent Street, but I can't get access to those cameras at the moment because the Met's using the footage to find a gang of Ukrainian shoplifters, then out at Russell Square at four fifteen p.m., which points him in the direction of Coram's Fields. I think he spent the day looking for the kid or waiting to get her alone, and it might not have been the first time he did that. His Tube card has similar times and destinations on other days.'

'Hm. I imagine he was so busy watching out for the girl that he didn't notice someone was following him. Amy O'Connor died in St Bride's Church. This has to be connected.'

'You don't know that.'

'O'Connor spoke to two small children before she entered the church. What if the little girl Waters met was one of the kids who were there that day? I want the O'Connor case.' He picked up the phone and called Oskar Kasavian.

'Are you absolutely sure this is relevant to my wife's situation?' Kasavian asked after Bryant had put forward his argument.

'I think we're going to find there's a clear chain of events linking her to the earlier death,' Bryant replied.

'You mean you don't have evidence yet.'

'Not quite. Does your wife like children?'

'Not especially. Why?'

'I can't see how she would get to know a little girl. One doesn't tend to come across them in central London.'

'I'm sorry, you're losing me. What little girl?'

'Amy O'Connor spoke to two children shortly before she died.'

'What has that got to do with her death? Were they related to her? Did she tell them she wasn't feeling well or something?'

'No, I don't think she knew them. But nobody else came near her, and something made her die. Healthy young women don't just drop dead. That's why I need the case. I want to look into O'Connor's background, her medical records, her employment history, and I need Home Office sanction to do it.'

'All right,' said Kasavian finally. 'I'll do what I can. The City of London Police are bound to kick up a fuss, but I'll see if we can get things moving from this end. If you honestly reckon it will help Sabira I'll do whatever it takes, but you may have to leave it with me for a few days. Things don't move as quickly here as they do in your world.'

Bryant ended the call. 'It looks like he's going to get us O'Connor,' he said. 'Dan, how soon can you tackle Waters's apartment?'

'I'll go right after this.'

'Good. I need to find out what else connects Waters to Sabira Kasavian. Check his computer and his cameras, look for the pictures he was taking on the night they met. I'd like to know if she sent him to St Bride's Church.'

'Wouldn't it be easier just to ask her?' said Dan.

'I'd get clearer answers from the cat.' Bryant tapped his false teeth with a chewed biro, thinking. 'Speaking of which, ask Meera to see if Crippen has given birth yet. I don't want to be treading on kittens. You know, it would be better if we can find a link, because it doesn't sound as if Kasavian's department is going to come up with anything overnight. The more we're delayed, the more we risk.'

'You say there's risk,' said Dan. 'I don't understand.'

'I think Sabira Kasavian is right to believe that her life is in danger,' said Bryant. 'If we lose her, we'll never get to the truth. And we have to act before she finds out that the only person she trusted is dead.'

15

GHOST IMPRINT

'John wanted me to see how you work,' Jack Renfield explained as he watched Dan Banbury attempting to open the front door. 'He thought it would help me understand your thinking. For God's sake give me the bloody key.'

Jeff Waters lived in one of the bland new high-rises that surrounded Swiss Cottage. Clearly his photographic business paid well. The top floors had glass walls that faced south, overlooking the city.

'We're in the wrong bloody jobs,' Renfield grunted. 'Look at this place, a million plus, easy.'

'I'm going to tell you this once,' said Banbury. Now that they had entered the flat, they were on his turf. 'I have my own way of working and I

138

need you to follow my instructions. You remain behind me, don't deviate to the left or right unless I clear an area first. I work to a grid, but I'll create two cleared access paths through the site. After that—'

'This is boring,' said Renfield. 'Just go in and stop pissing about.'

'I need to explain this because Mr Bryant fails to understand the concept of site contamination. He's been known to leave sweet wrappers by a body. He can't resist *touching* things.' Banbury grimaced. 'And bits seem to fall off him. He sheds foreign material like a dog. I once picked up trace liquids at a murder site and followed them through three rooms before I realized that he'd made himself a cup of cocoa and dripped it through the flat.'

'What are you expecting to find here?'

'Waters said he never spoke to Sabira, never saw her anywhere except from behind the paparazzi barrier, but Mr Bryant thinks otherwise.'

'Why would Waters have lied?'

'Presumably because she confided something of importance to him, and instructed him not to mention their conversation to anyone.'

'Pillow talk.'

Banbury held up his tweezers. 'The woman Sabira had the fight with in Fortnum's accused her of having an affair with Waters. A long blond hair would be a good start. The last thing her husband will want is to be confronted with proof of her infidelity. But Mr Bryant reckons it might shock her into giving some honest answers.'

'Has it occurred to anyone that she might just

be having a nervous breakdown?' Renfield asked. 'Birds do, you know. It's not easy living in the public eye, as my sister can tell you after she got done for shoplifting at Ikea.'

'What did she take?'

'She put an occasional table up her kaftan. Now that she's gained weight she could probably get away with a lawn chair.'

'I hardly think Sabira's change of lifestyle can be compared to your sister's light-fingered habits.' Banbury eased himself down on to his knees, opened his forensics box and began taping the floor. 'Besides, her husband is clear about the date of her personality dysfunction. He says it started six weeks ago. If I can find something that approximates that date, we'll be able to give him a reason for her behavioural change.'

'It may not be something he wants to hear.'

'I'm going to do the bathroom first.' Banbury cleared a path to a bare, white-tiled corner shower room and began checking the toiletries cabinet. 'There's no woman residing here,' he said. 'Not recently, anyway.'

'How do you know that?' asked Renfield.

'Single men hardly ever remember to clean the insides of their bathroom cabinets. It's special territory, like your shed. How long has he been living here?'

Renfield checked his notes. 'Three years.'

'Cleaning lady?'

'Janice spoke to the neighbour. She says no.'

'Overnight guests?'

'I can nip next door and ask her.'

'Don't bother, I'll soon tell you. I'm only going

140

to grid the seating area in the lounge. I can see where he's been. Singles form more regimented patterns than couples. Let's do the bedroom.'

The apartment had been recently painted in soothing shades of grey, offset with lime-washed light oak floors, thick cream rugs, white walls and hidden downlighters. The bedroom was elegant and minimalist.

Renfield noticed that the forensic pathologist had a habit of peering about himself like a cat venturing into a stranger's flat. 'No clutter to deal with, no knick-knacks, all very masculine.' Banbury opened another of his cases and set aside a packet of brown paper bags.

'What are they for?' Renfield asked.

'Best way to avoid evidence contamination. Should get some nice Cinderellas off those rugs. I can tell if there are only his shoes in the wardrobe from checking the angle of the footfall, rubbed spots, weight distribution, stuff like that. I can do that without going to Forensics.'

'And by looking at the sizes,' said Renfield sarcastically. 'Unless she had massive plates of meat.'

'What if there are two males living here with the same shoe size? He works strange hours, could be subletting without the neighbour even noticing. Hang on.' Banbury lowered himself beneath the bed and emerged with a tiny fragment of broken glass in his tweezers.

'Blimey, how did you spot that?'

'Practice. Normally I'd send this off to the GRIM room at Lambeth FSS.'

'Grim room? What's that?'

'A Glass Refractive Index Measurement room.

141

If we'd found a glass fragment from Waters's clothing, Lambeth would stick the fragments in a special oil, heat it, then cool it down until the point when the bits refract light at the same point as the oil. So the glass vanishes in the oil, giving its refractive index. If this bit and the recovered sample refract light at the same point then they're probably from the same source, and you could say he was killed here and dumped there. But in this case we know he was killed where he was found because of the CCTVs and witness reports. Anyway, I wouldn't be able to use the Forensic Science Service now. The government's closing it down.'

'Why would they do that? I thought it was supposed to be the best in the world.'

'It's the best, but it's also losing two million a month, so they're going to outsource to private firms. A total disaster, in my opinion. The FSS built its rep on shared information, the very thing private companies don't do.' He rose and stretched his back. 'No one else has been here. We're lucky Waters had a hairy chest.'

'Why?'

'Hairy blokes can't help shedding as they move about. You wouldn't believe the amount of stuff that comes off the human body. There's not been anyone else in his bed. Look at that.' Banbury had folded back the cotton covers and was pointing to tiny curls of hair on the bottom sheet. 'Heavy sleeper.'

'How do you know that?'

'He sleeps on the left but deliberately keeps the alarm clock on the right-hand table. It's so he has

142

to cross the bed to turn it off in the morning. If it was on the left he knows he would just hit snooze and go back to sleep. So there was no one to the right of him.'

'I can see why you like this job now,' said Renfield. 'It gives you a chance to have a right old nose around.'

'I like it,' said Banbury, waggling a dusting brush between his fingers, 'because it allows me to build a picture of someone without me ever having met them. A ghost imprint, if you will.'

'All right, then,' said Renfield, folding his arms. 'Tell me what you know about Waters that you didn't when you came in.'

'He's tall, around six three. The apartment's bespoke, and he's had the cupboards, sink and counters raised above normal height. That fits with the size twelve trainers, comfortable shoes for standing around. He's a night person; he drinks brandy alone, which no one does early unless he's French, in my experience, and his TV viewing history will back that up. Never eats at home; likes to think he's fit: the cupboards have protein shakes and there's a note in the kitchen reminding him to renew his gym membership. He probably put his back out two years ago – there are old packets of diazepam and tramadol in the bathroom, strong doses.'

'That's easy stuff. Tell me something I don't know.'

'All right. He likes his women young. He's got serious commitment issues because of his brain-damaged four-year-old daughter.'

'You're reading that from his apartment?'

Banbury shrugged. 'He decorated it alone. This isn't the kind of flat women would hang around in without altering something. There's no bath, for a start. Have you ever met a woman who could live without a tub? Plus there are some internet sites on his laptop that tread a bit close to the legal age limit.'

'You got the computer?'

'In his bag.'

'You're thinking about him talking to the little girl? The porn doesn't make him a pervert.'

'I agree, I'm just pointing it out. His hours are unsociable and he likes to sleep in late, so he never brings anyone back because he'd have to talk to them in the morning. He hardly ever sees his daughter. From the number of Plaxo reminders about doctors' appointments and a few of his emailed replies my guess is that she suffered some kind of brain-trauma, maybe meningitis, and the stress wrecked his relationship with his partner. There are a few pictures of her up to the age of three, but they're in a drawer. She was healthy then, everything was fine. Then he put his past away, a coping mechanism. I've got an address for the partner; you can check it out. He's obviously still involved and concerned because there are over a dozen books in the lounge on the subject of coping with serious child illnesses, so I'd say he was still handling the fallout. He's got no enemies because he has no friends. All he ever does is work.'

'But he knew something that could get him killed.'

'If the information's not in his laptop it has to

144

have been in his head.'

'And he never has sex?'

'I didn't say that. He brought a woman back here eight days ago.'

'How do you know that?'

Banbury had lifted something from the top of a pillow. 'Here's your long blond hair. I've got another one.' He held up a clear plastic pouch. 'The laundry hamper holds a pile of identical T-shirts, his working uniform. This was between the bottom shirt and the one immediately above it. To my eye it matches the one from the bed. We need to get them under a microscope, and get a sample from Sabira Kasavian. And find out her where-abouts the Monday before last.' Banbury grinned. 'I worked back through the number of shirts. You see? The old-fashioned methods are still the best.'

'You don't think he followed the girl because she reminded him of his daughter, do you?'

'Interesting idea. People sometimes do things they don't understand. Ask someone to explain their actions and they usually find a justification, but often I think they make it up to cover for the fact that they don't know themselves. If Waters was just randomly following girls around it would throw everything out of order, and I wouldn't like that. I'm a very orderly person.'

'I bet you keep a special stick for stirring paint with,' said Renfield. 'The unit must drive you nuts.'

'Mr Bryant lives in a whirlwind of filth and chaos,' muttered Banbury. 'If anyone murdered him in his office we'd never find out who did it, that's for sure.'

16

WATCHING

Meanwhile, John May was briefing the remaining assembled staff in the common room. 'We need to find the girl,' he said. 'We have to build this case solidly, step by step. Otherwise we can't connect Waters's death to Sabira Kasavian. We have CCTV shots of the children in Salisbury Court. We can match the footage against the entrance camera in Coram's Fields. That gives us two co-ordinates. Waters spent half of his last day in Belsize Park, so there's a chance the girl lives in that area.'

Bryant dug through a stack of ragged notes. 'Janice, did you talk to the chap on the gate at Coram's Fields?'

'He saw Waters and the girl enter and assumed they were father and daughter. He thinks Waters was holding her hand but admits he wasn't paying attention. A big crowd of Chinese children was coming in, and he was checking to make sure they were supervised. Kasavian called back. We've definitely got the O'Connor investigation. They're sending the files over right now.'

Bryant rubbed his hands together. 'Good, I thought he'd drag his feet. Where's Raymond?'

'He had to go home,' said Longbright. 'Bad

news, apparently. He wouldn't tell me what was wrong.'

'Right, you two.' Bryant turned to his PCs, Colin Bimsley and Meera Mangeshkar.

'No bins,' said Meera. 'I'm not doing rubbish duty.'

'No, you'll like this one: warm weather, a leafy square. I want you and Colin to stake out the courtyard and surrounding alleyways tomorrow morning, starting before the offices start filling up, so you'd better be there by seven. You're on the lookout for someone who knows this little girl.' He handed them an enlarged still taken from the courtyard camera. 'There are no schools in the area. You hardly ever see kids around that neck of the woods, so she and the boy must have been with someone, probably waiting for a parent.'

'It shouldn't take long to check all the offices in the square and find out if anyone brings children to work from Belsize Park,' said Bimsley.

'Don't you want to wait for Dan to match the footage from Coram's Fields?' asked May.

Bryant shook his head. 'We wasted time before and a man died.'

'Wait, does this mean we're going on to shifts, because I'm supposed to be going out tonight,' said Colin.

'Where are you going?'

'I've got tickets for Coldplay at the Emirates Stadium. They're on at half nine.'

'I assume that's something to do with young people singing?'

Meera snorted. 'No, they're really old and rubbish.'

'Well, I'm sorry to disturb your plans for a musical evening, Colin, but this is rather more important. And get Dan back. And find out what the hell's going on with Raymond. Then call the Cedar Tree to check on Mrs Kasavian. And somebody make me some bloody tea!' Bryant stormed from the common room.

'Blimey,' exclaimed Bimsley, 'he's cheered up all of a sudden.'

'Of course he has,' said May. 'It's more than one murder now. He's got a conspiracy on his hands.'

'Are you all right?' May came back into the office and sat on the edge of Bryant's desk.

'No, I'm not all right. I'm very upset.'

'Who with?'

'With myself, obviously. I should have seen this coming. Waters went into St Bride's. What was he looking for? Did Sabira Kasavian send him there? And why did Amy O'Connor have to die in a church, of all places, when we know Sabira is a Muslim?'

'Why won't Sabira talk to us?' May wondered. 'If she really believes she's the subject of a witch-hunt, why won't she try to convince us it's true?'

'You know, back on Monday, when we first heard about O'Connor, I thought I knew what had killed her.'

'Go on, enlighten me.'

'It looked like there was a wasps' nest in the bottom of the Roman excavation, just under the tree in the corner of Salisbury Court. I was pretty sure we wouldn't be given the case, but I did a little checking anyway. After I saw Ben Fenchurch at St Bart's, I talked to the admitting officer who emptied O'Connor's pockets at the hospital. I thought she might have been carrying an epinephrine pen. If you're allergic to wasps you're supposed to keep one with you at all times, so you can give yourself an injection to stop an allergic reaction. Then I thought maybe she was stung and didn't notice – it can happen if the sting occurs in an area where there are few nerve endings – or perhaps she didn't know she was allergic. But Ben didn't report any broken skin, and something would have showed up in the PM. So we're back where we started. I kept thinking about St Bride's being the reporters' church, that her death was a message of some kind, but that can't be it.'

'Don't worry, we'll find the little girl,' May assured him. 'We're closing in.'

Just after 10.00 p.m. on Thursday night the fine weather broke, and the effulgent skies dropped across North London. The streets cleared and Hampstead Heath took on the sodden appearance of a beaten-down rainforest. At the Cedar Tree Clinic, water bent the trees, sluicing over the garden slopes.

Standing at her bedroom window, Sabira Kasavian looked out and watched golden needles passing through the spotlight over the back porch. Even though the room was overheated, she found herself shivering. She prayed that Jeff Waters had done what he had promised, and that she would be saved. She listened to her mobile and counted the rings, seven, eight, nine, and then voicemail.

'Edona, please call me back when you get this. Please, it's very important.' She couldn't remember if her old school friend had gone home to see her parents yet. It didn't sound as if she had. She closed the phone and slipped it back in her jeans.

The clinic offered a safe harbour for now, but she also knew there was no way out. She was caught in a race between the forces of good and evil, darkness and light. It was hard being patient, not knowing what was going on in the outside world.

Not knowing what was going on inside her own head.

She could hear the rain drumming hard on the roof. The trees were moving beyond the window, and for a moment it seemed there was something dark inside them shifting back and forth. She came closer to the glass and tried to see what it was, but the light in the room was too bright, so she switched off the bedside table lamp.

Now she could see down into the garden. And there he was, standing in the rain looking up at her window, watching, daring her to call the nurse, knowing that by the time she did so he would have slipped away into the dark wet greenery, and she would look even more disturbed.

Perhaps I am mad, she thought. *Perhaps this is their wish, to make me as mad as them. I'll show you some real madness before you get to me!*

17

DESTABILIZATION

At 8.00 a.m. on Friday morning, Meera Mangeshkar sat on a rain-sodden bench in the courtyard of St Bride's waiting for her partner to finish his second breakfast burger. In the branches of the tree above her head, people had tied coloured ribbons to commemorate the lives of journalists killed in the recent conflict in the Middle East.

'It's amazing how many of these little courtyards and alleys are still around,' Colin Bimsley said, sucking bits of bacon from his teeth. 'Mr Bryant lent me a book about them. You can still find old debtors' jails and the channels of underground rivers round here; they take a bit more digging out but they're there here all right. I walked past something called the Alienation Office on the way here; 1577 it said over the door, something to do with transferring feudal lands without a licence. And over in Fen Court there are loads of upright sugar canes covered in Old Testament quotes, something to do with the Stock Exchange and slavery. I was coming out of the Cock and Woolpack pub the other night and saw them. Amazing what you find when you get off the main roads.'

'It'd be even more amazing if you stuck to the job and found a murder witness,' said Meera, taking the lid off her cardboard cup. 'Starbucks

151

tea is horrible. Why hasn't the City got a decent chain of teashops? My gran still makes proper Delhi spiced tea.' She took a sip and grimaced. The flow of workers into offices was steady now.

'This is a chance to prove ourselves,' said Colin, balling up his fast-food bag and looking for somewhere to put it. 'Find the little girl and we'll come off bin duty and surveillance for good. Move up the ladder.'

Meera was doubtful. 'That's not going to happen. There is no ladder. We're at the bottom of the pile right now, and I can't see the unit hiring anyone else beneath us. They don't even have a teabag allowance. So, how do you want to do this?'

Colin looked up at the steel and glass buildings sandwiched between Georgian and Victorian brick houses. 'Looks like the offices go a long way back. We'll have to cover them all. We won't get much joy asking which employees bring kids in because it was a Saturday, so there would have been different receptionists working. It would be better to find out who was in each of the buildings at the weekend, then see if they brought children. And I think we need to keep it a bit vague. If we tell someone that their kid might have been a witness to two deaths, they're liable to prevent us from talking to them. City types can be dead arsey.'

'We're officers of the law, Colin, they can't "prevent" us from doing anything.'

'Maybe not, but we need a detailed account from a girl who looks like she's about eight years old.'

'OK – you take those two sides, I'll take these. And I'll find her first.'

Colin grinned. 'Why are you so sure?'

'Because if I was a parent who had to go into work on a Saturday and my kid wanted to play outside, I'd make sure I could see her from my office window, and those trees are in the way of the rooms on the south and east sides.'

'OK, you have a head start – do you want a little bet?'

'Not if it ends with me having to go on a date with you if I lose.'

'You read my mind. It's not like you haven't been out to dinner with me before.'

'Funnily enough, I don't count sitting on bins all night doing surveillance while you eat chicken jalfrezi out of a box. First one to finish calls the other.'

Meera headed into the nearest building on her side of the square.

Back at the unit on Caledonian Road, Dan Banbury went to see John May. 'We've got a match on the girl,' he said. 'It's definitely the same kid in both screen grabs, the shot from Salisbury Court and the Coram's Fields footage. It's just a piece of software that matches physical features and body shapes, so I don't have an ID for you, but we're working on it. I put a rush on the test fibres from the Waters apartment and we have a match on those, but it doesn't make sense to me.'

'You're talking about the hairs?'

'They're from Sabira Kasavian.'

'So they were lovers.'

'I didn't say that,' Banbury hedged. 'They just place her in his bed.'

'What, you think she came by to read the Sunday papers with him or something? If she isn't a murderess she at least cheated on her husband, which means she lied to us.'

'I don't know that she did.'

'What do you mean?'

'Something's not kosher. I tried to picture what happened. Waters invites her back to his flat, or Sabira calls on him. Women are more prone to shedding signifying evidence than men. Make-up and long hairs with traceable dyes, a wider variety of clothing materials; my missus leaves a trail of tissues and trash wherever she goes, and if she opens a handbag – well, it's like Vesuvius. It might have cost her a grand at a fancy store but basically it's a dustbin with a strap. God help her if she ever tries to have an affair, I'd be on her like–'

'Dan, get to the point.'

'Sorry, John. Kasavian often works late, but hasn't been out of the country in more than two months, which means she wouldn't have stayed over. Even so, I'd expect something else in Waters's flat – a visit to the bathroom, something from the lounge sofa or the kitchen, but there's nothing. And it's not just her, there's nothing from anyone else other than Waters in the whole place.'

'So you're saying someone planted the hairs.'

'More than that, I'm saying they cleaned the flat up so we'd only find the hairs. There's nothing else there to contaminate the evidence. It's like someone wants to guarantee that she gets

154

the blame.'

'Is there any way of proving it?'

'That's the problem, John, it's just a feeling. Even in the cleanest flats you find alien matter and have to eliminate it piece by piece, but not this time. Two perfect long hairs, one placed where it couldn't be missed, on the pillow, the other conveniently left in the laundry basket between shirts so I can easily date it. I could buy the evidence as it stands, but in my experience it just doesn't feel right.'

'So you think someone planted the evidence to discredit her?'

'If there was someone in her husband's circle who was determined to frame her, this would be a bloody good way to do it.'

'With the motive of destabilizing Kasavian just as he's trying to push through the UK side of the borders initiative.'

'Exactly. The crazier the wife looks, the worse it reflects on his judgement. I'd start looking into his department, and see who's got the most to gain by causing his downfall.'

'Home Office Security is notoriously secretive. I very much doubt there's any way of getting to their inner circle.'

'Then I think you need to find a way before something else happens,' Banbury warned.

18

LUCY

When she tried Royal Oak Recruitment Services, Meera Mangeshkar struck it lucky.

The receptionist immediately singled out one employee. 'Andrew Mansfield,' she said. 'A lovely man, but a real workaholic. He's here nearly every weekend, never takes his holiday allowance. His ex-wife works nearby and they look after the children between them, two boys and a girl.' She tapped the blurry photograph. 'And that's definitely little Lucy. She's wearing her favourite yellow top. She's – well, she's quite a handful. Knows her own mind, that one does.'

'Do you know if Mr Mansfield was working last Saturday morning?'

'Oh, he'd have been here. We had a rush job on all last week. Lucy was probably with him.'

'Could I see him?'

'He won't like being interrupted, but let me try.' She rang Mansfield's office and persuaded him to grant Meera an audience.

Meera called Colin and told him to come over. Together they headed for the fourth floor. The sight of so many tightly arranged cubicles made Meera feel claustrophobic. *Fancy working in here every day, she thought. Give me the streets any time.*

Mansfield could not have been older than forty,

but looked as if he was about to drop dead. His grey suit matched his skin and hung about him like a flag. His shirt collar was a size too big, and his dark eyes were sunken and lifeless. He seemed to find it an effort to speak, and had already forgotten who his visitors were.

'We're from a central London crimes unit investigating two incidents that your daughter may have witnessed,' Meera explained again. 'It may be the case that she didn't register seeing anything she considered to be out of the ordinary, so we need to talk to her in order to form a fuller picture of the events.'

'Where did these "events" happen?' asked Mansfield distractedly. His BlackBerry buzzed and he reached for it.

'You can leave that for a minute,' Meera warned. 'One was on Saturday last around lunchtime, out in the square.'

'She was here. She went downstairs to play with Tom Penry, one of my colleague's boys. If you want to interview him, I can probably arrange that. You said there were two incidents.'

'Yes, the other was in Coram's Fields in Bloomsbury yesterday afternoon at around four p.m.'

Mansfield shook his head blearily, as if trying to clear it of clouds. 'No, I don't think I know—'

'It's a park just opposite the Brunswick Centre.'

'Oh God, yes. She ran off to look at the animals. We'd stopped in the farmers' market. I was dying for a cigarette and trying to take my mind off it, so I stopped at a bookstall. It was very busy there. Lucy was watching a man making pancakes. When I turned back I couldn't find her.'

'How long was she gone?'

'I don't know – five or ten minutes, something like that. She's very independent, quite fearless, always going up to strangers and chatting. I try to stop her. She's smart, though, a good judge of character.'

'She's still a little girl, Mr Mansfield.'

'I searched the market, then remembered the park opposite. That joins on to Coram's Fields, doesn't it? There's a petting zoo there.'

'So you left the centre and headed there?'

'There's a crossing going all the way over from the Brunswick Centre to the edge of the park. I followed the railings down the side and then I saw her running towards me. She said something about seeing a friend. She makes stuff up all the time.'

'Did you see the friend?' asked Meera.

'No, I was a bit angry that she'd run off again, but we were late for her optician's appointment, so I let it go.'

'Would it be possible to talk to her later today?'

'I'm picking her up from school at four because she needs to go back to have her glasses adjusted. Could I leave you to take her and do the interview afterwards? I've got a lot of work on this afternoon.'

'No, Mr Mansfield,' said Meera firmly. 'You have to pick up your own daughter. I don't think she'd want to be met at the school by a complete stranger.'

'All right,' said Mansfield finally, 'but it's just adding to my problems today.'

Meera scowled back at the offices as they left.

'When Mansfield keels over and dies on the job, leaving his children without a father, I wonder if his bosses will show their appreciation for all the hard work he put in,' she said.

'Divorced working parents competing over the kids.' Colin gave a shrug. 'I bet little Lucy gets a lot of terrific presents.'

Colin checked the name he had written in his notepad. The boy, Tom Penry, attended the same school as Lucy Mansfield, but was in a lower year.

'Don't take this the wrong way, Meera, but I don't think you should interview the girl.'

'What, you think I'm going to scare her or something?'

'Sometimes you scare me. Get Janice to do it – she's brilliant with kids.'

'But I'm younger, I'm closer to the kid's age than her. Plus I'm a lot shorter, which kids like.'

'Yeah, but she's ... you know, more patient.'

Meera finally agreed to the idea, but Colin could tell he had hurt her feelings.

'There was somebody out there in the garden, I swear to you,' said Sabira Kasavian. 'He was staring up at me, watching my room, but when I looked again he was gone. Believe me, I know exactly how that sounds but he was there. Go and look at the ground if you don't believe me. It was wet; he must have left footprints.'

Longbright had looked in on Sabira because the Cedar Tree Clinic was just up the road from Lucy Mansfield's school, where she had arranged to meet the girl with her father. She had been instructed to break the news about Jeff Waters before Sabira had a chance to find out accidentally. It was rare for someone to be killed in one of London's public parks, and reports of the murder had started to hit the press, although details were vague.

Sabira was seated in one of the clinic's empty afternoon lounges. Her mood had changed to one of tetchy anxiety. It was as if she was coming down from a night of drug-bingeing. Longbright sensed she would have to go easy with her.

'Why would someone come here just to watch you?' she asked gently.

'They want me to know that I'm always being watched, that I'll always be watched until..'

'Until what?'

'Until I kill myself.'

'What makes you think these people want you to kill yourself?'

'They leave notes telling me to.' There was something sinister about the way in which Sabira seemed resigned to her persecution.

'Do you have any of these notes that I could look at?'

'No, I threw them all away.'

'Where? At home, in the kitchen bin?'

'Oh, in the street somewhere.'

'Do you ever have suicidal thoughts, Sabira?'

'Suicide is for people who can't see a way out of their situation. Even when we had terrible problems at home, I would always try to find a solution.'

'And now?'

'Now there really is no way out. I suppose I

160

could run away, go back to Albania, but I would not even be safe there.'

Longbright rubbed her arms. The room had grown suddenly cold. 'Sabira, I'm trying to think about this logically. What do you know that could make someone reach out and try to kill you in another country?'

'It's too big to talk about. As big as the world itself. A global conspiracy. They have people everywhere. They will track me down and kill me, then make it look as if I killed myself.' The sudden clatter of teacups in the next room made them both start. 'I had proof – I swear I did – but it disappeared without ever leaving my hands, just as if it never existed. They came and took it from me while I slept.'

This was textbook paranoid delusion, Longbright realized. Sabira didn't think one particular person was out to kill her, she thought the world meant her harm. 'If you don't tell us why people want to hurt you, it's very hard for us to help you,' she pointed out.

'There's no one I can trust. And if I could trust them, I wouldn't be able to protect them.'

'You can trust me.'

Sabira shook her head violently. 'No, you're the last person I can confide in – surely you must see that?'

Longbright had serious doubts about introducing the subject of Waters's death, but there were computers and televisions scattered throughout the clinic, and the last thing Sabira needed to see right now was a sensationalistic report on the murder of an acquaintance in broad daylight.

161

'Sabira, we know you befriended the photographer assigned to cover your public appearances. We spoke to him.'

'He has nothing to do with this.'

'You know what? If I had a problem and needed someone to help me out, he's the sort of man I would have picked to confide in. That's why I wanted to talk to you, before you heard it from anyone else. Someone attacked him yesterday.'

'Is he injured?'

'I'm afraid he's dead.'

Sabira said nothing. For a moment Longbright thought she had failed to understand. Finally she looked up at the detective sergeant and said, 'His killer is outside the window right now.' The casualness of her tone was chilling.

Longbright looked out, but the garden was veiled in rain.

'It's the same man who was there last night. Can't you see him?' Her voice began to rise. 'He's right there, you must be able to see.' And then she was yelling in a thin, high voice, 'He's there! Right in front of you! He's there!'

Longbright ran to the French windows and unbolted them, running out into the downpour, but there was no one in sight. The rain had beaded on the grass, giving it a silvered sheen that held no other footprints but her own. She searched inside the bushes and under the trees, but it was clear no one had been standing there. She headed back to the house, soaked.

Sabira had turned away from her, expecting failure. 'I knew he'd vanish before you got there.

You must go now,' she said. 'Go and never come back.'

'Sabira, if there's anything I can do—'

'Just go. You can see how mad I am. Even I don't know what I'm saying any more. Go fast. It is safer for you.'

There was no point in remaining any longer. Longbright slipped her business card into Sabira's hand. 'This has my home contact details on the back. Please use them at any time.'

She said goodbye and went to speak to Amelia Medway, the centre's senior nurse.

'It may be more than just mental exhaustion,' Medway told her. 'Sabira is free to come and go as she pleases, but she's exhibiting quite serious symptoms, and may require more specialized health care. We're not a psychiatric unit, Miss Longbright. We're not secure, and don't provide long-term pharmacological solutions.'

'How long do you think she'll be here?'

'Certainly until Monday, when she'll be assessed by a King's College psychiatrist who'll decide the next step. If he thinks there's a genuine risk of self-endangerment, he'll refer her to the private ward of the Bethlem Royal Hospital in Bromley. She'll be well cared for there. If he thinks she's out of danger he may allow her to return home, providing she remains under local supervision.'

'There's one last thing,' Longbright said. 'I know your concern is for Sabira's mental well-being, but we need to make sure that she's not physically at risk from anyone else.'

'The doors of the centre are locked at night, but we're not legally allowed to restrict her movements. If she wants to go out, we have no way of stopping her.'

'Then perhaps you could keep me informed of her whereabouts.' Longbright gave her a card with the unit's number, and then took her leave.

Lucy Mansfield's school was just off England's Lane in Belsize Park. It was privately run and so smart that it looked like an upmarket restaurant from outside. It was popular with executive couples, who placed their children's names on its waiting list years in advance.

Longbright caught up with Lucy's father by the main gates. The girl who came running up was slightly built and small for her years, but clearly filled with confidence and energy. Lucy had reached the age when she had just discovered the power of her opinions, and was already used to being heard.

They went to the Caffé Nero on Haverstock Hill. Andrew Mansfield bought his daughter low-calorie chocolate cake and explained why Longbright was here.

'I was playing with Tom,' Lucy explained between greedy mouthfuls. 'I didn't do anything wrong. It's a real game, with a rulebook and everything. It's called *Witch Hunter* and you have to ride across the countryside and find witches to kill.'

'She used to play the game with her brothers,' Andrew explained. 'It's an RPG. We vetted it, of course. My wife doesn't approve, but I don't see the harm in it. It's historically accurate, rather like those books, the *Horrible Histories*, so the kids learn about the English Civil War. I didn't know you still played it, darling.'

164

'I don't, but Tom had the cards on him, and we were waiting for you and Tom's dad so we played.'

'How do you play the game?' asked Longbright.

'You pick if you're going to be a witch or a hunter. Hunters ride to a town in a place called Suffork and listen to accusations from the villagers, and then they find the person who's a witch. It doesn't have to be Suffork. It can be wherever you like.'

'How do players know who's a witch?'

'There are lots of questions you have to ask, but you can tell 'cause of the way they look. We couldn't ask a lot of the player questions because we didn't have a witch, because Tom wanted to be a witch hunter as well as me.'

'So you found someone you thought was a witch? Why did you pick her?'

'Because she was pretty and witches can change their skin, and she was reading a book about eating babies.'

Longbright remembered that a bookmarked paperback of Ira Levin's *Rosemary's Baby* had been found in Amy O'Connor's handbag. 'Then what did you do?' she asked.

'We pretended to be playing ball so we could get up very close, and I had a good look at her, but I still couldn't tell if she was a witch. And then we killed her. Can I go now?'

Longbright frowned. Lucy had deliberately skipped the part she needed to hear. 'Why would you kill her if you couldn't tell whether she was a witch?'

'I talked to Tom and he thought she was.'

'How did you kill her?'

'We put a curse on her.'

'How do you do that? Did you talk to her?'

Lucy shook her head. 'No. We did this.' She rubbed her fingers together. 'And we said the thing on the card called an incant ... an incant–'

'An incantation.'

'Yes, but I can't remember what it was. Tom has the cards.'

'I think you did talk to her, Lucy,' said Longbright.

'No – she just told us off. That's not talking, is it? Ask Tom, he'll tell you about her.'

'Then what happened?'

'She got up from the seat, put her sandwich box in the bin and went into the church. And then me and Tom went back into the office.'

'All right, what about yesterday, when you went to Coram's Fields? Why were you in the park?'

'I was bored of waiting. Dad was being a grump and wanted to look at the books on the stall, so I walked away.'

Longbright addressed Lucy's father. 'Had you taken your daughter to Coram's Fields before?'

'No. I knew there was a garden square opposite but I only had a vague idea there was a children's park there.'

'Lucy, how did you find the park?'

'I crossed the road and there it was.'

'Have you seen it before?'

'I can see it when we drive to Waitrose. We never have time to stop.'

'There's a camera by the road that photographed you with a man. Who was he? How did

166

you come to meet him?'

Lucy thought for a moment, but there was something too pantomimic about her performance. A finger on the chin, a roll of the eye. 'Oh, I remember now. He asked me where the farmers' market was so I told him.'

'Are you sure? How did he get into the park?'

'I don't know.'

'Because the camera shows the two of you entering through the gates at the same time.'

'He must have been walking close to me or something.'

'And that's all that happened? He didn't say anything else to you?'

'No. He asked me the way and I told him.'

'Why would he think you knew the way?'

'Don't know.'

'And then what happened?'

'I heard Dad calling and ran back to the road, but I had to go all the way around because there's no gate on that bit.'

'Did you see what happened to the man?'

'No. Daddy, we have to go now or I'll be late for the optician.'

She's lying by omission, thought Longbright. *She spoke to Waters, but maybe he told her not to tell anyone. She might even know why he was killed. Something else must have happened at St Bride's when the children were putting a curse on Amy O'Connor.*

Lucy glanced back at her with wide innocent eyes, then picked up her pink rucksack and got up from her seat. 'Daddy, come *on,*' she commanded.

All right, Longbright thought, *we'll see what your playmate Tom has to say.* She checked the number for Tom's mother, Jennifer Penry, and called her. 'I'm afraid you've missed him,' said Mrs Penry. 'Tom's with his grandparents.'

'Do you have a number for them?' Longbright asked. 'It's important that I speak with Tom.'

'I'm afraid not. At the beginning of the week they flew to Bodrum and boarded a gulet – one of those traditional Turkish boats? They're going along the coast and will be returning from Göcek, I'm not sure when. My in-laws fancy themselves as free spirits. All very annoying. I don't suppose there's any way of contacting them until they stop in Rhodes, and I'm not sure when that is.'

'Don't you have a number for Tom's grandparents?'

'They don't use mobiles. I thought we had one for the skipper but it doesn't seem to work.'

That's convenient, thought Longbright before checking herself. *Now you're starting to get paranoid as well. Maybe it's catching.*

'What about the travel company who arranged the trip?'

'I have no idea who they used. You'd have to ask them.'

'But I can't do that.'

'They may call in at some point. If they do, I'll get a contact number for them.'

As Longbright headed back towards Belsize Park Tube station, she found herself checking the glistening pavement behind her.

19

METHOD IN MADNESS

Arthur Bryant stepped into the narthex of the baroque Wren church and slowly made his way up the nave towards the altar.

It was early on Saturday morning and the place was empty. Sunlight shone through the modern design of the stained glass, dividing the marble floor into patterns as richly coloured as Tetris blocks.

Bryant consulted the church pamphlet and read:

In 1375 Edward III issued a writ in the Tower of London confirming the Charter of the Guild of St Bride. Its first purpose was to maintain a light to burn before the statue of St Brigide the Virgin. The Guild continued until 1545, when it was swept away by Henry VIII.

He folded out another section.

St Bride's is known as 'the cathedral of Fleet Street'. After its devastation in the Blitz the parish rose again, as it had so many times before. Little of import-ance that has happened in England's story has not been echoed here in St Bride's. From Celts and Romans to Angles, Saxons and Normans, the church has acted as a parish pump to the world.

As the journalists' church, it facilitated the spread of information. Was that why Amy O'Connor had chosen it, to make a point?

It was certainly not her local parish. O'Connor had lived in Spitalfields. Before that she had resided in Wiltshire from the age of seven. Banbury had been up to her apartment, but the City of London officers had already conducted a search and submitted a report, and he had not uncovered anything new.

Bryant eased himself on to a wooden chair and looked up at the great stained-glass window. The entire ground floor of the church had been searched inch by inch. If O'Connor's death had been planned somehow, why did it occur here? O'Connor's family might have originally come from Ireland but they were Protestant, not Catholic. Amy may have visited St Bride's before the day of her death, but no one recalled seeing her. The question rose again: Why this particular church? *A parish pump to the world.* A message of some kind?

There was an answer drifting like a raincloud at the back of his brain, but every time he tried to focus on it the damned thing dissipated. *The perils of age,* he thought bitterly, *you have to think twice as hard as you did when you were younger, and it will just keep getting worse unless you force yourself to make connections. Everything is connected. Step back and see how it all fits.*

Jeff Waters had come here after talking to Sabira Kasavian. It could only be because she had told him something about the O'Connor death. That had to be the link. It was nothing to do with the little girl.

But now Oskar Kasavian's wife was stashed away in a clinic and seeing ghosts emerging from the walls. After psychiatric evaluation she would probably be on her way to a more secure unit. She refused to co-operate with the State or the police because she was scared, but her claims made no sense.

Bryant shifted on the hard seat, his old bones aching. He was used to dealing with the aftermath of death, not the problems of the living. All right, he decided, *do what you do best: approach it instinctively. What do you naturally feel about Sabira Kasavian?*

The answer came back: *That she's innocent, and that she's telling the truth.* No matter how crazy she sounded, no matter how ridiculous her claims were, what if he assumed they were real? Then the key question became: What did she discover that could possibly make her so fearful?

He asked himself, *What would you do if you discovered something unthinkable?* You might run away, bury your head, pretend you didn't know anything. But if you were brave enough you would try to get proof, to stop people from implying you were mad. And that was exactly what Sabira said she did, stealing a file from Edgar Lang's office, but somehow her evidence turned into a bundle of taxi receipts. Either she had made a mistake, or somebody switched the folder to make her look crazy.

If you decide to go down this route, old boy, Bryant told himself, *you had better be damned sure of your facts, or you'll end up looking as loopy as she does.*

171

'Are you ready for more bad news?' asked John May a little later. 'Sabira smashed up her room at the clinic in the early hours of this morning. When the duty nurse arrived she attacked her with a knife, then tried to cut her own wrists.'

'Both wrists or just one?'

'One, the left – what does it matter? She tried to kill herself, Arthur. They've been forced to sedate her. It looks like she'll definitely be moved on Monday, no matter what the psychiatric report has to say about her condition. And don't bother calling the clinic, because the staff are under strict instruction not to talk to us or any-one else until they've conducted their own internal investigation.'

'Who allowed that?'

'Who do you think?'

Bryant picked up the phone and called Oskar Kasavian's direct line. 'Why have we had our access to the clinic cancelled?' he asked.

At the Home Office Department of Security, the call was recorded.

KASAVIAN: Do you understand the serious condition my wife is now in, Mr Bryant? It's quite clear to me that your detective sergeant upset her with news of the photographer's death.
BRYANT: It would have been worse if she had discovered the news for herself. It's all over the papers. If we can't talk to her directly, can you answer some questions?
KASAVIAN: I don't suppose you'll desist until I do.

172

BRYANT: How did you find out what had happened?

KASAVIAN: I received a call to say that my wife had attempted suicide, and had tried to stab her carer. The poor woman was trying to calm her down–

BRYANT: Do you remember the exact time this happened?

KASAVIAN: No, and I hardly think it's relevant.

BRYANT: Do you have any idea what sparked off her attack?

KASAVIAN: She was apparently difficult at dinner, refusing to eat and so on. I looked in on her in the day lounge at around eight thirty p.m. and found her asleep in her chair. She went up to her room at half past ten, and the nurse was disturbed by the sound of furniture being thrown about a couple of hours after that.

BRYANT: So the nurse went up to the first floor and found your wife in a state of distress.

KASAVIAN: That's right. She had overturned her dressing table, smashed a wall mirror and torn her clothes. It appeared she had also started to cut her wrist with a knife.

BRYANT: Where did she get the knife from?

KASAVIAN: She had taken it from the dining room. She warned the nurse not to come any closer or she would kill herself. When Miss Medway took a step forward, Sabira lunged at her. Luckily, Medway managed to disarm her. She called a doctor, and one of the other nurses stitched and bandaged my wife's wrist.

BRYANT: Why didn't Medway see to her wound?

KASAVIAN: My wife wouldn't let her near.

173

BRYANT: Did she give any reason for her actions? Make any demands?

KASAVIAN: Nothing. The nurses agreed there were no warning signs. There's no rationality behind my wife's actions. Mental instability is unfathomable by its very nature, although I understand it can be inherited. I assume you are cognisant of the fact that both her aunt and grandmother suffered mental breakdowns and were institutionalized for periods?

BRYANT: So you informed me. I ran some checks but was unable to verify the details.

KASAVIAN: Then I suggest you check the files more thoroughly; it's all on record. There seems to be little more I can do for my wife now, so if you have no more questions–

BRYANT: Can you tell me: the cut on her wrist, was it transverse or vertical?

KASAVIAN: Across, I believe, although I don't see what that has–

BRYANT: And you saw the knife?

KASAVIAN: Yes.

BRYANT: How sharp was it? Was it serrated, very sharp, a bit blunt?

KASAVIAN: They use them in the dining room so I suppose it's rather blunt, but it clearly served its purpose.

BRYANT: That will be all for now. Thank you.

'Are you aware of just how much Oskar Kasavian has to lose?' May asked after Bryant had rung off. 'It's not just his wife, although that would be enough. His government career, his entire future is at stake, and you're asking him

174

for details of how his wife cut her wrists.'

'The details are important,' said Bryant. 'I fear she won't survive much longer. There may be nothing we can do about that, but we may be able to save others.'

'I don't understand what you're talking about. There is no one else to save.'

'You're wrong. I want Lucy Mansfield watched night and day. Get Fraternity on it, he's a smart lad. And get in touch with the Turkish authorities, see if you can find a way of reaching her playmate, Tom Penry.'

'You still don't believe Sabira Kasavian is mad, do you?'

'Oh, I always thought there might be madness involved, but let's just say there's method in it.'

'We're supposed to be a team, Arthur. There aren't meant to be any secrets between us, and yet here you are holding cards to your chest.'

'I know I can be a little proprietorial about evidence,' Bryant admitted, 'but this time I have good reason.'

'Well, I'd love to hear it.'

'What I may be about to confirm about this case could place me at risk. I'm not speaking metaphorically or talking about risk to the unit, I mean it could physically harm me. And if I share that knowledge with you, it would place you in the same position.'

'So what am I supposed to do, let you go your own way until something happens to you?'

Bryant thought for a moment. 'There may come a time when I have no choice but to confide in you. Right now, though, it's better that you form your own theory.'

'I'm sure you have a good idea about what that might be.'

'Yes, as it happens. I need you to reach the conclusion that Sabira Kasavian has undergone a mental collapse due to the exorbitant pressures of her social life. Write it up in a report this weekend and submit it to the Home Office on Monday, ahead of the psychiatric report. Send copies to four people: Oskar Kasavian, Edgar Lang, Stuart Almon and Charles Hereward.'

'To do that, I'll need something more than anecdotal evidence,' said May.

'That's why you need to talk to Edona Lescowitz. Someone at *Hard News* had her surname on file.'

'The Albanian girlfriend? I thought she'd returned home.'

'So did I, until Jack Renfield ran a passport check and found that she never left the country. While you're at it, check out the records of Kasavian and the others' company, Pegasus. Give me something on the directors' background. I have to go to the British Library.'

May recognized the furtive look on his partner's wrinkled face. He looked like a Shar Pei tricking its owner out of dinner. 'And of course you can't possibly tell me what you're up to.'

'I'm conducting some research. It's rather esoteric, but I think it will turn out to have a bearing on the case. I have some books on the subject, of course, but they don't cover the particular time period I want.'

'Which is when?'

176

'The early thirteenth century. I won't bore you with the details.'

May was mystified. What could his partner possibly have found that would be relevant to a murder case over seven centuries later?

'Fine,' said May. 'We'll conduct all the interviews while you go and poke about in a cobwebby old library.'

'It's not cobwebby,' said Bryant, nettled. 'It's a new building. Although I'll also be in the old archival annexe in Clerkenwell, which is not only cobwebby but partially flooded.'

20

A FATAL FLAW

Walthamstow is a north-eastern district of London that has lately become home to a large Polish community, spilling over from neighbouring Leytonstone. Bombing raids and development projects have replaced many of the terraced Edwardian houses with grey concrete blocks of flats. On a warm summer evening the local lads hang out in the scruffy high street beneath a riot of plastic signs offering cheap booze and easy ways to send money abroad. In this sense it is like any other working-class London borough.

John May found the flat easily enough, but was surprised to find Sabira's friend living in such straitened circumstances. Edona Lescowitz lived above an Indian shop that sold tinned vegetables, mobile-phone covers and alcohol from distilleries with unpronounceable names. May figured that calling first would only alarm her and decided to take his chances, but there was no answer from the door buzzer.

'She's gone to the laundromat,' said the tiny Indian boy behind the counter of the Am-La Late Nite Groceries Store.

'Where's that?' asked May.

'Turn left out of here, next corner.' He returned his vacant stare to a Bollywood rock video.

May followed the street to the laundry. The printouts taped to the window informed him that the proprietor was also available to unlock phones and could cater for hen parties.

He recognized Edona from her photograph, although she was without make-up now, dressed in torn jeans and a blue Dodgers top. Her auburn hair was tied back, exposing pale skin and high cheekbones. When she finished unloading her washing from the tumble-dryer and stood up, it seemed to May as if she had been expecting him and fearing the worst.

'It's all right,' he said, approaching, 'it's nothing bad, I just wondered if I could talk to you about Sabira Kasavian.'

'You are police, yes?' She closed her arms over her sweatshirt protectively.

'Yes, but we're an independent unit. We're doing all we can to help her. I thought, as you're her friend, you might be able to shed some light on Sabira's recent behaviour.'

Edona sat down on the bench with a defeated

look on her face. 'I knew you would come eventually. She called me to say they had locked her away.'

'She's been sent to a clinic to recover, but I'm afraid she's not getting any better. I think she's in good hands, but I'm not a doctor. I want to understand what's happening to her. I'd like to ask you a few questions.'

'She's not crazy, if that's what you're thinking. But she is...' Edona chose her words carefully. '...vulnerable.'

'How long have you known her?'

'All my life. Our fathers grew up together. My uncle married her cousin. We used to be very close. Weddings, funerals ... despite everything, we managed to be together for family occasions.'

'But you're not so close now?'

'A lot of things happened. She was determined to move to England and find herself a rich husband, and that's exactly what she did. Meanwhile, I met an Albanian man who said he was a TV producer and I moved to Tirana to be with him. We laughed about it, said we had both met the men we were going to marry.'

May moved back to let a woman through with a plastic tub of washing. 'But you came here,' he said.

'It turned out my future husband didn't have a job but he did have a wife and three small children, so I left. And before you ask, no, I don't see much of Sabira any more, because of her husband. When she married Oskar, he turned her into someone I don't recognize. Me, I'm a reminder of her past, so I'm not welcome. I am too

179

low class.'

'But surely he can't choose his wife's friends?'

'All the government husbands do it,' said Edona wearily. 'They can't afford to make mistakes. The wives aren't invisible women who sit in the background any more, they help to lift up their husbands' careers. It's the same in my country.'

'Do you think Sabira believes in her husband?'

'I don't think she believes in the power of the British government.'

'Why do you say that?'

'She's seen it from the inside now, the way it works. When we were small, we dreamed of living in England, the lovely gardens, the friendly police, *please* and *thank you* and everyone saying *sorry* all the time. So proper, so well behaved. The well-spoken county ladies, confident and sure of themselves. We thought that to be English was to be fair, to be decent. *Reasonable*. Now she knows this is a lie. To survive in the English government, it is to hide, to cheat, to bury the truth. This is what she told me.'

'Was there some specific incident that changed her mind?'

'Something – yes. I don't know what it was. Something I think she discovered.'

'From her husband?'

'No, from the wife of one of his colleagues. Her name was Russian – Anastasia.'

'Edgar Lang's wife.'

'I think so, yes.'

'Do you remember when this was?'

'Maybe two months ago.'

'That was when her behaviour started to change?'

'Yes. She had a relapse.'

'A relapse? What do you mean?'

'Do you not know this? How Oskar and Sabira met?'

'She was here on holiday, wasn't she?'

'She came here for treatment,' said Edona. 'Sabira was ... well, she had an addiction problem. Nobody knew. She had never broken the law. But there had been bad episodes. Sabira is the one person who should never take drugs. She's very emotional, very highly strung.'

'What was she taking?'

'At first, prescription medicines, painkillers, antidepressants. She trained as a figure skater but hurt her back when she was sixteen. Then later, I think it was cocaine and ecstasy.'

'You think.'

'I don't know for sure. But I have seen such behaviour before.'

'How did these "episodes" of hers show themselves?'

'She became paranoid, thought everyone was out to get her. Oskar cleaned her up, kept it out of the papers, looked after her. She's one of those people who has everything going for her: brains, drive, beauty; but she has this one fatal flaw. So you see, Mr May, Sabira is not having a breakdown. She's having a relapse.'

Janice Longbright was arranging interviews for Kasavian's colleagues. While Jack Renfield went off to meet Charlie Hereward, she met up with

Edgar Lang at the Athenaeum Hotel on Piccadilly.

Seated in a wing-backed green leather armchair sipping coffee, Lang looked like a dissipated film star. He was an advertisement for old-school grooming, wrong for television but right for government. His eyes were hooded and half-shut, useful for hiding secrets, his skin too frequently buffed by red wine. Longbright sensed his type and involuntarily recoiled as she shook his hand. Lang seemed like the kind of man who would humiliate waitresses.

'Thank you for taking the time to see me,' she said, seating herself. 'I'll only be a few minutes.'

'Good – I'm due at the House of Commons for a meeting in about half an hour.' He checked his watch, an unobtrusive but vintage silver Cartier.

'So it's not a Monday to Friday job.'

'The government part is – you won't catch civil servants working late unless they have to. At the weekend I operate in a private capacity.'

'That's right, Pegasus. Security arrangements?'

'You make it sound as if we repair locks. We act as the link between scientific institutions and the press.'

'Like a PR company?'

'It's more to do with the government-sponsored prevention of negative publicity.'

'I'm sorry, I'm being a bit thick...'

'Scientific breakthroughs are achieved by the global sharing of information, or at least they used to be. Now that information is in the hands of private companies, it has to be safeguarded rather than published.'

'We were discussing a similar problem with the privatization of forensic laboratories.'

'Then you'll understand the issues at stake. But I thought you wanted to talk about Sabira Kasavian.'

'We were unofficially appointed by Mr Kasavian to uncover the reasons behind his wife's behaviour. Excuse me.' She felt her phone vibrate and saw a message from John May: 'SK former addict may have relapsed'.

As she talked, she texted back: 'Find out what Ana Lang said to SK that upset her'.

'I understand she's had issues with substance abuse in the past. The obvious conclusion is that she's using drugs again.'

'There are stringent precautions taken to protect everyone in the department against coming into contact with dangerous substances, Miss Longbright. The country is on a high alert from the threat of terrorism. All packages are opened; all rooms are checked.'

'Does that include home premises?'

'On occasion, yes.'

'But there are a great many social events to attend. It is feasible–'

'If someone is desperate enough, they'll always find a way. If you were to ask me, is there drug-taking in the House of Commons, I would have to answer yes. One has to be realistic about such things.'

'How often does Mrs Kasavian see you or your wife?'

'Once a week or so, sometimes more often. We cover the same ground.'

'Do you discuss your work in front of her? Does she know what you do?'

'You mean, is she a security risk? No, we don't discuss the Home Office or our private work with spouses. I doubt they'd understand it if we did. To outsiders, it would seem abstruse and tedious. Now, if that's all...'

'Just one more thing. Do you like her?'

'What do you mean?'

'I mean as a person? Do you like her?'

'I neither like nor dislike her. My business colleague chose to marry her, so my opinion hardly matters, does it?'

'I'm sorry to have taken up your time.' Longbright rose. 'I believe Mr Kasavian is putting up the UK's plans to revise Europe's border-control initiative some time in the coming week?'

'Indeed, on Friday morning, at the conference in Paris.'

'I read that you oppose his views. I assume there are others in the department who share your opinions?'

'I rather think that's outside of your jurisdiction,' said Lang curtly, closing his briefcase and rising. 'You shouldn't listen to gossip.'

'My point is that it might be in his opponents' interests to discredit Mr Kasavian through his wife.'

'If you're planning to make a case of that, you'd better be very sure of your facts.' Lang abruptly turned away from her.

'Well, I'll make sure you're the first to know if we do,' Longbright couldn't resist adding.

Renfield was having a little more luck with Charles Hereward. They met late on Saturday afternoon in a cramped coffee bar used by barristers behind the Inns of Court.

Hereward was a blunt, broad-beamed Yorkshireman with a spectacular comb-over, an old-school former Labour politician who still went for a beer with his pals on Saturday night and a kickabout with his kids on Sunday morning.

'She's a smart lass,' he told Renfield. 'Gives as good as she gets. But she's not the sort of woman the other wives take to. They support their men unreservedly but they can be a bunch of vituperative bitches when they get together. I tend to stay out of their way.'

Renfield didn't really understand why he had been asked to interview Hereward. There were two unsolved deaths to investigate, and he thought they should be concentrating on Waters's friends and relatives first. Taking the obvious route of inquiry had never been the way at the PCU.

O'Connor hadn't made any close friends in London and even her workmates barely seemed to remember her, so they had drawn a blank there. The photographer, though, he must have made plenty of enemies. Renfield didn't think the deaths were related, and certainly didn't believe that Sabira Kasavian's breakdown was connected in any way, but who was he to argue with his bosses?

'She nicked a file from your office,' said Renfield. 'It was full of taxi receipts. How did she get hold of it?'

'The registered headquarters of Pegasus is not at the Home Office, obviously,' said Hereward, looking suspiciously at his minuscule coffee cup. 'It's in Whitehall Place. Sabira knows the place well enough. She sometimes comes there to meet Oskar. I can only assume she picked it up when she was last in.'

'Security a bit lax, is it?'

'Well, I don't pat down my wife's pockets each time she leaves, but then I don't leave stuff lying about.' He sipped his coffee and was shocked to find the cup now empty. 'I doubt an outsider would be able to make much sense of anything unless they knew exactly what they were looking for.'

'I suppose you must have a lot of sensitive documents locked away,' Renfield pressed.

'Enough to bring down this and the last three governments,' Hereward admitted. 'I probably shouldn't say this but we'll all feel a bit safer with Sabira locked up, away from her junkie friends. Lean over and ask the waitress for two more, bigger cups this time.'

'You mean people gave her drugs?'

'That photographer who got stabbed in the park, he was supplying her with cocaine.'

'You know that for a fact?'

'It's common knowledge he was knocking her off and paying her with coke. It's no skin off my nose what people get up to in their own time, but she should have remembered who she was married to.'

'You think it's damaging Mr Kasavian's career?'

'Not if he acts fast and puts her out of harm's

way. I'm on record as being in favour of Oskar's border-control proposals. It's in my interest to make sure that he pushes it through.'

'Bit of a dilemma for him, though, isn't it? Choosing between his wife and his work?'

'You don't know the Home Office.' Hereward gave a graveyard chuckle. 'If you saw your spouse or your career falling out of a window, you wouldn't think twice about which one to save. The wife's replaceable, the job's not. Everyone thinks Oskar's a hard case, but I can tell you he's done everything he can to help her out. Depending on his performance in Paris, Her Majesty's Government will decide whether he'll take complete control of the initiative. That's why his wife has been taken off the streets. She can't do any more damage while she's banged up. The doctors will bring her to her senses, but it'll be too late by then.'

'What do you mean?' asked Renfield.

'If you ask me, one of the government's conditions to Oskar will be to keep his wife far away from the corridors of power.'

'You mean...'

'He'll have to file for divorce. Mental illness is good enough grounds.'

21

BREAKING FREE

Having planned her escape, she waited until they had finished serving afternoon tea.

There was no point in trying to get away at night because the front door was locked and alarmed. The shift ended in ten minutes' time, and the staff nurses would go to change out of their uniforms in five minutes. Sabira's screaming fit had not singled her out as someone to watch more carefully. The clinic's brochures didn't advertise the fact, but such behaviour was hardly out of the ordinary; much worse happened in the solitary first-floor bedrooms of the east wing at night. She had heard the nurses telling stories and laughing behind the patients' backs when they thought no one was listening.

And now they were heading off duty, down to the back of the house.

She listened for their tread and conversation on the stairs. The danger was that the first of them – Sheryl Cooper was the most gimlet-eyed of the clock-watchers – would reach the front door in under five minutes. Sabira searched about her room, trying to think what she might need, but her head was still full of clouds. She knew there was something she was supposed to take with her, but whenever she tried to think what it was the object of her attention slipped away.

She knew she was not at all well.

Being well meant being able to exert control over your actions, but it grew more difficult to do so with each passing day. It was much worse now than it ever had been before. If she remained here, in a place that encouraged so much intro-spection, she would never find her way back to the normal world. It was better to get out now and worry later about the consequences.

Taking a bag would only slow her down and make her more visible. It was a warm evening and she needed to travel light. She wished she had written the plan down somewhere, just so she could remember it, but at some point she had decided not to leave evidence.

Take it one step at a time, she told herself, fight-ing down panic. *The first thing you must do is get out of the building without being seen – if you fail to do that, there will be no plan.*

She had gathered the few things she needed in the top drawer of her dresser, and stuffed them in her pockets. Outside, she could hear footsteps in the corridor – not a nurse because they wore trainers, but one of the other patients.

Opening her door a crack, she peered out and saw the door on the other side of the hall close. That room belonged to Spike, an American musician with a shock of dyed black hair and a body so thin that he could surely feel his bones rubbing when he walked. He looked seventy but Sheryl had told her he was just forty-two.

Stepping into the silent corridor she ran quickly to the head of the stairs and looked down. At the moment there was a clear path to the front door, but the ground-floor hall was fed by four corridors. Any number of people could appear within seconds.

I could be going to the newspaper stand, she told herself, remembering the stack of journals that stood beside the front door. *That's what I'll say if anyone stops me. If I get caught this time I mustn't make them suspicious enough to report me. There won't be any second chances.*

She headed downstairs as if it was the most casual thing in the world. It was just five or six metres to the front door and the brass latch that could be popped smoothly and silently. She peered into the side corridors as she passed. Someone was laughing in the dining room but there was nobody in sight.

Dinner was being prepared in the kitchen – she could smell the usual stale aroma of warm potatoes and boiled vegetables. The clinic offered a full international menu including vegetarian and gluten-free options, but everyone seemed to opt for mash and pastry and gravy. Denied drugs and alcohol, they comforted themselves with carbohydrates.

She tried to imagine what would happen beyond the door, the path, the gate. She would make her way to Hampstead High Street and the Tube station, head south on the Northern Line. It was too risky to take a taxi. Taxis had talkative drivers.

She needed to do more than just get out of the clinic. She had to break free in her mind and start thinking clearly again, but try as she might she could not find a shape to her thoughts. Some-thing grey and cotton-woolly had soaked them up and wiped them away.

Her hand was on the lock, pressing down on the trigger that would spring it, when an image appeared before her. Less a man than a devil in black, watching and waiting for her to make an attempt at escape, knowing that she would try and fail.

She faltered, heart speeding, hand dropping, suddenly sure that if she stepped across the divide from captivity to freedom she would be playing into his hands. She saw a thin crimson line ex-tending and dripping, staining the floor, and realized that the wound on her wrist was bleeding through the bandage.

She pushed at the lock and heard it pop, felt the cool evening draught come in around the lintel. But there was nothing she could do to make the black figure step aside. He was smiling benignly at her, amazed by her capacity for self-delusion, blithely coming to this country and marrying into the upper echelons, and then happily assu-ming she could destroy reputations and wreck the status quo without any risk to herself.

You are dead to us now, he told her.

I am dead, she repeated, losing her resolve and lowering her hand from the lock as the door to the outside world began to swing open.

'Where are you going?' asked smiling Amelia Medway, the senior nurse who was just arriving to start her shift. 'You know you're confined to the clinic now.'

She gripped Sabira's arm firmly and led her

away to the dining hall, passing her over to the annoyed Sheryl, who was now out of uniform, thinking that her duties were over for the night.

'Take Sabira back upstairs and keep her there until the dinner bell,' said Nurse Medway, adding softly, behind Sabira's back, 'I don't want her left alone this evening, do you understand? Not after what happened last night.'

'I'm off duty now,' said Sheryl, who was going on a date, and didn't get them very often. 'I made sure she took her medication at three. I can get someone else to take over.'

'No, I'll do it,' said Medway, raising her voice to the patient. 'You can have dinner in your room tonight, Sabira. Would you like that? We usually have a special treat on a Saturday.'

Sabira stared dumbly back, barely seeing the face before her. Nurse Medway didn't like the lack of focus in her patient's eyes, and made a mental note to check her prescription dose. Paroxetine was an anti-depressant that helped treat panic disorder and social anxiety, just part of the cocktail of drugs her doctor had insisted on administering, but she wondered if it was cross-reacting to cause somnolence.

'Let's not take the stairs,' said Nurse Medway cheerfully. 'We'll use the lift for a change.' Looking down, she noticed the freshly stained bandage. Sabira felt her hand being raised, but offered no resistance. 'And we'll get that nasty old dressing changed for you while we're at it.'

22

AT HOME

Nobody answered the doorbell.

As usual, it was a war of nerves to see who would last out the longest. Alma Sorrowbridge was elbow-deep in kitchen soapsuds and Arthur Bryant was on his hands and knees, trying to reach an eyeball that had rolled under the bed.

The doorbell rang a third time, staccato and impatient. 'Can you get it?' called Bryant. 'I've lost Rothschild's eye.'

The outcome of any battle with Bryant was pre-ordained. With a sigh, Alma dried her hands and headed for the front door. She opened it to find a bull-necked man in a stained white wifebeater vest. He was staring angrily past her. 'Where the bloody hell is he?' he demanded to know.

'Mr Bryant, it's for you,' said Alma, heading back to the kitchen.

Bryant stuck his head around the door and raised an eyebrow. 'Who are you?'

'I'm Brad Pitt,' replied their next-door neighbour, 'and I want a bloody word with you.'

'I'm rather busy right now,' said Bryant, still appearing as little more than a disembodied head. 'Do you want to come back when you've got dressed?'

'Are you trying to be funny?'

Bryant's brow wrinkled in puzzlement. Why did people always ask him that? 'Brad Pitt the actor? You don't look anything like him, not unless he's been in prison. Very well, I suppose you'd better come in for a moment.'

The neighbour, whose overdeveloped body clearly kept him from walking with his legs together or his arms by his sides, made his way down the narrow hall. When he looked into Bryant's study, his mouth fell open. 'What the bloody hell are you up to?'

On the desk in front of him was half a cat. To be precise, the bottom half of a stuffed, sandstone-coloured Abyssinian cat. The top half lay on its side, filled with straw and old newspapers. 'Oh, that's Rothschild, my old friend Edna Wagstaff's spirit medium. I'm afraid he's past his peak condition. I was trying to restitch him, but this popped out.' He held up Rothschild's glass eye. 'Edna sometimes used him to summon the ghost of Dan Leno.'

The neighbour gawped at Bryant as if he had started speaking Chamicuro.

'Of course, Leno was a music-hall comic, so his advice wasn't very useful. But he did give us the details of his clog-dancing routine. You can sit down if you don't get dirt on anything. Who are you again?'

'The poor sod who lives next door to you.'

'Do you have a name?'

'Just Joe to you.'

'Well, Just Joe, what seems to be the trouble?'

'Do you want a list?' Joe scrubbed a hand through his stubbled hair, then ticked off his fingers. 'One, there was a smell like burning rubber and rotten fish coming from in here at three o'clock yesterday morning. Two, there was a noise that sounded like someone rupturing a duck just as I was trying to get my kid to sleep last night. And I'm guessing it was you who left the pig outside my front door yesterday.'

'Ah. Well, they tried to deliver it while we were out, you see.' Bryant had arranged for his old butcher to drop off a pig carcass that was past its sell-by date, but the butcher had been forced to dump the meat outside Bryant's new flat after a traffic warden threatened to have his van towed away. Pigskin was genetically close to human flesh and ideal for experimentation. Bryant attempted to push a trotter under his desk as he was talking but the pig rolled into view. It had a dozen pub darts sticking out of its flank. 'I'm trying to prove something,' he explained lamely.

'I think you've already proved enough, mate,' said Joe. 'When they took the last bloke out of your flat I told the council to warn us if they were thinking of renting to another nutcase, but I must have missed the call.'

'I think we've got off on the wrong foot,' said Bryant, forcing Joe to shake hands with him. 'The smell caught me by just as much surprise as you. I needed to reach the boiling point of an ammonia-potassium compound and accidentally burned through one of Alma's saucepans, so I set it down on the hall table, but the varnish melted and reset, so I had to unglue it with a blowlamp. And the noise you heard was actually atonal avant-garde German music from the school of Schoenberg.'

'It sounded like it was from the ironmongers down Chapel Street market, and if you do it again after lights out I shall come round and fetch you a punch up the bracket,' warned Joe. 'Are we seeing eye to eye on that? What are you doing with a dead pig, anyway?'

'That's something I can't tell you while the case is still open,' Bryant admitted. 'I'm a police detective.'

The news alarmed Joe, who in his time had been no stranger to the world of stolen goods. 'How long ago did you retire?'

'I haven't.'

'Well, you might want to think about it before we come to blows.'

'There's no need for that, we'll be fine from now, I assure you. It's just that I'm new to all of this.' Bryant waved his hands around the wall with vague distaste.

'All of what?'

'You know – tenement living. Here. Slum dwellings. The stews. The rookeries.'

Joe looked at Bryant as if trying to tune in a broadcast on a broken radio. 'What do you mean, rookeries?'

Bryant sighed impatiently, struggling with the effort of communication. 'Poorly constructed low-quality housing with third-rate sanitation constructed in overcrowded, impoverished areas for the poor, often occupied by criminals and prostitutes,' he recited, 'named after the nesting habits of the rook, a bird that constructs large, rowdy colonies consisting of multiple nests–'

He got no further, because Joe had lifted him two inches off the floor by his shirt collar. 'Are you saying I'm a criminal who lives in a dirty house?'

'No, I'm referring to traditional Victorian definitions of working-class accommodation, although Albion House is technically an Edwardian construction dating from 1909, I believe. Could you put me down? I have a weak bladder.'

Joe quickly lowered the elderly detective to the floor. 'So why are you staking the place out? Who are you after?'

'Nobody. I live here. Mrs Sorrowbridge and I were left destitute after the council placed a compulsory purchase order on our old property in Chalk Farm, so they rehoused us here. We're your new neighbours.'

'I'm pleased to meet you,' said Alma, shyly coming forward with an outstretched hand. 'I'm just making cabinet pudding with ginger tea, if you'd like some.'

Joe was flummoxed. 'Er, no thank you, ma'am,' he said politely. 'I'd best be getting back.' He glanced uncertainly at Bryant. 'As for you, try and keep the weird noises and funny smells down after midnight, will you?'

'My fault entirely,' Bryant called back. 'I'm not used to community living, but I'll soon get the hang of it. Do drop by again some time. You never know, you might be able to help me in my investigations.'

This last remark only served to quicken Joe's pace to his front door.

23

THE FOURTH SOLUTION

As Bryant watched his neighbour go, his attention was caught by a man standing below the balcony in the street, looking up in puzzlement. 'Raymondo, is that you? What are you doing here?'

It being a Saturday, Raymond Land was attired in civvy clothes, which consisted of the kind of trousers one saw advertised in the backs of local newspapers, and a Marks & Spencer's shirt that would have looked unfashionable on Denis Thatcher. It was as if, after his brief flirtation with youthful fashion, he had thrown up his hands in defeat and fallen into a sartorial black hole.

'I couldn't remember your door number,' he called up. 'I needed to see you.'

That was Alma's cue to head for the kitchen, leaving Bryant to welcome the acting chief of the Peculiar Crimes Unit. 'If any more of your little pals are going to drop in,' she called, 'could you let me know?'

'Is it all right to leave my car down there?' said Land, arriving up the staircase. 'It won't get broken into, will it?'

'Certainly not,' said Bryant, ushering him in. 'This is a semi-respectable neighbourhood.

198

Don't tell me you were passing by and thought you'd drop in.'

'No, I had an appointment with Edgar Lang.' He looked around. 'This is very nice, better than your last place. Very homely. Lang asked to see me. Not about Kasavian's wife – there's nothing much that can be done on that score until after the psychiatric assessment. About his boss's appearance before the European Commission.'

Bryant was amazed. 'Since when did important people start asking your advice?'

'My opinion is valued in some circles,' sniffed Land. 'He wanted to know how Oskar was bearing up.'

'Why would he want to know that?'

'I suppose he's protecting his assets.'

'What happens if Kasavian messes up and the Deputy PM fails to award him a new senior position?'

Land thought for a moment. 'He won't be able to remain as chief security supervisor. He'll have nailed his colours to the mast, trying for a new department outside of the Home Office. I imagine he'll be reshuffled.'

'And who's next in line for the position if he goes?'

'Well, I imagine it's Edgar, as he's technically Kasavian's number two. After that, it would be Charles Hereward.'

'So you could say it's in Lang's interests to see that Oskar's initiative fails. And if the wife is sectioned and Kasavian is forced to take time off to look after her, there'll be a no-confidence vote and Lang can step in again. In fact, every way you play it, first Lang and then Hereward and the others win, because even if the doctor decides that Kasavian's wife is fit enough to go home, she'll still require special attention.'

'Not everyone's as Machiavellian as you,' said Land, exasperated. 'Lang just wanted to know how the investigation was progressing.'

'I hope you didn't tell him,' said Bryant. 'I'd love to bottle your innocence and sell it to old streetwalkers. You do realize this initiative has been in various planning stages since the 7/7 bombings? It was pushed on to the last Labour agenda by the US, then redesigned by the Tories. It's a total overhaul of the UK's terrorism security system, and one man will be in charge of it. Except that now maybe he won't be, because seven weeks ago his wife started going mad.'

'I hadn't thought of it like that,' said Land in a very small voice.

'No, of course you hadn't,' said Bryant, giving him the sort of valedictory pat one would give a horse just before having it shot.

'I have to admit, I'm at a total loss with this one.' Land accepted a consolatory plate of cabinet pudding from Alma, who had decided he needed feeding. 'Death, madness and political suicide, all knotted together in one unfathomable bloody case. I mean, I know Oskar Kasavian is a hatchet man but he's losing the love of his life. Believe me, I know how that feels.' He chewed ruminatively. 'She's left me, Arthur. I don't suppose you know how to use a microwave oven.'

'I thought you and Leanne were getting on better after you confronted her about her affair?'

'So did I. But now she's told me she wants a divorce, and she'll be moving the rest of her stuff out next week. I've been married for twenty years. I always assumed we'd be together for ever. Before she met me, she'd never even been on a caravan holiday. She had absolutely no idea how to change the rotor blade on a lawn mower. She didn't even know that you could save a fortune by shopping with coupons. I taught her every-thing.'

'Perhaps she wants to go places you can't take her.'

'What – Barbados?'

'I don't mean literally. I mean in her head. Maybe she needs more mental nourishment.'

'She won't get it from a flamenco instructor in Cardiff.'

'Perhaps we'd better stick to the case for now,' said Bryant, exhibiting rare tact.

'Good idea. It'll take my mind off the thought of having to do my own washing. What are your new neighbours like?'

'Brad Pitt lives next door.'

'He's come down in the world. So, what's John's take on all this?'

'My partner thinks more logically than I do. He reckons there are only three possible solutions. One: Sabira Kasavian is genuinely undergoing mental problems brought on by a return to drug dependency, which would mean it's nothing more than unfortunate timing that she should become ill during the most important month of her husband's career. But we can rule out that possibility.'

'How so?'

'First, cocaine stays in the system for three days, and the clinic ran a urine test as part of her admittance procedure. She was clean, so the rumours about her are false. And if this was all just coincidence, it would mean that Amy O'Connor died a natural death and Jeff Waters was attacked in the park by chance. Now, there are fifty-five churches in the Square Mile alone, and that's not counting the non-English ones, yet O'Connor used the same one that Waters visited.'

'OK, unlikely, I agree.'

'Ben Fenchurch at St Bart's recorded an open verdict on O'Connor, but Waters was hit by a professional. The attacker didn't touch his wallet and mobile, and kept him out of the line of the CCTV cameras around the park. We're still checking Waters's electronic diary and address book, trying to find out if anyone hated him enough to have him killed, but it's not looking good. Which means that it's unlikely these events were entirely coincidental.

'This brings us to solution number two: Sabira Kasavian is faking her madness in order to destroy her husband's career. Now this is an interesting one. First, it fits with what we know about her. She boasted to her best friend that she would come to England and find herself a rich husband. She grew dissatisfied with him, and came to hate all of his friends and the world in which they moved. She felt trapped and shut out of society, and decided to take revenge for the way in which she had been treated. She could do this by wrecking her husband's career and paving the way for a favourable divorce settlement. The next step requires a leap of the imagination.'

'Go on.' Land sat wide-eyed with a forkful of pudding halfway to his mouth.

'One person knows too much about her. The man in whose apartment we found two of her hairs. So she has to ensure he won't ruin her plans. She pays to have him killed. This leads to two problems. First, how did she pay Waters's killer? We have no evidence of money being transferred from her account. Second, where does that leave Amy O'Connor? Is she entirely coincidental to the whole sordid business, or did Sabira meet her and possibly fall out with her at some point in the past?'

'Well?' asked Land. 'What's the answer?'

'Janice and Jack are still working on that one. It's not easy going through personal histories when, of the two people involved, one is dead and the other appears to be in a state of nervous collapse. Which brings us to the third solution.'

'That Sabira Kasavian is being framed,' said Land.

'Well done, you. Now the pieces slot together much more easily. This time the motive is power. Someone wants Kasavian's position as the man with the ear of the Deputy Prime Minister, and sees a way to achieve it. We know from our own dealings with the security supervisor that he's not a man to be trifled with. But he has one weakness: his beautiful, fragile young wife. If she can be taken out he'll be weakened, and if this can be done publicly so that everyone knows of his difficulties, there can be no cover-up. Oskar Kasavian used to date Janet Ramsey, the editor of *Hard News*, but even she refused to hold off the damaging stories – like all dyed-in-the-wool journalists, she's a scorpion who can't resist the chance to sting.'

Alma popped back in and left a fresh pot of tea from sheer force of habit.

'Where does this solution leave the deaths of Waters and O'Connor?' asked Land.

'We already have a connection between publisher and photographer; she employed him. It might be that Waters had a big mouth and too much inside information. The same goes for O'Connor, who is connected to Waters by the child who was at both death sites.'

'I'm getting confused,' Land admitted. 'How does all this connect to Mrs Kasavian?'

'It seems likely that Ana Lang talked to Sabira about work matters, although she doesn't recall any specific conversation that might have set her off. So we have two deaths and a case of mental instability, and it's possible there are threads between them all. Unfortunately, the most feasible solution is also the hardest to prove, because in this scenario the killer appears to have thought of everything. We've been unable to form a proper link between Amy O'Connor and Jeff Waters, and the evidence has been carefully stacked against Sabira Kasavian. It appears she slept in her photographer's bed, and will be responsible for destroying her husband's career.'

'But there's a flaw to the killer's plan,' Land pointed out. 'All we'd have to do to catch him is wait until he achieves his ends.'

'Ah, *cui bono*, precisely. Once it's possible to identify the victor with the spoils, the case solves itself. Unless that's part of the plan too.'

'What do you mean?' asked Land, deflated.

'We're dealing with politicians,' said Bryant. 'People who are capable of formulating schemes over a long period of time and studying them from every angle. The most successful crime is the one that nobody knows has been committed, yes? Let's imagine that next week, Kasavian's wife is sectioned and Oskar fails to reassure the European committee, so he's reshuffled and Edgar Lang is appointed in his place. This doesn't necessarily prove that Lang is the culprit.'

'It doesn't?'

'Oh, Raymond, do try to think. Who benefits?'

A light went on above Land's head. Quite literally, as it happened, because at that moment Alma came in and switched on the standard lamp behind him. 'Hereward, Lang or Almon would be poised to take over,' he said. 'They might even have hatched it between them. Or they could have another partner we've yet to meet, someone who has successfully kept themselves out of the limelight.'

'You see, now you're using the parts of your brain you don't usually use, which in your case is pretty much all of it,' said Bryant cheerily. 'I mentioned that it was John who came up with the Three Solutions theory.'

'It doesn't matter whose idea it was–'

'In this case it does, because I intend to propose a fourth solution. The Arthur Bryant solution.'

Land groaned silently, but even so a little bit of disappointed noise came out.

'And this solution involves witchcraft, madness, secret codes and an ancient London myth – perhaps its greatest and most terrible secret.'

'Oh no...' Land buried his face in his hands.

'But I don't want you to worry,' Bryant reassured him. 'I'm on the case. Although in the coming week, you may find me doing some very strange things.'

Land winced. 'How strange?'

'Oh, strange even by my standards.'

'But why?'

'Because I think we have to chase down the culprit in order to prevent the deaths of others,' said Bryant. 'I knew we were wrong to try and do this by the book. There's no more time left for strategies and suppositions. We need to start fighting back.'

Land looked faintly unwell. 'Is this likely to get us into trouble?'

'I should think so, yes.'

'But you think it's the only way?'

'I'm afraid so.'

'What should I do?'

'Get ready to take cover,' said Bryant. 'There'll be a lot of flying debris.'

PART TWO

The Chase

24

THE ESCAPE

Sabira Kasavian was beset by devils.

She opened her eyes to find them crawling up the bedspread towards her face. Tiny blood-blackened imps with scratchy claws and seed-like eyes, they pulled at the counterpane and tried to slip under the sheets with her.

Screaming, she awoke.

Amelia Medway appeared at the door within seconds. 'Were you having a bad dream?' she asked solicitously.

Sabira decided not to answer. Speaking to the enemy would only place her in danger. She checked under the sheets and scratched furiously at her hair.

'Come along, then, sleepybones, it's nearly nine o'clock.' Medway parted the curtains on the kind of glorious summer morning London sometimes springs on the unwary, momentarily fooling them into believing the weekend will be fine. 'You can have breakfast in your room today. We have some new arrivals. Everyone's rushed off their feet downstairs. Get yourself into the shower and I'll bring you up something nice in a few minutes. I think it's time you washed your hair, don't you?'

She looked around the room, checking that

everything was in order. A pair of nail scissors had appeared in the top of Sabira's make-up bag. 'I think I'll have to take these for the time being,' she said, pocketing them. 'Just in case of accidents.' She wasn't going to be caught out twice.

Medway was not prepared to take any nonsense today. Spike, the burned-out musician across the hall, had already thrown his toys out of the pram this morning after having his tattooing needles confiscated. It always surprised her how many of them were like children, squabbling over places at the dining tables, accusing others of taking their seats and stealing their magazines. Much of it was connected to the physical symptoms of withdrawal, of course, a rising and falling ache that contracted the muscles and burned the stomach lining.

Sabira Kasavian had dabbled with drugs, but wasn't an addict. She was clever and bored and fearful, but there was no craving in her eyes. Medway knew all the signs and found few in her new patient. So much rubbish was talked about addiction, now that everyone was an expert. Just last night some television doctor had been telling his audience that there was no way of stopping someone who wanted to do drugs, that addicts had to hit rock bottom before they could start healing, that they had to want help; all stupid, wrong advice in her opinion.

Sabira puzzled her, though. In one way she seemed exactly the type who might end up inadvertently escalating her use of recreational drugs, but there were glimpses of a steelier

210

woman inside. It didn't add up. And it seemed there was a pattern to her behaviour, an erratic but calculable change of mood as each day progressed.

She took one last look at the wild-haired young woman sitting lost on the edge of the bed and resisted the urge to reach out to her. Some of the patients were devious, and if you became involved in their power plays they would make sure you'd suffer. She went to get the breakfast.

Sabira walked to the window and looked out at the day. The milky mist was burning off, and would unveil a pitiless blue morning too grand to last. Such mornings were dangerous; everything could be seen. She pinched the skin on her right arm hard, rousing herself from her torpor.

It was time to move fast.

There was no point in heading for the front door in daylight. The manager's office was right beside it, and she always kept her door propped open. Sabira pulled on jeans, a sweatshirt and trainers, added a scarf, and then went back to the unbarred window. The room beneath hers had a bay, which meant she could climb down on to its slated roof. It belonged to a woman called Francina who was in thrall to some vague pervasive sorrow and never got out of bed before noon. With any luck she would still be asleep.

Sabira opened the window as quietly as she could and climbed out. The drop seemed greater from the outside and she had second thoughts. But even falling and breaking her ankles would be preferable to another night spent with the tiny crawling creatures that invaded her dreams.

She stretched as far as she could and let her trainers find purchase on the angled roof of the window. She could see that the room below still had its blinds closed, so she was able to take her time, gripping the guttering and carefully lowering herself on to the sill before dropping to the wet grass.

She felt sure she would be seen if she went up the garden, so she ran down the alley at the side of the house and opened the gate into the front, quickly swinging behind the box hedges, where she could not be seen from the manager's window.

Then she set off down the hill towards the Tube station.

London starts slowly on Sunday mornings, but the walkers were up and out in Hampstead, reining in their straining dogs until they were within sight of the woodland, then slipping their leads and yelling out names intended to show that their owners were also from good breeds: 'Jasper!', 'Montmorency!', 'Florinda!'

Sabira kept her head lowered and her pace steady. She had her mobile and purse, but no credit cards and just a small amount of cash. She needed to formulate the next part of the plan. If she had stayed at the clinic they would have found a way to kill her before the psychiatric hearing, just to be on the safe side. She had to make the detectives understand. Mr Bryant seemed the most sensitive to her situation. But she had to let him know without alerting his superiors. What could she do?

Her enemies had occult powers, of course, ways

of watching her from afar, ways of turning her purpose and changing her direction. They could cloud her brain and render her dumb, or invisible, or simply mad. They could reach her anywhere. But this morning something had gone wrong. They were still asleep, perhaps, for she could see things clearly for the first time in days and act upon her instincts.

She had a chance.

Behind Hampstead's white pillars and grand porticos were council estates, flats for the porters and nurses of the Royal Free Hospital, lives less celebrated but more essential to the running of what residents still termed 'the village'. Sabira had to be suspicious of them all. No turning head could be trusted. Trotting briskly to the Tube, she descended in the lift and found a southbound Northern Line train waiting at the platform with its doors open. She avoided the most obvious carriage and moved further down, watching to check that no one else boarded, but her view was blocked by an immense woman festooned with shopping bags.

The train sat in the station with its doors wide while the driver apologized for the delay. She had no clear destination in mind, and badly needed to order her thoughts for the day ahead. She needed to be somewhere calm and safe.

But that's what poor, scared Amy O'Connor had told herself. She had gone into her church and died. Even there, they had got to her.

Well, it wouldn't happen again. She could think properly now, although who knew how long this clarity would last, and she wasn't scared but filled with righteous anger.

Alighting at King's Cross she changed lines, heading for Great Portland Street. There was one place where she would be safe long enough to come up with a stratagem.

The unit was usually closed on a Sunday, but today Raymond Land had asked for all staff to be on hand.

At Bryant's request, the emphasis was on May's third solution: that someone in power was framing Sabira Kasavian to destroy her husband's career and advance themselves. But everyone could sense that even as they made calls and conducted interviews, the traces of guilt were being covered over. It was a race they could feel themselves losing.

Raymond Land usually enjoyed being in the office when it was like this: quietly humming with purposeful activity. If he was honest with himself, he was no longer upset that the case hadn't been solved after a week; being here stopped him from thinking about his suddenly empty home. People only really cared about themselves. It wasn't their fault – Banbury always said humans were hard-wired that way. If you applied that to the case, for example, a real survivor would do everything necessary to keep a secret, and keep on keeping it until it was truly buried again...

He hurried to Bryant's office.

'Arthur, I've been thinking. If we accept your idea that everything is linked, this has to have started in O'Connor's past, and it occurs to me that we still know nothing about her.'

214

'I'm way ahead of you, old sausage,' said Bryant. 'That's why I'm going to Bletchley this afternoon.'

'That's somewhere near Milton Keynes, isn't it? I've no details of her ever living there.'

'She didn't. I'm looking up an old friend of mine. Didn't I tell you? I've received a most suggestive communication from Sabira Kasavian.' He held up a Hallmark greetings card featuring a cartoon duck and the words 'Thank You!'

Land was puzzled. 'Did Banbury find that in O'Connor's flat?'

'No, it's from Sabira to me. Posted to the unit yesterday. I'm afraid I only just got to it.'

'It looks like a thank-you card.'

'That's exactly what it is.'

'I don't understand.'

'I do. She's sending me a message.'

'Yes, it says thank you.'

'No, it says something else. I'll be back with the answer in a couple of hours.'

The London Central Mosque stood at the edge of Regent's Park near the top of Baker Street. It had been founded during the Second World War in recognition of the British Empire's substantial Muslim population and their support for the Allies during the war. The Churchill War Cabinet requisitioned the site and King George VI opened an Islamic cultural centre. A mosque was the crowning touch, adding a golden dome to the London skyline.

It was the first mosque Sabira had visited in London, and still the place where she felt most at home. The minaret and dome provided a change from the surrounding 1970s architecture, and on a Sunday morning the park opposite was filled with walkers.

Slipping off her shoes and placing them on the rack, Sabira covered her head with her scarf and slipped inside. The thick red carpets and great gold chandelier above her reminded her of the mosque in Tirana; unlike the churches she had visited in England, most mosques were fundamentally the same, the better to concentrate one's attention upon prayer and reflection, but this one had immense windows filled with peaceful greenery.

She made her way up to the women's balcony, thinking, *This is how she died, ending her fears within the sight of her God. If I am to be taken, do it now and cleanse me of my fears.*

But she did not die. After an hour of reflection, Sabira rose and left the mosque. Now that she was thinking clearly once more, she considered calling the PCU to check that they had received the card – but what if her calls were being monitored?

While she had been in the mosque an idea had formed in her head; she had no proof of any kind to offer, and yet there might still be some gesture she could make that Mr Bryant would pick up. It had to be something her tormentors would never understand. Assuming the detectives were smart enough to appreciate her motives, she would give them as much as she dared, then head for Victoria Station to lose herself somewhere in its rural branch lines.

She set off in the direction of London's law courts.

At Holborn Tube station she alighted and tried to see if anyone was following her, but the platform was crowded with Sunday tourists now, and she had no idea whom she might be looking for.

Slipping behind the station, she headed into the green square of Lincoln's Inn Fields. Here, in the dappled shadows of the great plane trees, she felt protected. It seemed that fate had drawn them all in this direction. It had brought Amy O'Connor to St Bride's Church just up the road, and Jeff Waters to Coram's Fields, within five minutes' walk of here. Now she too had returned, to leave a trail that only someone with a very particular turn of mind might think of following.

Across the road was number 13, Lincoln's Inn Fields, one of the strangest buildings in London. Without looking back she climbed the steps and pushed open the front door.

There was nobody at the reception desk. The great room to her right appeared to be empty as well. Ahead was the narrow hallway that led to the stairs and the secret gallery. But now that she placed her foot on the first stone step, she started to feel a familiar dizziness.

She could not allow the imps to return. Swallowing hard, she rubbed at her arms and climbed the gloomy stairway, but she could see them suddenly swarming in from every corner of the dark, divorcing themselves from the dusty shadows, the heavy velour curtains, the bookcases and skulls, the busts and statues.

You don't exist, she shouted silently. But the house was designed for ghosts, and she realized she had fallen into a trap. There was no worse place to be in the whole of London for having tricks played on the mind.

Fighting blindly on, she made her way to the first floor, but the imps were batting at her face and arms, scratching at her legs, and now the voices began, urging them on.

I know what I must do, she told herself, *and all the demons of hell can't stop me.*

25

DEATH'S PUZZLE

Longbright broke the cordon of yellow plastic tape and rolled it up. 'Let's not draw attention to this,' she told Renfield. 'Keep the door shut. If anyone wants to come in, they can knock.'

She stepped into the hallway of number 13.

'There's supposed to be somebody on the door all the time,' said Renfield. 'She's a voluntary helper. Things were a bit slow because the listings magazines had the place down as closed. Usually it's open from Tuesday to Saturday, but they just added Sunday mornings. She went off to get a cup of tea. Said she wasn't gone longer than a couple of minutes. She's very upset. The EMT couldn't hang around; they had an emergency call to Holborn tube station so I let all but one of them go. He's upstairs.'

'Wait until Kasavian finds out what's happened,' said Longbright. 'Have you managed to get hold of Arthur?'

'His phone's off, or maybe his train's in a tunnel. He didn't drive to Bletchley, did he?'

'God, I hope not. John's on his way over with Dan. He's trying to find a place to park. Security's tight around here.'

London's legal centre consisted of two Inns and two Temples, each complex with its own great hall, chapel, libraries and barristers' chambers, built around a garden covering several acres, like an Oxford college. They operated as their own local authorities, a miniature city within a city.

May was not far behind them. 'Arthur's going to blame himself for this,' he said, looking around as he entered the hall. 'What the hell was she doing in here? Are there any other visitors?'

'A few of them on the lower ground floor,' said Long-bright. 'Chinese architectural students.'

'Nobody on the first floor or above?'

'No, just downstairs.'

'You'd better go and take statements. Does everyone have to sign in when they arrive?'

'It's not compulsory.' Longbright pointed to an old-fashioned leather-bound visitors' book lying open on the hall desk.

'I'm thinking the killer probably wouldn't have signed in,' said Renfield sarcastically.

'No, but I want to see if the victim did.'

May checked down the brief list of the morning's names and found Sabira Kasavian's signature clearly written. It was the sort of thing

Bryant would have checked at once. 'Five past eleven,' he noted. 'She left the clinic at nine. Why did she take two hours to get here? Where else did she go? No sign of the City of London Police, then?'

'I think as soon as they got the victim's ID they stepped back. Home Office turf.'

'I presume someone's spoken to her husband?'

Renfield looked blank. 'We figured you would do it. Not sure anyone else is up to the job.'

'Great, thanks for that. I can't wait to tell our client that his wife is dead.' He checked his watch. 'Where's Dan? I need to get some idea of the situation before I talk to him.'

Banbury was coming up the stairs with an aluminium box and a large clear plastic object that looked like a giant breadboard.

'What's that?' May asked.

'It's an anti-contamination stepping plate,' said Banbury. 'It means you can walk within the crime scene without messing it up. I thought Mr Bryant might be here. You know what he's like.'

'Go on, then, lead the way. We need to get started as quickly as possible. What else did you bring?'

'I didn't know what we were dealing with so it's a bit of a grab bag for now.' He slapped the side of the box containing a swab dryer, biohazard pre-cautions, chain-of-custody labels, a haemostat, a trace-evidence collector and presumptive blood IDs. 'I meant to bring a laser measurer – the wife bought me one for my birthday, but my nipper flattened the battery trying to confuse the cat with it.'

Everyone followed Banbury. 'Is it possible to get some more light in here?' he asked.

'There is, but not in the normal way,' said May. 'What do you know about this place?'

'I've walked down this street loads of times but I've never noticed it. Some kind of museum?'

'Sir John Soane was an architect. This is his house and his shrine. There are classical, medieval and renaissance antiquities here, a lot of paintings and drawings, death masks, statuary, artefacts, glassware ... you name it. You won't be able to take anything away without a lot of paperwork.'

'What did you mean about the light?' Banbury asked.

May pointed up. 'You know how dark terraced Regency houses can be. When Soane used to teach students here he wanted them to be able to see their work properly, so he arranged a system for reflecting light down through the atrium from the skylight via a series of tiltable mirrors hidden throughout the floors. I think there's one in the pedestal of a statue.'

The house was an extraordinary clutter of alabaster, marble, gilt, ironwork, stained glass and wood. Every wall, every pillar, every arch, every ledge and surface was covered with arcane pieces. The corridors and open-sided rooms all appeared to be interconnected, turning the house into an indoor maze. Once it had been entered, first-time visitors were rarely able to find their way out easily.

'I'm glad Arthur isn't here,' said May. 'We'd never have been able to pay for the breakages.'

221

They were met on the landing by Catherine Porter, one of the current custodians. London's more personal museums were guarded by an army of middle-aged ladies who knew how to get chewing gum off plasterwork and orange juice out of tapestries.

Porter clearly took what had happened as a mark of personal failure. 'I feel dreadful about the poor young woman,' she said. 'I never leave the front door but it was so quiet this morning. Usually there's a queue outside before we open, but people haven't got used to the Sunday hours yet. She came in and must have gone straight upstairs to the picture gallery.'

'You don't have cameras?'

'No. We're old-fashioned; we have attendants. Visitors were always allowed to open the gallery by themselves, but we were worried about wear and tear so Terry, our chap on the first floor, operates the display himself every fifteen minutes. But he called in sick this morning.'

She led the way through the claustrophobic maze of artworks and unearthed treasures until they reached a tall, perfectly square windowless room of unnatural height, lined with wooden panels. On each of the walls, paintings were displayed beneath each other in pairs.

The body of Sabira Kasavian lay crumpled in one corner of the room, her legs folded beneath her, right arm tucked beneath her torso, the left raised above her head.

'Has anybody touched her apart from the EMT?' asked Banbury, kneeling.

'You mean the ambulance man?' said Porter.

'No, he checked her for signs of life and immediately called you. I just touched her sweatshirt. I thought she'd fainted and fallen, but I could see she wasn't breathing. I thought it best not to try and move her.'

'You did the right thing. You're sure there was nobody else on this floor or above it?'

'Positive.'

'Are there any other exits up here?'

'No,' said Porter. 'There's only one way in and out, through the front hall. The back door leads into a small courtyard, but you can't get out from there.'

'So she died alone. Poor kid. She came to London looking for a better life, and all she got was ridicule – and this. What an end.' Banbury turned to the young Indian medic who waited at the edge of the room. 'Does that look like cyanosis to you? Her skin colouring's wrong.'

'We checked for blockages,' said the boy. 'There aren't any outward signs of trauma. The wound on the wrist–'

'We know about that. Anything else?'

'You'll have to get a toxicology report.'

'And this is the exact position you found her?'

'We put her back after checking her status. She was like that, the left hand extended.'

'Seems wrong to me,' said May. 'She was right-handed. And why would she have taken the dressing off?' He looked back at the livid red slash on her wrist, then knelt down. 'Shoes.'

Banbury looked at the black leather trainers. 'What about them?'

May pointed to the left. 'Looks like she tried to

kick one off.'

'It might have come loose when she fell.'

'No, Dan.' May slipped his hand into a baggie and wiggled the toe of the shoe. 'Look how tight they are. She pulled it off.'

'I don't see what you're getting at.'

'Neither do I, but let's take them anyway. Bag them up for me, would you?'

Banbury finished documenting the body position and allowed the technician to step in and shift the body into a slender white bag with carry-handles. Together they carried it down to the hall passage to await the return of the ambulance.

May checked Banbury's pictures. 'It couldn't be clearer if she'd written in blood,' he said. 'She fell but still had the presence of mind to point at something. That wasn't a natural position.' He thought about the line of her extended hand and found himself looking at a sixteenth-century engraving of Covent Garden and a drab painting of Bristol's Avon Gorge Bridge. 'But that's not a lot of help.'

'Sorry, there was one other thing,' said Porter. 'We closed the walls because I thought it wasn't a good idea to have visitors looking in.'

'What do you mean?'

The curator pointed to the polished brass handles that were set in the walls. She reached over and pulled the first one.

The wall was hinged in the middle and folded back, revealing a second wall of paintings. She proceeded to walk around the little gallery opening each of the walls in turn until she had revealed a completely different set of pictures. May was amazed to see another set of handles on these inner walls. Porter pulled at these and the second set of walls folded back on three sides. The fourth pair revealed that the room was, in fact, open to the atrium on one side. From here you could see into the rest of the house, up to the skylight and down to an empty Egyptian sarcophagus in the basement.

'Sir John Soane had trouble storing all of his treasures,' she explained, 'so he arranged for the paintings to be hidden behind each other.'

'Wait – which one of these sets of walls was open when you found the body?'

'The middle ones.' She closed the set of doors above the spot where the body had lain.

May found himself looking at William Hogarth's paintings of *The Rake's Progress*. 'Tell me she wasn't leaving us a clue,' he groaned. 'Nobody does that for real.'

'It's either the paintings, the ceiling or heaven,' said Banbury, opening his kit and setting to work. 'Ask Mr Bryant. If it's something to do with one of the pictures, he's bound to know.'

26

THE CARDANO GRILLE

Arthur Bryant's taxi brought him from the station to Bletchley Park at 11.45 a.m. The mansion had been built by a wealthy city financier in 1883 and finished in a bizarre mix of architectural styles, crenellated and gabled, with Tudor beams, decorative cream stonework, turrets, arches and redbrick octagonal rooms, one with a green copper dome.

In the Second World War it had been rechristened Station X and filled with MI6 codebreakers who masqueraded as 'Captain Ridley's Shooting Party' to disguise their true identities. Here Alan Turing and his colleagues had cracked the secret of the German Enigma machine, following a path of discovery that would eventually lead to the birth of the modern computer.

Angela Lacie was a former MI6 cryptography expert who had retired to help raise sponsorship for the restoration of Bletchley Park. As she swung down the stairs Bryant saw her as he had first seen her not long after the war: an elegant no-nonsense scientist in a boxy suit, with her blonde hair in slides made from wire clips tied with beads; there had been no money for fashion items, and the MI6 girls had made their own.

Her hair was ash-coloured now but she had

kept her figure and her smile. 'I wonder what it's taken to get you to visit me,' she asked, giving him a hug. 'You smell of disinfectant.'

'Wintergreen mixture.' Bryant bared his false teeth to reveal a bright green boiled sweet. 'I need your help.'

'I rather thought you might. You know I'm still under GCHQ employee rulings, so there won't be much I can tell you.'

'This won't compromise you, I promise,' Bryant assured her.

'Let's go to the day room. There's less chance of appearing in the background of tourist photographs in there.'

They walked through the ground-floor visitors' centre to the rear, where Angela pushed open a door leading to a small sunlit conservatory fitted with empty refreshment tables. She poured tea from an immense urn.

'I can't be long,' she warned. 'I've got a big Polish delegation in shortly. Polish cryptographers were fundamental to the breaking of the Enigma Code, and we're seeking to honour their contribution.'

'You mean you're trying to get money out of them,' said Bryant. 'I wonder what poor old Alan Turing would say if he could see how ubiquitous computers have become.'

'I imagine he'd be thrilled.'

'Funny how it's always society's outsiders who create the things that bind society together. Other countries venerate their national heroes. What did we do to one of our best minds? We chemically castrated him. Any biscuits going?'

227

'Here.' She passed him some Garibaldis. 'I suppose you're still smoking that disgusting pipe. And I'm sure you were wearing that scarf the last time I saw you.'

'Remind me when that was?'

'The winter of 1985. Something to do with a woman found strangled in a Carnaby Street shop window. How are you?'

'Well, it never gets any easier. Sometimes I doubt myself. I'm probably having a mid-life crisis.'

'You've left it a bit late.'

'I didn't say which life.'

Angela laughed. 'Come on, then, what have you got for me?'

Bryant poked about in his overcoat and pulled out the thank-you card and envelope. 'This was sent to me in yesterday's mail. Take a look at the inside.' He passed it over.

Angela carefully opened the envelope, and holding up the card between her thumb and forefinger, raised it to the light. The back half was striated with two sets of narrow slits, the top four vertical, the bottom four horizontal. 'Oh Arthur, you didn't need to come to me with this, you could have gone to a toyshop and figured it out.'

'I'm assuming you haven't been near a toyshop in a very long time, Angela. Children only like flying robots that fire lasers now.'

'When I was a little girl I spent my days with bits of paper, making up codes.'

'And I built Spitfires, but children aren't allowed knives and glue any more. This also

228

requires the use of a sharp knife – or a pair of nail scissors, which I believe the sender has.'

'Then I guess you already know what it is.'

'I wanted confirmation.'

Angela turned the card over and examined it carefully. 'Well, it certainly looks like a Cardano grille. A four-hundred-year-old cryptographic technique. They were still in use during the last war. I often made them with my schoolmates. I read somewhere that kids still play with them in parts of Eastern Europe. Not having money for toys makes you inventive.'

'So how does it work?'

'Easy. You cut some slots the height of a line of text in a piece of card, write in a ciphertext, remove the card and fill the rest in with anything you like. To decode the message the receiver places a similar card over the text. Where's the other part? Your friend, what did she put these over?'

'I don't know. There wasn't anything else. What's the difference between a code and a cipher?'

'A cipher's an algorithm, a series of steps for encrypting a message, and a code usually uses a key. There are hundreds of ways of doing it, but the simplest is to use a key like the Caesar shift.'

Angela took out a pen and began lettering her napkin. 'You write out the alphabet, then under-neath it you do the same again, but change the order of the letters. Julius Caesar kept his mess-ages secret by shifting the second line three places to the left. An additional trick is to start with a short keyword, then follow it with your text. If that eludes you, there are still various ways to decipher the message. You could "garden" for it, which means you contact the other party and ask them questions which encourage the use of certain words in their reply, or you can look for common repeats – words like "can", "you" and "today". Or you can overlay a second encryption. It was a great Victorian pastime, coming up with ways to hide messages. The personal columns of The Times were filled with cryptic messages sent between couples, sometimes over decades. One of Edward Elgar's best-known compositions became known as the Enigma Variations because he wrote part of his programme notes in a code that has never been broken.' She handed the card back to Bryant. 'You need the message page that goes with it.'

'I don't know what she did with that.'

'Then why bother to send this if she didn't tell you where you could find the other part?'

'She wasn't thinking clearly. She's been unwell for a while.'

'I'm sorry I couldn't be more helpful.'

'This message – what would it look like?'

'Well, the lettering would be of a point-size that could fit into those card slots. An old trick is to retype it and bury it in a bunch of other throw-away stuff – notes, receipts and so on.'

'In that case I think I might know where to find it. Angela, you should take off the "a" – you're an angel.'

'Well, you'll never know, will you? You had your chance once, long ago, but you didn't take it.'

'Didn't I?'

'No, you arranged to meet me and never

230

showed up.'

'No, I distinctly remember showing up – you didn't.'

'I most certainly did, Arthur. I waited for you on Waterloo Bridge in the rain for a whole hour.'

'You should have been able to see me, then. I was on Blackfriars Bridge. I waited for ages. You must have failed to understand my message. Not very impressive for a codebreaker.'

'Oh, *Arthur*.'

'We could always pick up where we left off.'

'I think my husband and my five children might object to that.'

'Ah. No doubt.' Bryant rose and planted his hat on his head. 'Well, you were very helpful.'

'Give my regards to your lovely partner. And, Arthur...'

'Yes?' Bryant's watery blue eyes swam up at her so sweetly that she wanted to give him a cuddle.

'Please' – she picked a piece of lint from the frayed collar of his coat – 'do try to look after yourself.'

Bryant smiled vaguely and set off back to London, still thinking about being on the wrong bridge.

27

THE WARNING

Bryant was amazed to see the unit's common room in a hurricane of activity. 'Why the hell is your phone turned off?' May asked. 'We've been trying to get hold of you for ages.'

'It's not turned off,' said Bryant. 'I even re-charged it before I left. Oh.' The object he removed from his pocket bore very little resemblance to a mobile. It was covered in what appeared to be sticky black tar.

'What on earth is that?'

'Liquorice Allsorts. I had a bag of them in my pocket. I left my coat lying on a tea urn at Bletchley.'

'Sabira is dead. I've just come off the phone from talking to Kasavian. He's – well, you can imagine. They're taking the body to Giles at St Pancras.'

'Lumme, that's horrible,' said Bryant, not sounding unduly surprised.

'Obviously, there are going to be horrendous repercussions. Take a look at these.' May passed Banbury's laptop to his partner and thumbed through the photographs of the crime scene.

'What killed her?' Bryant asked.

'We've no idea yet. There are no obvious marks on the body, but the EMT think she had trouble breathing. We've already managed to track her movements through her Oyster card and her phone. She slipped out of the clinic first thing, caught a Tube to Baker Street and went to the Regent's Park mosque, then headed down into Holborn and was found dead on the first floor of the Sir John Soane Museum.'

'The Soane? Why would she go there?'

'We've no idea yet. The duty nurse at the Cedar Tree said she'd been behaving more strangely than ever, talking to herself, exhibiting signs of paranoia.'

'That can't kill you, John. Something else must have happened. Who else was in the museum?'

'We've no idea. There was just one custodian on duty. The other was off sick. Four Chinese architectural students, a young German couple and a very old lady who restores frescoes in Italian churches. They're all in the clear.'

'Nobody else got in or out?'

'It doesn't appear so. There are no cameras inside the house but there's one on the wall next door and it didn't pick up anyone entering or leaving the front door.'

'No other exits?'

'The back door leads into a walled courtyard three storeys high.'

Bryant studied the photograph, tracing the livid crimson mark on Sabira's wrist. 'Did someone remove her dressing?'

'Not at the clinic. They think she must have taken it off after she left this morning.'

'Interesting. The arm. She's pointing. What's above her hand?'

May flicked to the next shot showing the muddy sepia paintings.

'Hogarth. *The Rake's Progress*,' said Bryant. 'She's been trying to leave evidence for us.'

'What do you mean?'

'A few weeks ago Sabira was as sane as you or I. Do you remember how vivacious she was when we first met her? I'm an idiot, I should have been able to prevent this.'

'I don't see how you could have done. Why didn't she confide in us?'

'She couldn't tell anyone connected with her husband's office. That's why she talked to Jeff Waters, and possibly to Edona Lescowitz. They were both outsiders.'

'No, Waters had a connection. He was employed by Janet Ramsey, Kasavian's former girlfriend.'

'I don't think that has a bearing on it. Those kinds of connections sometimes just happen, even in a city the size of London.'

'When you say she was trying to leave evidence, what do you mean?'

'Sabira broke out of the clinic prior to her psychiatric examination and tried to show us what was happening to her.' Bryant tapped the screen. 'She'd studied art history. She told us so herself. She headed here deliberately. I'll show you.'

He went to his room and returned with an immense, sooty, leather-bound volume, throwing it open and thumbing carelessly through the pages.

'Look. Hogarth's pictures tell stories. All you have to do is study the allusions in each one of the series, and you have a tale as complex as any novel. Look at them: each picture peppered with tiny details, signs and maps, globes and scrolls and what-have-you, all these bits and bobs mean something. There are classical references, of course, but any first-year art history student could figure out what's going on. It doesn't take a genius to tell you that when there's a black dog in the painting it means the subject is suffering from depression. *The Rake's Progress* tells the story of a spendthrift son wasting his father's fortune in boozers, marrying the wrong woman for her fortune, going to debtors' jail and ending up here, in scene eight, the painting Sabira was indicating.' His index finger stabbed at the page in question.

'In Bedlam,' said May, studying the picture.

'Indeed. The Bethlehem Royal Hospital where the mad were committed, and where Sabira was also to be sent. I think that's why she tore her dressing off. Look at the red ring around her wrist. The mark of madness. She wasn't trying to kill herself; she was sending us a message. No, more than a message – a warning. But I didn't pick up on it the first time, so she gave us another chance. She was far too frightened to talk, but if we reached the same conclusion by ourselves that was a different matter.'

'I don't understand,' said May. 'What was the message?'

'Amy O'Connor was found in St Bride's with a red cotton thread around her left wrist. I knew that it was once considered a treatment for madness, although in olden times you were supposed to attach a clovewort to the cord. Clovewort was a herb that supposedly cured lunacy. Sabira may not have known what the cord signified, but was leaving a mark on her wrist to link herself to O'Connor and the condition of madness.'

'That makes absolutely no sense. She didn't know she was going to drop dead in the museum, did she? So what was it – suicide? How did she think this "message" was going to reach us?'

'Er, I don't know.'

Bryant turned back to Banbury's photographs of the body. 'We don't know why her left shoe was half off?'

'We think it happened when she fell,' said Banbury, 'but I'm going to examine the shoes as soon as I have a chance.'

'Kasavian has demanded to see us first thing tomorrow morning,' said May. 'I assume he's going to throw the book at us.'

'Then we have to stall him while we look into this.'

'I don't see that we can do much until Giles has obtained permission to carry out an autopsy.'

'Sabira sent me a clue, a very simple code-reader, but I don't have the document it was intended to read. I think it might be in the folder of taxi receipts she brought back from the Home Office. Do we still have it?'

'It's on my desk,' said Renfield. 'Hang on.'

He brought it in and emptied it out on the common-room table.

Bryant pulled on his spectacles, withdrew the Cardano grille and started running it over folded pages of figures. 'There's something you can do,' he said while he checked the slots for codes. 'Go back into Amy O'Connor's history. Get inside her life. We need to know how the pair of them came to meet. That's the key to this. Whether she was mad or sane, Sabira left evidence that would lead us to the truth. She can still help us even though shc's gone.'

The door opened behind them with a bang.

'Well done, lads, seems like you've done a grand job.' The tone was sarcastic. Charles Hereward studied each of them in turn, as if he was seeking to memorize their faces. He appeared to have been drinking. 'You couldn't manage to keep her alive, though.'

'We didn't exacerbate the problem by shutting her away in a private clinic,' said Bryant angrily. 'Who let you in?'

'We own you, pal. Oskar was under pressure from the Deputy PM to do something about his bloody wife before the Paris summit. All you had to do was keep an eye on her until she could be sectioned, you realize that, don't you? You weren't *supposed* to do anything.'

'Look here, you can't blame my team,' said Raymond Land. 'They were acting under Mr Kasavian's instructions.'

'Yes, to keep his wife under lock and key for a while, not to let her die and let the Paris talks die with her. I'm sorry, does that seem callous? Putting our work ahead of a dim, unfaithful cokehead who decided she wanted a bigger wardrobe than her Albanian leks could buy her?'

'We've done nothing that should affect Mr Kasavian's meeting,' said Land, alarmed.

'No? I put six years of my life into building the case for stronger border controls.' Hereward drifted between them like an untethered blimp. 'I started work on it three years before Kasavian even joined the department, and now all that work will be wiped away, and the clock will be reset to zero because Oskar will be in no fit state to present his case, and there's no one who can deputize for him.'

'I thought you were a supporter,' said Renfield. 'Why can't you do it?'

'Because it's more than just a change in the law. He's the one who's up for the job of co-ordinating the entire initiative, not me. He's the one who's meant to keep every tax-dodging immigrant and would-be terrorist out of this country. And now he's in no fit state to do it. Instead of studying the protocols of twenty-seven member states this week, he'll be burying his wife. And you know what? He blames himself for not being there for her when she needed him, instead of blaming you.'

'It's not our fault that—'

'I want you to know that we're going to take you down, no matter whose fault this was.' Hereward looked like an unpricked sausage about to explode. 'It's time you learned something about the department that pays your salaries. When it comes to getting rid of its enemies, it's a vindictive, irrational son of a bitch. We'll grind you into the dust, then blow the dust away. It'll be as if you never existed.'

He turned to leave, but then stopped. 'Don't think I dropped by just to threaten you. I happened to be in the neighbourhood.'

'I didn't know the currency of Albania was the lek,' said Bryant, stacking his books in the stunned silence that followed Hereward's departure. 'Where were we? Ah yes, I think we need to conduct a search of the Sir John Soane Museum.'

Raymond Land was not a violent man, but he shot Bryant a look that could have blasted his desk into splinters and stripped off the wallpaper behind his head.

'What?' asked Bryant innocently. 'Have you never seen a civil servant explode before? You'd better get used to the sight. This is just the start.'

28

THE STRANGENESS OF CHURCHES

Bryant sent the rest of the demoralized team home at 10.00 p.m. on Sunday night. John May stayed behind, settling into his partner's huge leather armchair to keep him company, trying to stay awake while Bryant attempted to break encrypted messages in the taxi-receipt folder.

Two problems stood in the way of his success. If Sabira had been leaving a message for them, she would have written the encryption herself; he knew he wouldn't find it in a receipt or a company document unless she had forged it. Second, if it was written with the commonplace Caesar shift, he would need the keyword that preceded the coding.

'It's no good,' he said finally, poking May awake and handing him a Calvados. 'It's far too elaborate. If Sabira hid anything at all, surely she would have kept it simple. It only needed to be something her tormentor wouldn't spot. Until I can understand the nature of the algorithm, I'll have to pursue another tack. Would you see Kasavian by yourself tomorrow morning? I need you to buy me some time.'

May was exhausted and depressed. He had never felt closer to taking retirement. 'What for?' he asked. 'You heard Hereward. Whatever happens now makes no difference. We're done for.'

'That may be, but we have to right a wrong. Sabira Kasavian was hounded to her death.'

'If you believe that, you're accusing everyone of complicity,' said May. 'We're talking about conspiracy to murder, cover-ups, perverting the course of justice and God knows what else. Don't you see what's happening? We've finally come up against something that's utterly impervious to investigation. All we can do is react to each new disaster.'

Bryant tapped his teeth, thinking. 'I need to understand the nature of madness.'

'No, Arthur, we need basic evidence, cause of death, witness IDs, not some fanciful research into the history of bloody Bedlam.'

'You're wrong,' said Bryant simply. 'No traditional approach can possibly work against something like this. I'll prove it to you in the next twenty-four hours. I'm so close, I can feel the answer shifting beneath my hands. The threads –

those red threads that cured madness – they're coming together but I can't see why.' He held out his hands and examined their backs. 'It's right in front of me. Whoever did this has done it all before. It's second nature to him. I just need to find a way in. I know I'm probably not making any sense right now, but–'

'You're right,' said May wearily. 'You're not making any sense at all. It's late; let's go home.'

'No, you go. I'll stay.'

'Then I'll stay too.' The light in the old warehouse at 231, Caledonian Road, burned on through the lonely night.

May felt lousy. He washed in the unit's leaky, cantankerous bathroom and had a shave, but still felt ill prepared to face Kasavian's wrath first thing on a Monday morning.

To his surprise the security chief's assistant called to tell him that Kasavian was walking on Primrose Hill and would meet him on the bench at the top in half an hour, so that was where he headed.

The day was cool and pinkly misted. From the height of the emerald mound, London was softened in a silky haze that smoothed out its mean-spirited edges. Some of the city's buildings appeared to have been speared with cranes in order to keep them from floating away.

Oskar Kasavian was slumped on the bench in his long black raincoat, looking like an abandoned umbrella. May sat some distance from him in case he decided to lash out. There was a coiled power in the security supervisor that almost everyone found threatening, but today his mood caught May by surprise.

'I used to come up here with her,' he said, looking down towards Westminster. 'I never saw the beauty in it myself. I asked her, why this park? It's so small. She told me that when she was a little girl she saw a Disney cartoon at her local cinema, *One Hundred And One Dalmatians*, and this park and the surrounding houses were in it. She liked it because it looked so neatly organized. She arrived here expecting it to look different, but it was exactly as she'd seen it in the film. That's the difference. I looked and only ever saw the exits, the railings, the inadequate lighting, the signs and the bins. She saw what this place represented. An image of Englishness, something she craved.'

May had no response. Words of comfort would sound false, so he waited.

'I don't hold you responsible for what happened. I should have spotted the signs and done something about it. I should have been there for her. One gets focused on work to the exclusion of all else. It becomes very hard to live a normal life.'

'You'll have to sign the autopsy consent today,' said May. 'There's no obvious cause of death.'

Kasavian sighed, an exhalation of air that sounded like defeat. 'I'll be at the office. The Belgians and the French are planning a final attempt to derail the border-control process.'

'Nobody needs to know about your wife just yet. We'll keep it out of the press for as long as we can.'

'John – may I call you that? There's no point in you continuing the investigation. My wife is dead. I'm withdrawing you from the case. I'll make sure there's no reflection on your abilities.'

'It's a murder investigation, Mr Kasavian. I'm afraid even you don't have the power to stop it now.'

'But your unit is under the jurisdiction of the Home Office.'

'You have the ability to direct prosecutions and investigations, but not once a murder inquiry is under way. We have a responsibility to the public. If we call a halt it means that somebody out there is tempted to kill again. Each time we catch a criminal the desire is lessened in others. Prevention of public disorder; it's a fundamental part of our remit.'

'Then you must do what you have to do. I'm going ahead with the presentation of the initiative. It won't be easy to get the work done in time, but I can't lose this as well. I'll need your findings before I leave. I can't go into the chamber of representatives without knowing what happened. I have to start putting it behind me as soon as possible.'

'Then I'll personally provide you with the report before you set off,' said May.

Maggie Armitage acted as a PCU contact point for crimes containing elements of mental and spiritual abnormality. In addition, she offered advice on anything from ghostwriting to rhinoplasty. What she lacked in logic she made up for in a kind of deranged effervescence that some-

243

times shed light into penumbral corners.

Today Bryant had arranged to meet her at Liverpool Street Station. The white witch and self-proclaimed leader of the Coven of St James the Elder turned up in a purple woollen tea-cosy hat, a green velvet overcoat and orange leggings. Her glasses, winged and yellow-tinted, hung on a plastic daisy chain around her throat. She looked like a small seaside town celebrating a centenary.

'The colour of vitality and endurance,' she said, pointing to her tights. 'I thought we might need it today, judging by the tone of your call.'

Bryant explained the case as they passed through the diaspora of commuters. 'The remains of Bedlam were uncovered here, right beneath Liverpool Street Station in 1911,' he explained. 'It had been on this site since the thirteenth century. The workmen found dozens of layers of human skulls. The patients had died of sweating sickness. I thought you might pick up some useful vibrations.'

'At the moment all I can feel is the Tube trains through my trainers, but I'm pretty insensitive until I've had my first cup of coffee,' she replied, taking his arm. 'I would have worn blue had I known – it was Bedlam's trademark colour.'

Bryant barely heard her. 'Madness, melancholy and distraction, that's what they attempted to cure. The so-called "moon-sick" had a red thread tied on them. Kasavian's wife didn't have any red thread – Janice looked through the clothes in her wardrobe – so she scratched a red line around her wrist and died pointing to the picture of Bedlam. She was telling me that her madness held the key to this.'

'I don't know why you thought I'd know more about being barmy than one of your textbooks,' said Maggie. 'OK, I've lit the teapot instead of the kettle occasionally and I once used Strangeways in a revivification ritual by mistake.'

'How could you revive a cat by mistake?'

'I thought he was dead but it turned out he was asleep. The ritual had a reverse effect and put him in a trance for the entire winter. I just stuck him in a box with the tortoise and he woke up in the spring. I'm not really the person to ask about madness. You'd be better off with Dame Maud Hackshaw. She's been inside, you know. Bethlem, the real one, now in Bromley. That was back when she was still getting visits from Joan of Arc. The hospital's still going strong, although they've got rid of people poking the patients with sticks for a shilling a time.'

'Tell me anything you know about madness.'

'I know a few bits and pieces. The hospital was called "Bethlehem", from the Hebrew meaning "house of bread", because its founder got lost behind enemy lines during the crusades and followed the Star of Bethlehem back to camp. Let's see, what else? Madness is known as the English Disease. Wasn't Hamlet sent here because it was thought his behaviour would go unnoticed? Bedlam was used to incarcerate political prisoners, which sounds apt to your case.'

'My thinking precisely. They considered her a political danger.'

Maggie gripped his arm more tightly. 'I'm

feeling something now. Yes, a definite sensation. We must be over the site. Something's pulling me back. I'm rooted to the spot.'

Bryant looked down. 'You've trodden in chewing gum.'

'Oh.' She looked for somewhere to scrape it off. 'Did you know there were once two great statues over the entrance of Bedlam, *Acute Mania* and *Dementia*? Can you imagine how that made arriving patients feel? Half of the problem with madness is its definition. Tell someone they're crazy and they soon start acting crazy. Look at the way they dose children up these days for merely exhibiting normal healthy high spirits. What signal does that send to them? We've always thought that the human body has to be balanced in order to work properly. It was said to be made up of four humours that matched the seasons and elements: yellow bile and fire for summer, black bile and earth for autumn, phlegm and water for winter, blood and air for spring. A lot of alternative therapies still conform to those rules.'

'I've been trying to understand why Amy O'Connor died in St Bride's Church,' said Bryant. 'It has to mean something.'

'You know, there's hardly a church in the whole of London that doesn't have something unusual about it. St Bartholomew the Great in West Smithfield has the ghost of a monk who's said to haunt the church looking for a sandal stolen from his tomb.'

'They must have been very good quality sandals.'

'And there are wonderful puzzles in churches. St Martin-within-Ludgate has a seventeenth-century font with a Greek palindrome inscribed on it. *Nipson anomemata me monan opsin.* "Cleanse my sin and not just my face." And I suppose you know about the devils of St Peter-upon-Cornhill? In the nineteenth century its vicar noticed that plans for the building next door extended one foot on to church territory. He bullied the architect into adding three leering devils to frighten his neighbours. You can still see them.'

They threaded their way past WH Smith and Accessorize, two senior citizens discussing eso-terica in the most mundane of settings.

'Churches have become almost invisible in London,' Maggie said with a sigh, 'but they hide their own secret codes. There are compositions of hymns hidden in stonework and all sorts of runic curses, but it all comes down to man's clumsy attempts at balancing good and evil. Madness is always seen as evil. So perhaps someone was just trying to blacken your victim's name. Did you search the church?'

'Yes. There was nothing,' said Bryant. 'Sabira's husband is about to transform Europe's attitude to policing its borders. But after a week of psy-chological torture, culminating in the death of his wife, it's possible he won't have the strength to succeed in pushing through our government's demands. I think Sabira knew a hawk from a handsaw. Behaving strangely allowed her to say what she felt more easily, but that isn't why she died.'

'Perhaps she was taking revenge for the way she'd been treated, and went mad in the process, like Hamlet.'

'I wish I knew. I followed the red thread and it led me to Bedlam.'

'But madness has no logic, Arthur, and you don't have a cause of death,' said Maggie.

'If anyone can find one, Giles Kershaw can,' said Bryant. 'And when it comes to being irrational you're the perfect person to talk to, so keep talking.'

'I suppose I'll have to take that as a compliment,' said Maggie, holding on to his arm. 'Let's walk a little while and go a little mad.'

29

CAUSE OF DEATH

Bryant met his partner at the St Pancras Mortuary and Coroner's Office, housed in the diseased gingerbread cottage that lurked behind the cemetery of St Pancras Old Church. He was always cheered by its connection to both Frankenstein and Dracula; in the adjoining graveyard were the tombs of Dr Polidori and Mary Wollstonecraft.

Rosa Lysandrou, Giles Kershaw's dour housekeeper, admitted them. Rosa was a natural Greek mourner. Her features appeared to have spent at least two-thirds of their life streaked with tears.

She eyed the detectives warily.

'Is that a new perfume you're wearing, Rosa?' asked Bryant, sniffing the air.

'It's incense from the chapel,' Rosa replied. 'For the dead. Their spirits are all around us.'

'That's nice. I suppose it's company for you. All in black again, I see. Did somebody just die?'

'It's a morgue,' said Rosa. 'Somebody has always just died.'

'I thought perhaps you were dressed out of respect for your country's economy. Is Giles in?'

She led them along the hall to the main autopsy room and pushed open the door.

Giles was excited to see them. 'Just in time,' he said, pulling off his hairnet and releasing a mop-head of glossy blond locks. An unnerving array of body-opening tools had been rolled out behind him like a car-repair kit. 'I started as soon as Mr Kasavian emailed back his consent form, and I have a result for you. I can explain why no one else was found near her in the Soane Museum, and can probably account for the fact that Amy O'Connor died alone in St Bride's Church.'

He was standing beside a silver Mylar sheet ominously concealing a human shape on one of the steel tables. 'You heard the EMT thought she might have had difficulty breathing?'

'That suggested a poison to me,' said Bryant. 'Nobody came near her in the building, but if she'd ingested something harmful it would have taken time to work, which means Sabira took it before reaching the museum.'

'Exactly so. The problem was administration.

She didn't eat breakfast yesterday morning. Her stomach was empty, so how could she have ingested anything?'

'A tablet and water,' said May. 'That would indicate suicide.'

'Unless a doctored tablet was disguised as something harmless, say an aspirin,' said Bryant.

'Come on, who knows when they're going to need an aspirin? Are you suggesting the killer gave her a headache first? I examined the stomach lining for residue,' said Kershaw. 'There was nothing. Obviously poisons have other ways of entering the body: gas, spray, liquid administered via an injection, so I looked for a break in the epidermis but found nothing. Until I looked here.'

He folded back the bottom of the sheet to reveal Sabira's bare feet.

'Look at the sole of the left foot. It's easy to miss because there's some hard skin, but there is a very tiny puncture mark here, near the heel.' Kershaw indicated the spot with the collapsible antenna he had inherited from the PCU's last coroner.

'I can't see anything,' said Bryant.

'No, but that's because you can't see anything,' said Giles. 'You need to put your glasses on. Trust me, it's an entry mark. Something entering the body here would have taken longer to feed into the main circulatory system, so by timing it back–'

'The mosque,' said Bryant. 'She took her shoes off to enter it and left them by the door.'

Giles removed a bag from beneath the table and carried it over to his desk. Opening it, he lifted out Sabira's shoes. 'Take a look at this.' He slipped on plastic gloves and carefully removed the inner sole of the left shoe. 'Don't touch, but if you look very closely you should be able to see it.'

They could make out a tiny indentation in the rear of the inner sole. 'This is what caused the mark,' said Kershaw, tweezering a crystalline sliver of glass from a microscope plate. 'She tried to kick off the left shoe because by the time the toxin started to take effect her foot would have been itching.'

'So Sabira was right,' said May. 'Someone was watching her at the clinic. They followed her to the mosque. She put her shoes in the rack, and while she was inside, they inserted a sliver of glass into the inner sole. She came out, put the shoe on—'

'Probably didn't notice anything beyond a faint irritation, because there are very few nerve endings there,' Kershaw added, 'and she continued to the museum, where she would have started to feel sick and disoriented, collapsing in the room upstairs.'

'Do you have any idea about the kind of poison that could do such a thing?' asked May.

'It was obvious to me that we weren't dealing with some street amateur,' Kershaw explained, 'so I started thinking about professional toxins, and immediately came up with TTX. Tetrodotoxin. It's an incredibly lethal neurotoxin that blocks the nerves by binding to the sodium channels in the cell membranes. There's currently no known antidote and, more interestingly, there are no biological markers to indicate that a sufferer has been exposed to it, which is why it proved so difficult to diagnose a cause of death. It occurs naturally in nature, and can be found in newts, octopi and those Japanese puffer fish people insist on trying to eat. Fugu.'

'I beg your pardon?' said Bryant.

'It means "river pig". The poisonous fish.'

'How much would you need?'

'If it's injected, you'd only have to use half a milligram to kill a normal-sized person.'

'What are the symptoms?'

'The victims experience numbness, shortness of breath, then complete respiratory collapse.'

'And how long would that take?'

'Could be anything between fifteen minutes and three hours, depending on various health factors and conditions. It's diagnosable in blood and urine, but that would involve mass spectrometric detection after liquid or gas chromatographic separation. In other words, not your average high-street cause of death. It's not easy to get hold of, but it's very much the sort of trick the Russians pull on foreign agents these days, using toxins that go undetected or remain misdiagnosed. In the last few years they've pioneered this method of assassination.'

'But if the same murder method was used on Amy O'Connor, why weren't there any puncture marks on her body?' asked Bryant.

'Are you sure there weren't?'

'I'll go back and talk to Ben Fenchurch again.'

'Toxins,' May repeated. 'Sabira Kasavian's mood swings had an irregular pattern, but it was a pattern all the same. She seemed perfectly fine some days, confused and angry on others. You think she was being slowly poisoned? Is there something that could have made her display symptoms commonly associated with mental imbalance?'

'You're talking about the administration of a drug cocktail on different days,' said Kershaw. 'She was in a variety of locations, at home, in restaurants, in the clinic...'

'Any number of people could have got close enough to her to do it, but for one person to administer a toxin on a regular basis – wouldn't she have noticed?' asked May.

'That depends on the method of administration,' said Kershaw. 'There are some highly sophisticated ways to deliver drugs to the system.'

Bryant was following the thought. 'Jeff Waters was killed by someone dressed as a motorcycle courier. If his killer was hired to do the job, why couldn't others have been bribed or blackmailed into giving Sabira medication?'

'That would imply a sizeable conspiracy,' said May.

'But that's exactly what she told us she was afraid of, isn't it? Something so big that she couldn't trust anyone, least of all us because we were connected to the Home Office.'

'Well, you said you wanted to go up against the government,' said May. 'It looks like you've got your wish. What do we do now?'

'Giles, perform whatever tests you have to do to find out if Sabira Kasavian was being slowly poisoned. John, can you get Janice to try Tom

Penry, the boy who was with the little girl at St Bride's Church? He should be back from his holiday shortly. I'm going to find out why Fenchurch failed to find a cause of death for O'Connor.'

As the trio set off on their tasks, Rosa Lysandrou looked at them and shook her head sadly, wondering why they couldn't leave the dead in peace.

30

THE WITCH TEST

Jennifer Penry knelt beside her son and smoothed his sun-blond hair in place. 'I don't see why you can't ask his friend about this,' she said. 'Lucy is older, and seems to have led him on.'

'Lucy won't tell us the truth,' Longbright explained. 'It's difficult with children.'

'Do you have children of your own?' Mrs Penry asked defensively.

'No,' said Longbright. 'My hours would never have suited motherhood.'

'That's your choice, of course.'

Longbright decided not to argue. She had never felt it was a matter of choice. Her mother had been a police sergeant, and so had her former partner. Public service was in her blood; there had never been a question of giving it up. 'Tom, how well do you know your friend Lucy?'

she asked, kneeling down to bring herself to his level.

'We have to wait for our dads,' said Tom, 'so we play.'

'*Witch Hunter* looks like a very exciting game. Did you make up your own rules?'

'No, course not. It's an online game and a card game. There are rules you have to obey.'

Longbright had spent a fruitless hour attempting to play the game with other online players, but had given up after realizing that she had no enthusiasm for absorbing hundreds of arcane rules and updates. It had been like spending the afternoon with Arthur and his books.

'Do you always follow the rules? Are you sure you didn't make some up?'

'Lucy makes things up 'cause she says she knows them all and I don't. But I think she cheats.'

'That's not very fair, is it? Did she cheat before you went on holiday, when you were waiting for your fathers?'

'Yes, she said the lady was a witch but I knew she wasn't.'

'How did you know that?'

'Because there are ways of finding out.'

'What ways did you use to try and find out if she was a witch?'

'One way is to tie them up and drop them in a pond and if they sink they're not a witch and if they float they are a witch, but we didn't have a pond.'

'So what did you do?' Longbright kept her tone chatty and light. It was important not to put the boy on his guard.

Thomas squirmed a little. 'There's another test. You can stick a pin in them and if they don't feel anything or make any noise they're a witch.'

'And Lucy knew about this?'

'Yes, but she didn't remember it until the man said it.'

'What man, Tom?'

'The one who came up to us. He asked us what we were playing and we said witches, and he said you can tell who's a witch by sticking a pin in them. And Lucy said she didn't have a pin but the man did, and he gave it to us.'

'What did it look like?'

'It had a bit of red plastic over the end. He took the plastic off and handed it to her.'

'Then what happened?'

'Lucy ran around behind the bench and crawled underneath it, and she stuck the pin in the back of the lady's leg.'

Longbright glanced at Tom's mother. 'The lady must have been very angry with her.'

'No, she was angry with the wasps. She thought it was a wasp. But she felt it so I knew she wasn't a witch. We ran away.'

'What happened to the man?'

'I don't know. He went away.'

'And what about the pin? What happened to that?'

'Lucy dropped it. And then the lady went off towards the church, and we waited a bit longer to see if she was a witch because Lucy still thought she was, but then I went upstairs to see my dad.'

'This man – can you remember what he looked like?'

'He was a motorbike man with a helmet.'

'Can I show you a picture?' She unfolded a printed frame from the CCTV camera that had caught Jeff Waters's attacker at Coram's Fields, and showed it to him.

'Yes,' said the boy without any shade of uncertainty. 'There's supposed to be a bike badge. Triumph. There.' He tapped the courier's right shoulder.

'How did he give Lucy the pin? Was it in his hand?'

'He took it from his pocket. It was in the plastic thing.'

'What is this all about?' asked Tom's mother, concerned.

'The children had a lucky escape, Mrs Penry,' said Longbright. 'You should be very thankful.'

On the way back to the unit, she took a detour to the courtyard of St Bride's and searched the pavement, but a receptionist in one of the offices told her it was swept every evening, and there was no sign of the toxic needle or its plastic cover.

'I had an idea,' said May, seeking out Bryant at his desk. 'The algorithm – you've got the means of solving the code but not the code itself, right?'

'I don't know where else to look,' Bryant admitted.

'I think Sabira posted you the Cardano grille as a precaution. Have you looked in her belongings? It would have appeared innocuous without the grille to complete it.'

'She had a case of clothes at the clinic,' said

257

Bryant. 'Dan will need to search her flat. It would help if we knew what we were looking for.'

'Maybe she left it with someone she could trust. How about Edona Lescowitz? She might not even know she has it.'

'I'll call Colin and Meera and get them to check with her,' said May. 'They're still keeping a watch on her flat.'

'I feel a fool,' said Bryant suddenly. 'I think I was wrong. I jumped in as usual.'

'What do you mean?'

'Sabira and the Hogarth painting. She died under a depiction of a madhouse. I assumed she was trying to tell me something about her mental state, that somebody drove her to it. But it was you who figured out that the madness might have been chemically induced, which means that Sabira wasn't aware of the cause. So that wasn't the message she was trying to leave.'

'Then why did she go to the museum? It makes no sense.'

'I don't know. Maybe she really was having some kind of relapse. I'm not sure I can rely on my instincts any more.'

'No,' said May. 'Arthur, if you think she was leaving you a message, then we failed to understand its meaning in time to save her. And that means we must keep looking.'

31

TUNNEL RUN

Colin Bimsley pocketed his phone. 'They want us to make contact.'

'With Lescowitz? Why?'

'They need to know if she was given anything by Kasavian's wife. Something no bigger than your hand, they said.'

'Why do I always get the feeling that we're being left out of the loop?' Meera complained. 'It wouldn't kill them to brief us properly for once. Or give us something with a bit more responsibility than babysitting someone who's not even involved in the case.'

'You don't know she's not involved.'

'Exactly. If we had more facts... Can you see her?'

'She must still be inside.'

Lescowitz was studying film design at Central St Martins. The pair had followed her to the South Bank, where she attended a screening of *The Parallax View* at the National Film Theatre. Now she was in the BFI bookstore looking at DVDs.

'Come on then, let's make ourselves known.' Meera led the way across the concourse towards the shop. The cinema was disgorging its audience, and they found themselves in a rapidly thickening crowd. Suddenly the area beneath Waterloo Bridge had become as busy as Piccadilly Circus. The bookstall owners were packing up their trestle tables and people were pouring into the bar at the front of the cinema. Colin pushed forward and managed to reach the shop, but there was no sign of Lescowitz.

Edona walked quickly away from the theatre complex, heading in the direction of Tower Bridge. She had tried calling Sabira at five to see how she was, but the call had gone straight to voicemail, and she couldn't help wondering if something was wrong.

Her friend had changed so much in the last few weeks that it was hard to believe she was the same person. The last time they had spoken, Sabira had deliberately distanced herself, warning Edona that it would be better to stay away from her. Her free-spirited friend had become haunted and fearful.

It was a warm evening, and the walkways of the South Bank were crowded with strollers. The river was a default destination for Londoners, as if it had a pacifying effect on them. They were such strange people that Edona doubted she would ever fully understand them. Why, for example, when they lived in such nice houses, did they leave their rubbish bins right by their front doors where everyone could see? And their language was so dense with allusions and references that it was often impossible to understand what they were really talking about.

She had no real destination in mind, but

walking cleared her head. After a while she found herself in a quieter reach of the river, past the Design Museum, where roads cut down to the water only to double back on themselves or suddenly come to an end. She passed a housing estate, its bright lamps emphasizing the emptiness of the streets. A forlorn pub appeared in the distance, standing by itself at the edge of the foreshore, its rear veranda overlooking the river. She decided to have a drink there, and see if they had something to eat.

Walking over to the low wall, she looked down into the pebble-strewn mud. Her grandparents had told her about coming to London and swimming in the Thames on a hot summer's day, but surely they could not have swum here, where the brown water raced between moored barges at such a speed that the river's detritus became trapped between them?

She heard the motorcycle before she saw it.

The Triumph was on the riverside pavement heading directly towards her, its rider leaning out at such an angle that it seemed he would over-balance.

There was something in his hand – something that gleamed brightly–

With the river wall at her back she had nowhere to retreat, so she dropped down instead, and his arm passed above her head, lightly catching at her hair. Braking hard, he swung the bike around for another pass.

But now there was another motorcycle, a Kawasaki ridden by a slender Indian girl with a crop-headed man on the pillion. As it slowed, the man jumped off, fell hard and righted himself, running between her and her attacker.

The Triumph tried to get close but was driven back as the Indian girl, who looked far too slight to be in control of such a powerful machine, blocked its path. The two bikes circled in an awkward display of attack and defence before the Triumph took off.

'Stay with her,' Meera called to Colin, heading off after the leather-clad rider who had just fishtailed around the corner. His engine was more powerful than hers, but she had grown up in these streets and knew every one-way system and cul-de-sac.

Throttling hard, she thought that if she could get alongside him, she might be able to force him into one of the roads that dead-ended at the raised river wall.

She and Colin had picked up Edona's trail again by covering the route along the embankment wall. They had just spotted her when the other bike had appeared. The rider's physique matched that of the courier in the CCTV shot from Coram's Fields, but he was wearing a different crash helmet.

Meera was in jeans and a nylon jacket, and didn't fancy her chances coming off at high speed. She needed back-up, but there was no way of radioing in the suspect without losing her concentration. The rider ahead left Cherry Garden Street and hit the busy dual carriageway of Jamaica Road, turning hard left into the traffic. Meera followed and was almost fendered by an immense refrigerated truck.

He hit the roundabout and came off at the first exit before hitting another hard left and doubling back. She knew he would try to head for the Rotherhithe Tunnel, passing under the Thames. If he made that, he would be able to reach the chaotic traffic on Cable Street and the Limehouse Link, and there would be a good chance that she would lose him.

He was forced to turn on to Bermondsey Wall, which right-angled into Cathay Street, heading back to Jamaica Road. If he missed the tunnel approach he would only be able to take the painfully misnamed Paradise Street, which she knew dead-ended at St Peter's Church.

The road was narrowed by parked vehicles and braced with speed bumps, but she needed to pull alongside. Accelerating as much as she dared, she raised herself and jockeyed over the bumps as he tried to go around them. The time she gained brought them neck and neck. The sound of their engines reverberated from the passing housefronts. The junction for Paradise Street came up faster than she had been expecting. He needed to cut straight across on to Jamaica Road to catch the tunnel.

Meera saw that there was no possibility of pulling up beside him without killing herself, and was forced to fall back. Checking his rear-view mirror, he roared ahead and crossed the junction.

Or at least, he would have done, if the refrigerated truck she had veered around earlier had not ploughed into him.

The Triumph rolled under the lorry's front

wheels and was mangled to scrap. She did not see what happened to its rider. Braking hard and skidding to a stop, she stood the bike down and ran to the junction. The truck could not brake fast without shifting its load, and came to a halt on the far side of Paradise Street in a blast of air brakes.

When she found the rider lying ten metres further on, she saw that he had been thrown into a wall and had compacted the vertebrae in his neck, severing his spinal cord. He had died instantly. With a hiss of anger, she sat down beside him as sirens surrounded her.

32

METHOD AND MADNESS

It was almost midnight by the time Meera and Colin brought Edona Lescowitz into the unit. The three of them had only been released by Bermondsey Police after direct intervention from Kasavian. Edona had been informed of her friend's death, and had agreed to come in on the condition that somebody drove her back to Walthamstow. She appeared accepting and unruffled by what had happened, as if she had been expecting the worst, although she was taken aback by the shabbiness of the police unit.

Longbright made her comfortable in Bryant's old armchair. May had warned his partner not to upset their witness, but he need not have bothered; for the moment she seemed surprisingly composed.

'We appreciate your help,' May said. 'You're taking this very well.'

'Mr May, I was raised in an Albanian orphanage. We were taught to expect the worst.'

'Well, I'm afraid it gets worse. We think your friend Sabira was being poisoned, which would have accounted for her changes of mood. But even before that process began, she was unhappy.'

'Of course she was unhappy,' Edona replied. 'She was losing her identity. You don't know what a shock it is to come here and build a life in a strange country, as she did. And then to be treated so badly by those conspirators.'

'Why do you call them that?'

'She told me how they hatch their plans. Always trying to destroy their rivals. And the wives, always looking for excuses to meet in fancy restaurants. Sabira was always trying to get out of the lunches.'

'Did she tell you anything about them?'

'She said the wives met in order to agree on certain things.'

'What kind of things?'

'How to protect their men from bad press and keep a united front. They could apply pressure on any wife who failed to conform.'

'You think that's why Sabira had the fight in Fortnum's? She was goaded into reacting?'

'I'm sure of it. She couldn't be controlled, so she had to go.'

'So the wives might know more than they've told us?'

'If they have any suspicions, I doubt they'll share them with you.'

'I wonder if we could get them to open up,' said Bryant. 'We'd have to field someone they would trust. That rules out anyone from here. We're all a bit too rough around the edges.'

May took exception to this. He had always had great success with women. 'What about Janet Ramsey?' he suggested. 'She used to go out with Kasavian.'

'They close ranks against former partners, divorcees and journalists,' said Edona.

'It would need to be someone they don't know,' May agreed. 'Miss Lescowitz, what do you think caused your friend's breakdown?'

Edona hesitated for a moment. Her natural instinct was to distrust the authorities, but it was hard to refuse May's friendly, open face. 'I think her behaviour was deliberate at first. It allowed her to say things that had no voice. But at some point it stopped being a method and became a madness. Whether this was real or induced is for you to find out, no?'

'Nobody ever figured out Hamlet,' muttered Bryant.

'Did Sabira say anything about the photographer who always followed her?' asked May.

'I saw him a couple of times when she and I went out together. He told her to be careful, and not to trust anyone.'

'Why would he tell her that?'

'I don't know. I got the feeling it was part of

266

another conversation they had had earlier.'

'Do you know if Sabira had any feelings towards Waters? Were they intimate?'

'No, certainly not. She was loyal to her husband. It was in her nature. Waters was a handsome man. He spent his life calling out to attractive women to get their attention, so I guess he had to be charming, and Sabira enjoyed being paid a little attention, nothing more than this.'

'Come on, let's get you home,' said May. 'We know how to contact you.'

'One last thing,' said Bryant. 'Did Sabira send you anything when she was in the clinic? An envelope, perhaps?'

Lescowitz thought for a moment. 'No, nothing.'

'I'm sending Colin back with you. There will be someone posted outside your apartment until this is over. Colin, you can take my car.'

The detectives arranged for Fraternity DuCaine to share shifts with Colin and Meera outside the flat in Walthamstow until they could come to an arrangement with local officers.

Bryant stood at the window watching Bimsley and Lescowitz crossing the Caledonian Road, heading for the car spaces the PCU rented from the aged Russian extortionist who had been smart enough to buy up empty lots in the seventies, when the area had been a violent no-go zone. 'We're running out of time to uncover something that will probably kill us off for good,' he said. 'Not much of a deal, is it?'

'It's your call, Arthur,' said May. 'We could take Kasavian's advice and drop the whole thing right now.'

'Amy O'Connor's killer is dead, but other lives may be at risk. Someone's cleaning house to stop information from getting out. They're in the habit of hiring thugs, so they won't think twice about hiring another.' He rubbed his eyes wearily. 'I have to go home. Tomorrow's going to be a tough day.'

33

CONSPIRACY THEORY

'I don't need to be coached on how to behave like a lady,' said Longbright, straightening her jacket in the full-length mirror she had installed in her office. Looking over her shoulder, she caught Meera trying not to laugh. 'What? This jacket's a Biba classic.'

'It's not the jacket,' said Meera, 'it's how you wear it.'

'And how's that?'

'With your shoulders hunched up. You look like a boxer, or a tranny. Try to relax a bit.'

'That's rich coming from you. I've never seen you in anything but jeans and workboots. You don't exactly exude femininity.'

'It's not about being feminine, it's about looking classy. Like you were born to the style. Don't you ever watch any makeover shows?'

'No, of course not.'

'Drop your shoulders. What have you got on

your hair?' Meera reached up and touched Long-bright's blond mane. 'God, there's enough lacquer on that to create a new hole over the North Pole.'

'It's Silvikrin Twelve-Hour Hard Hair with Highlights. They stopped making it in 1968. I found some in a warehouse off the Edgware Road. Lady Anastasia has already agreed to introduce me to the rest of her coven today. She said she's happy to gather them at short notice.'

'Why would she agree to do that?'

'Because I represent an organization that's setting out to limit the freedom of the press in the wake of the recent phone-hacking scandals, and need to canvass opinion from women in the public eye. John came up with that one. She was very impressed by the CV he wrote for me.'

'What's the organization called?'

'Dunno, I'll come up with something. We're meeting in a Mayfair restaurant called La Cuisine des Gourmets. It's the closest I'll ever get to being taken out to a posh dinner, I can tell you.'

'You'd better eat something first. They'll order green salads. You'll be the only one asking the chef if he can knock up a cheeseburger.'

Longbright's hands went to her hips. 'Is that what you think of me? I admit I was born into a family of public-service-industry employees, but I do actually know how to eat with a knife and fork, thank you.' She checked herself in the mirror. 'Maybe I'll ditch the Bowanga Jungle Jaguar lip gloss, though. It's a bit too Ruth Ellis.'

'Who's she?'

'The last woman to be hanged in Britain. Call

yourself a copper? Blimey. I mean, goodness gracious.'

Arthur Bryant found his way back through the corridors of the Robin Brook Centre at St Bart's Hospital, looking for Dr Benjamin Fenchurch. He spotted his old friend through the smoked-glass panel of the mortuary door, hunched over his desk as usual, and quietly entered. Creeping up behind the coroner, he tapped him on the shoulder.

Fenchurch jumped. 'God, you gave me a fright,' he said. 'It's a good job I wasn't holding a scalpel.'

'It's funny,' said Bryant, shaking some Dolly Mixtures out of a paper bag and offering them, 'I didn't startle you last time. But then you heard my shoes, didn't you? You made a comment about me still wearing Blakey's. You didn't see me reflected in the mirror above your desk. And then there was the mix-up with the cadaver drawers. You had trouble finding O'Connor. How long have you been having a problem with your eyes?'

Fenchurch looked devastated. 'Don't say anything, Arthur. Please. I've got eight months to go before retirement.'

'But it's affecting your work, Ben. You didn't spot the puncture mark on O'Connor's left calf, did you? She was stabbed with a needle-tip coated in Tetrodotoxin. You had no assistant but still went ahead with the post-mortem, and you missed it.'

'I started having trouble with my right eye a year ago. I knew it would exempt me from finishing my

270

term if it got on to an official medical report, so I delayed my check-up. I'll lose my payout if they make me go early.'

'Is O'Connor still here?'

'The funeral parlour is due to pick her up tomorrow morning.'

'Let me see her. My eyesight's not much better than yours, but I know what I'm looking for.'

Fenchurch led the way to the cadaver drawers and they extracted the chilled bag containing O'Connor's remains. Bryant donned gloves and turned her left leg without waiting for Fenchurch's permission. He was always surprised by the way in which the absence of life left bodies looking smaller and less substantial, as if the soul could be weighed.

Leaning forward, he saw that a tiny but definite lump could be found now that the skin had lost its elasticity and started to retract.

'OK,' said Bryant, 'I won't say anything about your eyesight on two conditions. You need to change the report, and promise me that any further post-mortems you handle in your remaining time are conducted in the presence of a qualified medic.'

'Of course,' said Fenchurch gratefully.

'And I'm still expecting you on my bowling team next Saturday,' said Bryant, tightening his scarf in anticipation of the sunlit streets.

Meanwhile, Dan Banbury and Giles Kershaw were at the St Pancras Mortuary with the remains of a black Triumph Thunderbird and its rider, bagged and labelled with scanner codes.

'You know how many of these we see a month?' said Kershaw. 'Trucks still have blind spots that let them take out bikes at corners.'

'He was really travelling,' said Banbury. 'It must have been like driving straight into a concrete wall. No tags in his clothes. The bike was bought through an online site, and the seller was given an alias. Think it was the same guy who went after Waters?'

'Well, he's right-handed, and his build is consistent with Waters's attacker. He recently took anabolic steroids and cocaine.' He held up the rider's left wrist and turned it over to reveal a dense, smudged square of deep blue ink. 'That's a Russian prison tattoo, made by repeatedly jabbing yourself with a darning needle dipped in household ink. He tried to remove it with a razor blade but it looks like it went septic. If you're thinking of a criminal career, it's not a good idea to trademark yourself with something traceable.'

'What is it?'

Kershaw drew closer and shone a penlight over the patch. 'A church or a monastery. The crucifix at the centre indicates that the wearer is the prince of thieves. Four spires on the church. That's either the number of years or prison terms he's served. And that looks like a spider at the base. The joints on the legs are irregular, see? That gives us his admittance date. Russian prisoners take great pride in tattoo codes, and they're evolving all the time. I've seen these coming out of St Petersburg.' He snapped his gloves off. 'You should be able to fill in the rest, shouldn't you?'

'An ID won't be enough to link him to anyone

at the Home Office. They're covering their tracks.'

'My dear fellow, you give up far too easily,' said Kershaw. 'This chap wasn't supposed to go under a lorry. That was a mistake, and mistakes leave a trail you can follow.'

'You say that, but I can't even check to see if he ever contacted Kasavian's department because we can't access their phone records, and this guy wasn't carrying a mobile. We retraced his route on the off chance that he dropped it somewhere, but no luck.'

'There'll be a mistake,' Kershaw insisted. 'I can't be doing with conspiracy theories; they really are the province of crackpots. Just how many could be in on this? I mean, really?'

'I don't see that it would have to be that many. We're talking about, I don't know, five, maybe six people who are already signed up to the Official Secrets Act.'

'So what's the big international secret they're all protecting?'

'You tell me. Amy O'Connor worked in a bar. Anna Marquand, if it goes back that far, was a biographer. Jeff Waters was a *paparazzo*. And Sabira Kasavian, when it comes down to it, was an Eastern European bride coming to the realization that she'd made a bad marriage. They *must* have shared a piece of knowledge that got them all killed, but I can't begin to think what it might have been.'

'You've linked them,' said Kershaw. 'Good. Let's go from there.'

34

DOXIES AND RAKES

Longbright checked her reflection in the glass-covered menu outside La Cuisine des Gourmets and barely recognized herself.

She was dressed in a high-necked grey trouser suit she had only worn once before, to her aunt's funeral. Meera had tied her hair back with tortoiseshell clips. In gold earrings, a single strand of pearls, a tiny gold Cartier watch Bryant had borrowed from the 'unclaimed' drawer in the PCU's evidence room, low patent black heels and a matching bag, she looked like the Thames Valley wife of a professional golfer.

The restaurant was hung with gleaming copper pots, bunches of dried lavender and other pastoral French knick-knacks. And there they all were, seated at a long table by the largest window, the Home Office wives.

Longbright still had Sabira's notes about them. She could identify Cathy Almon, whose spouse headed the HO's Workforce Management Data System, and Lavinia Storton-Chester, whose husband Nigel was the security division's public relations manager. She also recognized a high-born woman named Daniella Asquith, wizened and birdlike, from staff files Dan had downloaded. At the head of the table sat Lady Anastasia Lang and Emma Hereward. The empty chair beside Ana Lang had clearly been left for Longbright.

Introductions were made, but the swirl of conversation was barely interrupted by Longbright's arrival. Apparently the chef had prepared a set menu for the group. Longbright's dietary requests – not that she had any – were obviously not to be taken into account. A first course arrived, something with asparagus tips and quails' eggs fussily laced with a crimson sauce that reminded her of blood-spatter patterns. Longbright trotted out her prepared mission statement about building evidence against the press.

'If you could do something about the *Guardian* journalists,' Emma Hereward piped up, 'we get a very rough ride from them.'

You picked the only left-wing newspaper out of nearly a dozen national dailies, thought Longbright, who had been in the public-service sector long enough to be able to spot a table of union-busters at a hundred paces.

'All our expenses have to be checked now,' Ana Lang agreed. 'All this rubbish about the taxpayer having to fork out to have MPs' moats cleaned. The lack of trust is appalling.'

Inflamed by the topic, Daniella Asquith became so animated that there seemed a chance she might be going into cardiac arrest. 'I think we behaved impeccably,' she said. 'You know what it's about? Jealousy. We have got a very, very large house. Some people say it looks like Balmoral, but it's a merchant's house from the nineteenth century. It was Labour who introduced the Free-

275

dom of Information Act and it is Labour who insisted on the things that caught us on the wrong foot.'

The wives chorused their dissatisfaction with the press reportage of the expenses scandal. The irony was that the story had been brilliantly uncovered by the *Daily Telegraph*, traditionally a bastion of right-wing journalism, but this appeared to have passed them by.

'They won't leave us alone,' Ana Lang told Longbright. 'It's because we've publicly voiced support for our husbands. They think we're fair game now.'

'I imagine Mr Kasavian's wife made the situation worse,' said Longbright.

'Well, of course it was terribly sad that she chose to kill herself, but she was unstable,' said Lang.

'I didn't know she killed herself.'

'They'll keep it out of the press, but it was an overdose. She was taking so many prescription drugs that she couldn't keep track of them all.'

'You know that for a fact?'

'No, but it was common knowledge.' All the wives nodded agreement.

'Did anyone actually see her take pills?'

Ana Lang spoke for the others. 'Not as such. But she told us she was taking them. She couldn't even remember what they were all for. She said something about not wanting her doctor to find out. In fact, I advised her to stick with her prescribed regime and avoid taking anything else.'

'When you have a situation where one wife

doesn't fit in,' Longbright said carefully, 'what usually happens?'

'We never exclude,' Ana Lang pointed out. 'We just don't go out of our way to *in*clude.'

As Longbright watched everyone playing with expensive meals that didn't really interest them, she suddenly felt sorry for the government wives. She could see their endangered lives laid out like forgotten biological displays: winter in Barbados, summer in Tuscany, kids at Eton and Harrow, lunches at the Delaunay and Hawksmoor, an endless round of preparations for cocktail parties and charity dinners that nobody actually wanted to be at, an atrophying existence of slow and steady strangulation until divorce or dotage beckoned.

'So you'll do what you can to help us limit press intrusion,' said Ana Lang, as if a decision had been reached by consensus. '*Hard News* has been especially tiresome about publishing pieces that don't have our approval. I suppose you know that the editor, Janet Ramsey, had an affair with Oskar? We simply had to put a stop to that.'

'How did you do it?'

'We leaked information about her unsuitability. She had an abortion a few years ago. We couldn't have him going out with a leftie.'

'Surely public servants have to undergo vetting and are required to be non-partisan?'

'Our spouses are required to make public displays of even-handedness, but that doesn't affect their beliefs,' said Emma Hereward. 'Whether they realize it or not, they do what we tell them. The public thinks we simply turn up at photo opportunities to support our husbands, but I assure you, we are the power behind their thrones.' She pointed at Ana Lang and laughed. 'And she is our Lady Macbeth.'

'Edona Lescowitz was right,' Longbright told her fellow detectives that afternoon. 'They are witches, all of them. They honestly think they can make or break their men, and I get the feeling that the fourth man in the Pegasus set-up, Stuart Almon, isn't long for this world. They want him out.'

'Why?' asked Bryant.

'Because he's weak. He's "not performing", whatever that means. The husbands all toe the line around their women, if the wives are to be believed. They do what they're told. Except when they go to their club, which they're allowed to do no more than once a week.'

'Where do they go, the Garrick, White's, the RAC Club? I'll bet most of them still don't allow women members.'

'Exactly. I can't blame the wives for forming their own society, so long as men want to play their little power games behind closed doors. Apparently the boys belong to a place in Westminster called the Rakes' Club.'

'You have got to be joking,' said Bryant. 'The Rakes'? The club founded around the time of Guy Fawkes – *that* Rakes' Club? How could I have missed it?'

'What?' asked May.

'The Hogarth painting Sabira died beneath. She wasn't trying to tell us something about the nature of madness, because she wasn't indicating the picture of Bedlam. I was misled by the red string around O'Connor's wrist and the red wound around her own. She was drawing attention to the series, not a specific painting. *The Rake's Progress*.'

'Now wait a minute,' said May, raising his hands, 'this sounds like one of your loopy–'

'It's obvious, isn't it? The directors of Pegasus Holdings all belong to the Rakes' Club.'

'So they're the kind of men who belong to clubs. What does that prove?'

'You don't understand the Rakes',' said Bryant. 'That's why she went to the Hogarth room. We have to go back there.'

With the second layer of doors closed, the high-ceilinged, wood-veneered room was too poorly lit to reveal its corners. May used his Valiant torch and shone its beam into the cracks and crevices. When he examined the base panels he saw the sliver of an envelope sticking out.

'This is why she came here,' said May, carefully extracting the paper.

Bryant seized the envelope and examined it in the torch beam. 'She must have slipped it behind the Bedlam painting.'

'Then when she fell against the doors it shook loose and slipped down between the lower layers. It looks like it matches the one that was posted to you. Sabira took a chance leaving it here. We might never have come across it.'

'Except that she knew we would follow her route,' said Bryant. 'I wonder where she was planning to go after this.'

'She didn't have her passport. I guess she could have hidden out somewhere, waited to get straight in her head. Maybe she suspected she was being poisoned.'

'And with any luck, this will give us the poisoner's identity.' Bryant pocketed the envelope with a flourish.

35

BRING IT DOWN

At 11 p.m. on Tuesday night, the staff of the PCU were still at their desks.

Banbury and Kershaw were collating notes when they received an ID confirmation for the Triumph rider. His name was Luka Terebenin, a 32-year-old Russian who had spent four years of a twelve-year sentence in the Kresty Prison in St Petersburg for armed robbery before having his sentence commuted. Emerging from the overcrowded jail when he was twenty-six, he disappeared from state records before turning up in the UK eighteen months ago.

'Sounds like somebody recognized his talents and recruited him,' said Kershaw. 'What have you got on his residence here?'

'Bugger all,' said Banbury, checking through the online file. 'No residential address, no employment stats, nothing except a visa entry. It looks like he had a sponsor to take care of his file for him. I'll try to contact his family in St Petersburg.'

'It seems unlikely that they'll know anything about his life here.'

'It's not that. If they want his remains shipped home, they have to pay for it. Not our responsibility.'

Everyone looked up as Bryant sauntered in looking more at peace with himself than he had for a while. He was definitely less wrinkly. 'This is what you're all waiting to see, I take it.' He removed Sabira's envelope from his pocket. 'The card. I need to compare it to the Cardano grille.' He held out his hand.

'I don't have it,' said May. 'You must have it.'

'Ah yes, I think you're right. I put it somewhere safe.' He stroked his stubbled cheek, thinking for a moment, and then wandered out to the kitchen, returning with the card. 'I hid it in the staff refrigerator.'

'Why would you do that?' asked May.

'Oh, my mother always used to keep the rent money in the larder, where my old man couldn't get at it.'

'Why can't you do things the normal way, just once?' asked Land, irritated.

'I find your emphasis on conformity hard to fathom,' Bryant replied as he donned his glasses and matched up the cards. 'Really, if you look at the average family there's no such thing. People behave in the most extraordinary fashion and think nothing of it. They have weird food habits and funny sleeping arrangements and rituals: "Oh, we always go to Grandma's the day before

281

Guy Fawkes Night to lock the cat up" – that sort of thing. You know the butcher on the Gaily Road, the big bloke with one eye? When he's not chopping up cows he plays gypsy accordion with three other fat butcher-musicians who call themselves the Gastric Band. Is that normal? Of course not. There's no such thing as normal.'

'Well,' said May, 'does it fit?'

'Perfectly. Take a look.' Bryant had placed the card with the cut-out sections over a pencilled panel of random letters on the inside of the second card. 'It clearly isn't just a Caesar's shift. We need a keyword.' He grabbed a pen and wrote out a list of names. 'Let's try everyone in the security department first.'

'Your notions of normality fascinate me,' said Land, unable to drop the subject. 'You formed your opinions in London in the second half of the twentieth century, you must have some idea that they go against the generally accepted flow of things.'

'*Au contraire*, old sausage, I've lived through Marilyn Monroe, the Suez crisis, the Kennedy assassination, Watergate, Edward Heath, the Jeremy Thorpe scandal–'

'Jeremy Thorpe?' said Land. 'That name rings a bell.'

'It should do. A fairly definitive example of political lunacy,' said Bryant without looking up. 'Thorpe was the Old Etonian leader of the Liberal Party in the early 1970s. He was alleged to have had an affair with a male model, Norman Scott, and to have hired a hitman to murder him. The hitman shot Scott's Great

Dane, Rinka, but the gun jammed before he could kill his target. Thorpe was forced to resign and was eventually acquitted in a very peculiar trial, while the hitman married a woman who fell nine hundred feet off a mountain in the Alps. This was the chairman of the United Nations Committee, and this is British politics, not some tiny Mexican town where the mayor is sleeping with the chief of police's daughter. You think you know normal? You have no idea.' He slapped down his pen. 'I've tried everyone's names and none of them work. Anyone got any bright notions?'

'Try "Pegasus",' said May.

'Hang on.'

The room went quiet as it became clear that Bryant was transposing letters.

Bryant creaked back in his green leather arm-chair, looking at his partner in alarm. He showed none of the satisfaction that usually crossed his features when he knew something the others did not.

'I think we're in more trouble than we realized,' was all he said.

He refused to speak to any of them. When May approached, he shook his head and left the room.

'Tell me,' said May, stepping over Crippen as he tracked his partner along the corridor, 'what's wrong? What did it say?'

'I thought I might be putting you in danger before,' said Bryant, 'and now I know it. Sabira was killed by her knowledge. I don't want any of you to be targeted.'

'Arthur, how long have I known you? How

many times have we been threatened? Have we ever backed down or given in? Of course not. What can you achieve by yourself?'

Bryant's silent glance chilled him. He had only seen his partner like this twice before in their long careers together.

'All right, I'll put it another way,' tried May. 'Nobody knows we have both the cards, do they? So long as they're not aware of their existence, we're safe.'

'Has Dan gone?'

'No, he's still at his desk.'

'I want the unit swept for bugs. The phones, the walls, under the floorboards, everywhere. He needs to check the cars as well.'

'With all this clutter? Aren't you being a little–'

'I know, John. Do you understand? I *know*.'

'You know who's behind all this?'

Bryant quietly folded the card away inside his jacket.

May held out his hand. 'Show me, Arthur. I'm in this with you. We agreed to see it through, didn't we?'

'I'll deal with it by myself,' said Bryant. 'There's no need for us all to go down.'

'Let me see what you've got,' May persisted, 'and I'll decide what to do. You have to trust me. I've always been the sensible one, haven't I?'

Bryant held his partner's gaze with a long, steady look, and then removed the envelope from his jacket pocket and handed it over. May took out the card and read the decoded sentence that Bryant had highlighted.

It said: 'OSKARKASAVIANMURDERER'.

May went to the window and opened it wide, setting a flurry of pigeons to flight and allowing the late-night traffic noise to flood the room. 'That isn't possible,' he said. 'It can't be him. Why would he hire us to find out what was wrong with his wife if he was secretly destroying her?'

'Oh, you won't find his fingerprints on anything. He's made sure he's untouchable. Think about it. He hired a thug, Terebenin, and got hold of untraceable toxins. He has all the right connections. He was with his wife every night. He's convinced we can't solve the case, and he'll be ready to damn us when we fail. He's lied to everyone. Sabira discovered something that could destroy him, and was removed because she was too difficult to manage. You know it's true, John. In your heart, you've always known it couldn't be anyone else.'

'I don't know...'

'Think about it. Why didn't Sabira tell us outright? Because she was being watched, and everything was overheard and reported. Whatever she discovered about her husband was so big that she knew he'd do anything to keep it hidden. If she'd communicated with us directly, he would have found out about it and acted with even more celerity. What on earth could she do? When we met in Smith Square, I told her I was good at breaking codes, remember? I gave her the idea.'

'So she used the only code she remembered from her childhood and sent you a message.'

'But the two envelopes were separated in such a way that we might never have found the second one.'

'What you're saying is that we have nothing, and he knows it.'

'He knows how to cover his tracks, John. Even if we did get physical proof, he'd make sure that everyone closed ranks against us. His wife's meeting with the photographer made him realize she was on to him, so he had evidence planted in Waters's flat to damage her reputation. And when that didn't work, he knew he would have to get rid of her.'

'I suppose Sabira's message wouldn't hold water in a court of law?'

'Of course not. Even if we could prove she sent it, she's on record as having psychological problems. We have evidence but no proof. If Giles can show that she was being systematically poisoned, we would still need to trace the trail back to Kasavian.'

'All right,' said May. 'We'll put this to the vote.'

He walked back into the common room. 'Listen up, everyone, I need your attention. Arthur and I have new information, but if we share it with you it could put everyone at risk. The two of us are prepared to go it alone. If you choose to abstain from taking the investigation further, your decision will be treated without prejudice.'

Renfield was the first to speak. 'This is a police unit, not an insurance office. We didn't sign up for the health-and-safety aspect of the job.'

'Jack's right,' said Meera. 'I don't see why we should let you have all the glory when it's cracked.'

'Hear what we've got first.'

'No,' said Renfield. 'Does anybody want to opt out?'

No hands went up.

'Very well. Arthur will brief you on the latest turn of events.'

'Right,' said Bryant. 'I just want you to know that we'll all be going to hell for this. This is the sort of thing that can undermine an entire government.'

'I knew it,' said Renfield. 'Bang goes the knighthood.'

36

RUNAWAY

It was 2.30 a.m. when the briefing session finished, and the detectives sent everyone home. 'We can't protect them all,' said Bryant. 'It's spreading fast and it's going beyond our control. There are already too many people who know too much: Edona Lescowitz and the children, Lucy Mansfield and Tom Penry. Perhaps the kids are safe – no one would believe them.'

'Then we have to wrap it up fast, before Kasavian gets wind of anything,' said May. 'And every step of this case has to be solid. I suggest we keep the PCU operational as a safe house for anyone who needs it.'

Banbury had run a check on everything emitting an electronic pulse in the building, and had been able to account for all devices except Bryant's radio, which continued working even after it had been unplugged and had had the batteries removed. It was agreed that no unknown callers would be admitted until they had closed the investigation, which needed to be before Kasavian headed for Europe, when he would move beyond their reach.

'I suggest we hit the Rakes' Club tomorrow, as soon as it opens its doors. Sequester their accounts and membership log. We're dead without evidence.'

They headed out to collect May's BMW. The light rain was sheening the roads with yellow diamonds.

'What's so special about this particular club?' asked May, unlocking the car door.

'The Rakes' was founded by a group of classically educated young Catholics who agreed to meet together on certain nights and kill the first man they met on the city streets,' said Bryant. 'For three years they literally got away with murder. London magistrates tried to find legal precedents to curb them but failed to do so, and of course there were no police. There's evidence linking the ringleaders to the so-called Jesuit Treason, or Gunpowder Plot, of November the fifth 1605, after which most of them were eventually transported, but the Rakes' Club survived. In fact, several other versions of so-called Hellfire clubs appeared in Europe, mainly in the Netherlands. Secret clubs demanded a level of loyalty that ranked above that to the Crown and the State. They terrified governments because of

288

their ability to destabilize the population.'

'But that's the most fundamental tenet of the PCU's remit, to prevent the disintegration of society.'

'Indeed. The Hellfire clubs in their original form petered out at the end of the eighteenth century, when the old libertine ways died. The Napoleonic wars distracted everyone. But the clubs continued in new, more acceptable forms. Their members became wealthy landowners. In many ways they represented the very things that the Peculiar Crimes Unit was created to oppose.'

May pulled out into Euston Road and turned on the windscreen wipers. 'Hellfire – didn't they practise Satanism and witchcraft?'

'They did by the time Sir Francis Dashwood was remodelling West Wycombe House in the style of the Temple of Bacchus. They were the opposite of guilds and Masonic lodges. I suppose you could say they sought to encourage disorder, anarchy, drinking, gambling and above all promiscuity, strictly for the elite – peers, military men, the gentry. The Wig Club in Edinburgh required its members to make a toast from a penis-shaped glass after donning a wig made from the pubic hair of the royal mistresses from Charles II to George IV. It was full of lice, so they all ended up infested.'

May laughed.

'The concept of anarchic clubs still continues in other forms. For example, Churchill's Special Operations Executive, the 'Ministry of Ungentlemanly Warfare', encouraged espionage and sabotage in Nazi-occupied Europe. I think a sense of anarchy exists deep within the English bloodline, and a good thing too.'

'How on earth do you know all this?' May asked.

'Remember all those years when you were out late at night in West End supper clubs, chatting up young ladies? I was at home reading.'

Ahead the lights were turning red, but when May applied the brakes his foot went straight to the floor.

'Do you want to slow down a little bit?' said Bryant. 'There are several things going through my head at the moment, but I don't want one of them to be the windscreen.'

'Can't,' said May. 'No brakes.'

The BMW shot past a truck, heading towards the red lights.

'It's the big pedal in the middle, if memory serves,' said Bryant.

'Not working. Get in the back seat.'

'Certainly not. I'm not going to leave you up here in the front. What if you take the key out of the ignition?'

'That would engage the steering lock.' The BMW raced through the lights, narrowly missing a Marks & Spencer truck and a very angry cyclist.

'There are at least seven sets of lights on this stretch of the road,' said Bryant. 'The cabbies reckon you can hit something called a "golden run" when all of them are aligned green.'

'I think we're going to be hitting something else,' May warned. 'The next ones are turning red. We're going to catch all of them.'

'Wait – look.' Bryant pointed at the ambulance in the next lane. 'It's heading for University College Hospital. Get behind it and stay as close as you can.'

May swung the BMW in behind the ambulance and followed it across the next intersection, racing through the red lights. A police patrol car swung in behind them and started its siren.

'Elderly detectives crushed in multiple pile-up,' said Bryant. 'I was planning to die in my sleep, not in the Euston Road. I don't want to be remembered by a Sellotaph.'

'Will you shut up a minute and let me concentrate?' May warned. They rode another red light. Miraculously, the next cross street was deserted. The ambulance was starting to slow in preparation for its left turn into the hospital. The BMW bumped its rear fender as the medics looked out of the window in alarm.

The ambulance turned. May tried to turn with it, but felt his tyres start to slide.

'I read somewhere that you're supposed to turn into it.'

'Thank you,' said May tetchily, 'I'm trying to.'

The BMW slipped off the wet road and bumpily mounted the pavement.

'Go over there.' Bryant airily waved his hand at the windscreen. 'Between the lamp-post and the wall.'

'I don't think there's enough of a gap.'

The BMW shot into the space and was brought to a jarring, grinding stop as wall and lamp-post scraped the sides of the vehicle, dragging it to a standstill. Behind them, the patrol car halted and

291

two officers jumped out.

'I'll let you talk us out of this one,' said Bryant. 'Then I'm going to go home for a cup of strong tea and a change of trousers.'

37

THE SICKNESS OF THE MOON

'The next time you decide to go stock-car racing, you might not want to do it in the Euston Road,' said Banbury the next morning.

He had been called into the unit early, and still looked half-asleep. 'I've just been over your car, John,' he said. 'The brakes weren't cut. It looks like the shoes were oiled with some kind of industrial lubricant. Unusual molecular structure, like the sort of product NASA used to develop for the space program. Nice job, very professional. We'll run a trace. There can't be many people who could supply it. I think your repair bill is going to be more than the resale value. I hope you were insured.'

'I don't think my insurance covers assassination attempts,' said May. 'I need you to try and link it back to Kasavian.'

'I hope you're joking. There are no prints, nothing to suggest tampering.'

'But you said a lubricant—'

'There's a lot of high-intensity industrial work going on in the backstreets around here. It could have been picked up from a spill. That's the way these jobs are pulled off, John. They're designed to leave room for interpretation.'

'But you could check around the area, and if no one was using–'

'How long have you got?'

'Fair point,' May conceded. 'Giles reckoned he'd get clear proof that Sabira Kasavian was being slowly poisoned. Anything on that?'

'Well, I spoke to him on the way in – didn't see why I should be the only one up – and I think he's run into trouble. So far all the isolated chemical components he's had back from the Institute of Tropical Medicine are commonly found ingredients. They need to run further tests, which is going to take time and be expensive. Knowledge and proof are different states.'

'But the only person who could consistently get close enough to her was Kasavian.'

'That's purely circumstantial.'

'What about Waters's death?'

'That trail's already gone.'

'Then what else do we have? It sounds like O'Connor is our best bet.'

'We could start at the other end, with the culprit.'

'Except that he knows how we work,' said May. 'He's been studying our methodology like a hawk for years, waiting for us to slip up.'

Bryant sat up with a start. Everyone had thought he was asleep. 'We still have a few tricks up our sleeve. There's someone we can use: Leslie Faraday.'

Faraday was the Home Office liaison officer,

and the budget overseer of London's specialist police units. Answerable only to Kasavian, he had *carte blanche* to investigate anything that failed to meet his approval. In the hands of someone intelligent this power would have been absolute, but Faraday was the sort of man whose mental circuitry had been soldered into place.

'Faraday? He's an idiot. What can he do?'

'Oh, I absolutely agree. He's W.S. Gilbert's original "Disagreeable Man" – you know:

Each little fault of temper and each social defect
In my erring fellow-creatures I endeavour to correct.

'But that's the beauty of it; he'll never spot what we're up to. He can help us nail Kasavian. We need the Home Office agenda for the Paris presentation. I don't think he's just going to sign off on the initiative, I think he's going to bury something else there, something he doesn't ever want to surface here.'

'How can he do that?' asked May.

'By placing security information under one of the Europe-wide anti-terrorism secrecy laws. If it's neatly knotted with red tape and locked in an EU filing cabinet, we'll never be able to get our hands on it.'

'That gives us less than forty-eight hours.'

'Then we'd better get a move on. We need to get into the Rakes' Club. We're not the only ones being set up for a fall; Stuart Almon's card has also been marked. He'll be our ticket in.'

'Why would he agree to do it?'

'You heard what Janice said. Almon is being

294

sidelined. He'll be there. Anyone who fears Kasavian is a potential ally. See if you can arrange to meet him when I get back. I want to be there.'

'Why, where are you going now?'

'I have to catch up with someone at the British Museum. I need some more specialist knowledge.'

As always, Bryant's thought processes were as mysterious as Mars and just as hard to reach. Gathering up his hat, stick and scarf, he set off for Museum Street.

Georgia Standing did not look like an archivist specializing in the study of Roman lunar symbolism. She looked like a Goth who had come to London for a Cure concert and, having accidentally got locked in the British Museum, had decided to make the most of it. Her jet mane was sewn with Egyptian beads that glittered darkly as she swung towards him on high rubber boots. 'Hey, Grandpa,' she called, 'you're looking good. Still wearing my favourite scarf. Long time no see.'

Bryant waved her hands away. 'Don't call me Grandpa and don't try to do any complicated young-people handshakes with me. How are you getting on?'

'Oh, you know. The female archivists try to trip me up with smart remarks and the married men have a tendency to hit on me. Meanwhile I haven't had a decent date since the Queen Mother died. How's the PCU?'

'Still going, although at this rate we may not make it to the end of the week.'

They strolled together across the gravelled forecourt, passing through a miasma of roasted frankfurters from the stall permanently moored at the museum gates.

'I went to visit Harold Masters in the Royal Bethlem Hospital last month. The doctors don't think he'll ever fully regain his sanity,' said Standing. Masters had been her predecessor at the museum before attempting to strangle someone. 'It amazes me how many academics have nervous breakdowns or start believing that God is speaking to them through the fireplace.'

'It comes with the territory,' said Bryant, taking her arm. 'They focus their attention on one area of study for so long that they lose their perspective. Poor Harold. He was always rather highly strung. Speaking of madness, I need your help.'

'I'll do my best. What's the problem?'

'Murder victims with crimson cords tied around their left wrists.'

'You're talking about the cure for lunacy, the sickness of the moon. A very clerical concept, the evil of the mind, just as illness was to the body. Was there clovewort tied on to the red string?'

'No. The cord wasn't there as a remedy. It was a warning to others.'

'Or a remembrance, perhaps. You know, madness has inspired some pretty irrational cures. Doctors tried to teach patients "therapeutic optimism" while attaching leeches to them, and when that failed they gave them blood transfusions from animals. The bloodline carried insanity, so I guess it made a warped kind of sense to try and bleed it out.'

'I thought this case must be about madness at first, particularly as the victim was found underneath Hogarth's painting of Bedlam from *The Rake's Progress*.'

'Was she wearing anything blue?'

'You mean the colour of Bedlam? No, she offered no other clues.'

'We were once the nation of the Mad Monarch, poor old King George. After that, Bedlam became a dumping ground for political prisoners.'

'Well, it appears to have become so once again,' Bryant explained. 'Which is why I'm rather more interested in the other meaning of the Scarlet Thread.'

'Oh no, you don't believe all that old claptrap, do you?' Standing led the way up the last flight of museum steps. 'My co-workers keep telling me Harold Masters believed it too. Wouldn't shut up about it, by all accounts.'

'He was interested in its mythology, just as am I. After all, the Scarlet Thread runs through the Bible as the blood of Jesus Christ, shed on the cross to wash away sin. But it also seems to run between a number of murder victims and the government.'

'I think you'd better tell me what you know.'

'To do that I have to take you to a part of the museum with which even you may not be familiar.' Bryant pointed across the Great Courtyard with his walking stick. The vast arc of the glass roof glowed even on the dullest days. 'Far end, down the stairs at the rear, then turn left, right and left again. According to your predecessor, at the heart of the myth surrounding the Scarlet

Thread is the idea that man can only be brought into a covenant with God through the spilling of blood.'

'Ah, the warrior Christians. Christ's own blood had magical properties. Stands to reason, if he could walk on water.'

'There's your first connection between madness and the blood of Christ, right there,' said Bryant as Standing clomped down the steps beside him. 'Goffredo de Prefetti was the Bishop of Bethlehem, and he supposedly brought Christ's blood to London. He put it on display at the opening of his asylum, and then placed it in the foundation stones of Bedlam at Bishopsgate. And somehow it ended up here in the British Museum.'

Standing gave a disbelieving laugh. 'No, that's not possible.'

'Oh, but it is. I'm about to show it to you now.'

As they headed back into the gloom between the interconnected rooms, they passed fewer and fewer visitors. 'I think people start getting Stendhal syndrome by the time they get down here,' she said. 'Too much choice; too much to try and understand. The permanent exhibitions in this section only appeal to academics.'

'It's probably what has kept this artefact safe for so long.' Bryant stopped before an illuminated glass case containing the six-inch-long reliquary. It was bottle-shaped, gilded and inset with precious stones, surrounded by a complex arrangement of enamelled angels, arches and sunbursts. There was a tiny inscription on the side reading *'Ista est una spinea corone Domini*

298

nostri ihesu xpisti.' At the base of the case was a small plaque:

Holy Thorn reliquary belonging to Jean, duc de Berry, created between 1400 and 1410 to house Christ's crown of thorns from the Crucifixion. In the possession of the British Museum since 1898.

'There's a lot of theorizing that the Romans invented Christ by writing the New Testament,' said Standing, 'but if you dip into some of the online discussions you'll find yourself in a world of serious lunacy.' She walked around the crystal vial, studying it. 'I guess it's interesting from a mythological point of view. I can see a thorn of some sort, certainly. But the "crown of thorns" was never meant to be taken literally. It's a traditional metaphor indicating immortality. Which makes this bauble a nonsense. But it's a very attractive nonsense, a wonderful example of *émail en ronde bosse*. Pearls and rubies alternately arranged around the compartment that holds the relic.'

Surrounding the relic were trumpeting angels, a scene of the Last Judgement and cherubs raising the dead. At its centre, crimson and indigo jewels flanked a tiny dark brown sliver. 'Take a look at the edge of the so-called thorn,' said Bryant.

A faint line no thicker than spider silk ran through the crystal like a fine molten seam. 'It's oxidization. The air got in through a flaw in the crystal. Oxidized blood goes the colour of wood. What if the contents of the vial only oxidized on the outside?'

'Mr Bryant, I don't really see what you're getting at.'

'That's all right, nobody ever does.' He looked around for a bench and sat down with a sigh. 'My knowledge of the subject is only what Harold Masters told me. Hang on.' He dug out a crumpled sweet bag and his spectacles. 'I made a note. On October the third 1247, the Knights Templar presented Henry III with a lead-crystal pot that they marked with the symbols of the knights. They told him it contained the ultimate relic of the crucifixion: the blood of Christ. The gift came with provenance, confirmed by a scroll holding the seals of the Patriarch of Jerusalem, signed by the prelates of the Holy Land. They considered it the holiest and most important of all gifts.'

'That's understandable,' said Standing. 'Christ's blood consecrates and bestows eternal life. It's an elixir that leads to the gates of heaven.'

'There's a rather different story about the creation of the reliquary. Apparently there was once an imperial crown decorated with four of the supposed thorns from Christ's head, but when times grew harsh the crown was broken up and its parts were reused to make more treasures. The possession of such items wielded huge political influence, so four new reliquaries were constructed. But it turned out that three of them were created by forgers. You can tell them apart by looking for enamelling on the backs of their doors. The fake versions don't have that. This one does. So it turns out there's only one known thorn, and that isn't a thorn at all. Given that the crystal vial exactly matches the descriptions of the gift to Henry III, it would appear to contain Christ's blood.'

'R-ight,' said Standing slowly, clearly deciding that she was trapped in the museum's basement with a mad pensioner.

'So now I have a problem,' Bryant explained. 'What possible connection could a female bar manager, a photographer and the wife of a Home Office official have with the blood of Christ? Is there anything else that the red cord might signify?'

'If the blood was at the birthplace of Bedlam, I think the fact that your victim was found under such a painting confirms the connection,' said Standing.

'But what does it *mean?* You see my problem?'

'Maybe it stands for something else. You know, in the same way that the "thorn" does. To be honest, this is out of my league.'

'Did Masters ever talk to anyone else about his theories?'

'I have no idea.'

'So none of the other archivists have ever mentioned the contents of that case to you?'

'I'd never even noticed it before.'

'Then I'm sorry to have taken up so much of your time.' Bryant rose to leave. 'I should be off. I need to find a toilet, anyway. At my age, you always need to know how far you are from one, like petrol stations.'

'That's all right,' said Standing. 'If I think of anything, how can I contact you?'

Bryant gave her his card. 'If you have any ideas

at all, no matter how strange, I'll listen to them.'

She watched as he jammed his trilby on to his head and set off by himself, as strange an exhibit as had ever graced the museum.

38

ROUGH MUSIC

The Rakes' Club existed behind a discreet ebony door with brass fittings at number 42, Dover Street, Mayfair. As Bryant had predicted, Stuart Almon had readily agreed to meet Bryant and May outside and show them around.

When the detectives arrived, they didn't spot the accountant at first. As thin as a chopstick, dressed in a loose grey Jermyn Street suit that matched the brickwork, he blended perfectly into the surrounding terrace.

Almon stepped forward and placed a cold, bloodless hand in each of theirs.

'I'll introduce you as prospective members,' he said. 'That way I'll be able to give you the tour. They can be spiky about who gets to see inside. We're a most venerable institution. It's said that to be accepted here you have to be a peer, a parliamentarian or a prick. Sadly we no longer have the ear of the government. It's an old-boys' network, and the boys are getting very old indeed. Many of London's landowners were members but they're dying off and being replaced by property developers.'

Almon led the way through a dun-coloured passageway lined with sepia portraits of austere-looking lords and dusty busts of sour-faced duchesses.

'What else can I tell you? Still no women allowed, of course. The house drink is still saltheen – that's hot whisky and melted butter with spices, guaranteed to thicken the arteries. And of course we still have a resident black cat that gets served lunch before any of the members. That goes back to the days when the Devil was believed to adopt the form of a cat, making him the club's oldest member and therefore the first to be served.'

He signed the detectives into the visitors' book and led them to the library, a tall oval room buttressed with leather-bound volumes that appeared not to have been opened in two hundred years.

'It's said to be modelled on the library in the abbey at Melk,' Almon explained. 'Can't see it myself. Upstairs are the meeting rooms, snoozers and bar: everything you fear about such a place – boarding-school food, brandy snifters and smelly old geezers bottom-trumpeting in wing-backed armchairs. It's the sort of place where you'll still hear a coloured chap referred to as a golliwog, although at least these days all racist claptrap is reprimanded by the management.'

'Why does the Home Office still use the place, then?' asked Bryant.

'Habit, I suppose, and the fact that it's a network, as rickety as it is. Oskar seems to like it.' He led the way to the brass-fitted bar and called the barman over to plot drinks. Bryant looked around, wrinkling in complete disapproval. It seemed unlikely that anything nefarious had ever been planned by a handful of bibulous, bulbous-nosed aristos frittering away the last rents from their estates. 'Anything at all unusual about the place?' he asked.

'Well, there are a few arcane rules. One states that no club member may ever resign, living or dead. Some rot about the place collapsing if a woman ever sets foot inside the building, that sort of thing. But there was once a Hellfire club based here. The Duke of Wharton met here with his cronies. Young men gathered to discuss the existence of the Trinity. Questioning these things goes against the teachings of the Church, so it was said that the blasphemers were "raking the fires of hell", hence the Rakes' Club. In those days you could lead the most extraordinarily debauched private life and still command respect from your peers, who were, after all, peers of the realm. They weren't subjected to rough music.'

'What does that mean?' asked May.

'They exercised parliamentary privilege,' said Almon. 'Had they been commoners, acting as they did, they would have been tied to donkeys and driven through the streets to the noise of the public banging on saucepans.'

'So there was no rough music here for miscreants.'

'Not as such, but there *is* another meeting room.' Almon tapped the side of his nose conspiratorially. 'Sort of a club-within-a-club.'

'Does Mr Kasavian use it?' asked Bryant.

'Yes, from time to time. It has a name: the Damned Crew, a traditional title going back to 1602, all loosely connected to the Gunpowder Plot. It's actually a sub-club, with its own membership, initiation ceremonies and an annual subscription, operating separately inside the Rakes'.'

'How do you qualify to become a member?'

'Now that *is* a political network. You need to have worked for the government. It helps if you've displayed leadership qualities in the past and are committed to certain – ideologies. By that I mean it's full of barking fascists.'

'Is there any record kept of what goes on here? Meeting minutes, anything like that?'

'Absolutely not. There wouldn't be much point in paying for an inner sanctum if it could be breached. You're looking to take Oskar down, aren't you?' A dark and eager light appeared in Almon's eyes.

'We're not at liberty to discuss–' May began.

'Yes,' said Bryant. 'Do you want to help?'

'I might be able to,' Almon replied. 'When men become arrogant they start to make poor choices.'

'Why would you help? Why now?'

'We always have to watch our backs, Mr May. My wife informs me of rumours when they become too loud to ignore. One currently circulating is that I will be scapegoated for certain failures of nerve within the department.'

'You mean there were things you didn't want to go along with?'

'The original members of the Damned Crew

used their positions to get away with murder. I'm not saying we did anything quite that dramatic. I have no personal enmity towards Mr Kasavian. It would be a purely business arrangement between you and I.'

'We're not here to give your career a leg-up,' May replied. 'If you have something on your boss, it's your duty to inform us.'

Almon knocked back his whisky and clearly thought devious thoughts. Bryant instinctively disliked him; the civil servant was weighing up his options in order to maximize their advantages, but was nervous about crossing into territory from which he could not return. 'There is – a certain matter,' he said finally. 'It's something he wouldn't want uncovered. Something rather nasty. Let's not talk in here. I can show you the clubroom used by the Damned Crew.'

Almon led the way back to the stairs, turned on the darkened landing beneath a bust of Landseer and withdrew a key from his pocket. Bryant looked for a door, but saw none.

Almon stepped close to the wall and slid the brass key into what had appeared to be nothing more than a small stain on the wainscoting. The door had been painted to perfectly match the tobacco-coloured wall, and tipped inward to a narrow brick passage. 'This runs behind the walls of the bar,' said Almon softly. 'It was used by the servants to deliver the meals, so that no one would have to run into them on the main stair-case.'

The passage smelled sharply of rising damp. Bryant and May followed the civil servant to its end, where a second door was unlocked to reveal an elegant smoking room lined with books. Six maroon leather armchairs stood on a sea-green carpet. There was a large globe, which Bryant suspected of being a bar, and a small walnut dining table. In one corner the conversation from the drinkers on the other side of the wall could be clearly overheard.

'I always assumed there were rooms like this in London, but I've hardly ever seen one,' whispered Bryant, barely able to contain his enthusiasm as he headed for the bookshelves.

'It's not as cloak and dagger as it appears,' said Almon. 'Enter any large building that once had plenty of servants and you'll always find rooms and passageways like these. The running of such houses depended on the efficiency and invisibility of the staff. We'd better be quick, Mr Bryant.'

Bryant forced himself to step away from the books. 'What do you have on Kasavian that's of practical use to us?'

'Before he came to head up our department, Oskar was employed as head of security for a biochemical company outsourced by the DSTL at Porton Down.'

'We know about that,' said May. 'It's old news.'

'How do you think he was able to step straight into a top position at the Home Office?'

'You tell us.'

'He knew how to keep a lid on things. He proved himself amply capable in his final months at Porton Down. There was a murder committed–'

'It was Kasavian?'

Behind them, the passage door opened. Oskar Kasavian stepped into the room. If he was surprised to find the detectives in his private sanctuary, he managed not to show it. Bryant, on the other hand, reacted as if Dracula had just appeared at a crypt entrance. He instinctively wanted to look around for a crucifix.

'Almon.' Kasavian smiled. 'I thought I might find you here. I do hope you're not planning to breach club rules. Gentlemen, if you would excuse us for a few minutes, my colleague and I need to have a private conversation.'

Unable to argue for a reason to stay, Bryant allowed his partner to steer him from the room.

39

BLOODLINE

The nondescript June weather had fractured into chill drizzle and darkness. Pustular clouds reached down to infect the top floors of buildings, sheening slates and blackening brickwork. Even the glass towers of the Square Mile were dimmed and streaked with condensation, as if they no longer wished to expose their interiors to the sinister streets.

Maggie Armitage furled her umbrella and huddled in the doorway of the Peculiar Crimes Unit, waiting to be admitted. Something had been bothering her ever since her meeting with Bryant at Liverpool Street Station. The sensation had grown with the passing hours, until she could bear it no longer.

Last night she had used her Ouija board to contact Starbuck, an unruly Edwardian child she occasionally used as her contact to the spirit world. He had proven impossible, throwing tantrums, tossing cups and vases, yanking at the tablecloth and tearing open the curtains, alternately angered and hurt by her questions. When she came to, she found herself shaking with cold.

The spirits were disturbed. *She* was disturbed. Death held no terrors for her; she had brushed against it too many times, but evil ... now that was a different matter altogether. Just as she believed there were forces for good in the world, it had to follow that there were forces for harm.

Janice Longbright opened the door with a look of surprise. 'We've never had you visit us before,' she said. 'Come on in before you get soaked through.'

'I had to come,' Maggie explained, bashing out the rain from her rainbow-wool hat. 'They're in danger, aren't they?'

'Someone sabotaged John's car last night,' said Longbright. 'We think it was intended as a warning.'

'I knew it. Are you brewing up? I'll think more clearly with a cup of tea inside me. Bags will be fine. Arthur will be on the first floor, to the right.'

'How did you know that?'

'He has to be able to look down into the street. Can you show me?'

'Of course.' Longbright led the way to the detectives' room. On the stairs they passed Jack Renfield. Maggie reeled, her spiritual sensitivity battered by unseen forces.

'Wow,' she said, staring after the broad-shouldered sergeant. 'So you're finally seeing somebody again.'

'Jack?' Beneath their Elizabeth Arden foundation, Longbright's cheeks coloured. 'We're colleagues. Well, friends. Well – I don't know, really.'

'There's a golden cord running between the two of you. I think he'll be good for you, although...'

'Although what?'

'There's something you have to discover about him first, a problem to solve. If you can surmount that, he'll be the one to save you.'

Longbright was becoming annoyed by the white witch's cryptic prognostications. Maggie reached Bryant's doorway and peered in, breathing deeply. 'Of course,' she said quietly. 'I knew it would be like this.'

Making herself comfortable in the green leather armchair while Longbright made tea, she took in her surroundings, studying the bindings of the books and folders, the chaotic spread of Eastern artefacts and Victorian bric-a-brac. She paid particular attention to a volume of Greek myths that lay on Bryant's desk.

'He knows more than he's telling you,' she told Longbright when the DS had returned with a tray. 'He doesn't want you to come to harm.'

'I'm sorry, I'm not with you,' Longbright admitted.

'The Greeks. Pegasus was the offspring of

310

Medusa. The horse sprouted from her severed head. It was a half-brother to Theseus.'

'Nope, still nothing, I'm afraid.' Talking with Maggie was confusing at the best of times, but Longbright feared the white witch was finally dropping off the conversational bandwidth.

'I knew there was a connection, but couldn't quite recall having the conversation with Arthur about it. He already has everything he needs to solve the case.'

'I don't see how you could possibly know that, Maggie.'

'Because we talked about it long before any of this happened.' She accepted the hot tea and drank, but had to steady the cup with both hands. 'It's the Scarlet Thread, the line of Christ's blood. He's been misled. There's no such thing. It's just another myth. But the danger is very real, and he will die if he fails to remember the past. Your cat's about to have nine kittens, by the way.'

'Maggie, you know I love you dearly but I'm very busy and to be quite frank you're making as much sense as a box of rubber kippers, so if you don't mind, I think I'll just—'

'Did he go to the British Museum?' Maggie asked suddenly.

'Yes, I think he did. Why?'

'He went to look at the blood. But you see, it's not Christ's blood at all. It's just a stupid old artefact manufactured by the Church to encourage their devotees. And yet when you think of all the trouble it's caused...'

Longbright pointed along the corridor. 'Look,

311

I'll just be in the next room, OK?'

'Your mother's with you, you know.'

Longbright froze. 'What do you mean?'

'I see Gladys standing behind you, almost as clearly as I see you. She never had the gift. It skips a generation, you see. She went to her death without knowing. But you have it, the power of second sight. You don't see it now but one day it will return to you.'

'Maggie, I'm a rationalist. I know you believe in … certain things, but I can't afford to accept that they're possible. My mother died in the course of her duty.'

'I know, dear. When I say I see her I'm speaking figuratively. I'll let you in on a little secret.' She leaned forward to impart the confidence. 'I don't believe in the supernatural either, not in its traditional form. I believe there are degrees of sensitivity that allow some of us to connect. I'm a connector. Think of me as a spiritual three-pin plug. And I've finally made the connection. Oskar Kasavian worked in Porton Down, didn't he?'

Longbright was taken aback. 'How did you know that?'

'Arthur once told me. You do know what they do there.'

'It's classified defence-of-the-realm stuff – biochemicals mainly, I think. They work quite closely with American military scientific units.'

'There's a reason why the Scarlet Thread keeps coming up.' Maggie searched the air, as if trying to catch the wavelength of a distant music. 'Madness. Loss. And blood, of course, always blood. A

312

bright red through-line, if you will. I see it shimmering.' She raised a ringed hand before her eyes. 'Just there in front of me. Oh, how it shimmers! I must stay until Arthur returns. He needs to understand.'

Longbright could take no more. She left Maggie to her whispering spirits, returning to her office, but a feeling of dread had settled deep in her bones and would not be easily shaken off.

40

THE THREAD

Stuart Almon was a frightened man.

Kasavian paced slowly before him, seemingly studying the shine on his shoes. The packed bookcases and heavy tasselled curtains turned the room into something decadent and claustrophobic. They might have been in some overwrought Victorian bathysphere, miles below the surface of the Thames.

'What I fail to understand', Kasavian said carefully, 'is why you would bring the police here. Those poor senile flatfoots are merely marking time until their enforced retirement. Why do you think I appointed them to investigate my wife?'

'You wanted to be seen to be doing something,' said Almon sullenly.

'I didn't want the Met involved because they would have started throwing their weight around

313

as they always do, ploughing through our company files out of sheer bloody-mindedness. There was never any likelihood of the Peculiar Crimes Unit doing the same, not with Bryant wandering off into old museums all the time. But you should know better. Or perhaps you thought you did.' He turned his hands, admiring their marmoreal sheen, and then wagged a finger at Almon. *Naughty boy.* 'You were pointing them towards something else, weren't you? Now, what could that be?'

'They knew about the club,' said Almon a trifle too hastily. Kasavian's sudden honesty made him nervous. 'I thought it would be better to bring them here, rather than just have them turn up. I only took them as far as this room. I wouldn't have taken them any further.'

'You know, Stuart, I've spent years listening to explanations about security breaches and I always start from the same position. I know people lie to themselves. They're hardwired to try and cover their mistakes.'

'This wasn't a mistake. It was damage limitation. I told you, they knew about the club. Your wife – she died beneath a painting of the bloody *Rake's Progress*, for Christ's sake. If that wasn't a clear enough pointer, I don't know what was. I don't know how or why it happened, but it did.'

Kasavian realized just how badly he had underestimated his accountant. Concern momentarily flickered across his features. Then the mask came back into place. 'They'll get no further. You can undo the damage you've caused to the company.'

'How?'

'You're going to destroy the only remaining file for me.'

'You know I have no idea what's in it, Oskar, and I don't want to know.'

'I appreciate that. It's better for everyone that the contents remain a secret. What you don't know can't hurt you. If you want to open a Pandora's box, I won't be able to keep you alive.' Almon blanched. 'I mean, in terms of your career,' said Kasavian.

'I don't understand. Why don't you do it?'

'Good God, man, you led them here.' Kasavian's raised voice came as a shock in the deadened room. 'I can't be connected to it in any way. I'm about to present the government's case in Paris. The file is the reason why we were forced to tackle the border initiative in the first place. You talk about damage limitation – you have no idea of the damage that could be wrought.'

'Where is the file? Is it in here?'

'No, it's in a secure location. You need to go there tonight, remove the contents and burn them. Don't look at them, just burn them.' He took out a pen and scribbled down an address and some numerals, handing the paper over. 'Obviously it's imperative that nobody sees you. For your sake. You'll need this.' He removed a small brass key from his pocket.

The parting was awkward. As Almon moved back to the door, Kasavian's eyes never left him.

'Goodbye, Stuart.' Kasavian remained motionless, watching him leave. As Almon fled the building, he found it hard to shake the feeling that his fate was being sealed.

'We can't leave Almon in Kasavian's hands,' warned May as they reached the PCU. 'There's no telling what might happen to him.'

'Kasavian wouldn't be that stupid,' said Bryant. 'Besides, we can't stop him. All we have is a note from a dead woman who was undergoing psychiatric evaluation.'

'But if Giles gets his evidence of systematic poisoning–'

'It could take days to get that information from the labs without Kasavian himself signing off the budget. Jack just texted me; Kasavian's on the six p.m. Eurostar to Paris tomorrow evening. We have to arrest him before then.'

'Couldn't we trump up something? They arrested Al Capone for tax evasion. Hold him on some minor infraction until the lab report comes back?'

'And what if it's inconclusive? He has the backing of the Deputy Prime Minister. It'll take a lot more than that to stop him catching that train.'

As the detectives were shaking the sooty rain of King's Cross from their jackets in the hallway of the PCU, Maggie found them and launched into a fragmented, frantic plea neither of them could understand.

'I'm sorry,' said Longbright, trying to stop her, 'she just turned up here. I have no idea what she's on about.'

'It's OK, Janice,' said Bryant, 'I'll handle this. Slow down, you silly woman, I can't understand what you're saying.'

'Come with me, I'll show you.' The white witch

seized Bryant's soggy arm and pulled him upstairs towards his office. Bryant shrugged back at
his partner and allowed himself to be led.

Throwing open his volume of Greek mythology,
she turned to the index and traced a finger down
the list. 'You told me Mr Kasavian and his team
own a company called Pegasus providing security
intelligence to the scientific community. Pegasus
and Theseus were half-brothers. You do remember
Theseus, I take it?'

'Of course. Peter Jukes, the whistle-blower who
died. That was where he worked.'

'Do you still have the file on him?'

'It's in the attic. Pass me my stick, the top stairs
are a bugger.'

'Would somebody please tell me what's going
on?' asked Raymond Land, hearing the commo-
tion. 'What is that woman doing here? She's a
bloody menace.'

'Yes, we know,' said Bryant. 'She's helping us
on the case. We'll be in the attic.'

The PCU's top floor ran the full length of the
building and was still partly filled with dust-
sheeted crates left by previous tenants. 'Walk on
the joists,' warned Bryant, 'or you'll fall through
the ceiling. Dan rigged up a couple of lights for
me. The switch should be somewhere on your
right.'

'Madame Blavatsky,' Maggie whispered, pressing her palm against the glass case housing a
yellowed fortune-telling wax effigy of the Victorian medium. 'So she *is* here.'

Behind the dummy were stored the memories
neither Bryant nor May had room for in their

apartments, items they had salvaged from previous notable investigations: a giant prop lightning bolt from the Palace Theatre; a lamp that had hung in an underground canal tunnel; one of the seventy-seven brass clocks; a highwayman's hat; a snow globe from Devon; a pub sign; a pair of antlers; a Tube-station worker's yellow pith helmet; and the latest addition – a Mr Punch doll.

Bryant burrowed into the boxes and attempted to drag a box of files out. 'John, give me a hand with this,' he instructed. 'I kept hard copies of our reports because you were always tinkering with the unit's technology.'

It took the best part of an hour to find what they were looking for among the mildewed blue cardboard folders, tied off in bundles with bits of twine. 'Here we are,' said Bryant. 'We need more light.'

May pulled down one of the cabled bulbs and held it over the file. "Dr Peter Jukes, Salisbury, Wiltshire",' he read, then précised: 'Body found by fishermen floating off Black Head on the Lizard Peninsula, Cornwall. He'd been missing for a week, but had only been in the water for a few hours. The local coroner gave a verdict of accidental death, although he acknowledged that there were unexplained injuries. Jukes's boat was found miles away, washed into a local harbour. There was a fair amount of dissent about the death. The coastguard concluded that he was unlikely to have been thrown from his boat, because local tides and currents would have taken them to shore together. I don't see what relevance–'

'Keep going,' said Bryant.

May held the light closer. 'Jukes told friends he was going fishing with a colleague named...' He stopped and looked up. 'Oskar Kasavian.'

'Read on further.'

Jukes had once belonged to some kind of Druid sect, and the press picked up on it. They tried to imply that he had fallen victim to Satanists. There was talk of a witch-hunt.'

'Now, there's an awful lot of misinformation about Satanists–' Maggie began.

'Don't start,' warned May, continuing hastily. 'Jukes's family admitted he had arcane hobbies, but were forced into denials to protect his reputation after it was suggested that there was some kind of connection between his injuries and his supposed interest in black magic. The press were curious because Jukes was a scientist involved with biological-defence experiments at the MOD's Porton Down laboratory. There had been a public scandal over part of the lab being outsourced to private companies. The police vindicated the coroner and agreed with the verdict of accidental death, promoting the idea that Jukes had become mentally unstable. He'd been suffering from clinical depression for a number of years, and had been recognized as a security risk.'

'The company he and Kasavian were outsourced to was called Theseus,' Bryant interpolated. 'It employed a number of epidemiologists studying the pathogenic spread of mutating viruses. The US National Science Advisory Board for Biosecurity wanted to shut the place down. They were worried that terrorists might be able to translate the scientific data into a weapon if it was published.'

'I remember that part – it was tangential to a case we were handling. But there's no real link between the drowning and Kasavian. He managed to prove that he was nowhere near Jukes's boat on the day.'

'Kasavian and his pals now run the sister company to Theseus,' said Bryant. 'One of the things they've been looking into is the protection of scientists developing genetic mutations of avian flu.'

'Arthur, there is still no direct connection. And you' – May pointed at Maggie – 'should not get involved in this kind of conspiracy theorizing. It only makes matters worse.'

'What if I told you that I'm holding the thread between the past and the present?' said Maggie.

'I don't care if you're holding the fireman's ball, if you're hiding any kind of information that could help us, then you're required by law–'

'I know where it can be found,' Maggie stated very loudly.

'I don't see how that's possible. There's nothing you could know about this case.'

'The girl who died in St Bride's' Church. Her name was Amy O'Connor, I believe.'

'That's right.'

'She was Peter Jukes's girlfriend,' said Maggie. 'She always believed he had been murdered. And she went to her death in London still looking for proof.'

41

THE BLOOD LINK

'How could you possibly have got hold of this information?' May demanded to know. 'We've been over everything time and time again and there was nothing...'

'You interviewed the churchwardens, then?' asked Maggie.

'Of course we did, all three of them.'

'But there are four. Jake Wallace was working in the basement that day. He and I have been friends for years. He used to attend my Mind and Spirit evenings when he was a penniless student, although to be honest I think he only came for the vol-au-vents. I mentioned I'd seen you, and he told me he'd seen Miss O'Connor on a number of occasions. She confided in him. People often do in churches, as you'd know if you weren't both such heathens.'

May looked flummoxed. 'I don't understand how we could have missed him.'

'I imagine nobody thought to tell you he'd switched to a different shift. Sometimes he took over the shop between one and two p.m., while the others were at lunch. Miss O'Connor said her boyfriend had told her to come to St Bride's if anything happened to him. Soon after he died, she visited the church, but couldn't find out why he had sent her there. A couple of months ago she returned and started visiting more regularly. I imagine by then she assumed his request was more of a spiritual nature. Jake said it seemed as if Miss O'Connor found peace there, just knowing her partner had been in the same place. He got the feeling she wanted to talk to somebody but didn't know whom to trust. And she was running out of money. I think she was working in a bar and had had her hours reduced.'

'She told the warden all this?'

'There's something open and friendly about Jake that people in distress respond to. That's why he's a churchwarden.'

'Why would Peter Jukes have sent her to St Bride's?' May asked.

'It's the journalists' church,' said Bryant. 'Perhaps he wanted her to discover something and spread the word. Had Jukes ever met your friend Wallace?'

'I don't know,' Maggie admitted.

'Dan checked every square inch of that place,' said May.

'What about the basement? St Bride's was badly damaged in the Blitz, but the bombs uncovered a sealed vault.'

'Nobody mentioned a vault.'

'No, it was closed up by the authorities in 1854, after a cholera outbreak. Dan only covered the ground floor. He was looking at a possible murder site, not studying archaeology. Is the basement open to the public?'

'I don't think so, no,' said Maggie.

'Then why is a warden posted down there?'

'Jake's helping an American radiography unit. There's a visiting professor analysing the bones and coffin plates.'

'An American scientist,' said May. 'Theseus had US connections. Perhaps Pegasus does, too. As much as I'm loath to allow you to go wandering off into church crypts, Arthur, I think you'd better get down there, if you're up to it.'

'Of course I'm up to it,' said Bryant, affronted. 'What are you going to do?'

'Someone has to keep an eye on Stuart Almon. I wasn't comfortable about leaving him with the Prince of Darkness.'

Samuel Simmons was a director of the Cincinnati Bioanthropology Research Unit, currently in charge of the Diagnostic Imaging Program being undertaken at St Bride's. Right now he was keen to analyse an abscessed jawbone belonging to a young girl who probably died of the pain alone. Instead, a rumpled old man in a sagging tweed hat was peering at him intently from behind a stack of coffin lids.

'Can I help you?' asked the bearlike Simmons, extending a paw.

'Arthur Bryant. Yes, you can.' He handed the professor his PCU card. 'I need that back, it's my only one.'

Simmons examined it and was clearly none the wiser. He returned it. 'You're a policeman?'

'As amazing as it may seem, yes. I understand you've been working down here for over two years?'

'On and off. It's a slow process.'

'Why, what exactly are you doing?'

'We're comparing the grave-marker plates found here with official death records to see if they accord. Then we X-ray the remains to see if the causes of death were accurate.'

'And are they?'

'Not very often. Between this and the charnel house crypt next door there must be the remains of around seven thousand bodies.'

Bryant leaned into one of the lead coffins as if choosing something from the freezer. 'Come up with any surprises? Found anything you shouldn't have?'

'Like what?'

'I mean before you started excavating. We're looking for – well, I don't exactly know what we're looking for. Something a visitor could have left in the basement.'

'No members of the general public are allowed down here,' said Simmons. 'Many of these coffins once housed cholera victims. There's no risk of infection, but the bylaws require us to keep potential contaminants away from the public.'

'How about visitors from within the scientific community?'

'Yeah, we get a few of those. None lately.'

'Have you found anything at all that shouldn't be here? I'm thinking someone came by, used their company pass to gain entrance and left something to be collected.'

'You have no idea what this item might have been?'

'I'm afraid not.'

Simmons pulled off his gloves. 'Come with me. There's a box of stuff in the back. Everything on the site has to be annotated, and the items that remain unidentifiable get put in a junk box.' He pulled at a mud-stained cardboard carton and opened its flaps. 'It's mostly just debris, plus sweaters and books left behind by employees. But please, knock yourself out. There's a table lamp over there.'

Bryant picked his way through lost Tube passes, gloves, a pair of football boots, unallocated chunks of coping stone, loose change, paperbacks and folders of unfinished notes.

He was about to give up when he saw it, a small steel memory stick sealed in a clear plastic bag. There was no label. There didn't need to be. The bag had been tied with a strand of red wool.

He held it beneath the lamplight. 'Do you know where this came from?' he asked Simmons.

'No idea,' Simmons replied. 'People sometimes dropped in to see their partners. We had quite a number of interns helping us at the start.'

'Do you have a record of their names?'

'No need,' said Simmons. 'I remember them all. Try me.'

'Amy O'Connor.'

'The woman who died last week? Nope.'

Bryant passed over the dossier on Peter Jukes and showed him a photograph. 'Does this chap look familiar?'

Simmons shook his head. 'I'm just one of the guys here. I guess he could have visited while I was back in the States. The company name rings a vague bell.'

'His name was Peter Jukes.'

'The guy who drowned? I wasn't here at the time, but I heard he came up from the MOD in Wiltshire to see what we were doing. Must have been soon after we started. Somebody read about his death and remembered the name.'

'Do you have any idea what he wanted?'

'Apparently we had a team project in common.'

'What was that?'

'Blood. Yeah, I know, weird, huh? In the early days of our research we thought we might find a blood link through the bodies interred here. It seemed we might locate a hereditary disease passed through bloodlines because there were so many fathers and sons, mothers and daughters buried together. It didn't take long for the Ministry of Defence to start sniffing around. A whole bunch of guys turned up and started asking questions. Some time later, Jukes followed them.'

'What do you think they were all looking for?'

'C'mon, Mr Bryant, you're the detective, I think you know the answer to that one.'

'They were interested in any biochemical discoveries you might make, particularly with regard to military applications.'

'Can't think of any other reason why they would be interested, can you?' Simmons gave a lopsided grin.

Bryant was amazed. O'Connor had come back, knowing that her lover had directed her to the church, but had not thought to check in the basement.

326

'This was intended for the woman who died,' said Bryant, indicating the wool-tied bag. 'Why didn't she come downstairs to collect it?'

'That's easy,' said Simmons. 'If you didn't know about the crypt you sure wouldn't come looking for it. You enter the church and look around, and the ground floor is all you can see. The vault door's kept shut.'

Given his fractious relationship with technology, Bryant didn't trust himself to run the contents of the flash drive on Simmons's computer equipment. Pocketing the bag, he thanked the professor and took his leave, heading back out into the rain.

42

THE ROOFTOP

'She's not going anywhere tonight,' said Colin, looking up at the windows.

'How do you work that out?' Meera asked.

'Stands to reason, doesn't it? There was a Lovefilm DVD in her mailbox and she's just gone in with a bottle of plonk. Bet you there's a pizza delivery within the next half-hour.'

The pair were still camped outside Edona Lescowitz's apartment. 'How do you know it'll be a pizza?'

'She's a skinny European bird. They can really pack away the nosh without ever putting on

327

weight. They eat green salads in restaurants and shovel down pasta at home, usually followed by a tub of ice-cream.'

'I've always been amazed by your sensitive understanding of women, Colin.'

'Thank you.'

'I mean you don't have any. We're an alien race to you, aren't we? A complete and total mystery. You're probably aware that we share the same number of limbs, if not appendages, and that's about it. So you and your mates down the pub can make up whatever you like about us and congratulate each other on being able to understand us. Incredible.'

'You'd be surprised, Meera. I understand more than you think. Especially about you.'

Meera folded her arms and leaned back against the dustbins. She waited while a drum-and-bass-deafened teen in a pimped-up van thudded past. 'Go on, then,' she challenged. 'Give me the benefit of your amazing male insight.'

'No, 'cause you'll get angry with me.'

'No, I won't.'

'Promise?'

'Yeah, just this once.'

'Say it. Full sentence.'

Meera hissed angrily through her teeth. 'I promise not to get annoyed with Colin Marlin Bimsley when he tells me what he thinks of me, all right? Is Marlin really your middle name?'

'It was my grandad's. All right. I'll tell you where your anger comes from. Your mum and dad favoured your sister. In their eyes she could never do anything wrong. Even though she always screwed up and let them down, especially when it came to fellas, they've always pretended not to notice or have quickly forgiven her, which winds you up, so they see you as the angry one. They were against you joining the force because they wanted you to get married to a nice Indian boy and give them grandchildren. When your sister said she wanted to open a restaurant they paid for it, even though they couldn't afford to, and you didn't speak to them for the best part of a year. Every time you try to put things right, they take it the wrong way. You try to control your anger, but you know it won't go away until your sister gets married and takes the pressure off you, and there's not much chance of that happening because she always picks the wrong blokes.'

'That is a complete load of the most – total...' Meera grasped for the words, fighting to control her temper.

'It's accurate, Meera. You know it and I know it.' He pointed at her accusingly. 'Every time you go home, you come back in a foul mood. Last time you even kicked Crippen, and it turns out she's a lady cat so that's not nice. And there's only one thing that ever calms you down.'

Meera's eyes narrowed. 'And what is that?'

'Being with me. I can lower your blood pressure in a matter of minutes. You know the first thing you always do when you come back from seeing your folks? You come into the common room to find me. You hang around scowling for a while, shooting the breeze, then you go to your room. And you don't even realize you do it. It's me,

Meera.' He slapped his chest. 'Ever since you joined the PCU, I've been the one constant loyalty in your life.'

'Colin, that is so—'

'Sssh.' He held a forefinger gently to her lips. 'Don't say anything that will make you break your word.' He looked up. 'There you go, pizza-delivery man, ten minutes ahead of schedule.'

A black Triumph had pulled up at the kerb. Its rider dismounted and opened his red pillion panier. He removed a pizza box and went to the front door.

'At least she's getting something to eat,' said Colin. 'I'm bloody starving.'

Meera looked across the road in puzzlement. 'Why hasn't he turned his engine off?'

'I guess he's only going to be a minute.'

'No, nobody does that. I should know. And it's not the kind of bike pizza places use, it's way too high-powered.'

Colin threw down his coffee and ran across the road. The rider had already been admitted, but the door buzzer was still keeping the main entrance open. The empty pizza box had been dropped just inside the doorway. Colin took the stairs three at a time.

She had already opened the door to him. Edona was in her dressing gown, money in one hand, but he had his arm across her throat. Colin's rugby tackle was spectacularly foolhardy even by his standards. He brought them both down, which couldn't be helped, but the rider was up and swinging something sharp in his fist. Colin was wearing his father's old police-issue Doc Martens with steel toecaps, and punched one leg out hard, connecting with the rider's groin.

The blow must have been off though, because his opponent was up again, vaulting over him, heading for the staircase above.

Each of the terraced buildings had a different kind of roof access. This one had a short flight of steps to a steel fire door, which was already being opened.

Colin found himself faced with his worst nightmare. The roofscape before him was a darkened obstacle course of steep tarred slopes and brick gaps. He tried not to look down as he negotiated the slates, tried not to think of the spaces between objects that would recede or elongate, tricking his senses.

Diminished spatial awareness was the inherited inability to judge heights and widths, a form of Ménière's disease caused by the interaction of the eye, brain and inner ear. The problem had initially resulted in his rejection from the Met, but he had largely learned to control it – except at night, when everything appeared to flatten out.

His quarry had jumped across an alleyway, landing on the next angled roof, and Colin gamely followed, but could feel a familiar giddiness starting to kick in. Screwing his eyes shut he made the jump, but barrelled into a chimney stack. Ahead, the rider climbed a slated peak with ease and jumped down the other side. Colin followed, but his left leg was burning and felt as if he had gashed it. He climbed, trying to gain purchase on the dirt-crusted slates, pushing himself up on the rubberized soles of his boots.

On a flattened section of the next roof a group of teenagers were lounging in deckchairs, drinking beer. As Colin skittered down the rider dropped into the surprised circle and landed among them, scattering cans. Grabbing one of them, a young girl, he swung her over the edge in a single movement, as if she was weightless. He extended his arm and she screamed, trying to reach his neck.

Colin held the others back. The motorcyclist appeared to be the same one that he and Meera had chased, although that was impossible. He wore the same riding leathers, helmet and boots, even moved with the same rolling gait. PCU members were unarmed; all Colin could do was force the others to stay back beyond the rider's reach.

Once he saw that they were not going to try and rush him, the rider lowered his hostage to the roof and pulled her with him towards the adjoining building.

Colin followed as closely as he dared, but the game had changed. His main purpose now was to make sure that no harm came to the girl. She was being dragged backwards to the roof doorway, but was not making it easy for her abductor, yelling and kicking as she went.

As soon as he saw a chance to get closer Colin ran forward, throwing himself at the pair with the same undirected energy that had got him banned from boxing matches. Crashing them all into a tangle of limbs, he tore at the rider's helmet, trying to reveal his features, and was struck on the side of the head for his efforts.

By the time he had recovered his senses, the rider was off again, a leather-clad rhinoceros thundering across the rooftops of Wahthamstow, smashing through a washing line, then another, then – incredibly – straight through a barbed-wire fence that separated two roofs.

Tearing the wires away, he headed doggedly on, jumping to the terrace of an apartment building where each flat was divided from the next by a wooden partition. They came down like draw-bridges beneath his boot, one after the other. Gnomes were scattered. A pair of plastic herons were poleaxed and a *faux* wishing well went for a burton.

What's it going to take to stop him? Colin wondered, trying to stay close. He would have kept the pace, too, had not an angry householder burst from his home to berate the detective constable over a flattened begonia bed.

As the old man blocked his path and threatened to call the cops, he could only watch helplessly as the rider dropped from the end of the terrace and vanished from view.

By the time he got free and managed to make his way downstairs, there was no sign of the pizza bike.

He found Meera in the stairwell. 'I wasn't close enough behind him,' she said. 'My bike was parked too far in the opposite direction.'

'Is she OK?'

'Fine – a bit shaken. Maybe we should take her back with us.'

'Take her on your bike,' said Colin. 'I'll follow behind. I nearly had him.'

'I know you did, Colin.' Meera smiled at him. 'Go on, I'll see you back at the PCU.'

43

LOW CASTES

'A whistle-blower,' John May exclaimed, 'that's what this is all about.' He had examined the material on the flash drive left in the crypt by Peter Jukes and was debriefing the team members in the chaotic common room. 'Jukes was worried that what he knew would place him in a dangerous position, so he copied the information and left it at St Bride's. The only person he was sure he could trust was his girlfriend. He told her part of what he knew but didn't give her proof. I guess he knew that doing so would have shifted the burden of knowledge to an innocent outsider. Instead, he left it in the church, thinking that he could send her there to collect it if things got bad.'

'But she didn't get the message?' said Land, confused.

'Perhaps she misunderstood, or he failed to make himself clear. He'd have been under a lot of pressure by then. Arthur believes she went to the church thinking he meant it was a place where they could connect on a spiritual level, whereas

Jukes had something more practical in mind.'

'So what's on the drive?' Longbright asked, 'or are we still being kept on a need-to-know basis?'

'Theseus was developing a bioweapon for Porton Down that appears to have been banned under international law. It was codenamed "Scarlet Thread".'

'They chose the name of a biblical myth,' said Bryant.

'A mutation of avian flu that could be air-transmitted to affect everyone with a particular characteristic. Not in the blood, though – everyone's blood is the same. Variations in race occur because of melanin and tiny differences in DNA. The idea was to develop a weapon that could be used against specific ethnic groups. For example, you could infect a town of insurgents and not harm your own people.'

'Something similar was once practised here in London, albeit in a very different form,' Bryant added. 'People from specific Eastern European countries, most notably Romania, were employed to shift the coffins of plague victims because they were genetically immune to a particular strand of the disease found here.'

'Now here's the really nasty part,' said May. 'Jukes wouldn't have known about the specifics of the bioexperimentation if it hadn't been for the deaths of a number of low-level workers at the plant. He started his career as a journalist, and couldn't help noticing two connected elements. Those who died were all from the Indian subcontinent, and all suffered mental problems followed by death from drowning. The more he uncovered, the more worried he became. He realized they had died as the result of testing the Scarlet Thread.'

'Let me get this right.' Land ticked off his fingers. 'Oskar Kasavian worked for Theseus, so you're saying he knew about this. Then he found out that one of his employees was about to turn whistle-blower, so he ordered Jukes's death and made it look like an accident.'

'It certainly seems that way,' said May. 'Jukes died because he was planning to go public on the MOD breach. He was killed, then smeared by the tabloids for having "satanic" connections. Sabira found out that her husband had sanctioned murder. Either she went through his belongings at home or read something at his office. She told the photographer, Waters, because he worked for a press agency and she had no one else to confide in. When Sabira led us to the painting I simply thought of madness, but she was smarter than that. She was pointing to the Rakes' Club and to the Scarlet Thread experiment, a bioweapon that could make its targets lose their reason and commit suicide. Those who had been experimented on drowned themselves; according to Giles here, it would have been the least painful way to alleviate toxic symptoms. They shared the information online with each other. When Kasavian discovered that his wife knew about his involvement, he realized that he needed to discredit her. Which is exactly what he did.'

'Is Kasavian explicitly named in Jukes's documents?' asked Land.

'Jukes was more concerned with laying out the legal breaches in the case than with blaming any one man. His documentation is dry reading, but it states a clear case. However, it doesn't help us make an indictment.'

'You're telling me you have proof of murder–'

'Effectively, yes.'

'–and there's no way we can use it to put Kasavian in court?'

'That's about the gist of it.'

'You do realize that he heads to Paris tomorrow? If we attempt to indict him after he's appointed head of this international initiative, we'll cause an international scandal. One of the purposes of the Paris meeting is to monitor the movements of terrorists and prevent their access to biochemical products.'

'I'm aware of that,' said Bryant. 'I did warn you. We could arrest him on suspicion, let him know that we have Jukes's evidence and hope that he indicts himself.'

'No, there has to be something else,' said Land. 'Some other way of reeling him in.'

'Stuart Almon is our only remaining informant,' said May. 'He was prepared to name his boss. We need to try him again.'

'Jack's keeping an eye on his movements right now,' said Longbright. 'Maybe there's a reason to bring him in.'

Everyone looked to Bryant for approval. The PCU staff were under no illusions about who actually ran the unit. Bryant did not look happy. To be precise, he had a face like a codfish with a liver complaint.

'What's wrong?' asked May.

'All the way through this investigation, we've been several steps behind the Home Office,' Bryant said. 'That was my fault, sending us off on a wild-goose chase, but we haven't been moving fast enough. Kasavian had us thrown out of the Rakes' Club and we simply bowed to his superiority and walked away!' Bryant shook his head angrily. 'He knew that his director was about to tip us off, which means he either has to get rid of Almon – which he can't do – or enlist his aid in clearing things up. There must be something that tangibly links him to the Scarlet Thread deaths. I'm betting he'll use Almon to get rid of it. Kasavian has to be completely clean before the Paris meeting begins. If there's any more dirty work to be done, it has to be done tonight.'

'How do you know he won't just get rid of Almon as well?' asked Longbright.

'Because Almon is a player, and the ones with power are never at risk. Look at the victims: a bunch of low-paid Indian workers, a researcher, a backroom biochemist and his girlfriend, a freelance photographer and the immigrant wife of a civil servant. These aren't people who hold influential positions within the class system. They're outsiders, lower castes, which means that nobody will be questioning their loss in the House of Commons. But someone has to bring the whole ugly business to light, and it has to be us.'

44

CONFLAGRATION

Stuart Almon had never been to Whitechapel before, and was dismayed by what he saw there.

He lived in one of London's most expensive streets, situated at the top of Campden Hill in verdant Holland Park. Now he found himself walking past shuttered shops that sold Asian DVDs, plastic washing baskets and money orders. It was almost midnight and the street was busy. Groups of Indian kids were hanging around on corners, looking at him, he thought, with menace and malice in their eyes. The accountant slipped his hand over the smartphone in his pocket as he walked past them. The boys, however, were concerned with their own lives and barely noticed him. To them he was just another awkward-looking white guy heading home from one of the fancy restaurants that had begun to border the area.

Almon wanted to check the streetfinder on his phone, but did not dare to withdraw it from his jacket in case somebody spotted the light and mugged him. In all honesty, the only time he ever saw this many black faces was when he had to pass through a railway terminal. What the hell was Kasavian doing leaving his 'Pandora's box' in such a poor neighbourhood anyway? Any number of private banks and financial institutions could have offered him twenty-four-hour access to a safety-deposit box. Of course they would have recorded the event, and there Almon had the answer. Around here half the street lamps were out and the CCTVs would fail to pick up identifiable images.

He looked for the warehouse and finally found it in a narrow backstreet that, over 120 years earlier, had been inhabited by the desperate women who had fallen foul of Jack the Ripper. Stepping over the sodden trash in the gutter, he searched for a way in. Someone had left a foil tray of curried rice on the steel code box, and it had leaked over the keypad. What was wrong with these people? Almon punched in the number Kasavian had given him and waited while the steel shutter rolled up.

He couldn't locate a switch inside, but his mobile had a torch app. Turning its beam around the bay before him, he found himself in the storeroom for the Spitalfields Art Fair. The smell of curry was pervasive.

A series of immense papier-mâché props peered out at him: Perseus, Heracles, Hippolyta and the Minotaur stared down from gold-sprayed pedestals. Behind them stood a pair of rearing stallions, a silver chariot, a scale model of the Parthenon, plus assorted braziers, columns and pediments.

This cloak-and-dagger stuff is absurd, thought Almon. He had not expected that his clumsy attempt to betray Kasavian would dump him in a rundown Whitechapel warehouse at midnight.

The safe stood in the rear corner of the bay, an absurdly theatrical affair made of green-painted iron, with a huge old-fashioned steel dial on the front. Using the code he had been given, he matched up the numerals and hauled on the safe's handle. It seemed to be stuck, but then it gave way with an agonized groan. Inside was a red wooden despatch box with a brass lock, into which he inserted the key.

At first he thought the box was filled with taxi receipts. There were lots of small rectangles of paper. When he saw the accompanying letter-headed notes from Porton Down, it crossed his mind that if he took the contents he might be able to gain the upper hand over Kasavian. But even as he considered the idea, he knew he would never be able to pull it off. He did not possess the Machiavellian gene. Something was bound to go wrong. If this was one incriminating box Kasavian had missed, there had to be others he'd managed to destroy, and even more he'd salvaged for his own purposes. It was better to follow the instructions he'd been given: burn the contents and have done with it.

Doing this was not as easy as he thought it would be. Almon was not a smoker, and had no lighter or matches on him. Searching around, he tried to find something on the shelves that would burn the paperwork.

Outside he heard footsteps and low laughter. Waiting in the shadows until a group of boys had passed, he tipped out one crate after another, searching for a light. Finally, in one of the artists' craft boxes, he found what he was looking for: a

341

can of petrol and a box of matches.

He sprayed most of the can into the despatch box and struck a light, tossing it in. He figured he'd let it burn through, then kick the box lid shut, but the fiery explosion caught him by surprise. A moment later the flames had leaped up to the oil-burnished papier-mâché statue of the Minotaur. The fire swept over its great bull-thighs, jumping across to Perseus and Hippolyta, and within seconds the entire back wall of statuary and model buildings was alight.

Before his eyes, an ancient civilization was collapsing. Almon jumped back, dropping his mobile and the paper with the code for the bay door. The fire was spitting oily droplets that spattered when they landed, spreading gobbets of molten lava. Acrid black smoke roiled across the low roof in silken folds. The statues were weakest at their legs and had already started to collapse, spraying more burning debris as they tipped and fell.

In the cramped rooms above the warehouse, Mandhatri Sahonta and his wife Jakari were asleep with their four children.

The couple had abandoned their village in Karnataka and moved to London to run a catering company. They worked long hours and sent most of their money home every month, with the result that they had not been able to move from the apartment they had lately come to despise. Jakari was the first to smell the varnish blistering on the flat's outer doors. Shaking her husband awake, she told him of her fears and they set about rousing the children.

Outside, Renfield saw the flames flare behind the warehouse windows. A light went on in the flat above, but was extinguished with a pop; the fire had already reached the building's electrics.

He needed to deal with Stuart Almon, but first there were families to warn. Renfield had spent some time behind the sergeants' desk at Bethnal Green Police Station, and knew how crowded many of these old houses were. Few had fire escapes, and most had only one narrow staircase in or out.

He reported the fire as he ran into the burning bay, seizing Almon just as his jacket caught alight. Swiftly cuffing him, he dragged the dazed, smouldering civil servant outside and left him against a lamp-post on the opposite side of the road while he went back in to find a way of reaching the building's imprisoned residents.

Stuart Almon watched in horror as the flames flared to extraordinary heights, splintering windows and filling the night with the cries of the trapped. He had no interest in the lives he had placed at risk. All he could see was his career going up in flames.

45

DEAD IN THE WATER

Early on Thursday morning, Edgar Digby, a lizard-eyed lawyer with hair as shiny as a mackerel and a suit that cost more than the average annual wages of a fisherman, turned up at the unit to give Stuart Almon some outrageously expensive advice, to whit: *Don't say anything that incriminates you.*

'Christ, Digby, I think I could have figured out that part for myself,' muttered Almon as the pair sat before Raymond Land, Renfield and May. 'You're here to get me out.' He needed to talk to Kasavian urgently and update him on what had happened.

'I don't think that's going to be quite as easy as you think,' warned Digby. 'You were observed entering the warehouse and torching it.'

'I didn't "torch" it, I was...' But Almon could not say what he was doing. He decided to follow his lawyer's advice and shut up.

'It's thanks to the sergeant who was following you that you're not here on a manslaughter charge,' said John May. 'If he hadn't managed to evacuate the building—'

'Well he did,' Almon snapped impatiently. 'So what happens now?'

'Before we get to that,' said May, 'perhaps you'd

care to tell us what you were doing setting fire to a Whitechapel warehouse in the middle of the night?'

'I was – it got out of hand. I dropped a match.'

'You don't have to say anything at this juncture,' reminded Edgar.

'Well, I'm not going to sit here and let myself be incriminated, am I?'

'Perhaps you would excuse us while I brief my client?' the lawyer asked Land.

'Forget it, that's not going to happen,' Renfield replied, turning to Almon. 'You nearly killed six people, matey. Four kids, two of them little girls aged six and four years old – they almost died because of you.'

'That wasn't my fault,' Almon complained unconvincingly. 'You can't keep me here without charging me. I know my rights.'

'We can hold you for thirty-six hours on the authority of a police superintendent, which we have,' said Land, 'but we can push arson under the Terrorism Act, which gives us the right to hold you for fourteen days. And we have all the evidence we need to keep you here without bail. So you can start by admitting the truth, or we'll make damned sure you're charged with attempted manslaughter.'

'There's no such thing as attempted manslaughter,' Edgar pointed out. 'You can't attempt to accidentally kill someone. In the event, nobody was hurt.'

'You were happy enough to name names yesterday,' said May. 'You struck a deal with Kasavian, didn't you? Clear up his mess and get back in his

345

good books, something like that?'

'I had no choice,' said Almon pathetically. 'You don't understand how the Civil Service works. It's all about reciprocity. You get caught up in the favours you owe, and I'm in deeper than I ever intended to be.'

'I would *really* stop there,' warned Edgar.

The accountant would not be interrupted. 'Kasavian buried the story, but it resurfaced.'

'I'm afraid we're ahead of you, Mr Almon,' said May coldly. 'We're going to give you a chance to do the right thing. We need evidence that your boss was directly involved. Did he send you there?'

'I never said that,' said Almon, trying to buy enough time to think.

'We're going to find proof that he is a murderer. The documents you burned can be reconstituted.' May had no idea if they could be or not, but it was worth a try.

Almon was shocked by the bluntness of May's words. The language of the Civil Service was tapestried with euphemism and allusion. 'Oskar never gets his hands dirty. Nothing sticks to him. He commissions the services of others. I can't imagine for one moment that he'd leave a trail that could be followed back to him.'

'Well, he's having to act spontaneously now. He can't have thought of everything.'

'You still don't understand who you're dealing with,' said Almon. 'He has all the resources he needs to cover his traces, and they're not accessible to you except through official government channels. Your unit is answerable to him. He's

346

made sure that it's impossible to bring him down. Why else would he have come to you in the first place? He knew you were incompetent.'

Renfield had never hit a civilian before but came close to it now. 'You were never going to give us what we needed,' he said. 'You were just trying to keep your own career from tanking. Well, it's over now. After this you won't be able to get a job cleaning toilets.'

'You still have nothing on Kasavian,' said Almon simply. 'And you won't find it, because there's nothing to find. He's wiped his prints from everything. You talk about my career being over? You're screwed, all of you. You've been played. You're floating corpses. Your unit is dead in the water, just how he planned it would be from the very beginning.'

That was when Renfield jumped at him.

46

SHADOW IMAGE

After Stuart Almon signed a statement negotiated to the satisfaction of all parties, he was charged with arson and reluctantly released on bail.

A sickly grey and yellow dawn broke over King's Cross. The clouds looked as if they had fallen down a flight of stairs and badly bruised themselves. The news reports promised heavy rain as the capital's traditional summer weather – squalls of disappointment with intermittent outbursts of gloom – returned.

The PCU team had worked through the night, but the atmosphere was one of defeat.

They knew they had nothing and would find nothing. As each lead was followed and came to a dead-end, the detectives saw just how carefully the web of their downfall had been constructed. Kasavian had clearly been testing them to see what could be uncovered, secure in the knowledge that even if his original crime was known, there was no way of connecting it back to him.

Colin and Meera had returned to tell of the night's events. 'They're ex-military lads, these bikers,' Colin told them. 'Freelancers, up for anything. I can tell the type. Guys like that used to come to our boxing club. They were lousy at playing by the rules but they were tough as nails, the kind of men who trained out in the snow in shorts and vests. Kasavian probably found them through his old MOD connections. They're taught to keep their mouths shut no matter what happens. They're as solid as railway sleepers. I checked to see if they had a shared base here, somewhere they might meet or train together, but they're real loners.'

'I'm getting a warrant to turn the Rakes' Club inside out,' said Banbury, 'but the chances of finding anything there now are unlikely.'

'What time is Kasavian heading to the station?' asked Land.

'He's got a car coming at four thirty p.m.,' Longbright told him. 'I'm sending out for breakfasts.' She pressed the heels of her hands against her eyes and rose from her desk, where a tundra of reports had spread in the last dark hours.

'Arthur, can I get you something?' she offered, looking in on Bryant's office.

'Just a cup of tea. I'm not hungry.'

'Perhaps you should try and get some rest.'

'If I fall asleep now I may not wake up again.' Bryant peered blearily over a stack of books and rubbed at his wrinkles. 'Why is it that we always run to the fifty-ninth minute of the eleventh hour? Just once, I'd like to close an investigation a few days earlier than expected.'

'You still think we're going to wrap it up?'

'Yesterday I felt sure we'd arrest Kasavian before his departure. But there's something wrong here. I keep asking myself: Why is there no evidence?'

'You know the answer: everything was pre-planned.'

'No, Janice. He didn't know that Jukes had left something for his girlfriend to find. Nobody did. Fancy leaving it in a bloody crypt!'

May passed Longbright as she was leaving. 'I hope she just convinced you to eat.'

'Food makes me sleepy. I've got a quarter of pineapple cubes here.' Arthur rattled a paper bag. 'The sugar will keep me going. Tell me, John, you're absolutely sure there's nothing on that flash drive that can convict Kasavian?'

'No. There are some classified reports on Scarlet Thread and the inquiry findings on the re-search scientists' deaths. Jukes was more con-cerned with damning the science behind the project. There's nothing to indict Kasavian because Jukes didn't know he was going to die and leave us with no bloody proof.'

'We still have a few hours left to find something. But we won't, and I'm beginning to think I know why.'

May seated himself and waited patiently, but could finally bear the suspense no longer. 'Do you want to tell me?'

Bryant dug out a grubby hanky and blew his nose. 'No, because you'll really hate the answer.'

'You always say that. It's an incredibly annoying habit.'

'I know, isn't it? Let me at least try to elucidate. Come and sit beside me.'

May pulled a chair up next to his partner. 'What's that funny smell?'

'I got kebab juice down my vest last night, so I sprayed it with air freshener from the toilet.' He turned back to an immense sheet of paper covered in scribbled names. 'You have a rough idea of how my brain works.'

'Sort of. Yes. But not always,' May admitted.

'You know how much I trust your instincts and working methods.'

'Of course.'

'Well, we differ on one major point. You believe that from the outset of every investigation the most obvious facts point to the right solution. Occam's razor. I don't. Fair?'

'Fair enough,' agreed May.

'In this case, what did our instincts tell us?'

'That Kasavian wasn't to be trusted.'

'Exactly. Whether we were conscious of it or not, that was the agenda we were pursuing. And we got the result we wanted. We proved his guilt to ourselves. We've followed the line all the way from the sanctioned death of Peter Jukes, right through to poor, dim Stuart Almon setting fire to the evidence.'

'Except that we still can't make an arrest.'

'Indeed. I've been over the timeline from beginning to end and it's solid – and yet there's a shadow image behind it.'

'What do you mean?'

'Another theme, as it were. An undertone that contradicts everything we know.' His words hung ominously in the still air of the office.

'But the one thing we know is that Kasavian is guilty.'

'Yes, nothing can change that fact. He's implicated in a murder dating back to his time at Porton Down.' Bryant rubbed his forehead wearily. 'But suppose there was something we missed right from the start? Not a direct fact – something foggier and more obscuring.'

'You're losing me.'

'I know. What I'm trying to say is that there's another agenda at work here. I think it may have something to do with class. Perhaps this whole thing is really only about class.'

'Arthur, I've seen you reach this point many times before, and I still don't quite understand the journey you take. And I don't know what you're trying to say.'

'You know that at heart I'm an academic, not a criminologist. I'm out of my depth when it comes to the construction of empirical data. That's your speciality. But when I look at the victims and the

351

suspects, you know what I see? Two entirely separate classes. Anna Marquand, living in a run-down council house with her mother. Amy O'Connor, working in an East End bar. Jeff Waters, a barrow boy turned photographer. Sabira Kasavian, a disadvantaged Albanian kid whose parents worked in a smelting plant. Then there are the attacks on Edona Lescowitz and even on you and me. The ruling elite consider everyone here to be several classes below them, and therefore thrashable. But they're wrong. They've misjudged us.'

May was anxious to return the conversation to more solid ground. 'Do you think you can get something concrete on Kasavian before his delegation heads off?'

'I honestly don't know. We're trying to indict our own supervisor for murder, John. If it doesn't stick, it won't be just you and I who'll be thrown to the wolves.'

'But if we get him, we'll be exonerated once and for all. There will have to be a new regime.'

'I wish I had your faith, but I know nothing will change. My parents always obeyed the instructions of the authorities, from town-hall officials to railway clerks. It was a working-class habit I was determined not to take into my life.'

'Kasavian doesn't intimidate you, does he?'

Bryant blew a raspberry of defiance. 'No, of course not. At my age the only thing that still commands respect is death. But Kasavian makes me fearful for others with more to lose. I have no right to risk their careers.'

'They already gave you their vote. If we let him

off the hook now, we'll be bowing to authority once more.'

'All right. There's something else that's been troubling me. Kasavian was involved in an illegal programme of research that resulted in sickness and suicide. But he couldn't have been alone in this; I imagine the whole thing was government sanctioned. His wife saw some papers that proved she was married to a man who was, at best, morally deficient. Why should he have cared? I mean, really? Nobody was going to listen to her. She could tell a couple of friends, and nobody would listen to them, either. She had no solid proof. So why would he still go to the trouble of killing her?'

'Arthur, you cannot be this full of doubt at this late stage.'

'I'm afraid I am.'

'Well, I'm going to stop Kasavian from leaving the country, whether you give me reason to or not. So you'd better get back into those books and find whatever it is you're looking for, before it's too late. Find me your assassin's shadow image, or whatever you call it. And you'd better get a bloody move on because I'm leaving soon.'

Bryant watched his partner blast out of the office and felt suddenly alone. May was right to force his hand, but he had no idea how to give his partner the evidence he needed.

47

MR MERRY

John May stood on the corner of Euston Road with Banbury and Longbright, trying to shield his watch from a light drizzle of sooty rain. He felt as if he could hear the seconds ticking by in his heart. *Of course you're anxious,* he told himself. *Who wouldn't be? You're heading off to commit career suicide.*

'We can't leave it any longer,' he said finally. 'Let's go and do it discreetly, without any fuss.'

'Are you certain we've got cause for arrest, John?' Longbright was still uncomfortable with their line of inquiry. Hell, it hung on a web of slender threads including a bizarrely encrypted note from an unstable wife and some research carried out by a supposed suicide who believed in witchcraft. It wasn't anywhere near enough.

'No, I'm not,' May admitted.

Giles Kershaw was still waiting for the St Pancras Biomedical Centre's verdict on the contents of Sabira Kasavian's stomach, and Dan Banbury had found nothing of a chemically hazardous nature in her room at the Cedar Tree Centre. Without evidence of poisoning it would prove impossible to link Kasavian to his wife's demise.

No further evidence had come from May's

wrecked BMW. Nothing more had come to light from Waters's flat. The delivery man's mobile phone had been found by the kids on the Walthamstow rooftop, but apart from that there was nothing. A sense of demoralization flooded over the melancholy group.

'We have enough to make Kasavian miss his train, but that's about all,' May replied. 'If we pick him up before he boards, we undermine his career and derail the initiative, he calls his lawyer and the burden of proof returns to us. I've never done anything like this before. It doesn't look like it will end well for anyone.'

'If we don't do anything and he gets his promotion, I imagine he'll become pretty much untouchable under European jurisdiction,' said Banbury. 'Did Mr Bryant say what he was going to do or how long he'd be?'

'He just said he was going out.' May checked his watch again. 'Why does he always have to cut it so fine? He was exactly the same in his early twenties, running for trains just as they were pulling out of stations.'

'I don't know where he's gone,' said Longbright. 'He just said he was going to follow up an idea. He wasn't in his office when I left, and his phone is going straight to voicemail.'

'Right.' May wiped rain from his face and headed towards the only spare staff car, a battered blue Fiat that Land kept for his exclusive use. Longbright had filched the keys. 'I guess we just have to pray he comes through with something in time. Dan and I will handle the actual arrest. You stay in the car. We make it as discreet as possible, call him down to the foyer and request that he accompanies us. He's going to go crazy but we have to hold our nerve.'

'Let's do it,' said Longbright, getting behind the wheel of the Fiat. 'I hope Arthur's really concentrating on getting us out of this.'

'Of course, one of the most common themes in early Christian writings was female subservience to men,' said Maggie Armitage, riding the escalator to the first floor. 'You'd expect it from the patriarchy of the Church. If any group chose not to conform to Christian teachings, they were immediately attacked. You know I'm doing this under protest, don't you?'

'I appreciate that,' said Bryant, stepping off the escalator and taking Maggie's hand as they made their way around the raised concrete circle. On either side, stone sections of the original London Wall thrust up between glass office buildings, preserved to remind the City's inheritors of their debt to the past. 'Go on.'

'There's nothing shared between the genders in traditional Christianity. Religious and financial power always returns to the hands of males, even now. You haven't met Mr Merry before, have you?'

'No,' said Bryant, 'I've only heard you speak of him.'

'He is my nemesis. It could be argued that we are of equal power, and therefore cancel each other out, but I believe he thinks he is stronger, which I can only pray is mere arrogance. He's certainly very bright. He teaches at the museum.

356

Many years ago we trained together, but we took different paths. My studies took me to the light and his led him towards darkness.'

Bryant studied his old friend with great affection. Maggie had donned legwarmers of different lengths and colours, one pinned with an ankh, the other with a Star of David. It was easy to get distracted by her wayward wardrobe choices. 'Are you saying he's a Satanist?'

'That's such a slippery word. Mr Merry believes he is Ipsissimus, an equal of the gods. He uses his abilities for personal profit and the cruellest of pleasures, whereas I cannot take a penny from clients, and I never venture towards that borderland of pernicious and sinister influence wherein he operates. He believes in something called Paradox Philosophy, a psychological system that involves freeing yourself from so-called "old impediments": right and wrong, true and false. I wouldn't be taking you to see him if I thought there was any other way, believe me. There'll be a price to pay.'

In his desperation to break the deadlock of his stymied thinking, Bryant had called his old friend to ask for advice. After some considerable soul-searching, Maggie agreed to lead the detective to Mr Merry.

'We'll be safe here,' she said, pulling Bryant ahead, 'he won't be able to hurt us, not in a public place. Listen to me, Arthur, I must give you some rules to follow. Under no circumstances should you shake his hand. At no time must you come into contact with his person. If he reaches out to touch you, step out of his way. If he tries to get you to take anything, you must politely refuse. If he drops anything, do not pick it up. If he looks you in the eye, break contact. If he asks you a question, reveal nothing of yourself. It would be better if you didn't speak and let me do the talking. At least I know how to handle him.'

'OK, I'll keep my distance. That sounds easy enough.'

'It sounds easy but it won't be.'

'Why not?'

'Because you have to tell him everything about the case, just as you told it to me. You must do so honestly, or he'll know you're lying, and you can leave nothing out because he'll sense that, too. As you talk together, he'll start to lower his voice until it seems barely audible to you, and you'll find yourself moving in closer, straining to hear. You must not do this, because he'll be trying to plant subconscious commands in your mind. He is extremely manipulative.'

'You're making him sound like some kind of monster,' said Bryant as they reached the entrance to the Museum of London. 'As a rationalist, I can't afford to start believing that such people have supernatural powers.'

'He certainly has a magnetic effect on people,' said Maggie. 'The majority of believers in Satanism are also avid readers of the Bible. Insecure people are drawn in by such readings as they look for something to believe in, and Mr Merry knows exactly how to exploit them. It's free admission: go around the ticket counter to the right and follow the stairs to the lower ground floor.'

The Museum of London does not merely hide

its light under a bushel. It extinguishes the light, and then buries the bushel inside a series of unrelentingly grim walkways, making the building entirely invisible from its exterior. Even those who know of its whereabouts venture there by following other lost visitors.

'What makes you so sure Mr Merry can help us?' asked Bryant.

'I'm not,' Maggie replied. 'But he has a strange way of getting to the root of things.'

They reached the bottom of the staircase and pushed open glass doors into a dimly lit exhibition space. Taking up the entire wall facing them, millions of plague rats scampered in a moving carpet down a flight of stone steps. The video projections were designed to disgust, and the sight was met with appropriate noises of horror from a party of schoolchildren.

'The Great Plague of 1665 was caused by the fleas that infested the Dutch cotton bales, then travelled on rats and jumped on to humans,' intoned a deep, mellifluous voice. 'They bit into the flesh and spread the disease by sucking in and spitting out blood. The fleas lived on the rats, and the rats lived on the ships, and the ships arrived at the London Docks, in the poorest part of the city.'

Bryant looked around but could not see anyone speaking.

'They hopped and jumped across filthy floors and dirty beds, into babies' cots and on to sleeping mothers, burrowing into unwashed hair and wriggling into sweaty clothes, and they bit and drank and spread their poison. The houses of the poor were close together, so the infection spread. The authorities ordered all the cats and dogs of London to be killed, and by doing that they destroyed the only creatures that could catch the rats. So then they told everyone to smoke, and to burn pepper and hops and frankincense, to kill the evil humours in the air. By now one-fifth of all the people in London had died. Then something happened that ended the plague – can you tell me what it was?'

'Fire!' shouted a few of the children.

'That's right, fire,' said the voice. 'The sparks leaped across the narrow lanes and the inferno roared through the city, gutting the grandest churches and the lowest slums, destroying ninety per cent of the houses it reached. And so one great evil cancelled out the other. So perhaps we could say that this second evil was a good one.'

From the centre of the schoolchildren rose an extraordinary figure, dressed as a pirate. Mr Merry was as round as a pudding. His barrel chest was covered by a gold-braided coat with turned-back sleeves. His great black bushy beard was sewn with coloured beads. He had smiling kohl-lined eyes and thick black eyebrows, possibly dyed. His large head was topped with a black felt tricorn hat, from which protruded a thick beaded ponytail. In his right fist he held a rat. The children screamed in delighted horror, but as many reached out to touch the stuffed rodent as fell back.

Before Maggie Armitage could stop him, Bryant had stepped forward to the edge of the children's circle. 'The Great Fire of London didn't end the plague,' he said cheerfully. 'The disease was already dying out before the fire started.'

Mr Merry slowly turned to look at him. The eyes missed nothing. He smiled faintly, and the smile grew, and then he laughed, patting children on the head and shooing them away. 'To your drawing pads, you homunculi,' he boomed. 'I want to see works of genius, or I'll send all your souls to the Devil.'

As the children dispersed he turned his attention to the small wrinkled old man wrapped in an olive-green scarf who stood blinking at him, waiting for an answer.

'Who's to say if the flames really burned away the germs?' he replied. 'We were none of us there to witness the events of that terrible year. You are Arthur Bryant, I take it?' He held out a welcoming hand.

Bryant ignored the proffered palm. 'I don't think we've ever met.'

'No, but your reputation precedes you.' Mr Merry dropped his hand and smiled again. 'I imagine you've come to talk to me about your problematic case.'

As Mr Merry took a step forward towards him, Bryant took one back. 'I don't believe I've discussed it with anyone.'

'Of course you haven't. Perhaps Oskar mentioned it to me. We're very old friends, after all. But you mustn't let that deter you. I value an open mind above all else. Tell me the facts of the case, and I'll see if I can offer you some advice.' He looked around at the children. 'Oh, don't mind them. I've blocked their hearing. Your

361

words will sound in their ears as meaningless gibberish.'

Despite Maggie's warnings, Bryant felt himself becoming unsettled. Whether or not Mr Merry actually possessed paranormal powers was beside the point. It was clear that, if nothing else, he was a devious psychologist.

Bryant glanced at Maggie, wondering how to begin. He could feel Mr Merry's black eyes fixed upon him, and sensed the importance of keeping the warlock within his peripheral vision, as one would an unshackled crocodile.

'Come, sit next to me.' Mr Merry dropped himself on to a leather bench and patted the space beside him.

Bryant felt the warning in Maggie's glance. 'I'll stand, if it's all the same to you,' he said. 'But I'll tell you what I know.'

Mr Merry crossed pale beringed fingers with black painted nails over his tight waistcoat while, behind him, his acolytes crawled on the floor with pens and paper. 'Please,' he said expansively, 'enlighten me.'

48

FINAL CALL

The foyer of the Home Office was as quiet as a fish tank. A cleaner was slowly wiping a rubber plant. The receptionist sat entranced by her desk monitor. She looked up at John May. 'It couldn't have been more than ten minutes ago,' she said. 'His car was early.'

'Who did he go with?'

The receptionist checked her screen again. She had very little neck and needed new glasses, so that craning forward to read it was an effort. 'Mr Almon, Mr Hereward, Mr Lang and a team of lawyers. He's not due back in the office until the middle of next week.'

'I've tried every route across London that exists,' said Longbright as they returned to the car, 'including one where you have to reverse a quarter of a mile down a one-way street, and I bet I can get there before an Addison Lee hired car.'

Slapping a siren on the roof of the Fiat that they were not technically entitled to use, they set off towards the north. Longbright drove like Ayrton Senna needing to find a bathroom. She overtook trucks on the inside, slid up on to the emergency lanes and shot through traffic lights with an abandon that made May screw his eyes shut tight.

'It's going to be a nightmare trying to find him in the station,' he warned.

'I don't think so,' said Dan Banbury. 'I borrowed his iPhone to check his contacts some while back. I reset it so that I could pinpoint him through my phone's SatNav. It's accurate to under a metre.'

'Why did you do that?'

'It was for his protection, so that if anything happened we could find him quickly. And I just wanted to see if it worked. I tried to do it to yours too, but of course that didn't work.' He turned his own phone on and checked Kasavian's progress. 'Looks like he's a mile ahead of us on the same road.'

The traffic was heavy, and fresh squalls of rain made the going slow. The only thing more depressing than driving to St Pancras International in a grey slush of drizzle, sprayed by the cars in front, was driving away from it in the knowledge that you weren't leaving the country.

Longbright parked on the pavement in Euston Road as a policeman ran up and warned her not to leave the vehicle there. 'You park it, pal,' she said, throwing him the keys and noting the ID code on his epaulette. 'I'll find you.'

'He's with a team of corporate lawyers,' said May. 'It's not the ideal situation for an arrest.'

The Paris counter clerk told them that Kasavian had already checked in his luggage and had gone through passport control to the business lounge. May took the others through the side office at immigration control and they made their way to the lounge, where the receptionist confirmed that Kasavian had just passed inside.

May hesitated before the glass doors. He could see the security head surrounded by lawyers from here. 'I'll go in and try to do this quietly,' he told Longbright and Banbury. 'I don't want it to look heavy-handed.'

'You're arresting him for conspiracy to murder, John, I don't see how it can be anything else,' said Longbright. 'The way everyone tiptoes around this guy is incredible. This is how people like him stay in power.'

'Yes, I know.' May pushed open the door. 'Try Arthur again and find out if he's got anything. Kasavian will be only too well aware of his rights. He'll soon see we haven't enough to hold him.'

The others watched as May crossed the floor and approached Kasavian. The ensuing confrontation unfolded in mime.

Kasavian passed through stages of puzzlement, incredulity and fury, and then summoned his lawyers. The momentary advantage May had gained through the power of surprise was swiftly lost.

'I don't know what Mr Bryant is doing, but he had better come back with something Kasavian isn't expecting,' said Banbury doubtfully.

Under Maggie's watchful eye, Bryant finished outlining the case, carefully keeping to impersonal facts. From time to time Mr Merry would lean forward on the bench, appearing to listen more intently to a particular detail, but it became clear that he was looking for something else as Bryant talked, a seam in the detective's

365

armour. Finally Bryant reached the point where his partner was heading off to carry out the arrest, and Mr Merry sat back, considering what he had heard.

'You realize your mistake by now, I take it?' he asked. His hooded eyes made him appear half-asleep.

'I'm hoping you'll enlighten me,' said Bryant.

'You should have trusted the children more at the outset – the young ones always see what is happening far more clearly than adults. We over-complicate matters. These dullard fathers walking around the museum have no understanding of their children. They hold the power to shape youthful souls and alter the course of destiny, and they waste the opportunity.' His dark eyes glittered with the thought of twisting young minds. He was Captain Hook and the crocodile rolled into one.

'The children,' Maggie prompted. 'What about them?'

Mr Merry's eyes refocused on the problem at hand. 'The game the pair of them were playing, *Witch Hunter*, it's based on the old precepts of medieval witch-finding in England. You understand how and why the creation of such witch-hunts came about?'

'We were discussing the subject earlier,' said Maggie.

Mr Merry was greedy for details. 'Where was this? How did the subject arise?'

'I don't understand why the principles of witchcraft keep recurring in this case,' said Bryant hastily.

'Come here and I'll tell you,' offered the black magician, beckoning. 'I shall whisper in your ear.'

A sharp warning glance from Maggie put paid to the idea. 'Tell me,' said Bryant.

'Very well, but it's nothing you don't already know, for your mind was set upon its subconscious course when you first heard about the death of the O'Connor woman. Do you remember what the children told you of how they picked her, and why? It was there that you got your first inkling of the truth.'

They spoke quietly together for some minutes while Maggie watched, carefully pushing Bryant back from Mr Merry's range whenever she felt they were drawing too close together.

'And now you see it, and must finish your work,' said Mr Merry, rising and looking down to where Bryant's scarf had fallen on the floor. Sweeping it up in his ringed hand, he handed it back. 'Yours, I think?'

'Why don't you keep it as a souvenir?' said Bryant.

'Very well, but if you succeed in closing the case now, I shall exact my fee,' said Mr Merry. 'Don't worry, I won't expect cash. There are other ways for you to pay.' Patting his tricorn back on to his head and pocketing the scarf, he clapped his hands and roused his children from their torpid studies.

'The thought of him working with children every day makes my blood run cold,' said Bryant. 'Why is he allowed to do so?'

'The staff say he's wonderful with them, but I'm not sure about that. I keep a watchful eye on him from a distance, and he knows it. I'm surprised he didn't affect you. You know how susceptible you are.'

'I turned down my hearing aid slightly,' Bryant admitted. 'I missed everything he said in a lower register.'

Bryant and the white witch exited the museum. 'Can I let you see yourself home?'

'Why do all my evenings with you end the same way?' Maggie sighed. 'Go on, be off with you. And a word of advice, keep Mr Merry's image out of your head tonight or he'll worm his way into your dreams. Where are you going now?'

'Claridge's,' said Bryant. 'I'm told they serve the most wonderful macaroons for afternoon tea.' Waving her off at the Tube station, he hailed a black cab and rang Longbright's number as one pulled over before him.

'Has John done it yet?' he asked, climbing aboard.

'He's in with Kasavian right now. It doesn't look as if it's going well. The lawyers are arguing and they've just announced the final call for passengers on the Paris train.'

'Janice, I need you to go in there and tell John something for me,' he said, settling back in his seat. 'He'll know what to do with the inform-ation.'

'What do you want me to say?'

'Tell him to let Kasavian go.'

49

WITCHCRAFT

There were few raised eyebrows as Arthur Bryant made his way across the thick grey carpet of Claridge's dining room. Shambling elderly men were part of the furniture in the esteemed hotel. Many of them were waiters. The pianist was tiptoeing through the tulips and planning a segue into 'Roses of Picardy'.

They were seated at their usual table in the corner, just where the maître d' had said he would find them. There were three of them: Anastasia Lang, Cathy Almon and Emma Hereward, halfway through a teatime spread of tiny fairy cakes decorated with lurid arabesques of intestine-pink and acid-green icing sugar, accompanied by diaphanous leaves of brown bread, compotes, salads, savouries and glasses of thick yellow Chardonnay. They barely bothered to look up when he arrived at their table. Bryant was just another member of staff, indistinguishable from waiters, cleaners and concierges, made a necessary evil by his usefulness.

'Mr – Brighton, isn't it?' said Ana Lang after a brief moment of thought. 'What a strange coincidence. Who are you with?'

'I'm not dining here, Mrs Lang. My wages wouldn't cover a sausage on a stick in a joint like this.' He took a chair from another table and dragged it over to theirs, which was something one might do in a public house but never in Claridge's. 'I hope you don't mind me joining you for a minute. I'm knackered. My knees are on their last knockings.' He peered at Mrs Lang's side plate of cheeses with interest. 'What are those leaves?'

'It's a rocket garnish,' she said through perfect clenched teeth.

'You know, that stuff was the first thing to grow back over bomb-sites after the war. My mum used to bundle it up by the bushel. God knows what she did with it; no greens ever found their way on to our plates. She mainly did cruel things to suet. And now I bet they charge a tenner for that.'

'I don't suppose you came here to discuss the cuisine.'

'Indeed not. I wanted to let you know that the funeral of Sabira Kasavian can finally be planned, and should be able to take place next week, depending on her husband's availability.'

'You mean you've concluded the post-mortem,' said Mrs Lang, insufficiently hiding her surprise.

'The verdict of the inquest will be made public later today,' said Bryant. 'I don't suppose there's any chance of a cup of tea? Nothing fancy, builders' will be fine.'

'Well, what was the conclusion?' asked Cathy Almon, withholding her pastry-fork.

'Oh, exactly what we thought it would be.' Bryant waved at a waiter and failed to catch his rheumy eye.

'What killed her?' Emma Hereward enunciated impatiently.

'Now, that's rather interesting. I can't remember these things, so Giles wrote it down for me.'

Bryant patted his pockets and located a rumpled piece of paper. Donning smeary reading glasses, he squinted at the page. 'Basically a mix of SSRIs. Or selective seratonin reuptake inhibitors, as they're known. She was stuffed to the gills with anti-depressant drugs. The problem with high-dose combinations of Prozac, Paxil, Zoloft, Luvox and the rest is that they can cause akathisia. It's – let me quote here – "a state of physical and mental agitation that can spark off fits of violent, self-destructive behaviour". Many of the terrible killing sprees that occur in America are carried out by people misusing prescribed drugs.'

'So I imagine you'll be looking to indict her doctor for over-prescription,' said Mrs Hereward.

'No, because her doctor didn't prescribe them.'

'Don't tell me poor Oskar is under arrest,' said Mrs Almon. 'I knew it.'

'No, not at all. I believe he's on his way to Paris at this moment.'

'Well, I don't understand,' said Mrs Lang. 'Why exactly are you here?'

'To be honest, I've always been a bit of a theatre buff, and sometimes we're offered free tickets. I was given a matinee seat for the new RSC production of *Macbeth* today, but I couldn't use it. People are always fascinated by the character of Lady Macbeth, but for me it was always about the witches.'

Miraculously, a waiter had heard his plea for tea and had crept over with a pot. Bryant poured and took a sip, but it was too hot to drink. 'Historically speaking, the number three has always had magical qualities. It appears several times through the play: three witches; three prophecies; three apparitions; and the "weird sisters" repeat their incantations three times.'

To everyone's horror he poured his tea into his saucer and slurped it through his false teeth. 'Of course, the word "witches" is rather ambiguous. The Folio text refers to them in stage directions and speech prefixes as witches, but really they represent the three Fates of ancient mythology, weaving the threads of human destiny, foretelling the future and altering the paths of men's lives.'

Anastasia Lang was visibly losing patience. 'If you have something to tell us, perhaps you'd be so good as to do so?'

'Sorry, of course. It would help if I explained my thinking a little. There's a governing rule of investigation: *lex parsimoniae*, the law of succinctness. It means that the simplest and most likely explanation, the one which feels organically right, is usually most likely to be correct. In this case we had an answer suggesting itself from the outset. Given our past dealings with Oskar Kasavian and knowing how Machiavellian he could be, it seemed highly likely to me that he poisoned his own wife. Even though he hired us to look into the case, and seemed genuinely distraught when he heard of her death, everything always pointed back to him.' The room's background banter and tinkling teacups receded into silence as he explained. It seemed that everyone was listening.

'But, you see, there was another, deeper level of *lex parsimoniae* at work, perhaps less rational, and it was something I began to realize I had sensed from the outset. A certain, shall we say, distaff element to the case. The subject of witches kept arising.

'Amy O'Connor was reading *Rosemary's Baby*, and had folded down the corner of page 145, in which Rosemary opens a book called *All Of Them Witches*. Lucy and Tom, the children who hunted her in the courtyard of St Bride's Church, were playing a game called *Witch Hunter*, loosely based on the medieval instructions for searching out witches. Sabira Kasavian told me it was witch-craft, that she had been placed under some kind of spell, but she was at a loss to explain how it worked. And whenever she talked about the cause of all her problems, she said "they", never "he". Which was odd, considering she knew her husband had covered up a government-sanctioned murder. Even Oskar told me that his wife was the subject of a witch-hunt.'

Now it appeared that even the pianist had ceased playing and was watching them with interest.

'Then, of course,' Bryant continued, 'the three of you told my detective sergeant you always protect your men. You described in some detail how you controlled your weak husbands from the sidelines. And yet there we were, ignoring this deeper truth for the more obvious idea that Oskar Kasavian was the culprit. After all, he had been responsible for covering up a whole series of deaths, although technically they were suicides. And perhaps Peter Jukes drowned himself too. For all I know, he may have been an unwitting part of the test group.

'Sabira Kasavian discovered the truth about her husband, as wives are wont to do. She named him in the code she sent us, but I should have realized that she wasn't referring to the architect of her own troubles. She was talking about his work. He had murdered in the course of duty. How did she find out about him, I wonder? Did he toss guiltily in his sleep, speaking of the terrible burden that still haunted him? That seems rather unlikely. It's obvious Oskar sleeps pretty easily at night. It was more likely something prosaic. Sabira often went to the Pegasus offices to wait for her husband, and it's likely that she read something she shouldn't. Little notes that looked just like taxi receipts. She was a bright girl. She quickly realized what he was hiding. But who could she tell? Not any of you, all of whom she hated, because you were a class above – and she knew you were searching for opportunities to advance your husbands.

'I don't know which of you first discovered that Mr Jukes's girlfriend was in London, but I imagine her arrival was enough to stir you into action once more. Your husbands were all on the board and in the club; any exposure would taint them. You had taken steps to hide the past before, hiring a former member of the Russian militia to remove my biographer. You didn't even need to get your hands dirty. Such men live invisibly, work cheaply and are untraceable, so why not do it again, and close the circle by getting rid of Miss O'Connor? You weren't to know that she knew nothing. You just knew that she was Jukes's girlfriend, and had started visiting his old haunts.

'That should have been the end of it. Except there was Sabira again, making accusations, talking to strangers, throwing tantrums, being *common*, and you couldn't just have her whacked. You hired someone to watch her and report back. No wonder she felt persecuted! As you took turns to visit her you poisoned her mind against her husband, and then you poisoned her body with your helpful ministrations. "Try taking two of these every morning, Sabira, they've always worked for me." "Take one of these before bedtime." As for Oskar, well, I imagine that when he heard about O'Connor's death he assumed the government cover-up was continuing without him, never realizing that you were taking care of the business, destroying his wife and undermining his career.'

The women stared and stared at him, frozen to their chairs, all thoughts of food forgotten.

'Apart from switching the folder of evidence Sabira found with one full of taxi receipts, all you had to do was make the odd phone call to an untraceable number and draw out some cash. But Sabira had a mouth on her. She talked to the photographer, who traced O'Connor to the church. She talked to her girlfriend, and things just kept getting more complicated. Best not to think of it as murder, you told yourselves, more like an act of self-preservation. But here's the funny thing. If you hadn't interfered in the first

375

place, you could have let events unfold naturally and most of your problems would have been taken care of.

'One thing puzzled me. If Sabira suspected the three of you, why on earth did she take your pills and your poisoned advice? And then I realized what I should have known from the start; that it was a class issue. Even though Sabira was afraid of you, she obeyed you because you were posh. Oh, she complained about you to me, but whenever you arrived full of apologies and turned on the charm and *deferred* to her, she thought that she might finally be gaining acceptance. But you weren't accepting her. You were killing her. The children were right. There really are witches.'

A waiter dropped a tray, making everybody jump. 'What children?' said Ana Lang, confused.

For once, the women were dumbfounded. They looked even more shocked when a pair of constables from Savile Row nick appeared at the end of the table ready to take them into custody, but Bryant suspected it was more to do with the embarrassment of being arrested in Claridge's than any real resentment at discovery.

'To save time and energy,' said Bryant, 'I'd rather we didn't have to go through the tedium of denials. You covered your tracks, but of course the Russians like to know who they're dealing with and did some checking up on you. They recorded your calls. Guess whose mobile just got handed in?'

The wives rose with the little dignity they could muster. 'John put this on my bill, would you?' Mrs Lang told the maître d' with an impressive level of imperiousness.

'Do you need a taxi, madam?' asked the maître d'.

'No, we'll probably walk if the rain has stopped.' Ana Lang leaned into Bryant as she passed. 'I'll tell you what will happen now, you nasty little old man. First, the lawyer. Then, your head.' She brought her hand up swiftly and would have slapped his face had not one of the constables been quick enough to stop her.

'On second thoughts,' said Bryant, 'you'd better handcuff the three of them together. They're clearly dangerous.'

So it was that the county wives of the Home Office were removed from the dining room of Claridge's locked to one another like common criminals, as the clientele watched in open-mouthed amazement.

50

THE OUTSIDERS

The detectives took everyone, including Crippen, to the Nun and Broken Compass that night. Oskar Kasavian was in Paris representing the views of the British government, and Raymond Land had agreed to stick the Home Office with the drinks bill.

Jack Renfield unloaded the beer tray and squeezed in beside Longbright as they raised their glasses. It was the British version of a midsummer's evening: rain fell against the windows and there was a fire in the grate. Through the window they could see umbrellas turning inside out.

'What do you think will happen now?' he asked Bryant, tearing open a packet of crisps.

'Oskar will get the new position, the wives will be indicted and the department will be swept clean,' said Bryant, sipping his porter. 'It's a perfect opportunity for HMG and GCHQ to be seen to be putting their houses in order while burying the past. Nothing will actually change.'

'Except that Kasavian will have to follow through on his promise to grant us full status under the City of London,' said May.

'In that case I'd like to propose a toast,' said Maggie Armitage, who had wedged herself next to Raymond Land. 'May the purple candle of friendship neutralize the effects of karmic retribution.'

As toasts went it didn't strike a very upbeat note, but everyone raised their glasses, and much beer was spilled. Did they realize, as they sat huddled together in the corner of the snug, that they were all outsiders in one way or another? Marked apart by the fierceness of their curiosity, they moved among the docile majority unacknowledged, mistrusted and unloved to the point where they only found solace in one another's company.

'Where did you suddenly disappear to this afternoon?' asked May.

Bryant glanced across at Maggie. 'I went to see someone who confirmed my theory. He told me to re-examine everything through the eyes of the children. They were hunting witches. And so were we. As soon as I changed perspectives, everything made sense.'

May's mobile suddenly rang. He checked the text and frowned. 'Arthur, it seems that somebody wants you,' he said, holding up the screen. The message read: 'Send Bryant outside'.

Just at that moment, something crackled and glowed beyond the pub window. Everyone rose and headed for the door.

On the rain-spattered pavement before them was a trail of fire. As it began to die down, they could read the words it had formed:

TIME TO PAY MY FEE – MR MERRY

'Do you have any idea what that means?' asked May.

Bryant caught Maggie's eye and silenced her. He turned to his partner, his wide blue eyes swimming with the innocence of one whom London has made truly devious. 'No idea at all,' he said. 'My round, I think.'

Back inside the pub, Crippen gave birth to nine kittens.

The publishers hope that this book has given you enjoyable reading. Large Print Books are especially designed to be as easy to see and hold as possible. If you wish a complete list of our books please ask at your local library or write directly to:

Magna Large Print Books
Magna House, Long Preston,
Skipton, North Yorkshire.
BD23 4ND

This Large Print Book for the partially sighted, who cannot read normal print, is published under the auspices of

THE ULVERSCROFT FOUNDATION

THE ULVERSCROFT FOUNDATION

... we hope that you have enjoyed this Large Print Book. Please think for a moment about those people who have worse eyesight problems than you ... and are unable to even read or enjoy Large Print, without great difficulty.

You can help them by sending a donation, large or small to:

The Ulverscroft Foundation, 1, The Green, Bradgate Road, Anstey, Leicestershire, LE7 7FU, England.
or request a copy of our brochure for more details.

The Foundation will use all your help to assist those people who are handicapped by various sight problems and need special attention.

Thank you very much for your help.